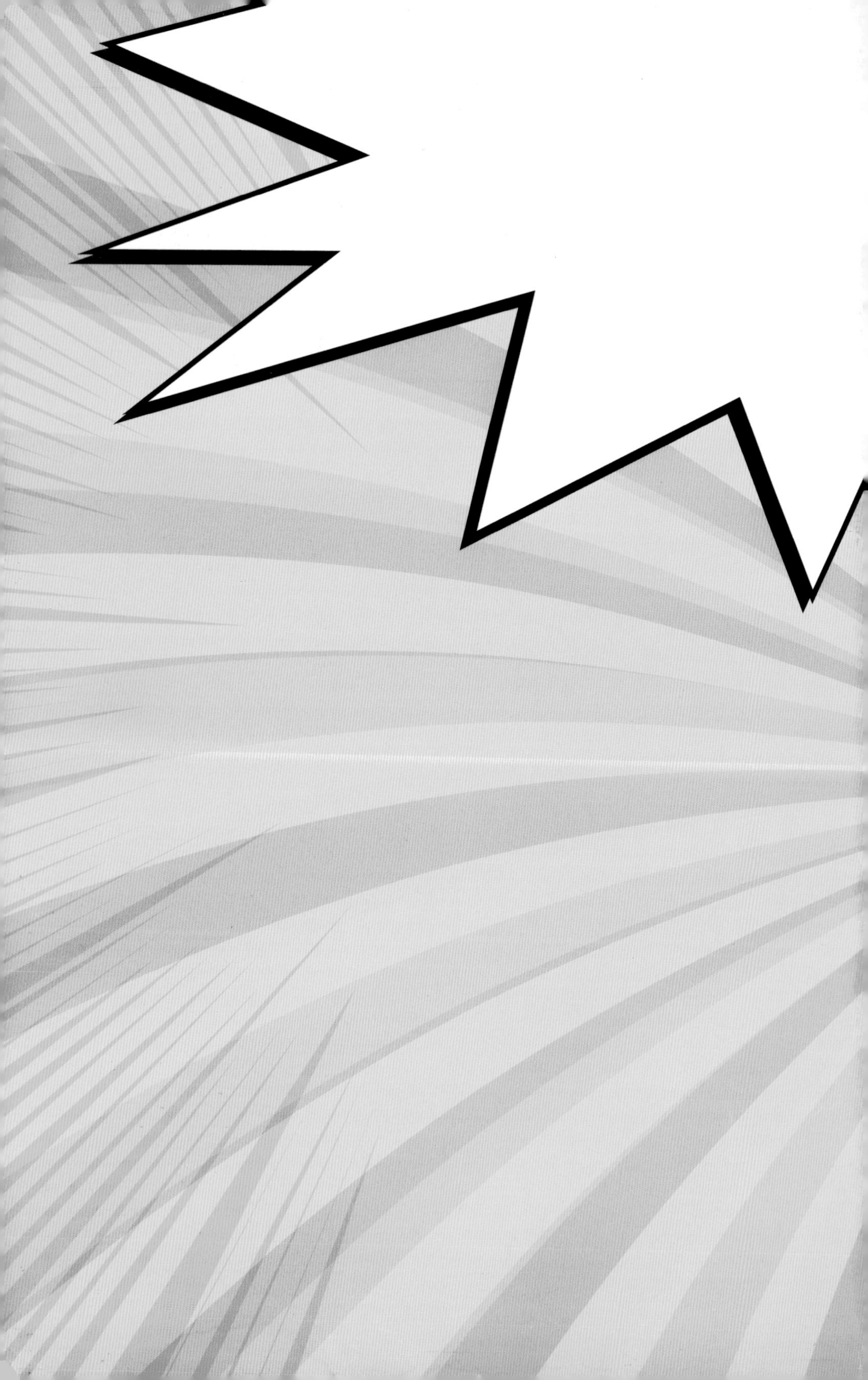

SUPER TURBO ★

AND THE FIRE-BREATHING DRAGON

WRITTEN BY **EDGAR POWERS**
ILLUSTRATED BY **SALVATORE COSTANZA**
AT GLASS HOUSE GRAPHICS

LITTLE SIMON
NEW YORK LONDON TORONTO SYDNEY NEW DELHI

LITTLE SIMON
AN IMPRINT OF SIMON & SCHUSTER CHILDREN'S PUBLISHING DIVISION 1230 AVENUE OF THE AMERICAS, NEW YORK, NEW YORK 10020 FIRST LITTLE SIMON EDITION SEPTEMBER 2021 * COPYRIGHT © 2021 BY SIMON & SCHUSTER, INC. ALL RIGHTS RESERVED, INCLUDING THE RIGHT OF REPRODUCTION IN WHOLE OR IN PART IN ANY FORM. LITTLE SIMON IS A REGISTERED TRADEMARK OF SIMON & SCHUSTER, INC., AND ASSOCIATED COLOPHON IS A TRADEMARK OF SIMON & SCHUSTER, INC. FOR INFORMATION ABOUT SPECIAL DISCOUNTS FOR BULK PURCHASES, PLEASE CONTACT SIMON & SCHUSTER SPECIAL SALES AT 1-866-506-1949 OR BUSINESS@SIMONANDSCHUSTER.COM. THE SIMON & SCHUSTER SPEAKERS BUREAU CAN BRING AUTHORS TO YOUR LIVE EVENT. FOR MORE INFORMATION OR TO BOOK AN EVENT CONTACT THE SIMON & SCHUSTER SPEAKERS BUREAU AT 1-866-248-3049 OR VISIT OUR WEBSITE AT WWW.SIMONSPEAKERS.COM. DESIGNED BY NICHOLAS SCIACCA * ART SERVICES BY GLASS HOUSE GRAPHICS * ART AND COLOR BY SALVATORE COSTANZA * LETTERING BY GIOVANNI SPATARO/GRAFIMATED CARTOON * SUPERVISION BY SALVATORE DI MARCO/GRAFIMATED CARTOON * MANUFACTURED IN CHINA 0621 SCP * 2 4 6 8 10 9 7 5 3 1 * LIBRARY OF CONGRESS CATALOGING-IN-PUBLICATION DATA NAMES: POWERS, EDGAR J., AUTHOR. | GLASS HOUSE GRAPHICS, ILLUSTRATOR. TITLE: SUPER TURBO AND THE FIRE-BREATHING DRAGON / BY EDGAR J. POWERS ; ILLUSTRATED BY GLASS HOUSE GRAPHICS. DESCRIPTION: FIRST LITTLE SIMON EDITION. | NEW YORK : LITTLE SIMON, 2021. | SERIES: SUPER TURBO, THE GRAPHIC NOVEL ; BOOK 5 | AUDIENCE: AGES 5-9 | AUDIENCE: GRADES K-4 | SUMMARY: SUPER TURBO AND THE SUPERPETS AT SUNNYVIEW ELEMENTARY TRY TO GET RID OF THE FIRE-BREATHING DRAGON IN THE SCIENCE LAB BEFORE IT DOES SERIOUS DAMAGE. IDENTIFIERS: LCCN 2020049522 (PRINT) | LCCN 2020049523 (EBOOK) | ISBN 9781534485372 (PAPERBACK) | ISBN 9781534485389 (HARDCOVER) | ISBN 9781534485396 (EBOOK) SUBJECTS: LCSH: GRAPHIC NOVELS. | CYAC: GRAPHIC NOVELS. | SUPERHEROES—FICTION. | HAMSTERS—FICTION. | DRAGONS—FICTION. | ELEMENTARY SCHOOLS—FICTION. | SCHOOLS—FICTION. CLASSIFICATION: LCC PZ7.7.P7 SF 2021 (PRINT) | LCC PZ7.7.P7 (EBOOK) | DDC 741.5/973—DC23 LC RECORD AVAILABLE AT HTTPS://LCCN.LOC.GOV/2020049522 LC EBOOK RECORD AVAILABLE AT HTTPS://LCCN.LOC.GOV/2020049523

CONTENTS

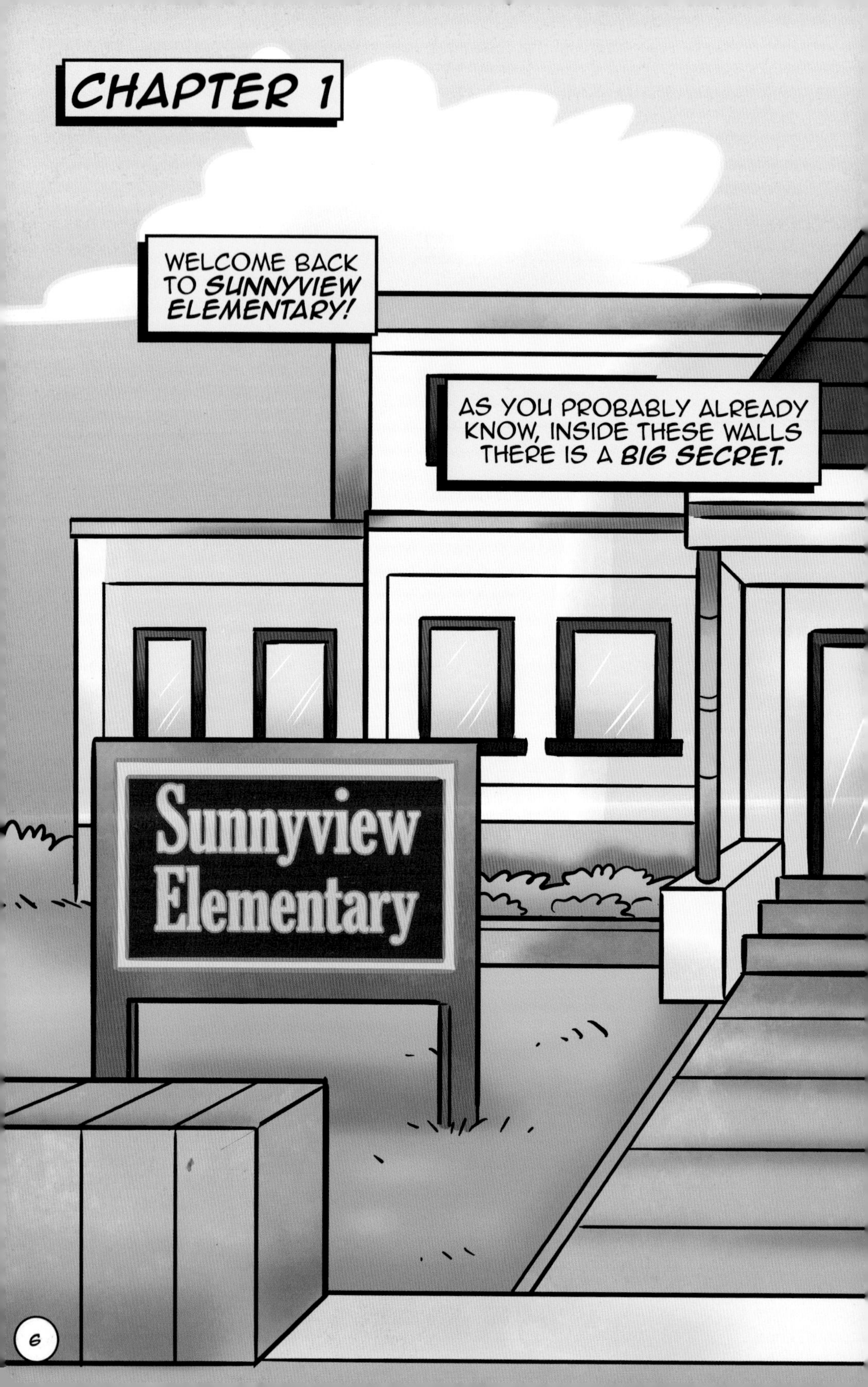
CHAPTER 1
WELCOME BACK TO SUNNYVIEW ELEMENTARY!
AS YOU PROBABLY ALREADY KNOW, INSIDE THESE WALLS THERE IS A BIG SECRET.
Sunnyview Elementary

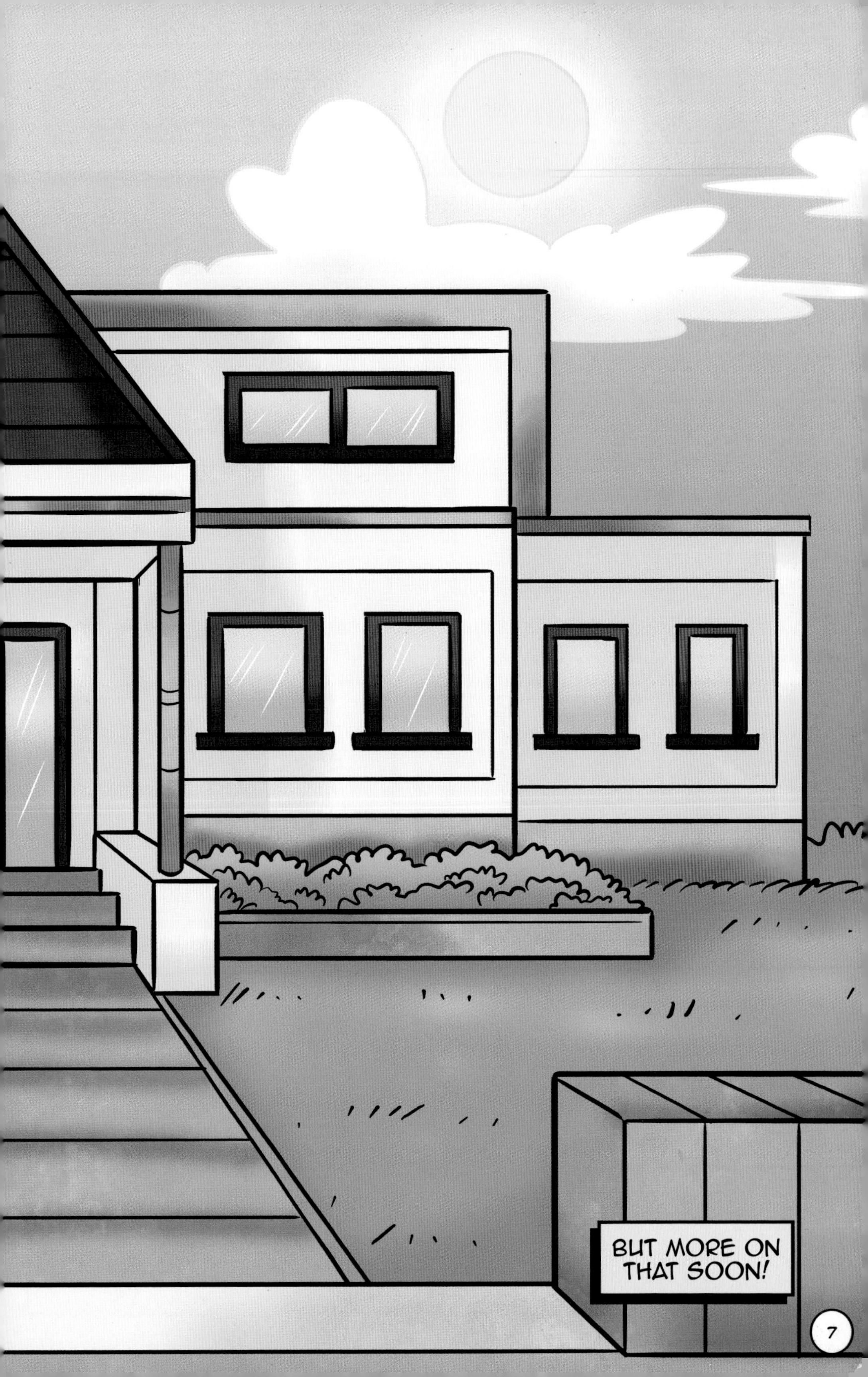
BUT MORE ON THAT SOON!

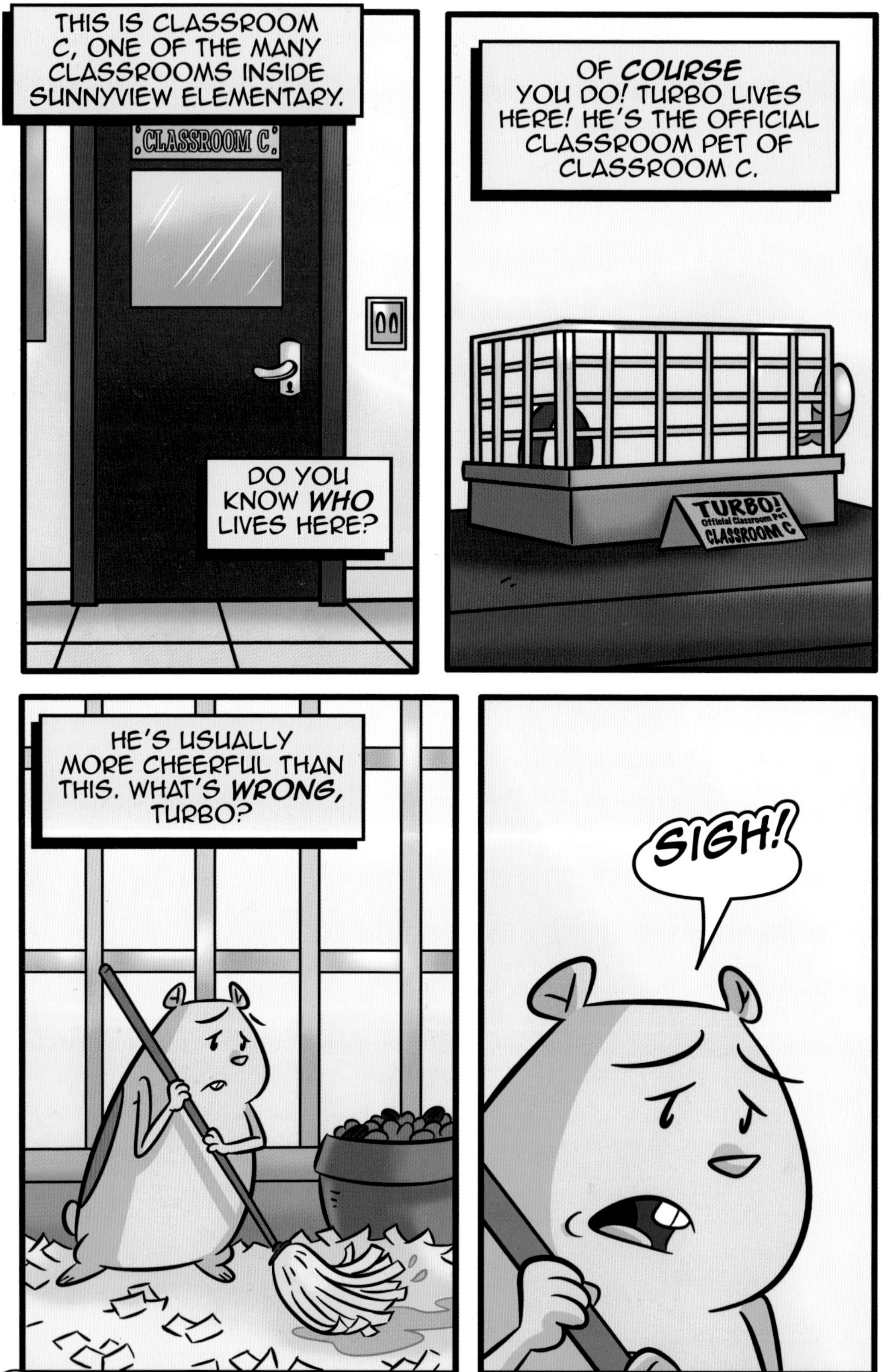
THIS IS CLASSROOM C, ONE OF THE MANY CLASSROOMS INSIDE SUNNYVIEW ELEMENTARY.
CLASSROOM C
DO YOU KNOW *WHO* LIVES HERE?
OF *COURSE* YOU DO! TURBO LIVES HERE! HE'S THE OFFICIAL CLASSROOM PET OF CLASSROOM C.
TURBO! Official Classroom Pet CLASSROOM C
HE'S USUALLY MORE CHEERFUL THAN THIS. WHAT'S *WRONG*, TURBO?
SIGH!

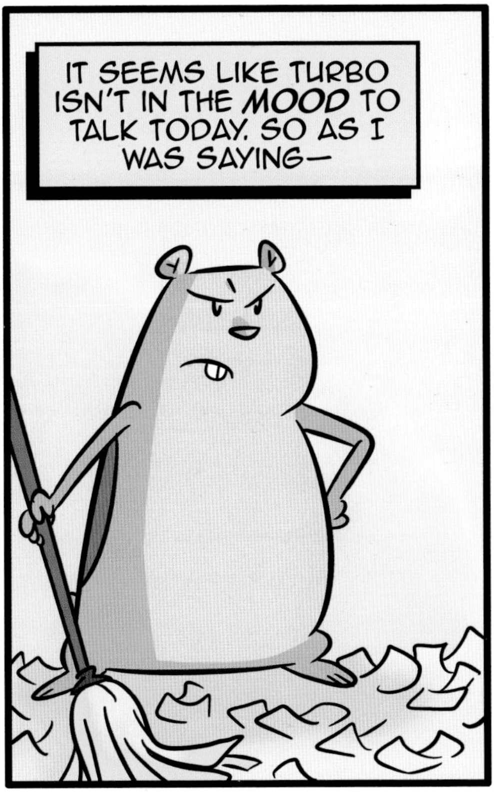
IT SEEMS LIKE TURBO ISN'T IN THE *MOOD* TO TALK TODAY. SO AS I WAS SAYING—

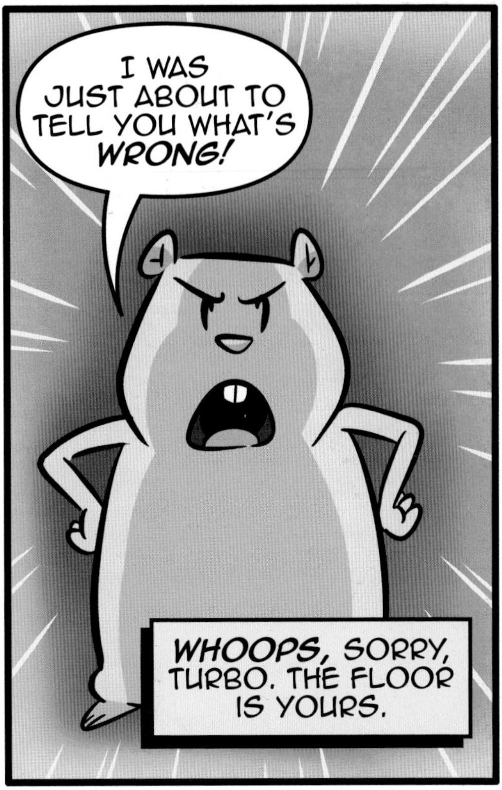
I WAS JUST ABOUT TO TELL YOU WHAT'S *WRONG!*
WHOOPS, SORRY, TURBO. THE FLOOR IS YOURS.

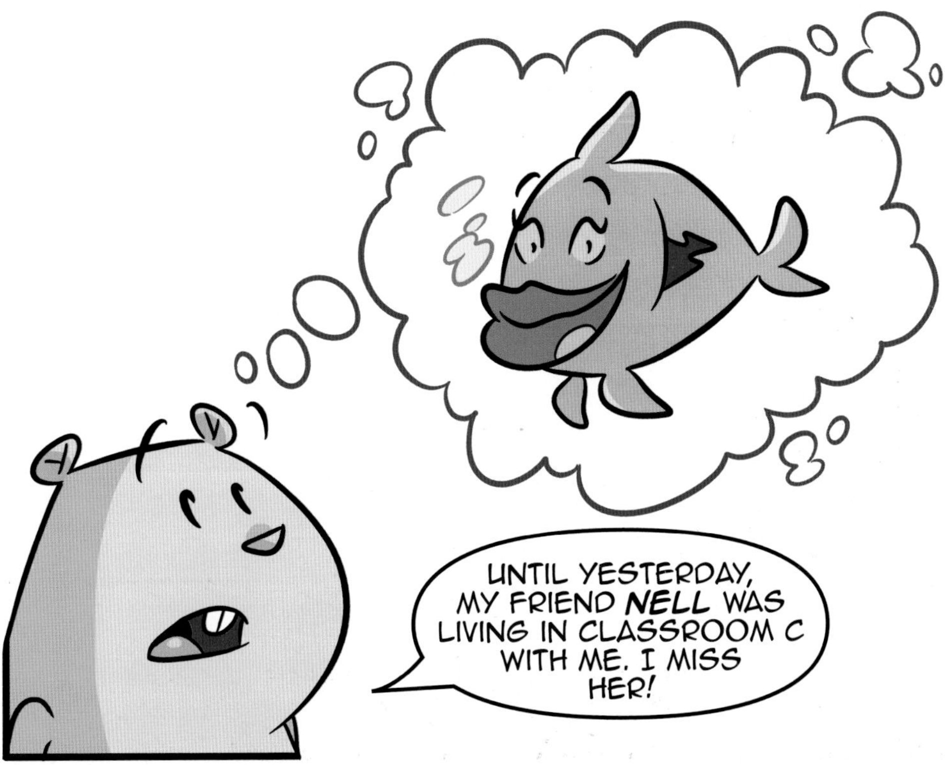
UNTIL YESTERDAY, MY FRIEND ***NELL*** WAS LIVING IN CLASSROOM C WITH ME. I MISS HER!

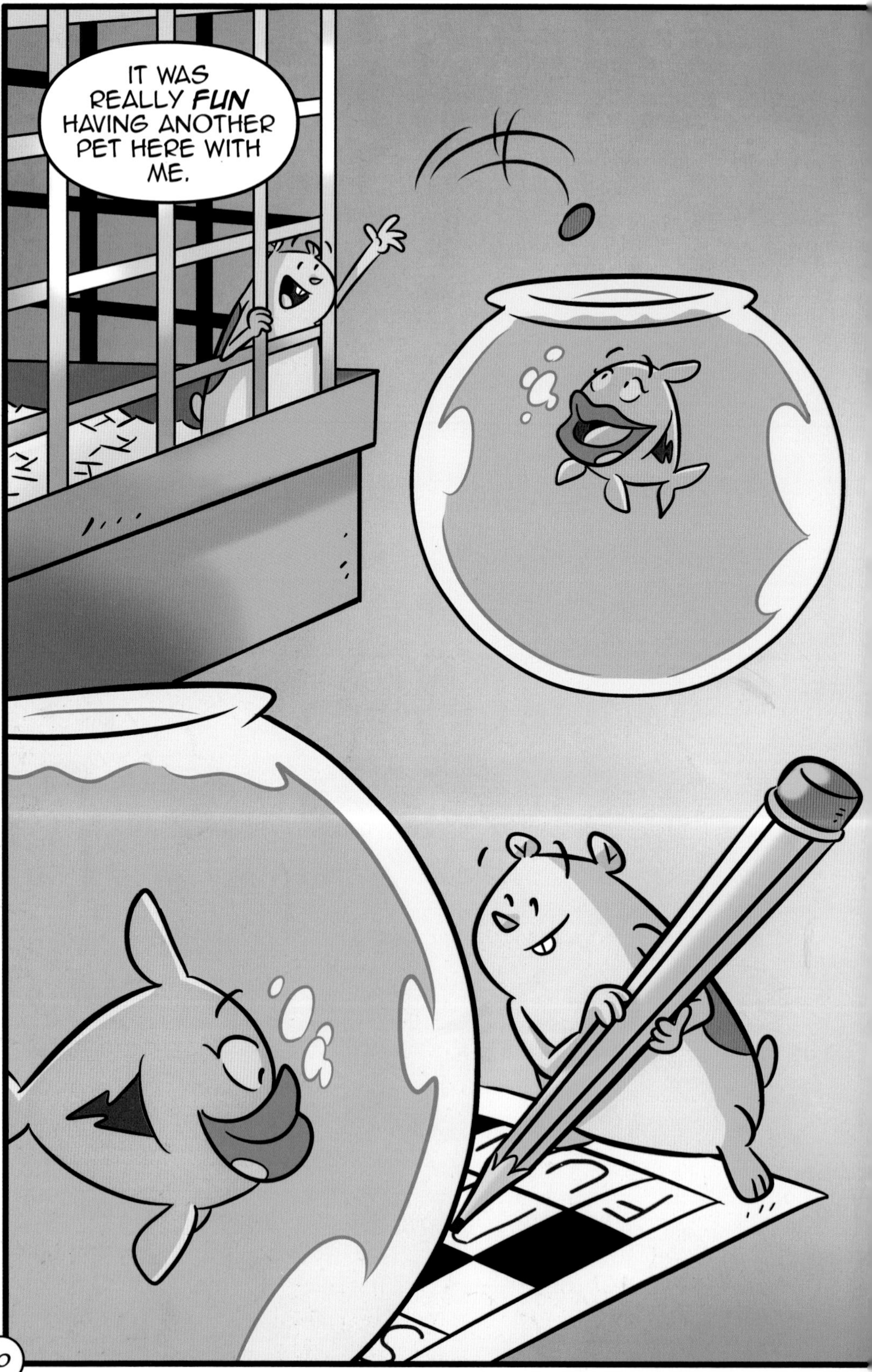
IT WAS REALLY FUN HAVING ANOTHER PET HERE WITH ME.

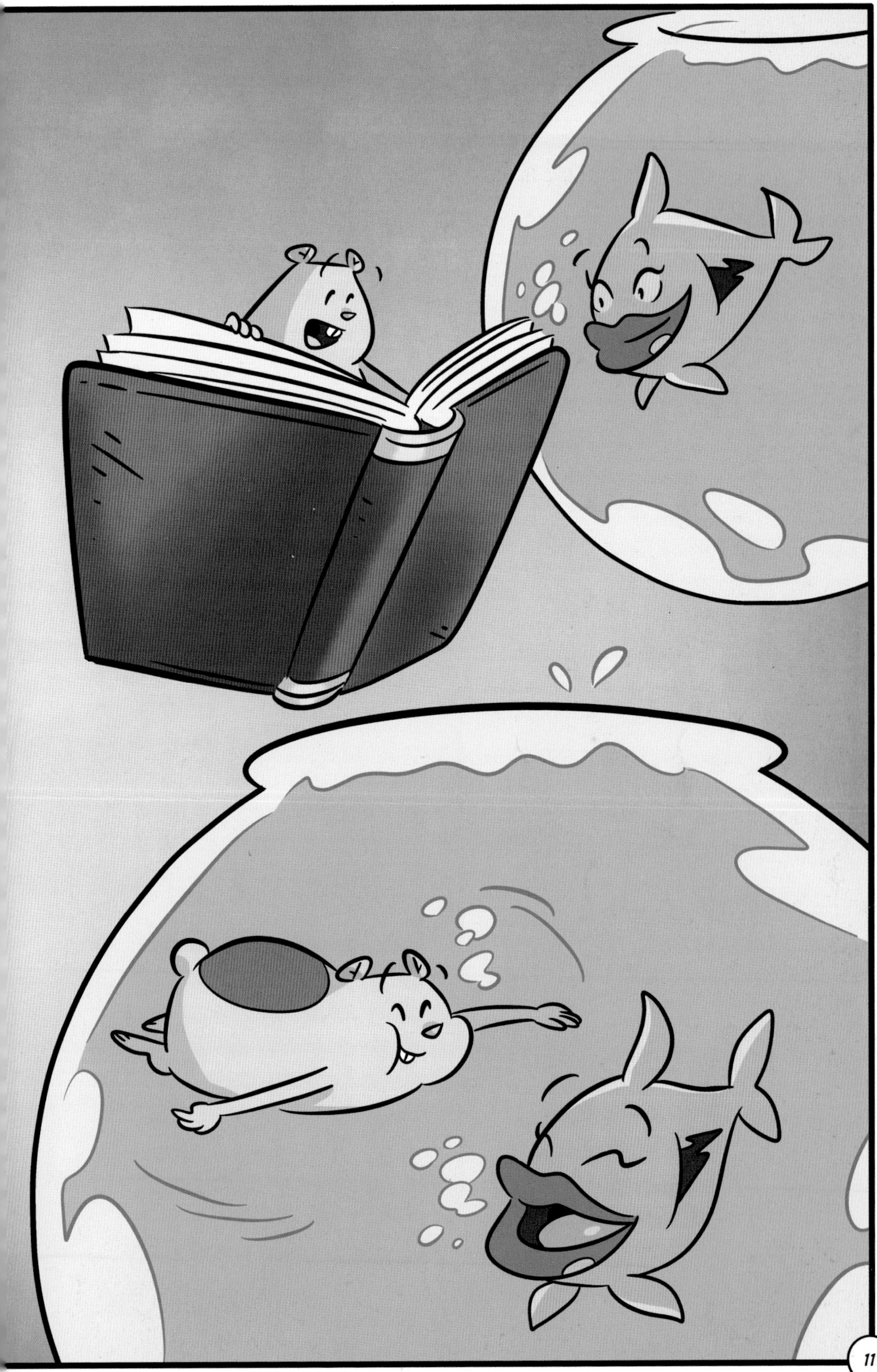

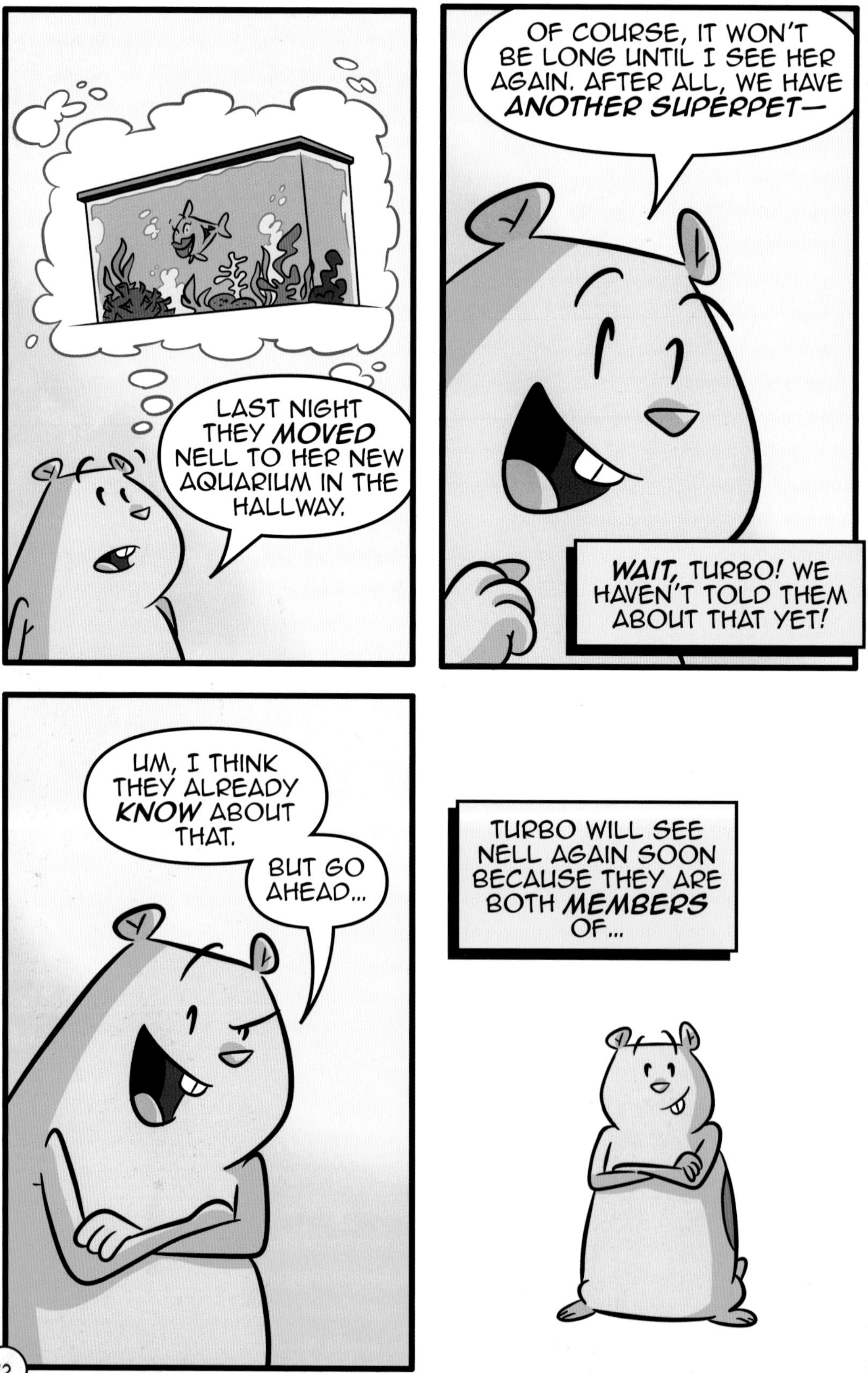
LAST NIGHT THEY *MOVED* NELL TO HER NEW AQUARIUM IN THE HALLWAY.
OF COURSE, IT WON'T BE LONG UNTIL I SEE HER AGAIN. AFTER ALL, WE HAVE *ANOTHER SUPERPET*—
WAIT, TURBO! WE HAVEN'T TOLD THEM ABOUT THAT YET!
UM, I THINK THEY ALREADY *KNOW* ABOUT THAT.
BUT GO AHEAD...
TURBO WILL SEE NELL AGAIN SOON BECAUSE THEY ARE BOTH *MEMBERS* OF...

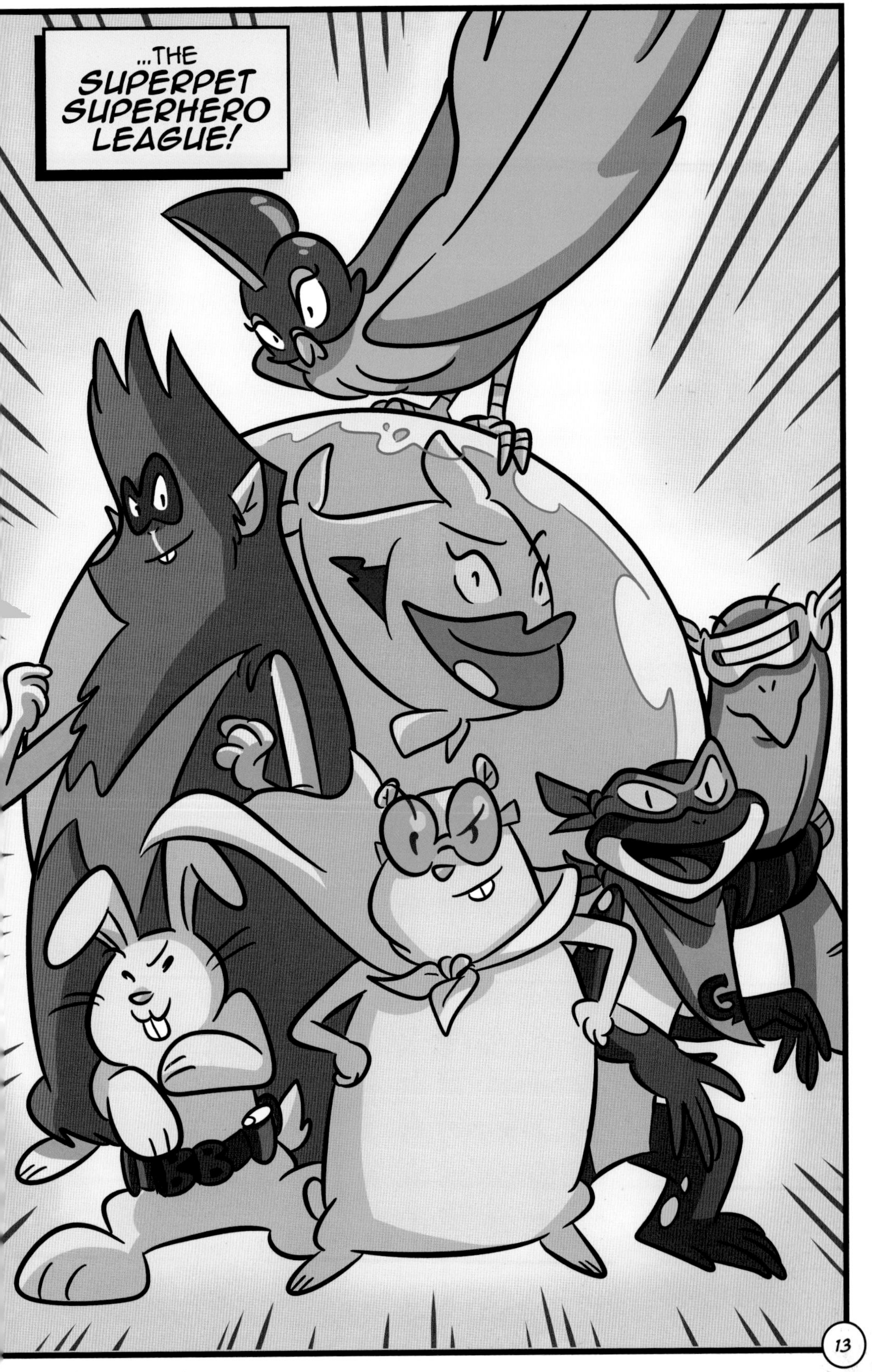
...THE SUPERPET SUPERHERO LEAGUE!

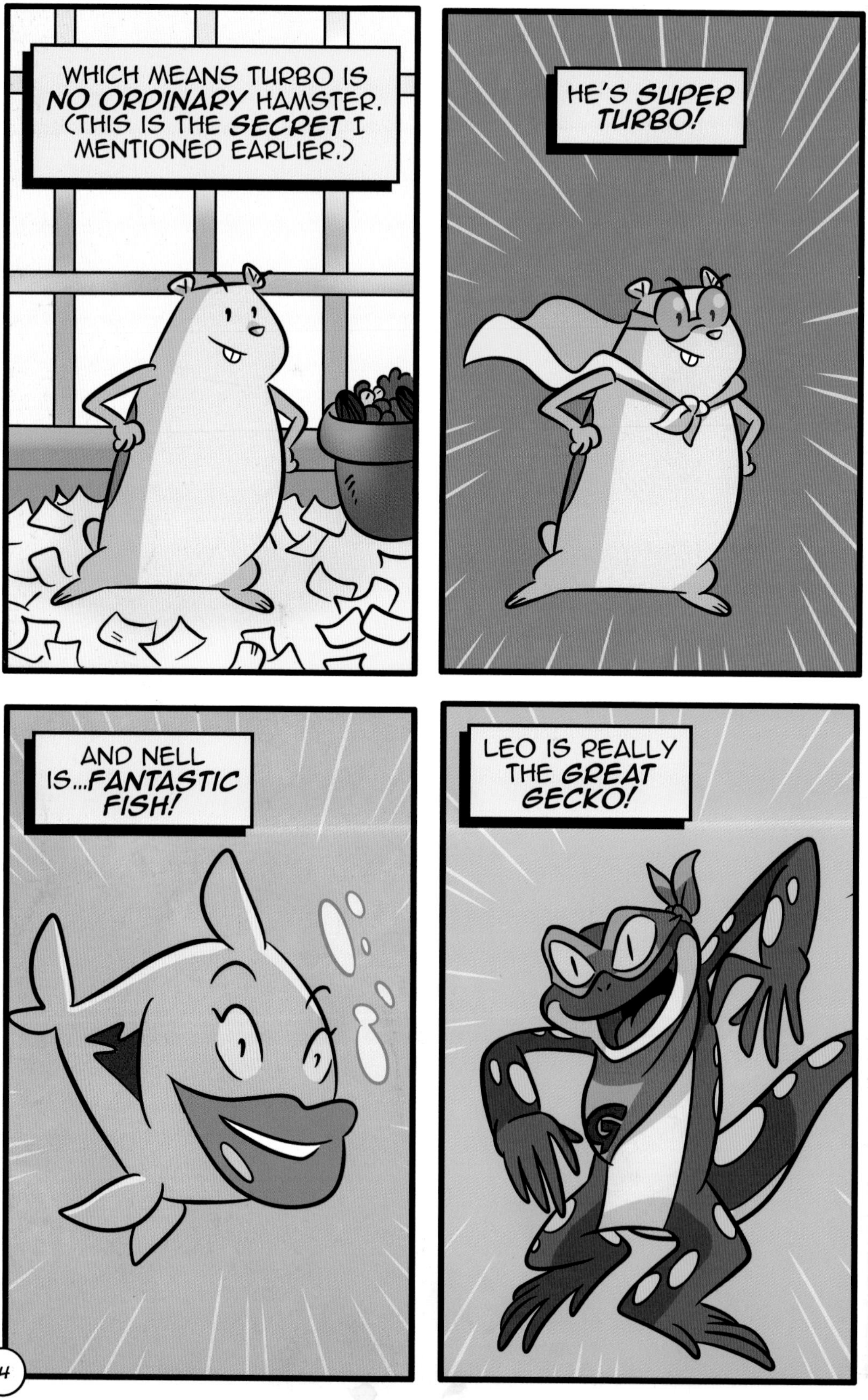
WHICH MEANS TURBO IS NO ORDINARY HAMSTER. (THIS IS THE SECRET I MENTIONED EARLIER.)
HE'S SUPER TURBO!
AND NELL IS...FANTASTIC FISH!
LEO IS REALLY THE GREAT GECKO!

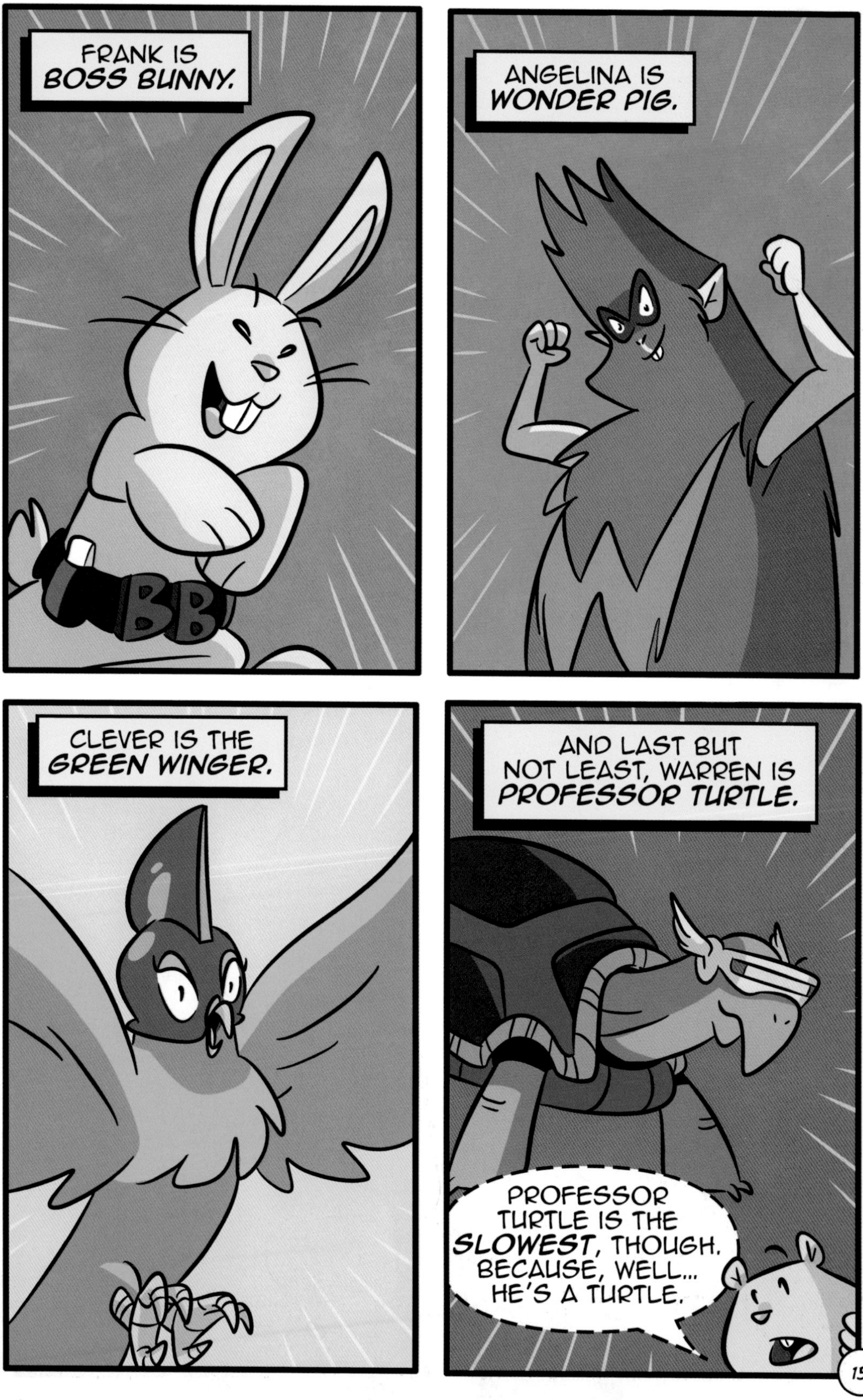
FRANK IS BOSS BUNNY.
BB
ANGELINA IS WONDER PIG.
CLEVER IS THE GREEN WINGER.
AND LAST BUT NOT LEAST, WARREN IS PROFESSOR TURTLE.
PROFESSOR TURTLE IS THE SLOWEST, THOUGH. BECAUSE, WELL... HE'S A TURTLE.

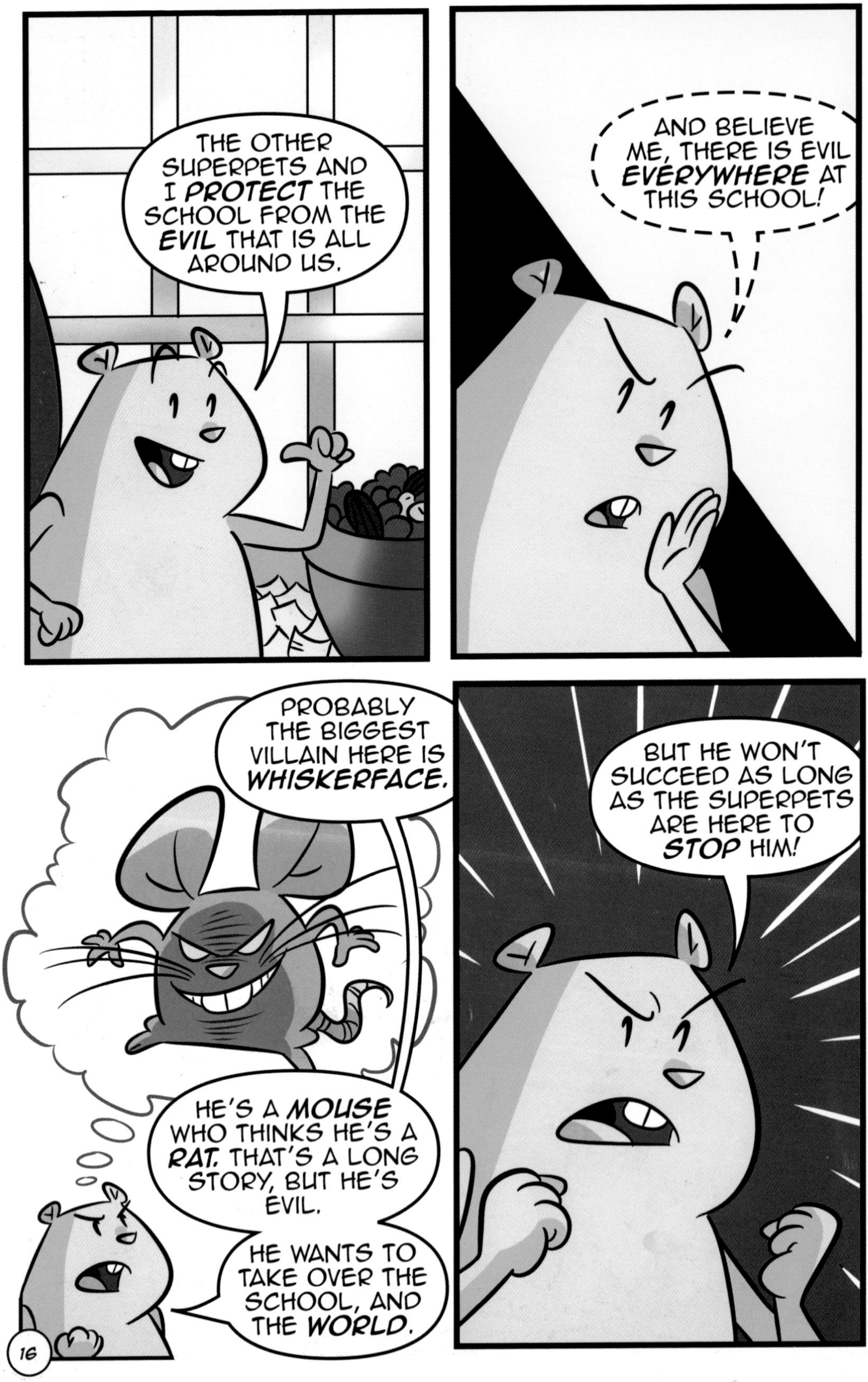
THE OTHER SUPERPETS AND I PROTECT THE SCHOOL FROM THE EVIL THAT IS ALL AROUND US.
AND BELIEVE ME, THERE IS EVIL EVERYWHERE AT THIS SCHOOL!
PROBABLY THE BIGGEST VILLAIN HERE IS WHISKERFACE.
HE'S A MOUSE WHO THINKS HE'S A RAT. THAT'S A LONG STORY, BUT HE'S EVIL.
HE WANTS TO TAKE OVER THE SCHOOL, AND THE WORLD.
BUT HE WON'T SUCCEED AS LONG AS THE SUPERPETS ARE HERE TO STOP HIM!

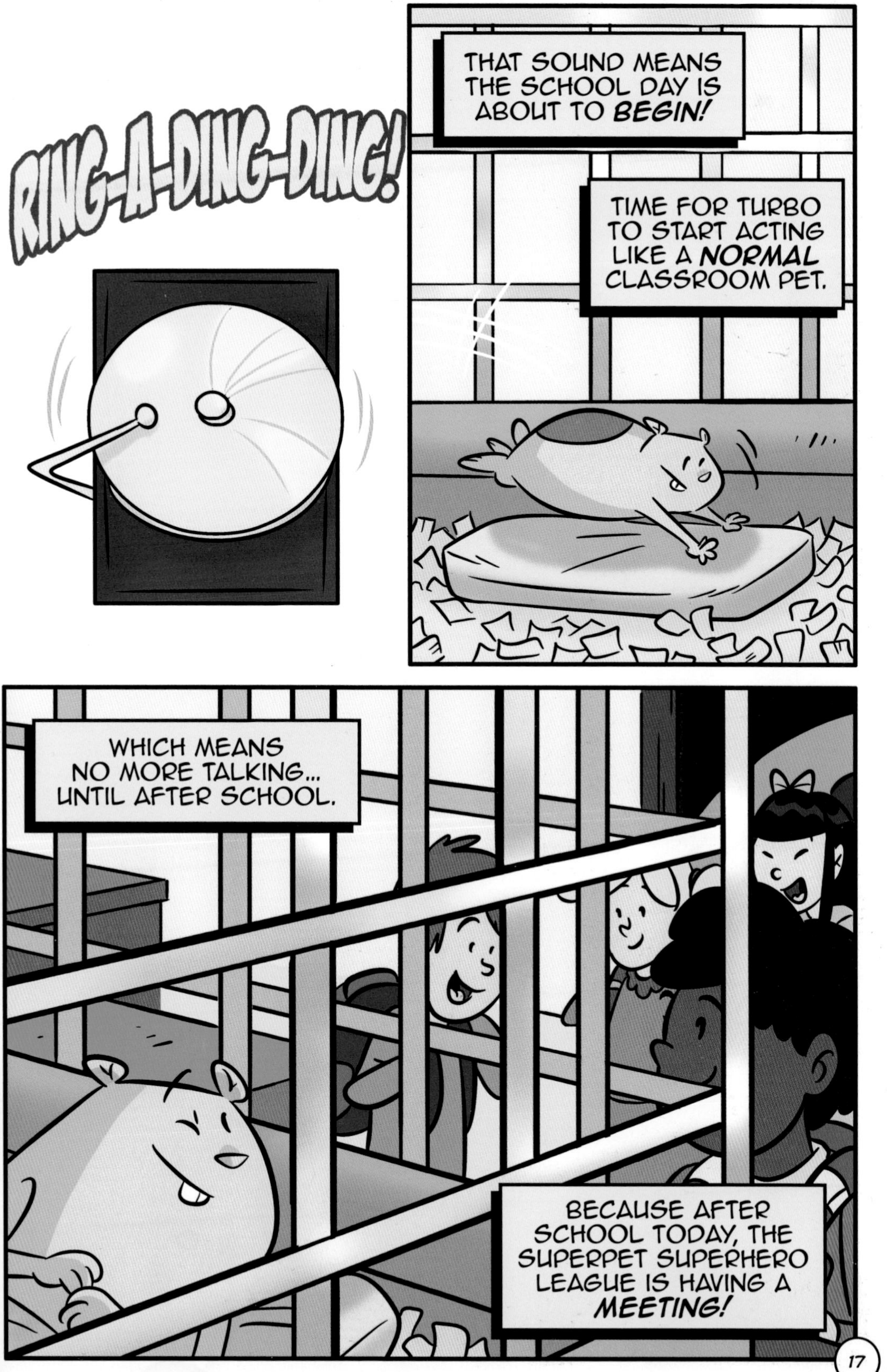
RING-A-DING-DING!
THAT SOUND MEANS THE SCHOOL DAY IS ABOUT TO BEGIN!
TIME FOR TURBO TO START ACTING LIKE A NORMAL CLASSROOM PET.
WHICH MEANS NO MORE TALKING... UNTIL AFTER SCHOOL.
BECAUSE AFTER SCHOOL TODAY, THE SUPERPET SUPERHERO LEAGUE IS HAVING A MEETING!

CHAPTER 2

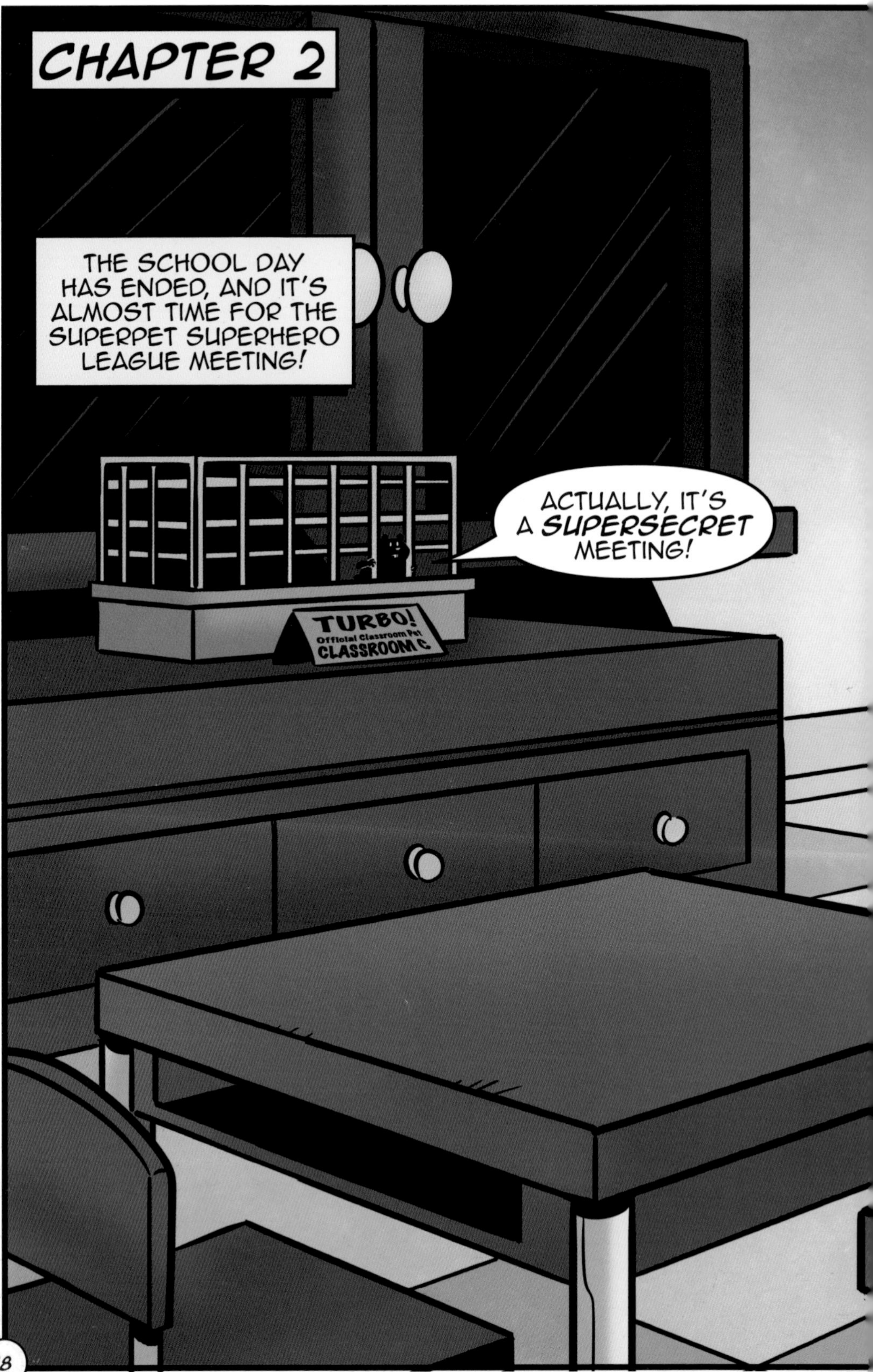
THE SCHOOL DAY HAS ENDED, AND IT'S ALMOST TIME FOR THE SUPERPET SUPERHERO LEAGUE MEETING!
ACTUALLY, IT'S A SUPERSECRET MEETING!
TURBO!
Official Classroom Pet
CLASSROOM C

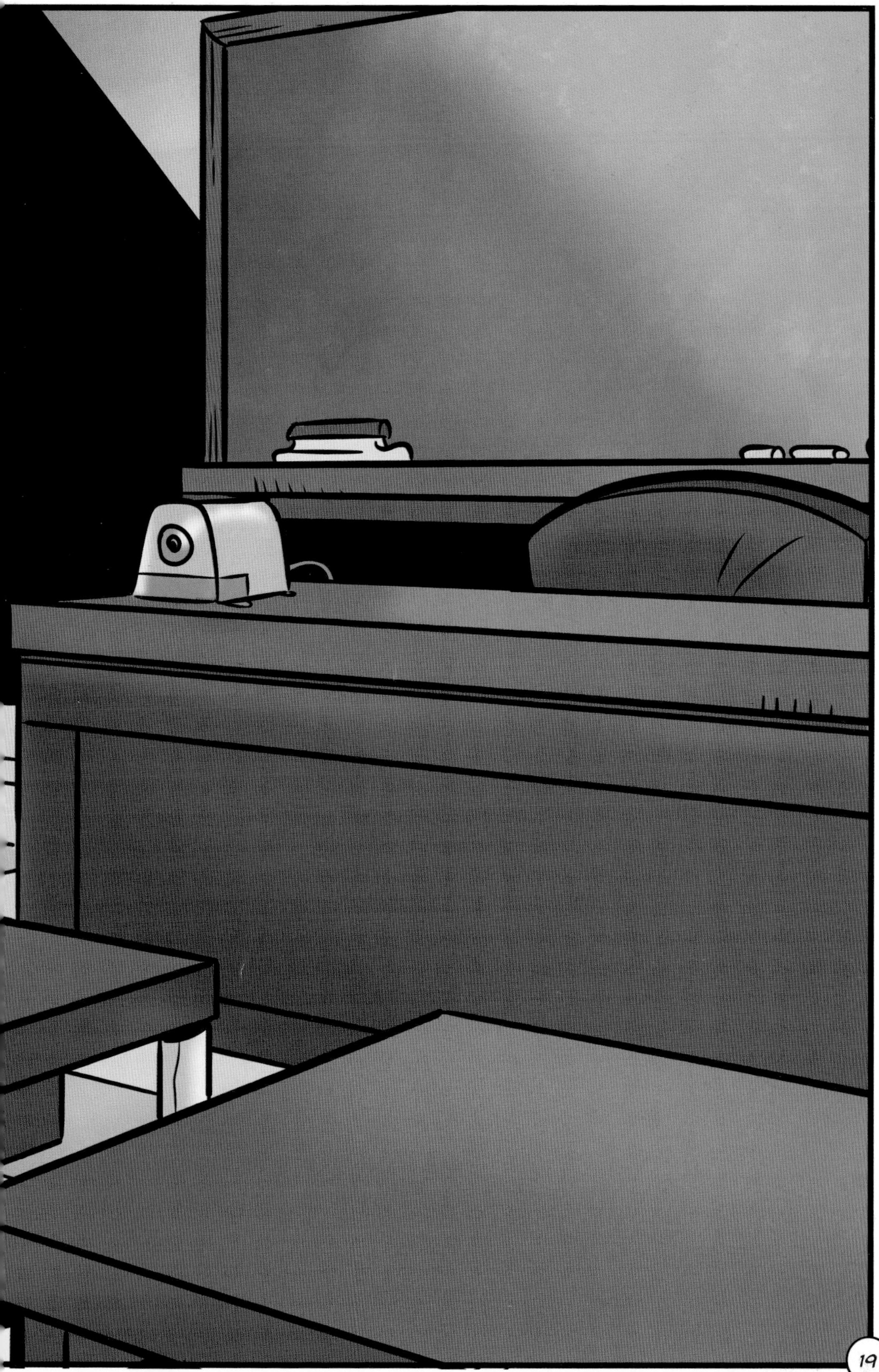

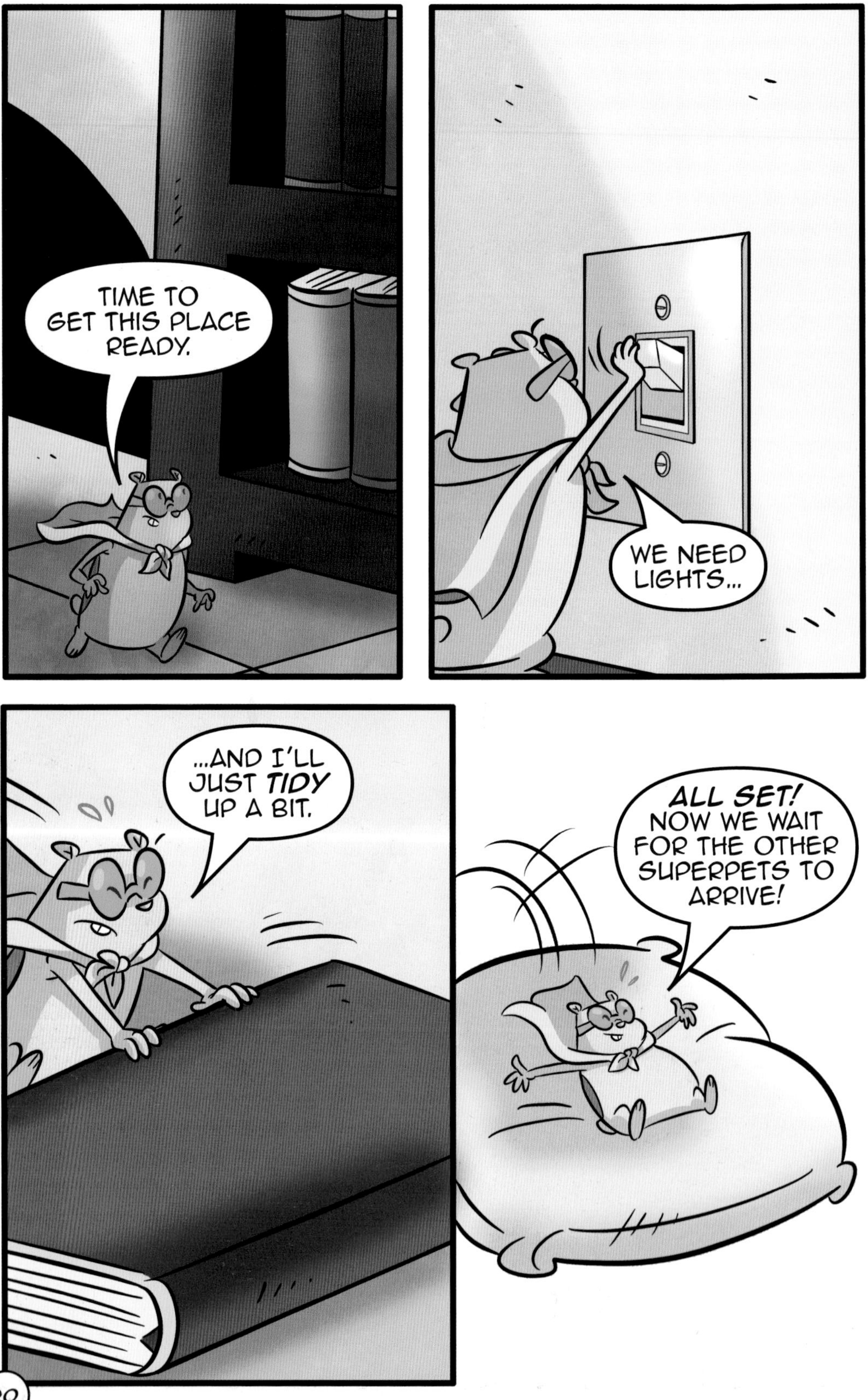
TIME TO GET THIS PLACE READY.
WE NEED LIGHTS...
...AND I'LL JUST *TIDY* UP A BIT.
ALL SET! NOW WE WAIT FOR THE OTHER SUPERPETS TO ARRIVE!

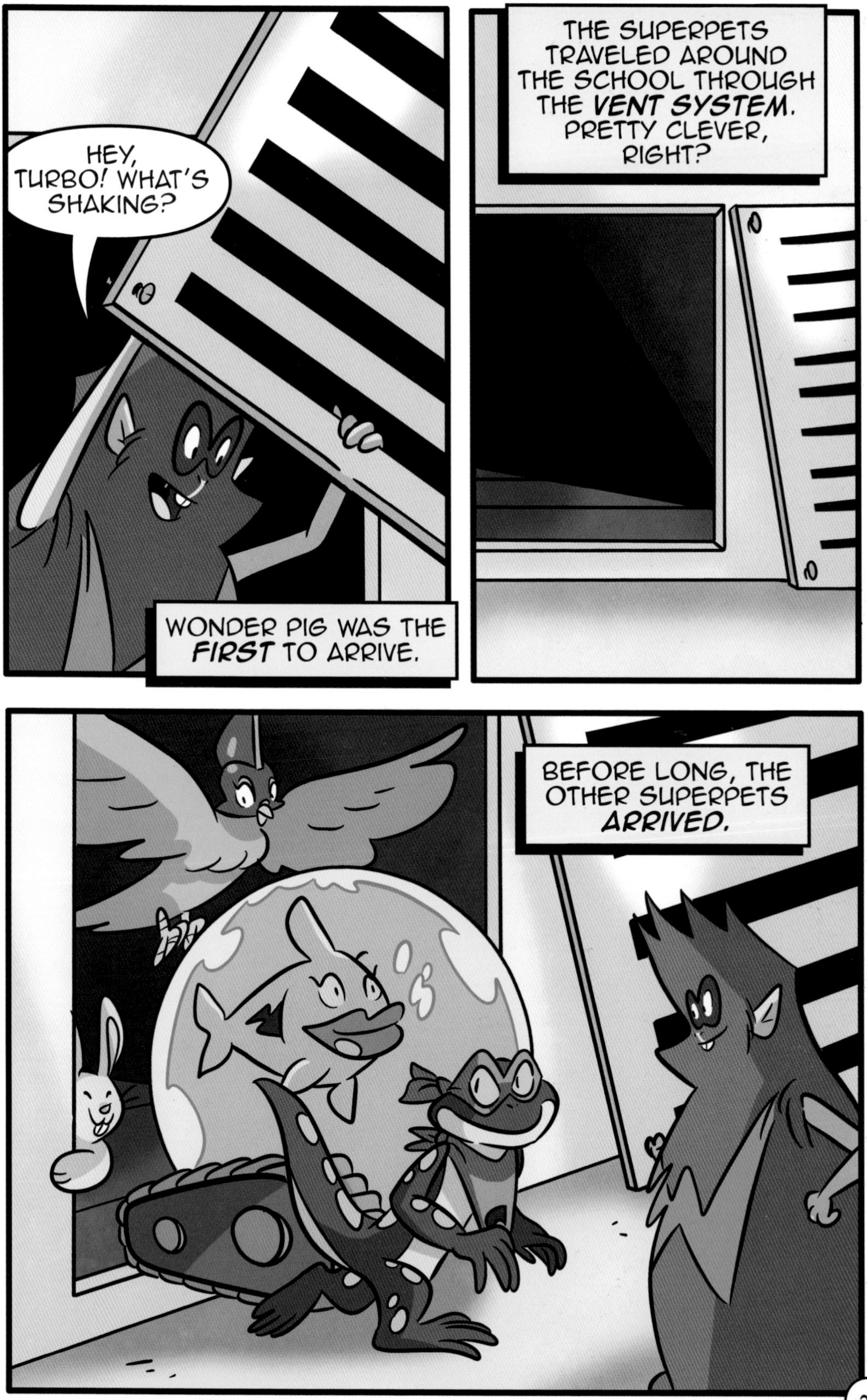
HEY, TURBO! WHAT'S SHAKING?
WONDER PIG WAS THE FIRST TO ARRIVE.
THE SUPERPETS TRAVELED AROUND THE SCHOOL THROUGH THE VENT SYSTEM. PRETTY CLEVER, RIGHT?
BEFORE LONG, THE OTHER SUPERPETS ARRIVED.

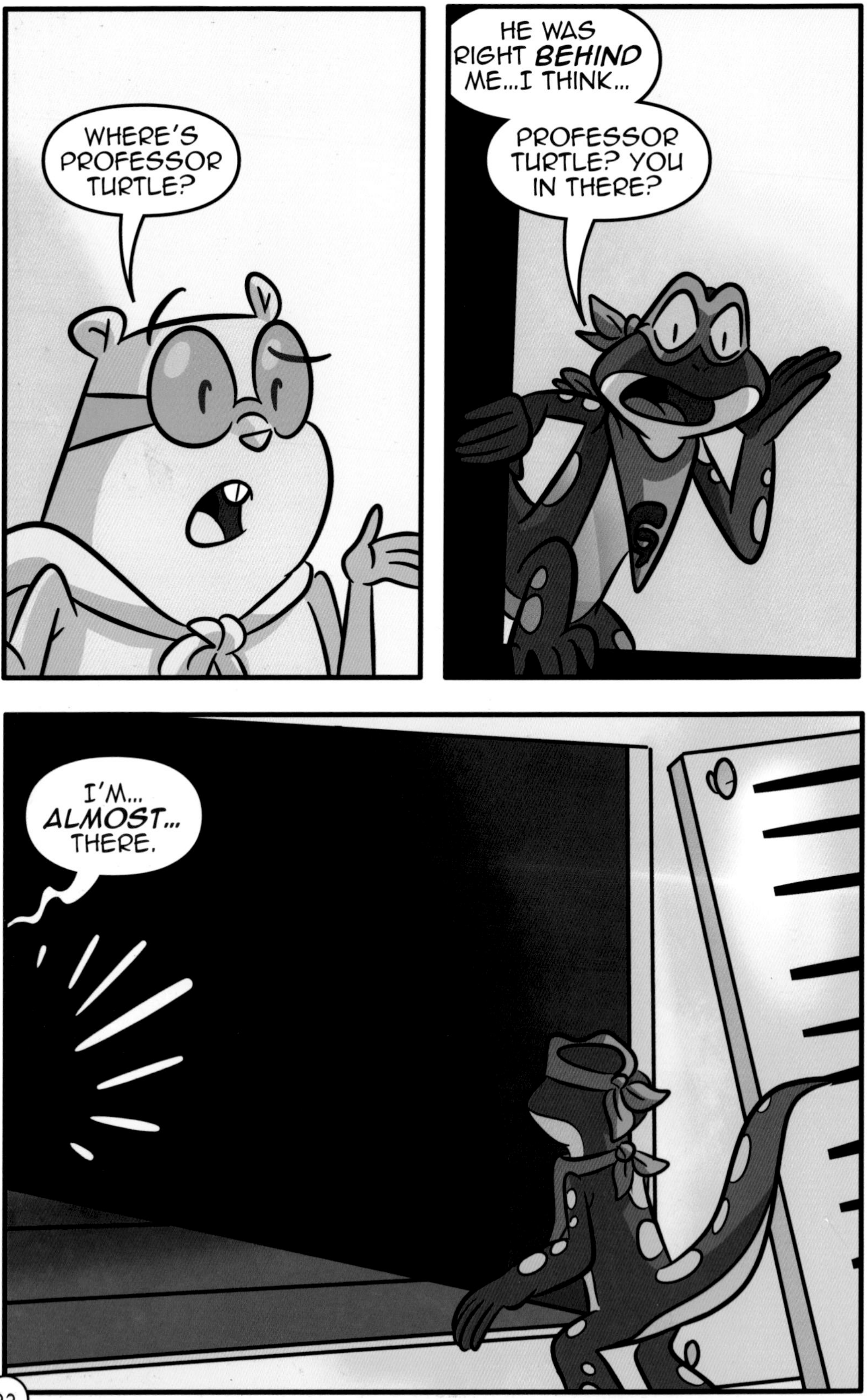
WHERE'S PROFESSOR TURTLE?
HE WAS RIGHT BEHIND ME...I THINK...
PROFESSOR TURTLE? YOU IN THERE?
I'M... ALMOST... THERE.

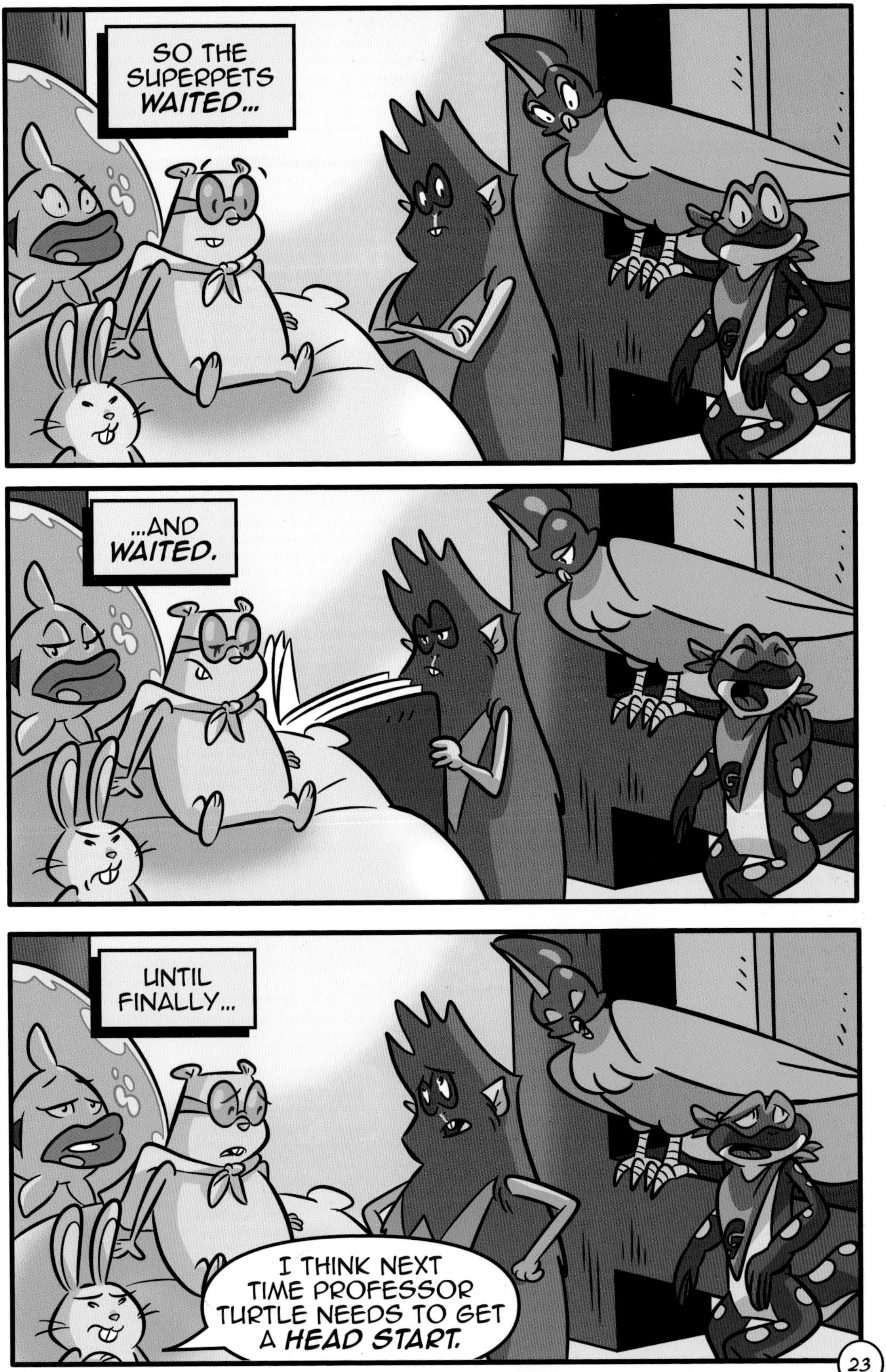

SO THE SUPERPETS WAITED...
...AND WAITED.
UNTIL FINALLY...
I THINK NEXT TIME PROFESSOR TURTLE NEEDS TO GET A HEAD START.

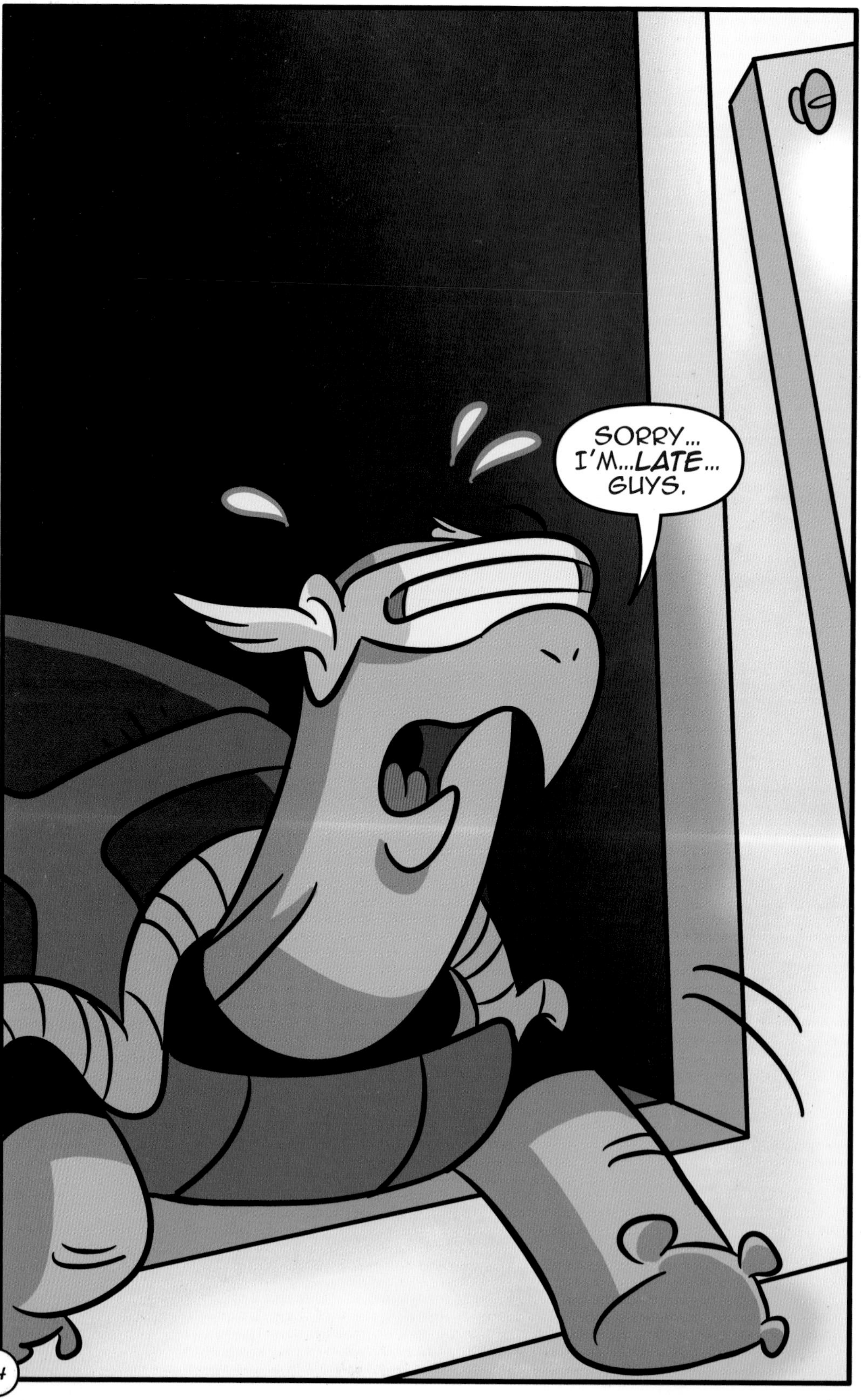
SORRY...
I'M...**LATE**...
GUYS.

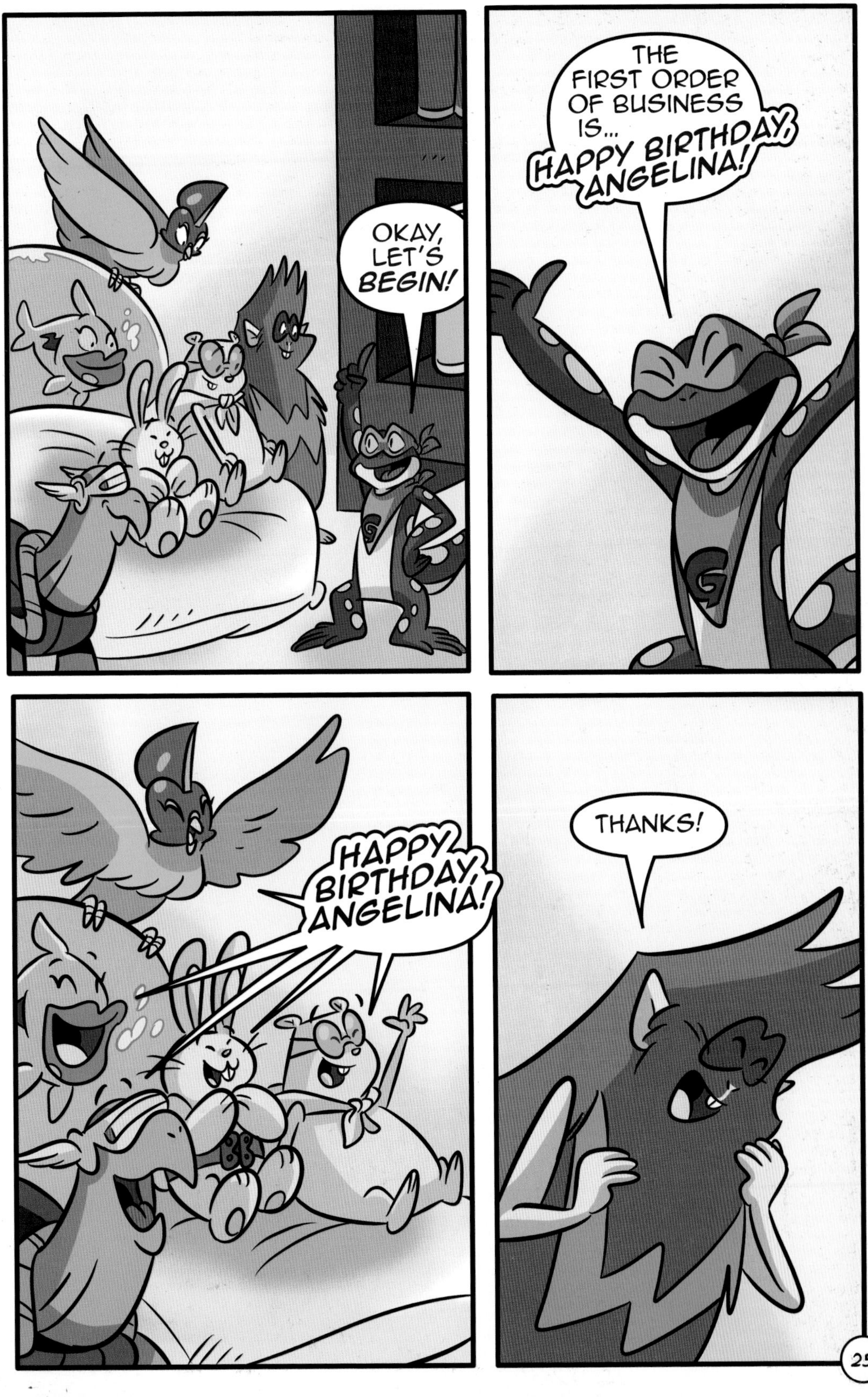
OKAY, LET'S BEGIN!
THE FIRST ORDER OF BUSINESS IS... HAPPY BIRTHDAY, ANGELINA!
HAPPY BIRTHDAY, ANGELINA!
THANKS!

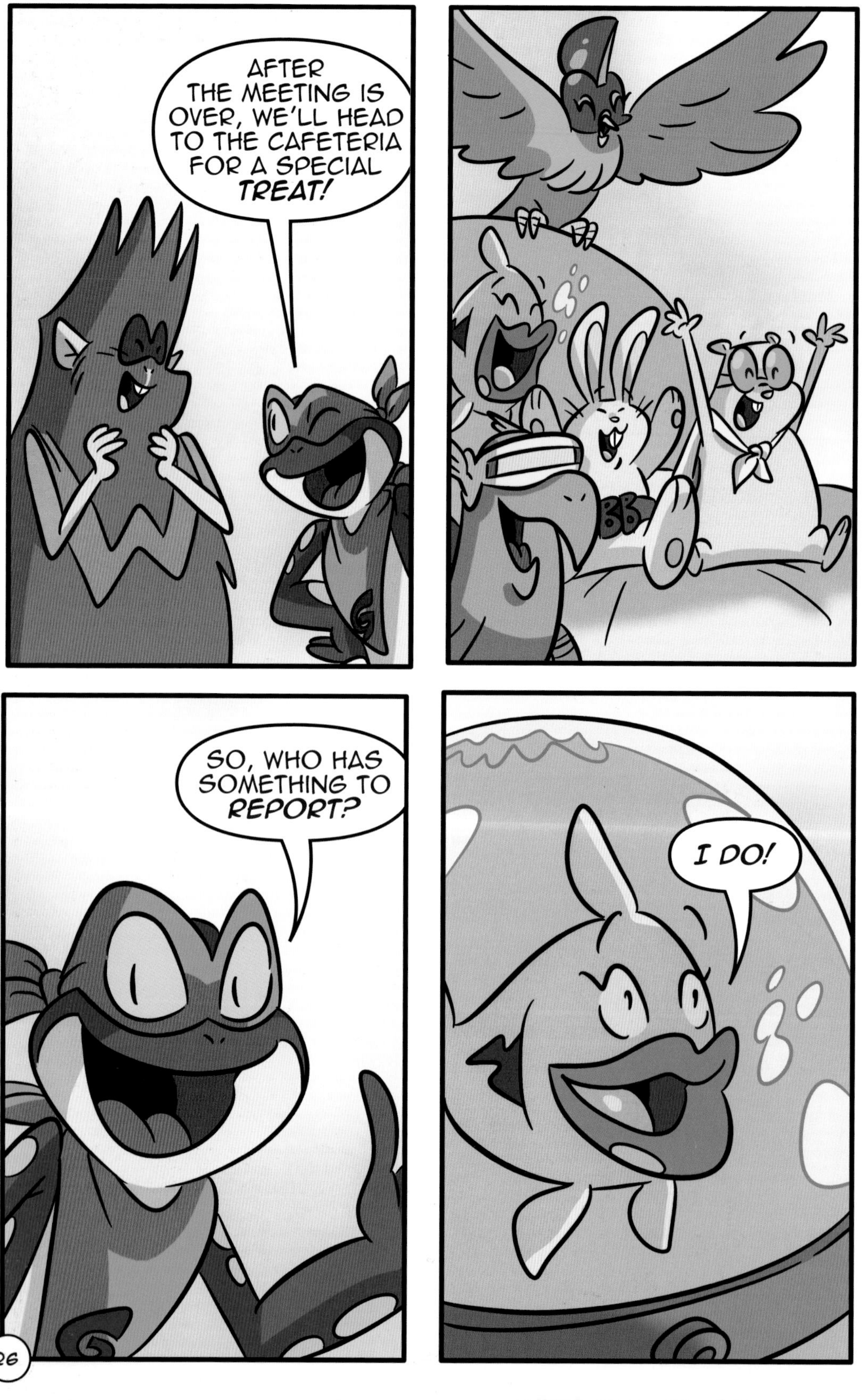
AFTER THE MEETING IS OVER, WE'LL HEAD TO THE CAFETERIA FOR A SPECIAL *TREAT!*
BB
SO, WHO HAS SOMETHING TO *REPORT?*
I DO!

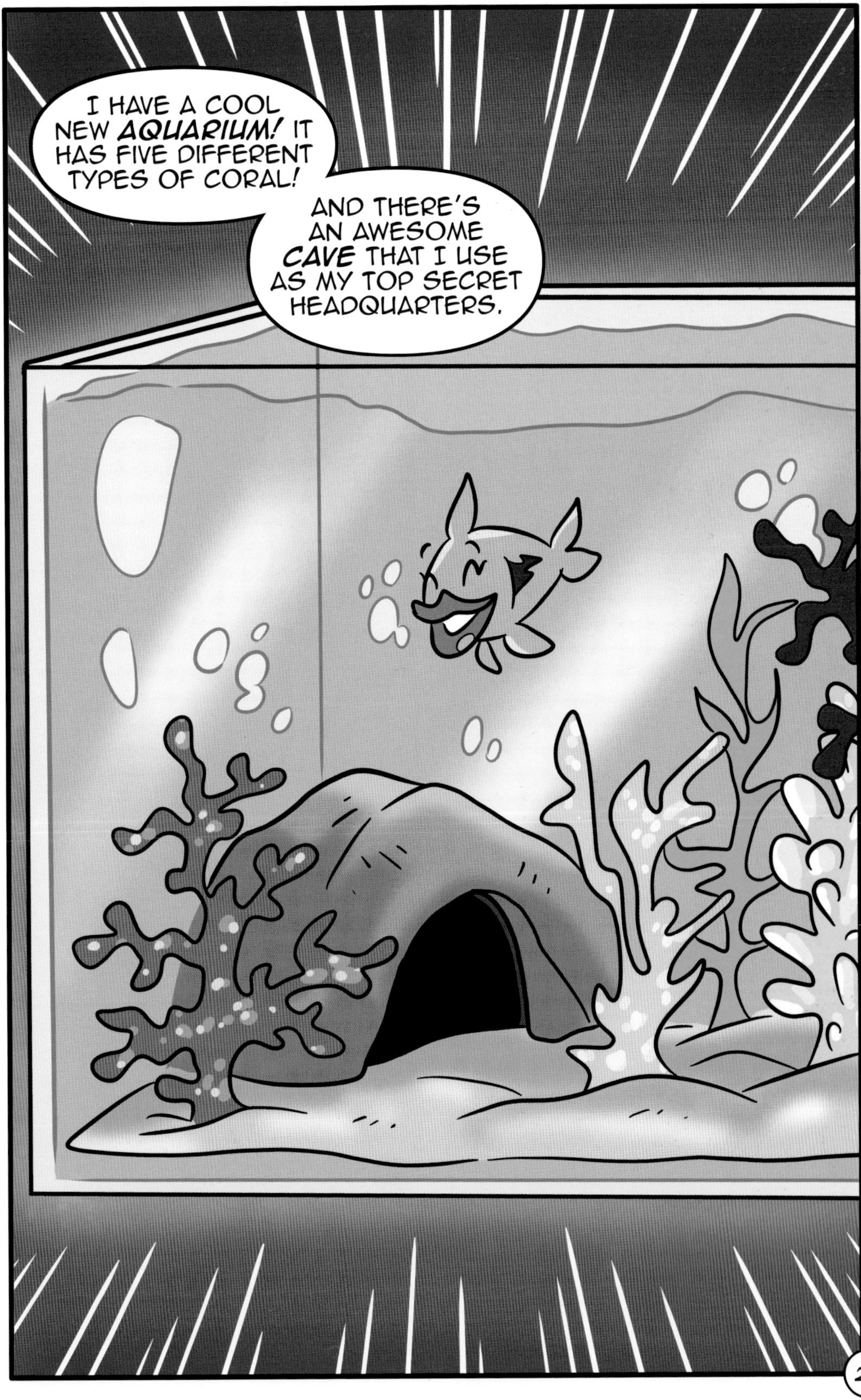
I HAVE A COOL NEW AQUARIUM! IT HAS FIVE DIFFERENT TYPES OF CORAL!
AND THERE'S AN AWESOME CAVE THAT I USE AS MY TOP SECRET HEADQUARTERS.

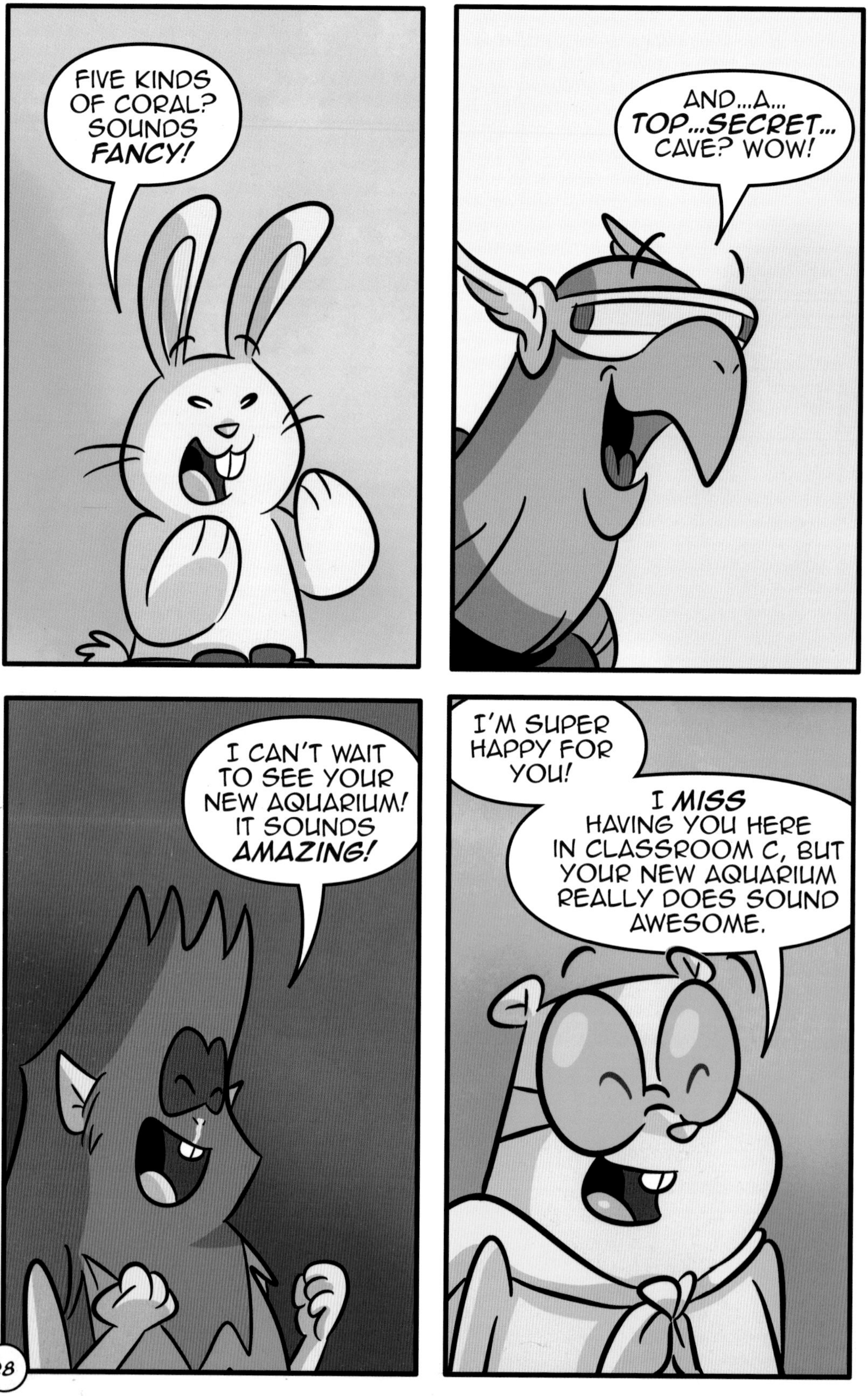
FIVE KINDS OF CORAL? SOUNDS *FANCY!*
AND...A... *TOP...SECRET...* CAVE? WOW!
I CAN'T WAIT TO SEE YOUR NEW AQUARIUM! IT SOUNDS *AMAZING!*
I'M SUPER HAPPY FOR YOU!
I *MISS* HAVING YOU HERE IN CLASSROOM C, BUT YOUR NEW AQUARIUM REALLY DOES SOUND AWESOME.

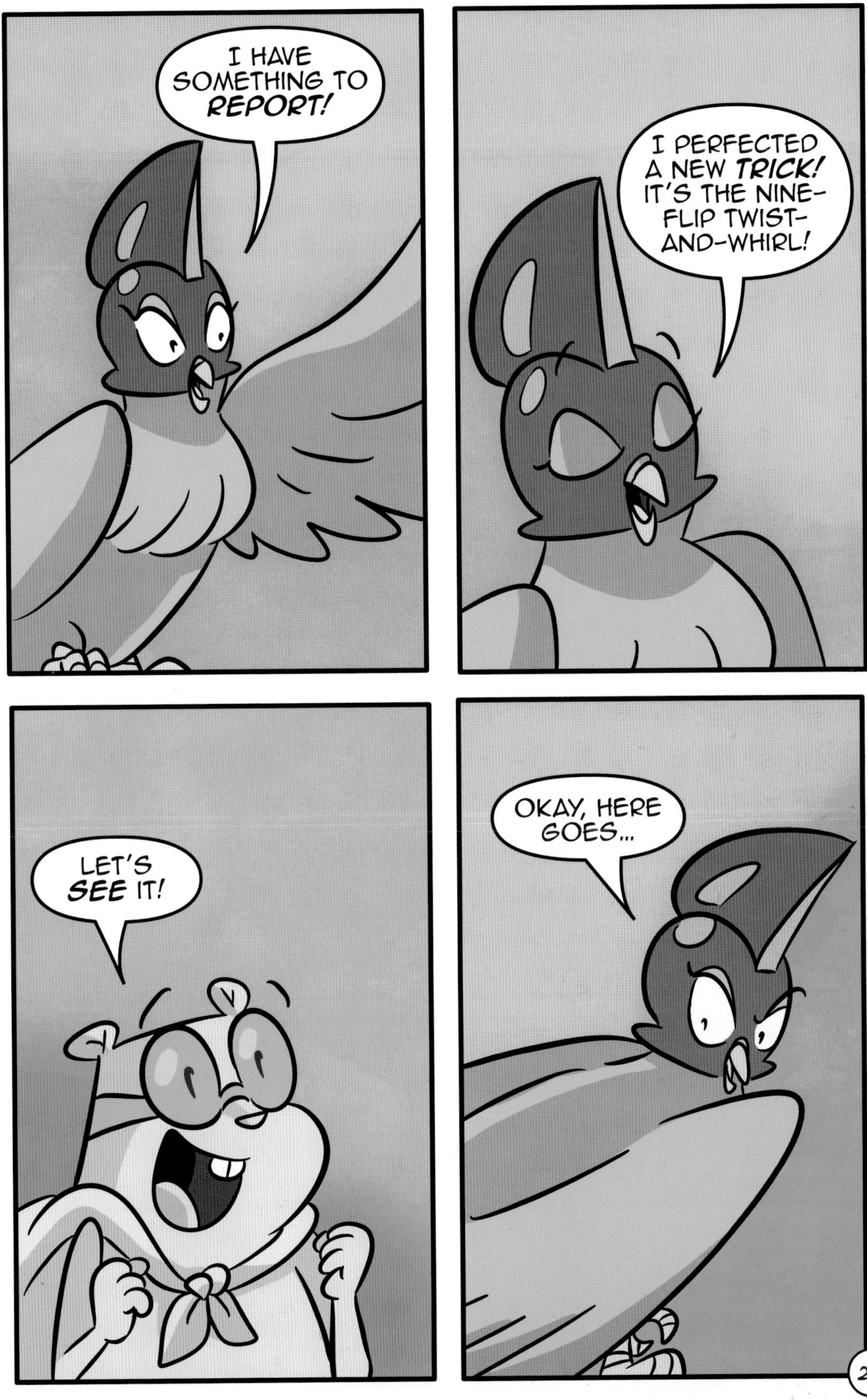
I HAVE SOMETHING TO REPORT!
I PERFECTED A NEW TRICK! IT'S THE NINE-FLIP TWIST-AND-WHIRL!
LET'S SEE IT!
OKAY, HERE GOES...

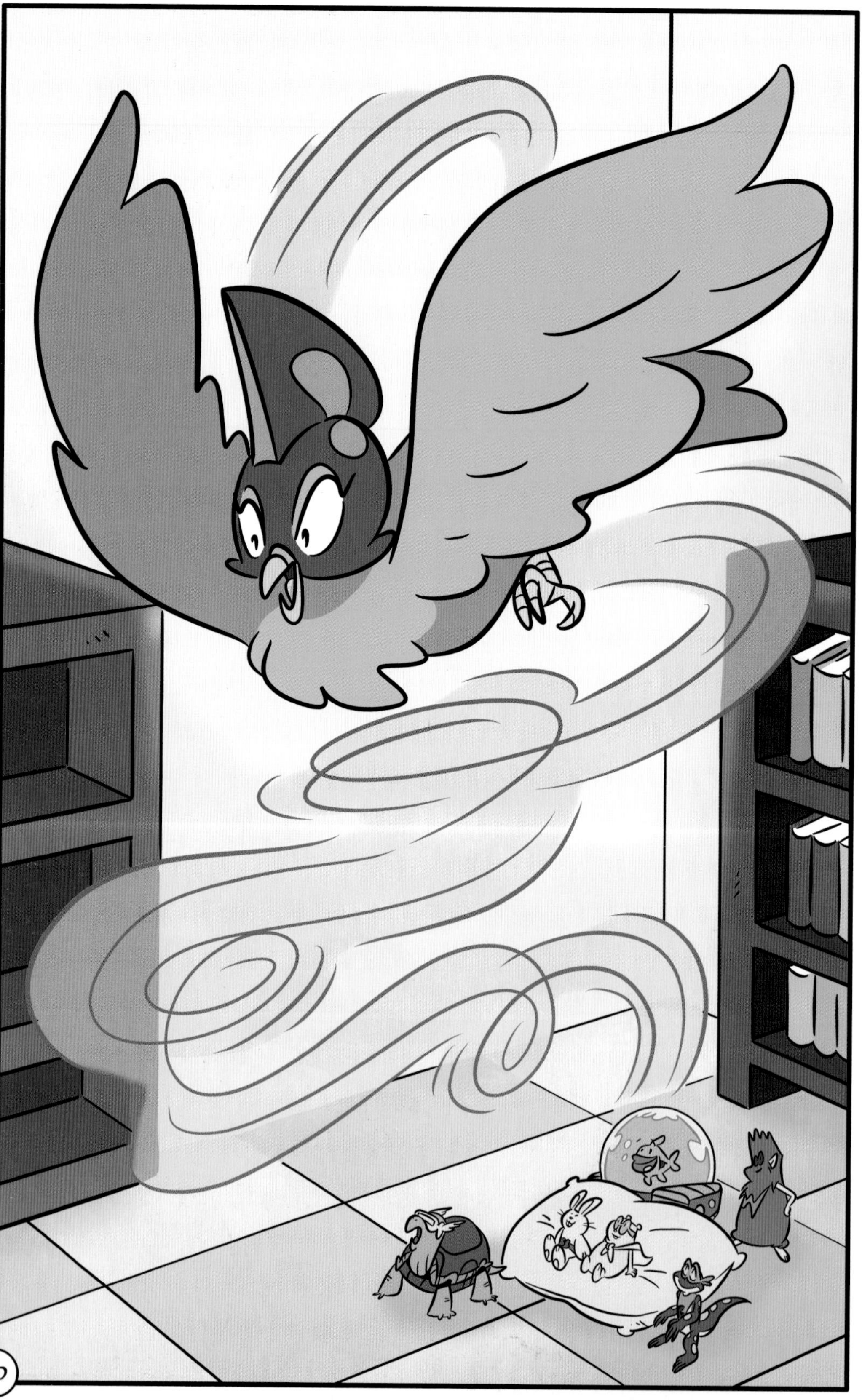

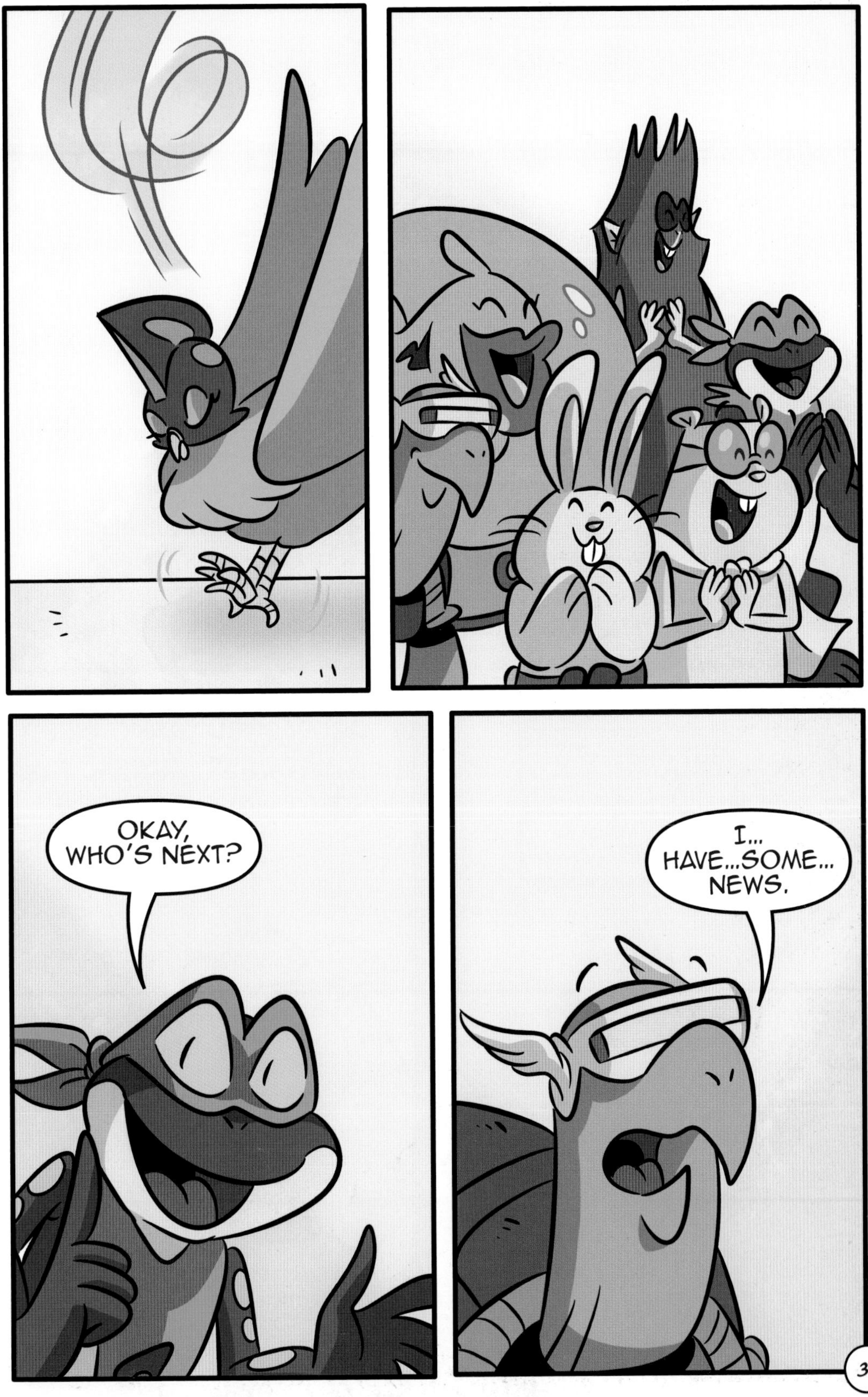
OKAY, WHO'S NEXT?
I... HAVE...SOME... NEWS.

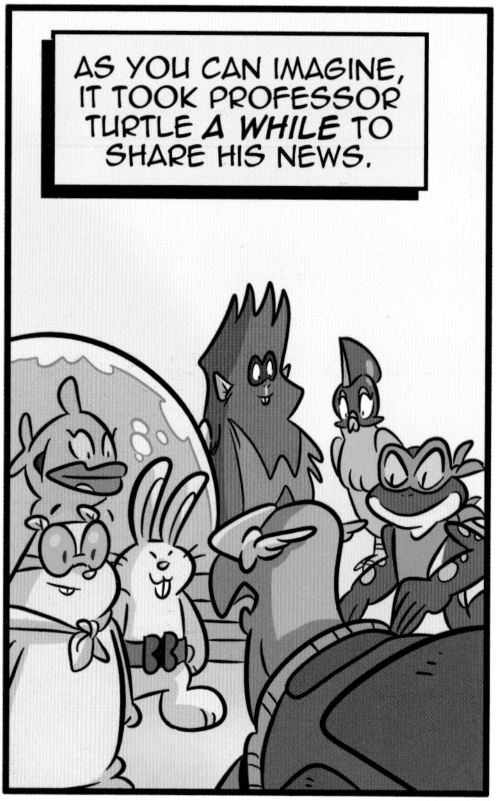
AS YOU CAN IMAGINE, IT TOOK PROFESSOR TURTLE A WHILE TO SHARE HIS NEWS.

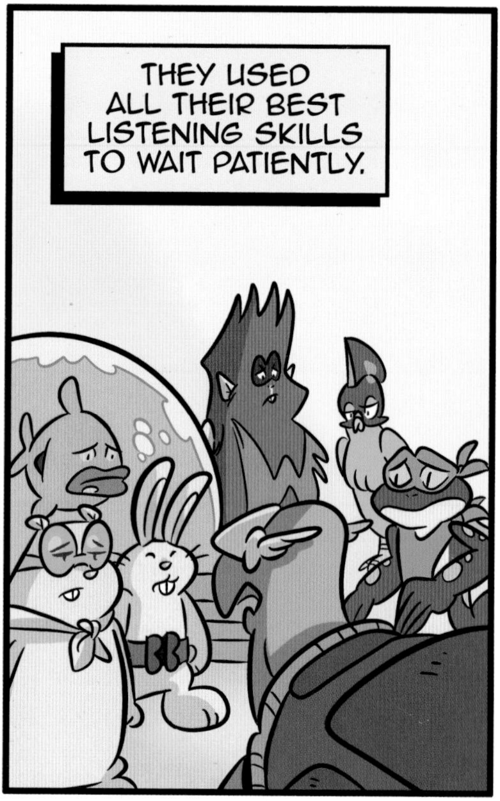
THEY USED ALL THEIR BEST LISTENING SKILLS TO WAIT PATIENTLY.

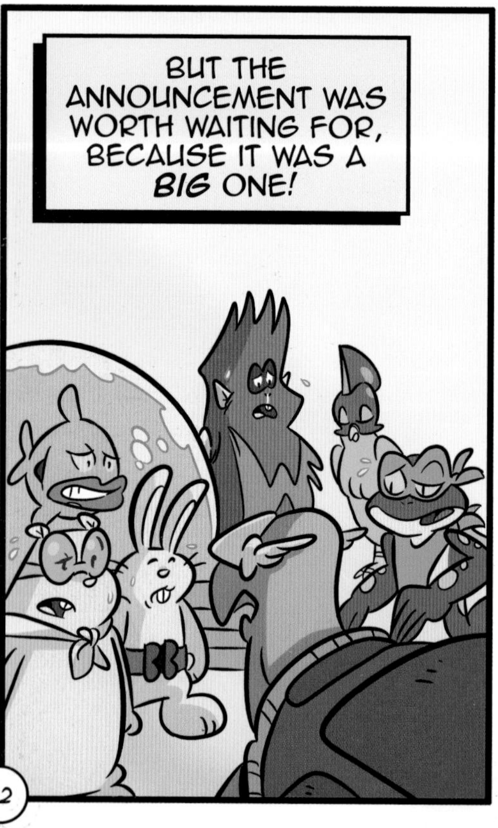
BUT THE ANNOUNCEMENT WAS WORTH WAITING FOR, BECAUSE IT WAS A BIG ONE!

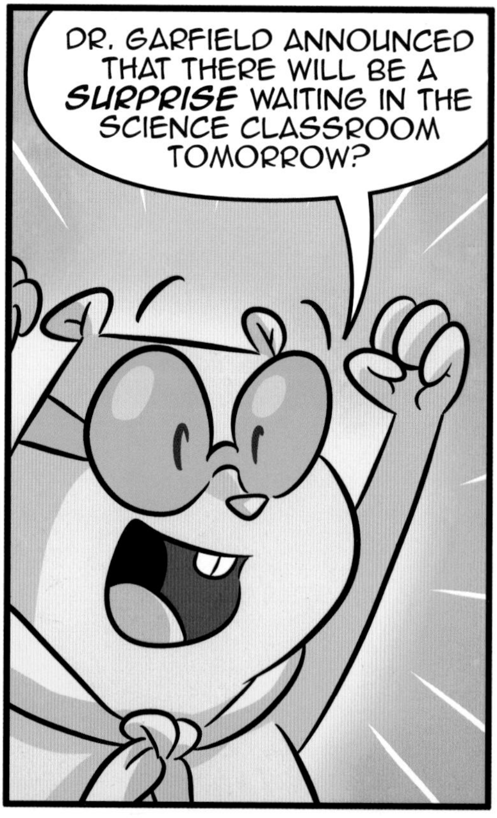
DR. GARFIELD ANNOUNCED THAT THERE WILL BE A SURPRISE WAITING IN THE SCIENCE CLASSROOM TOMORROW?

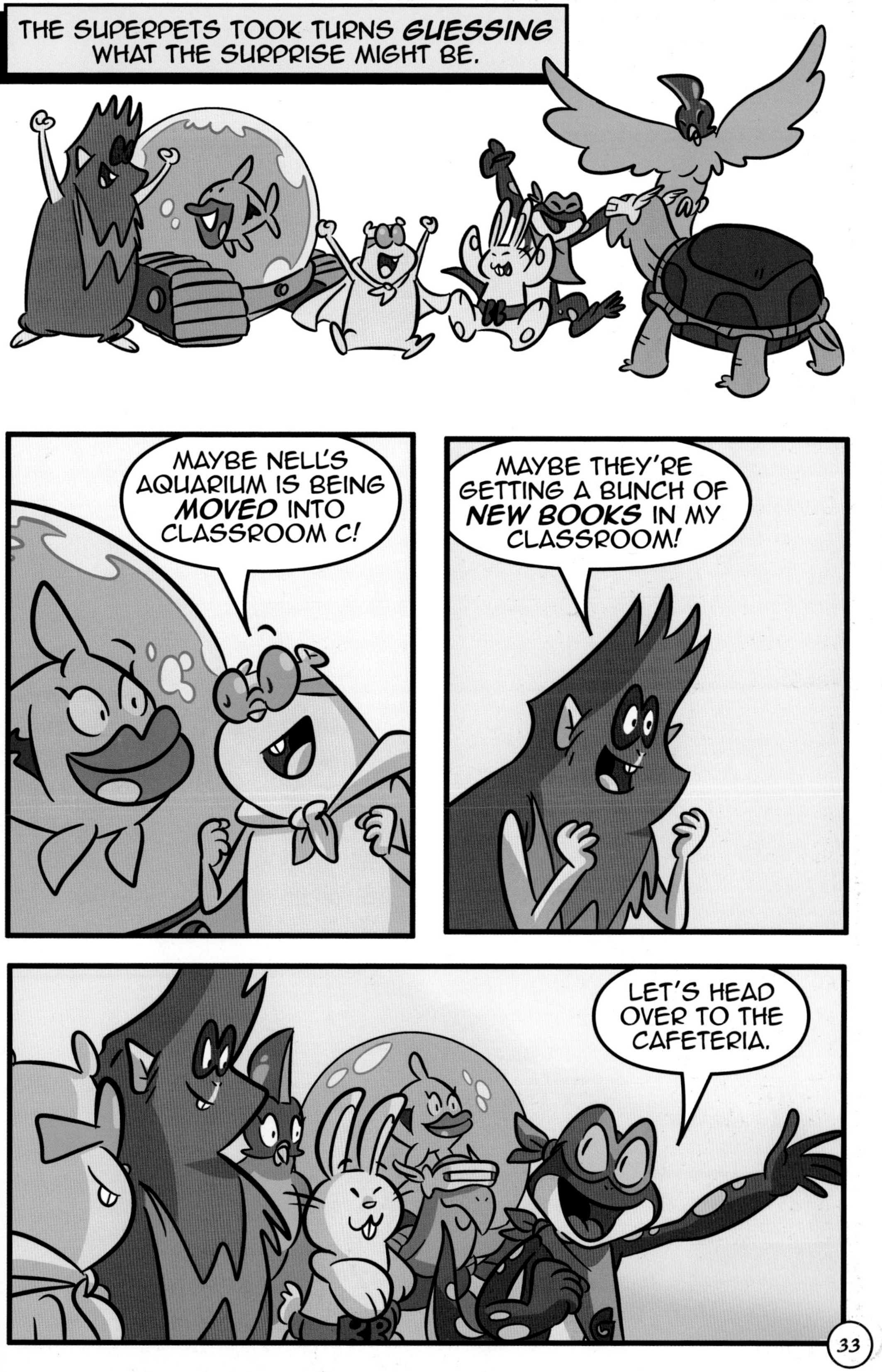
THE SUPERPETS TOOK TURNS *GUESSING* WHAT THE SURPRISE MIGHT BE.
MAYBE NELL'S AQUARIUM IS BEING *MOVED* INTO CLASSROOM C!
MAYBE THEY'RE GETTING A BUNCH OF *NEW BOOKS* IN MY CLASSROOM!
LET'S HEAD OVER TO THE CAFETERIA.

BEFORE LONG, THE SUPERPETS REACHED THE *CAFETERIA*.

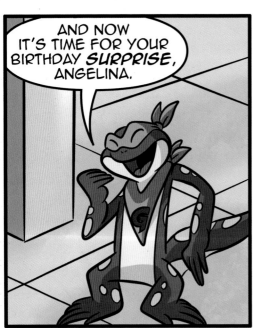

AND NOW IT'S TIME FOR YOUR BIRTHDAY *SURPRISE*, ANGELINA.

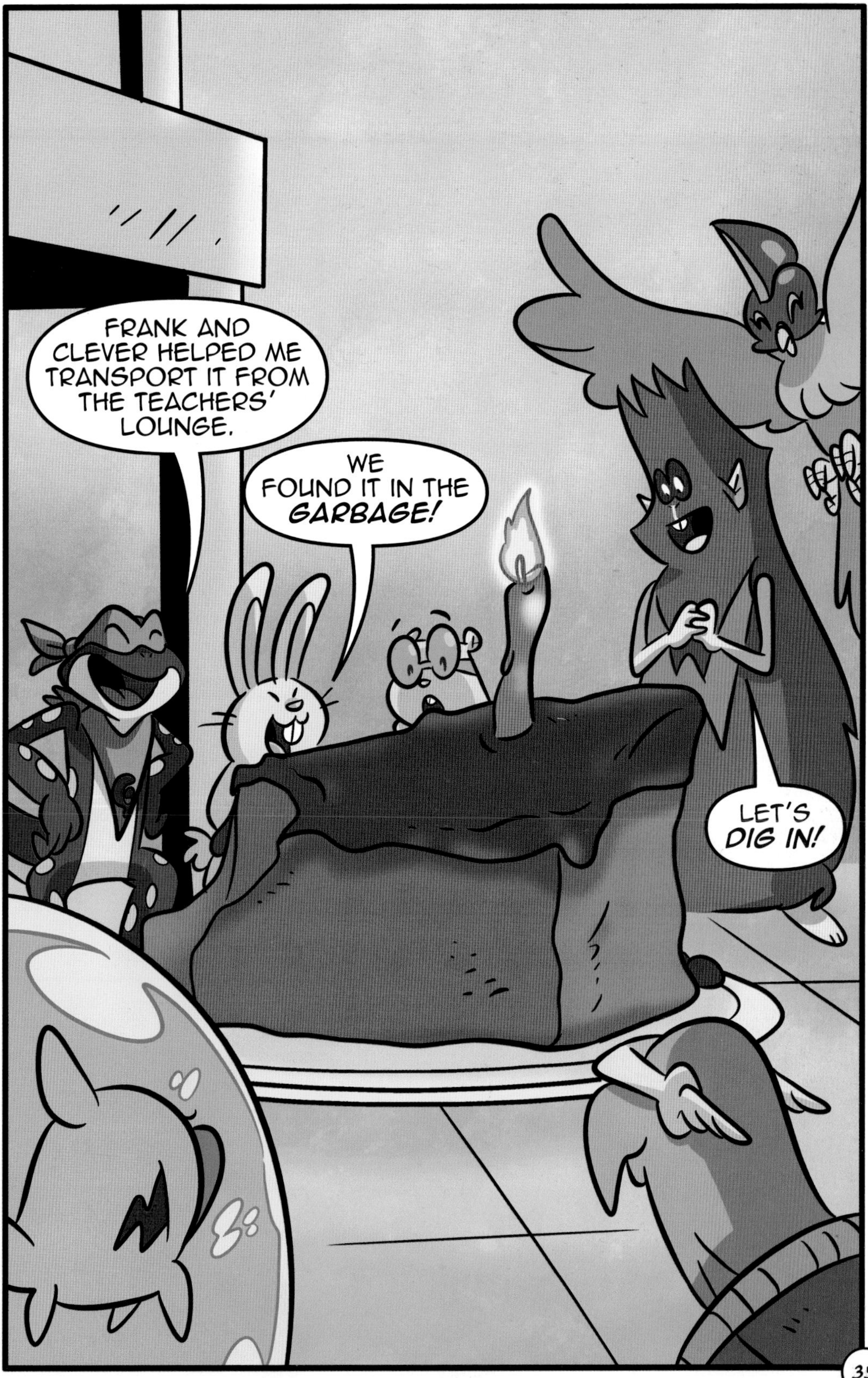
FRANK AND CLEVER HELPED ME TRANSPORT IT FROM THE TEACHERS' LOUNGE.
WE FOUND IT IN THE GARBAGE!
LET'S DIG IN!

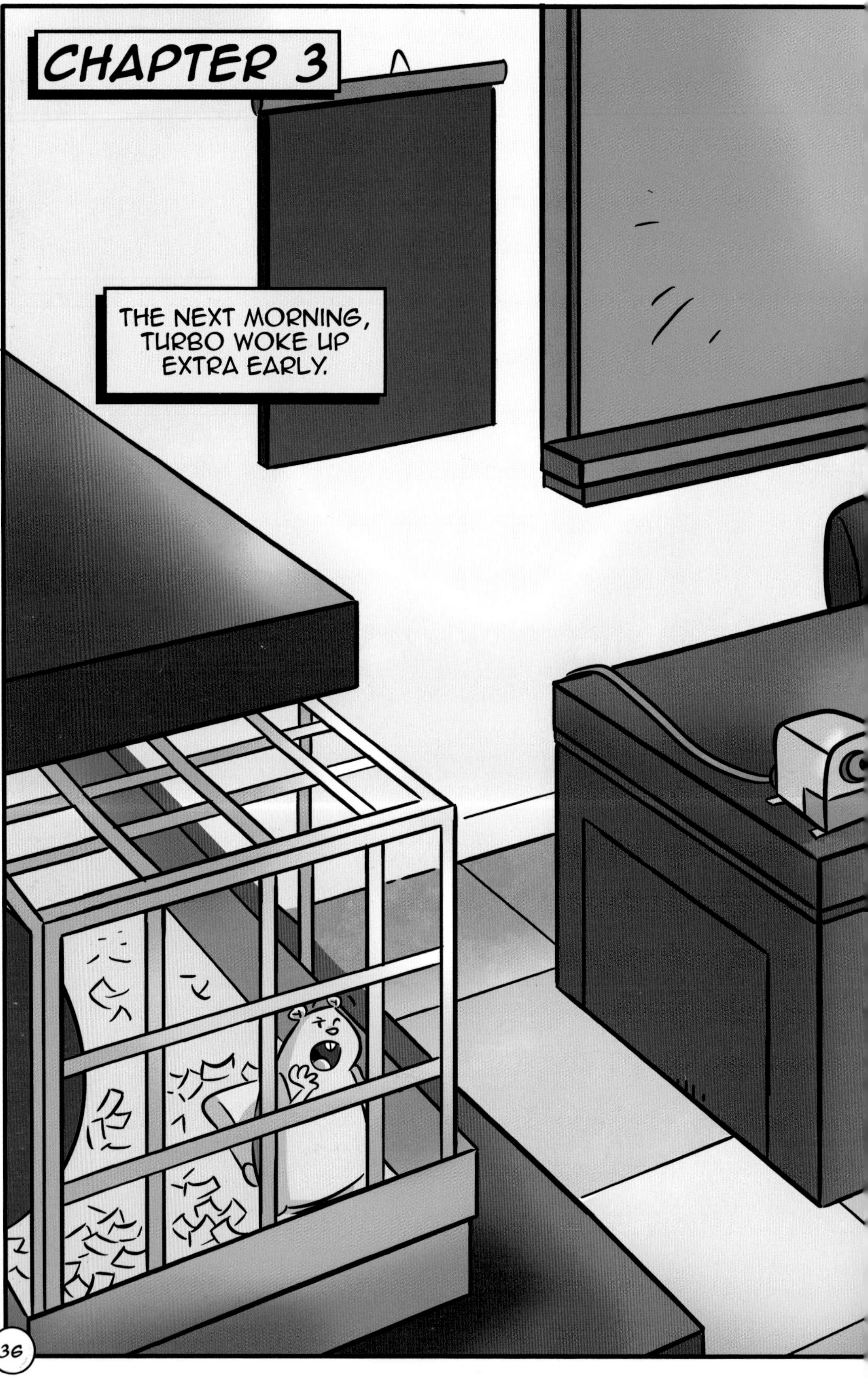
CHAPTER 3
THE NEXT MORNING, TURBO WOKE UP EXTRA EARLY.

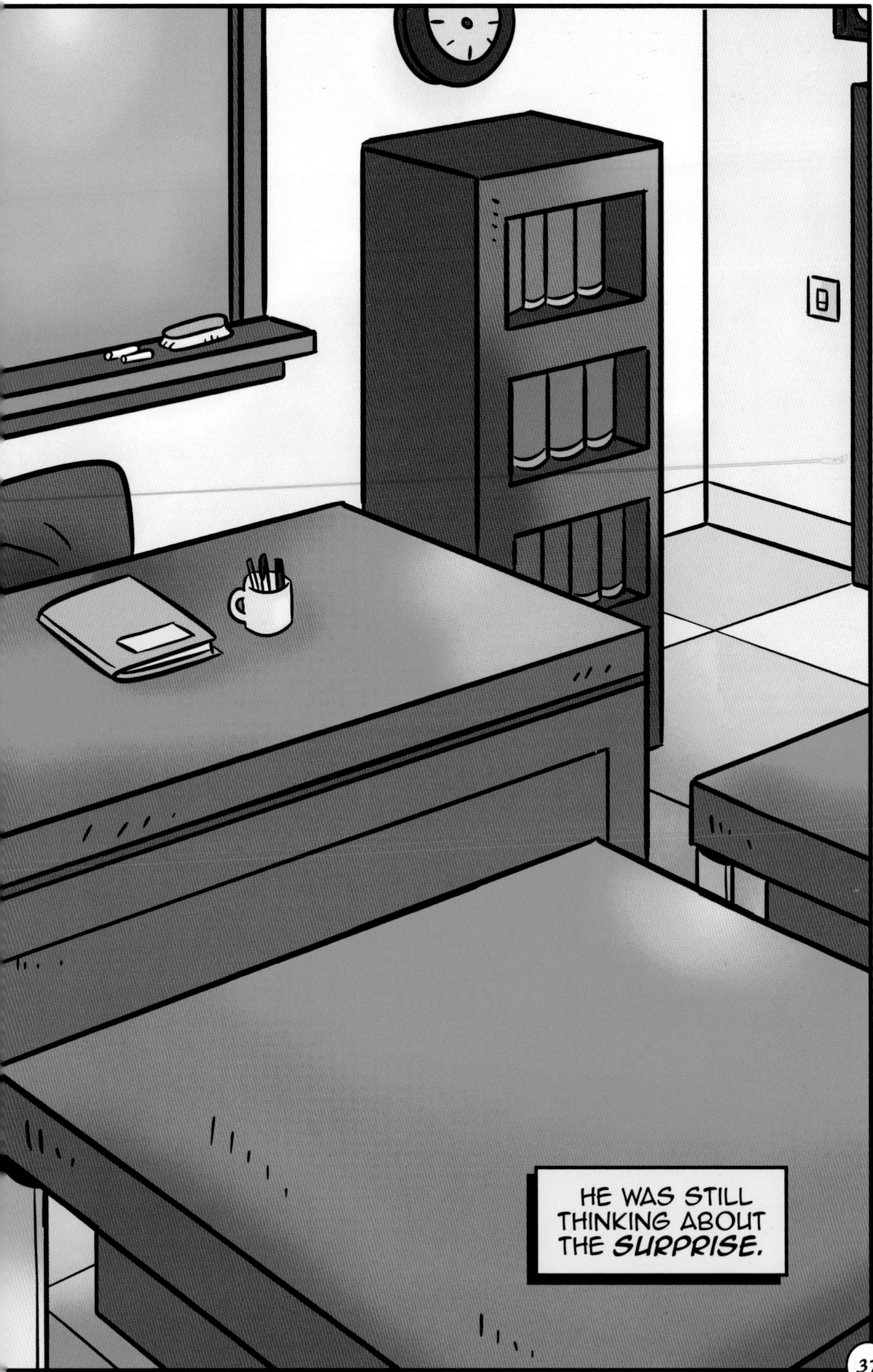
HE WAS STILL THINKING ABOUT THE *SURPRISE.*

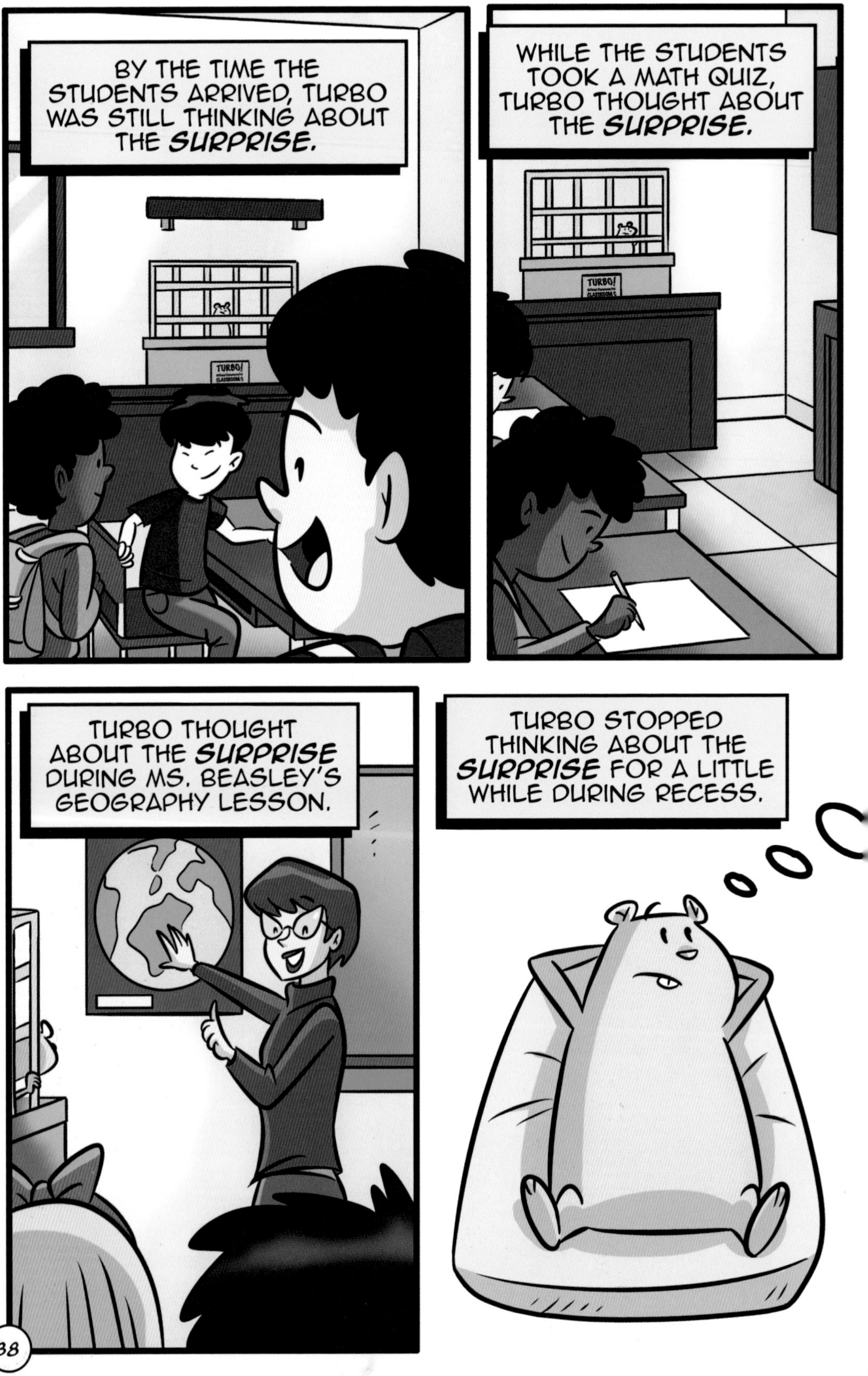
BY THE TIME THE STUDENTS ARRIVED, TURBO WAS STILL THINKING ABOUT THE *SURPRISE*.
TURBO!
WHILE THE STUDENTS TOOK A MATH QUIZ, TURBO THOUGHT ABOUT THE *SURPRISE*.
TURBO!
TURBO THOUGHT ABOUT THE *SURPRISE* DURING MS. BEASLEY'S GEOGRAPHY LESSON.
TURBO STOPPED THINKING ABOUT THE *SURPRISE* FOR A LITTLE WHILE DURING RECESS.

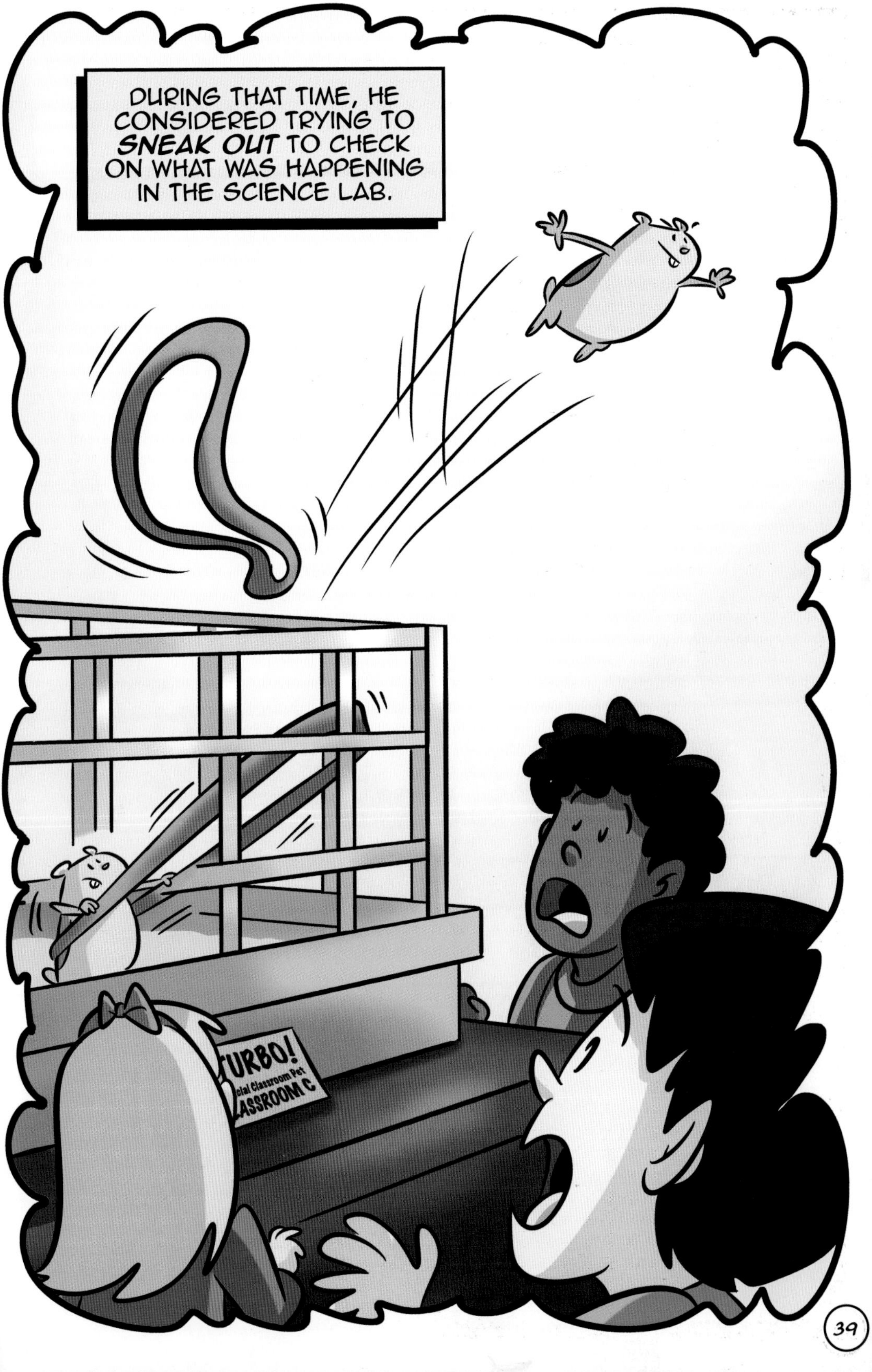
DURING THAT TIME, HE CONSIDERED TRYING TO *SNEAK OUT* TO CHECK ON WHAT WAS HAPPENING IN THE SCIENCE LAB.

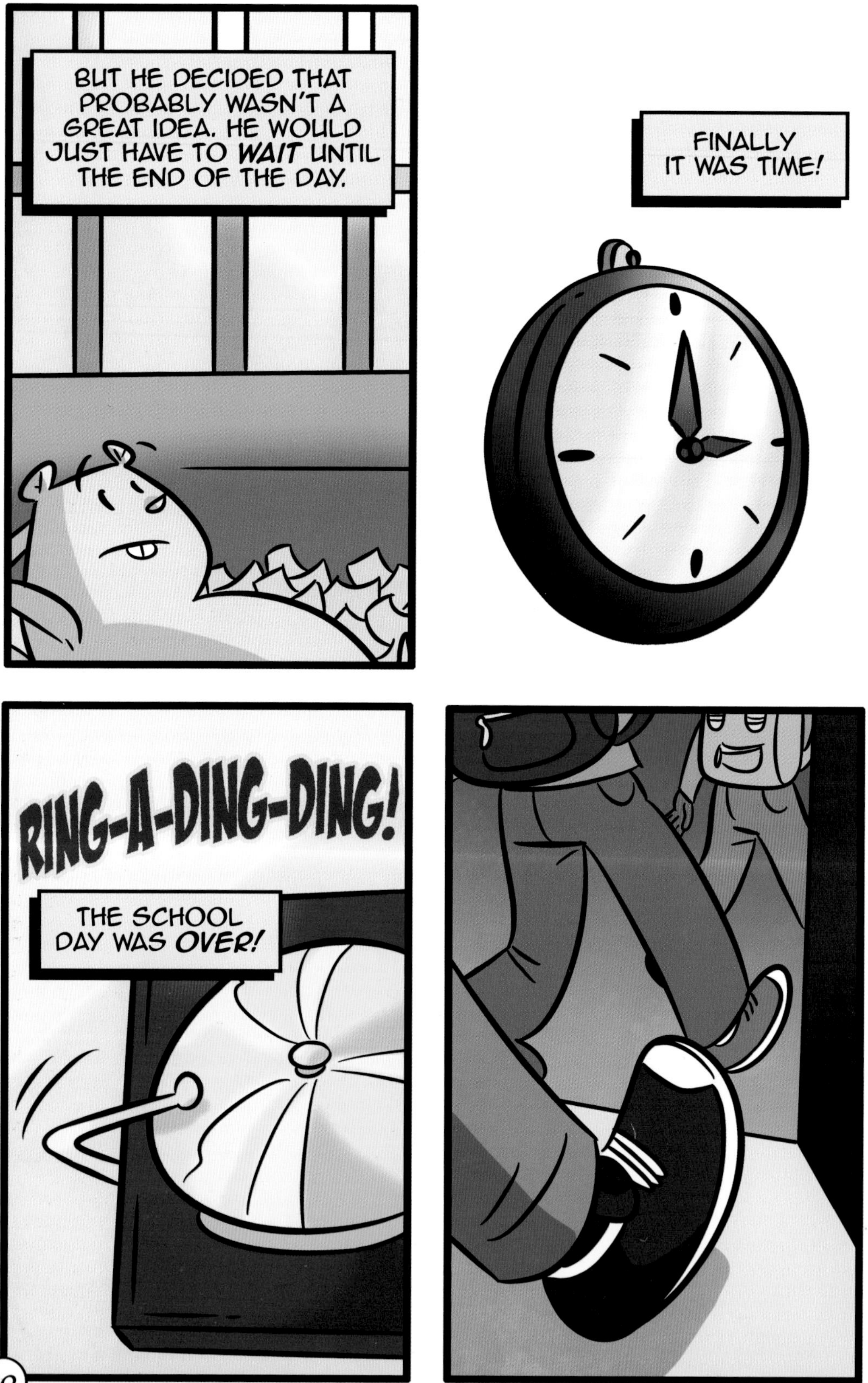
BUT HE DECIDED THAT PROBABLY WASN'T A GREAT IDEA. HE WOULD JUST HAVE TO *WAIT* UNTIL THE END OF THE DAY.
FINALLY IT WAS TIME!
RING-A-DING-DING!
THE SCHOOL DAY WAS *OVER!*

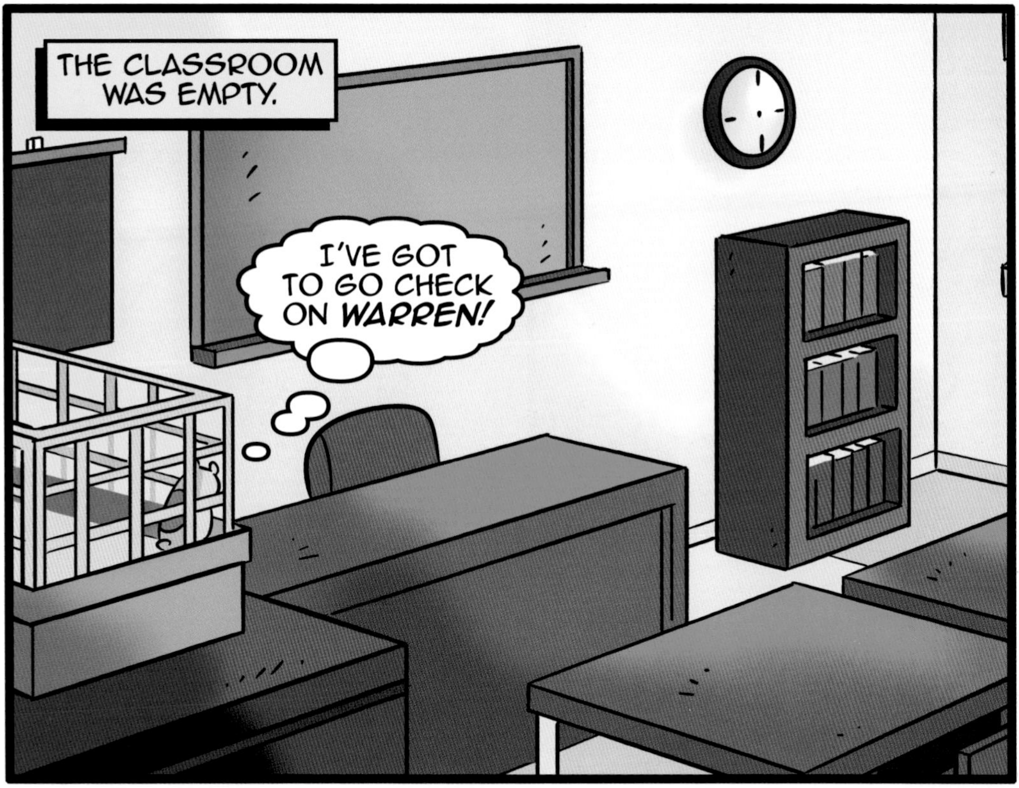
THE CLASSROOM WAS EMPTY.
I'VE GOT TO GO CHECK ON WARREN!

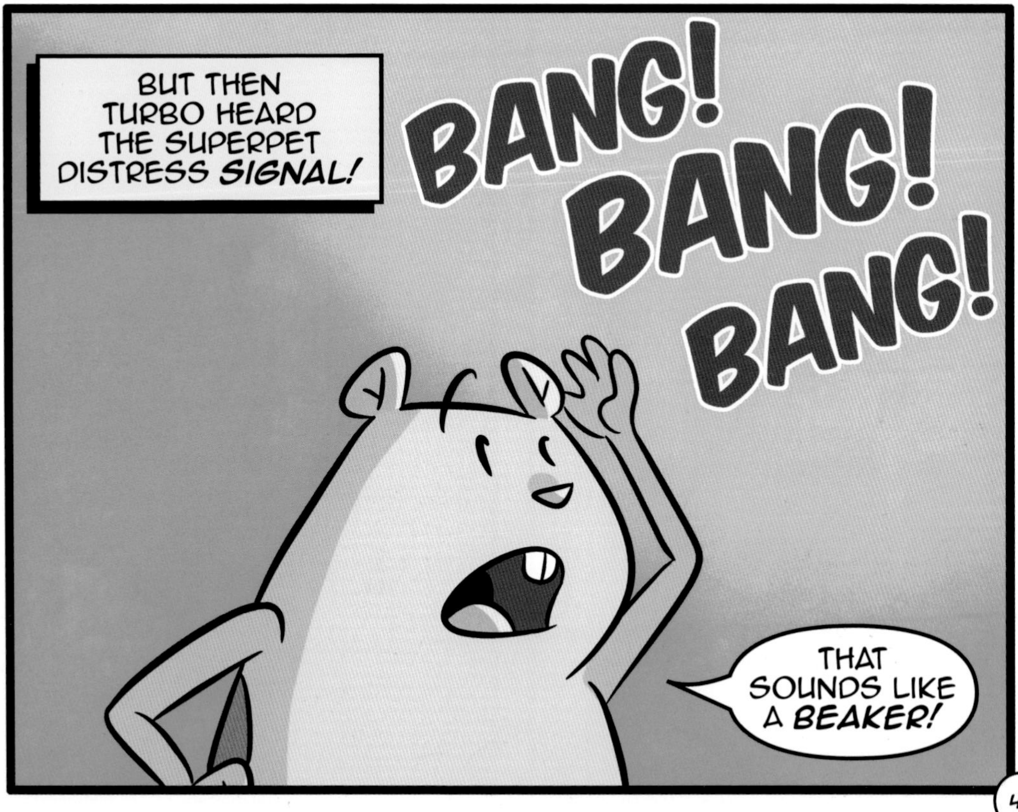
BUT THEN TURBO HEARD THE SUPERPET DISTRESS SIGNAL!
BANG! BANG! BANG!
THAT SOUNDS LIKE A BEAKER!

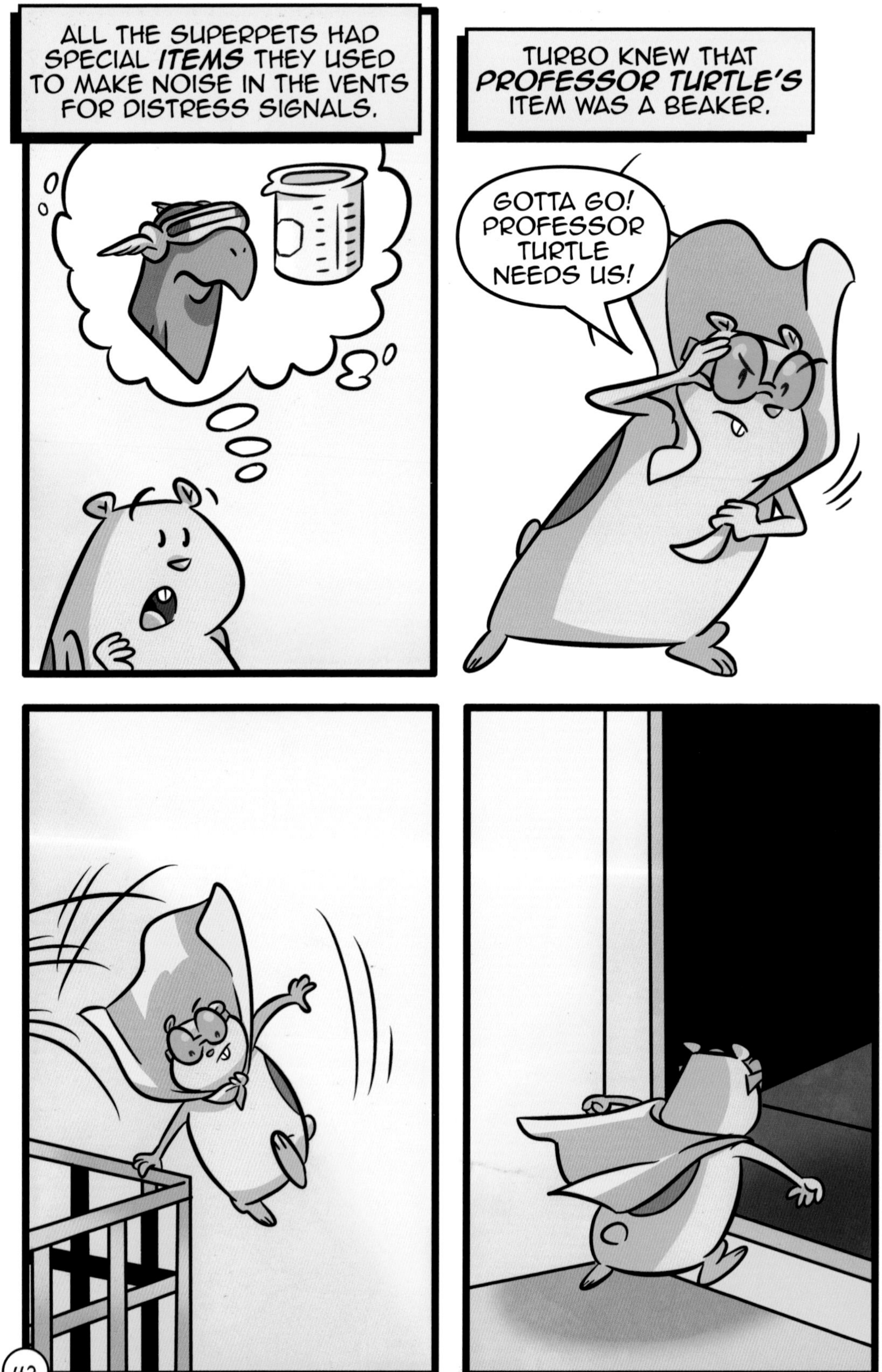
ALL THE SUPERPETS HAD SPECIAL *ITEMS* THEY USED TO MAKE NOISE IN THE VENTS FOR DISTRESS SIGNALS.
TURBO KNEW THAT *PROFESSOR TURTLE'S* ITEM WAS A BEAKER.
GOTTA GO! PROFESSOR TURTLE NEEDS US!

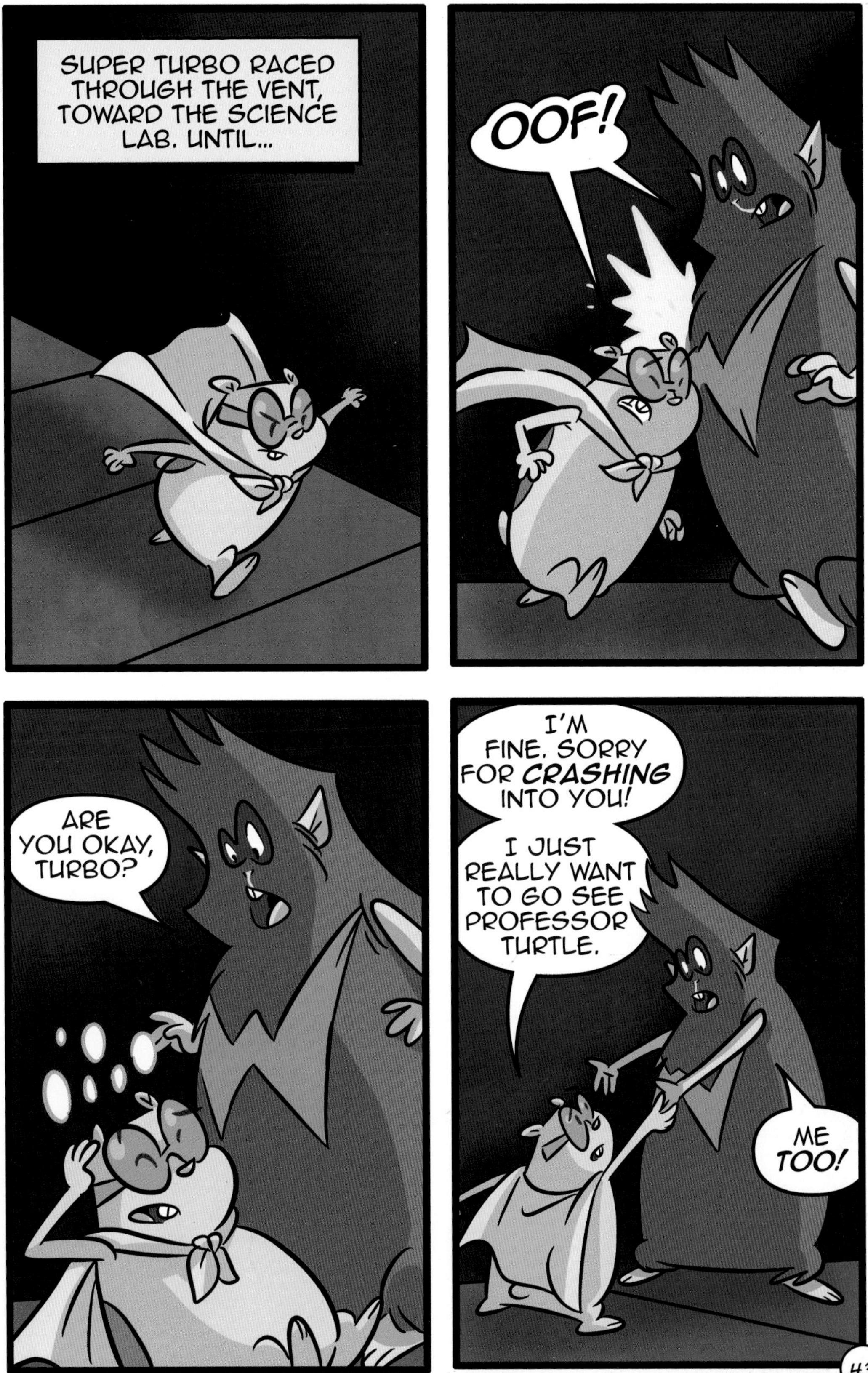
SUPER TURBO RACED THROUGH THE VENT, TOWARD THE SCIENCE LAB. UNTIL...
OOF!
ARE YOU OKAY, TURBO?
I'M FINE. SORRY FOR CRASHING INTO YOU!
I JUST REALLY WANT TO GO SEE PROFESSOR TURTLE.
ME TOO!

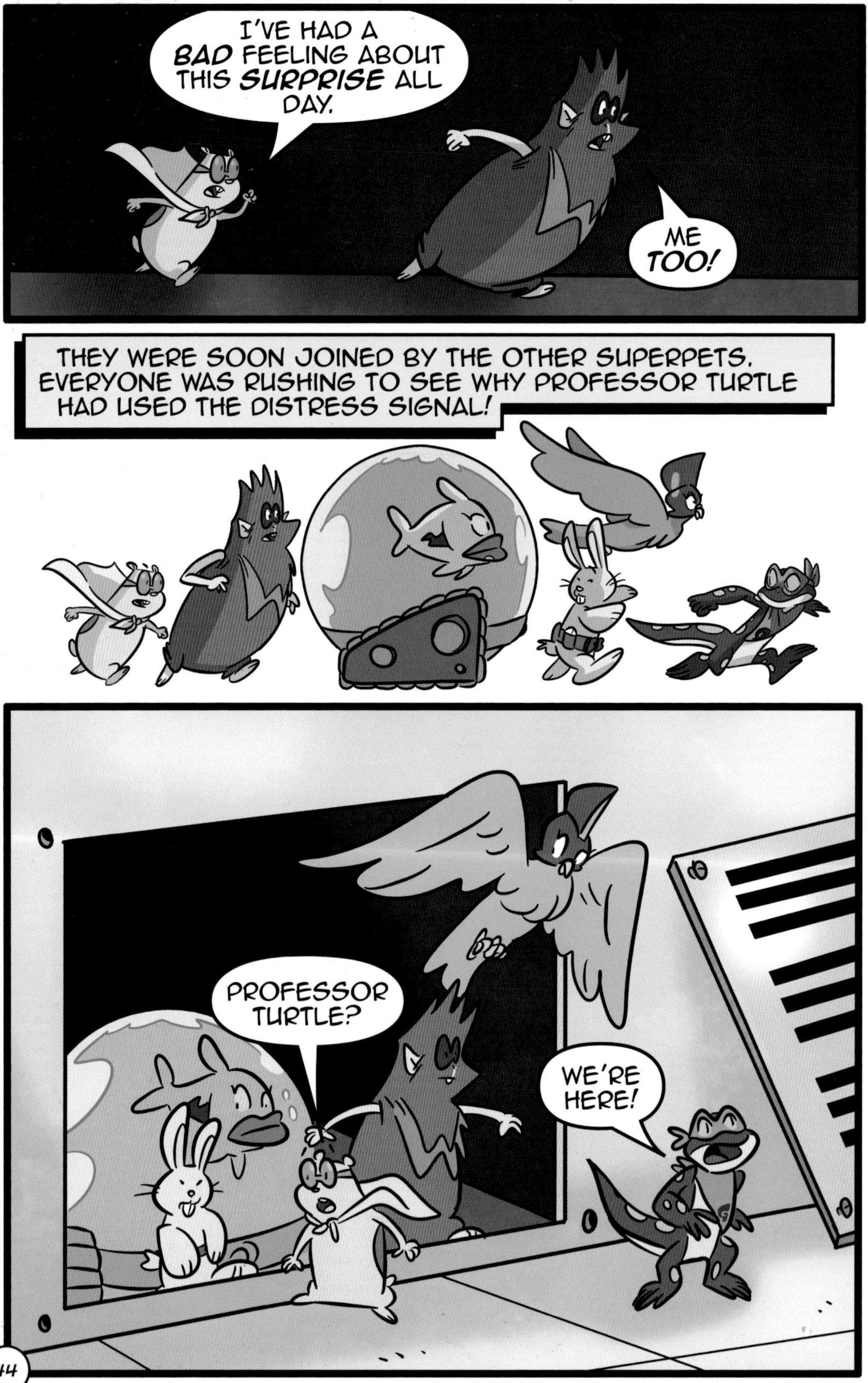

I'VE HAD A BAD FEELING ABOUT THIS SURPRISE ALL DAY.
ME TOO!
THEY WERE SOON JOINED BY THE OTHER SUPERPETS. EVERYONE WAS RUSHING TO SEE WHY PROFESSOR TURTLE HAD USED THE DISTRESS SIGNAL!
PROFESSOR TURTLE?
WE'RE HERE!

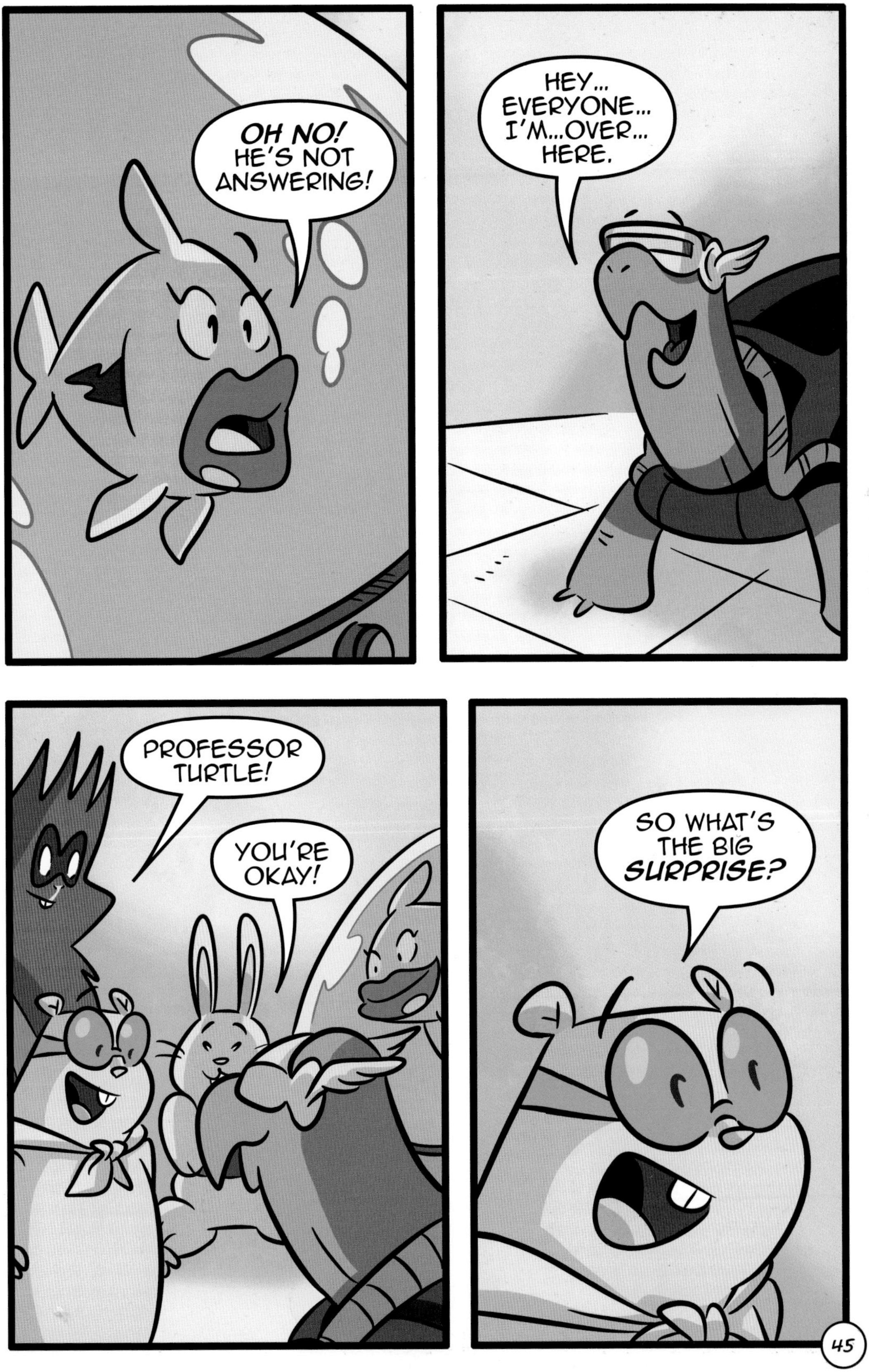
OH NO! HE'S NOT ANSWERING!
HEY... EVERYONE... I'M...OVER... HERE.
PROFESSOR TURTLE!
YOU'RE OKAY!
SO WHAT'S THE BIG SURPRISE?

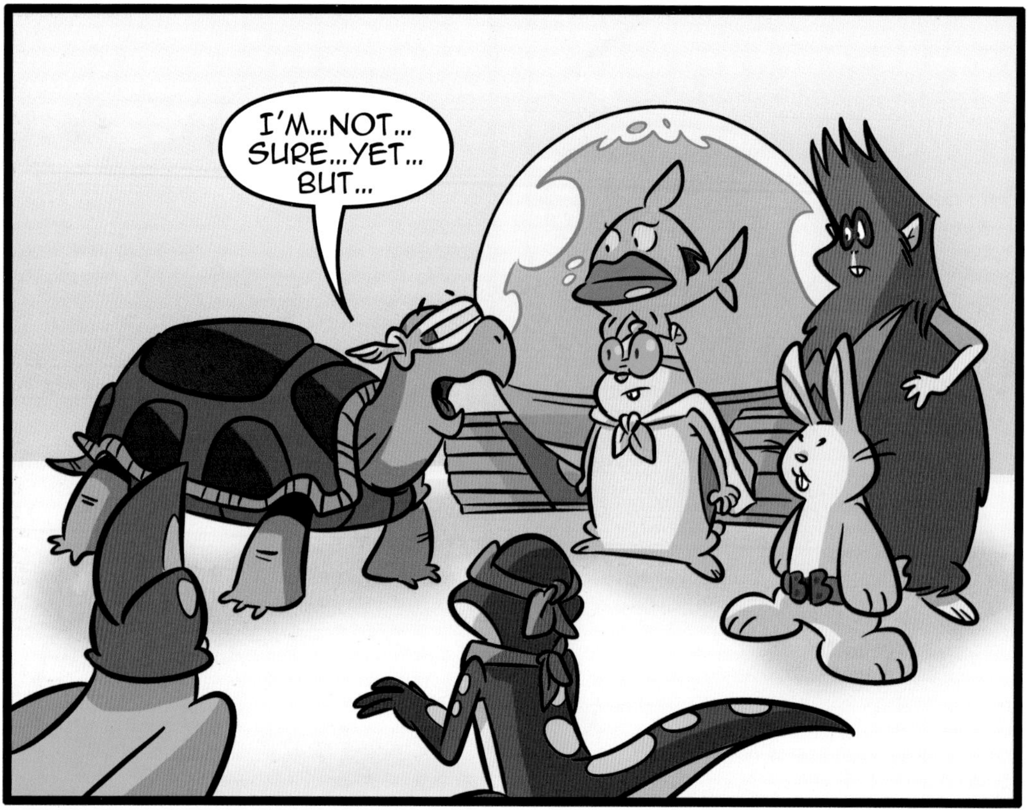
I'M...NOT... SURE...YET... BUT...

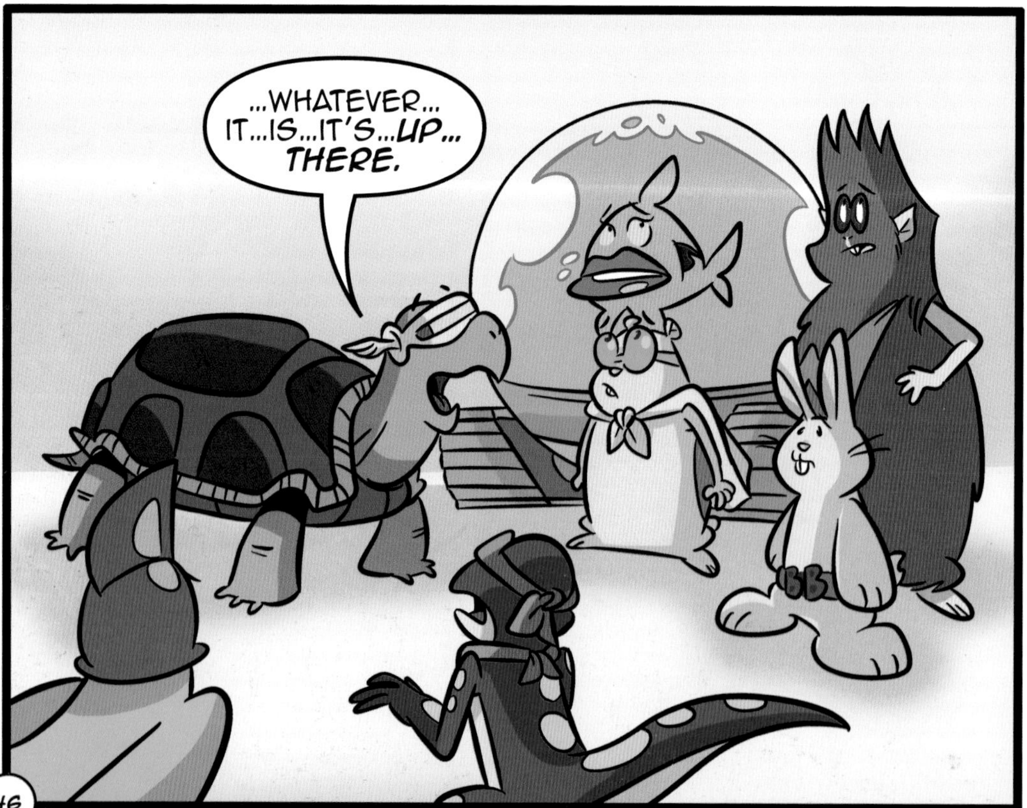
...WHATEVER... IT...IS...IT'S...*UP*... *THERE.*

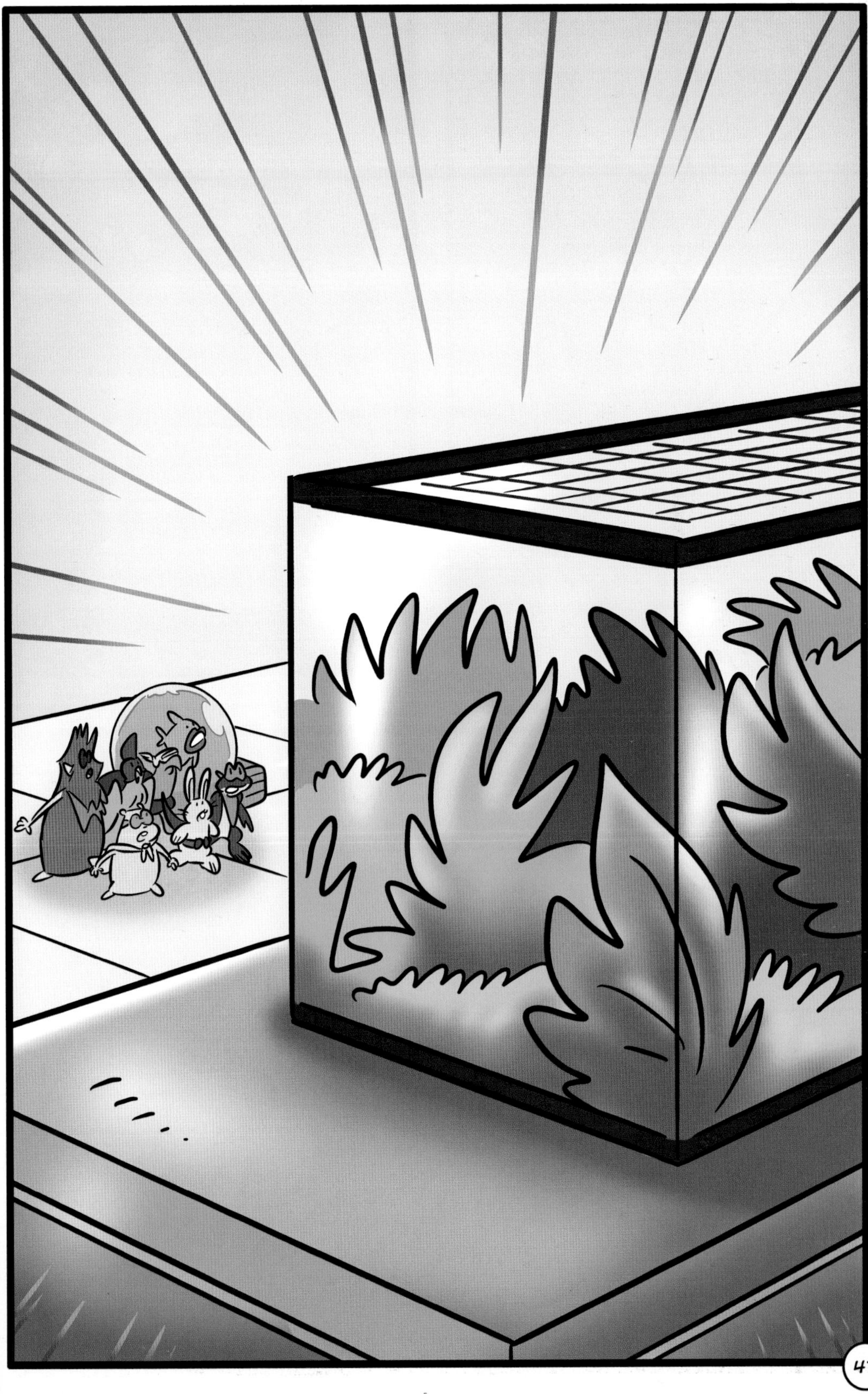
!!!...

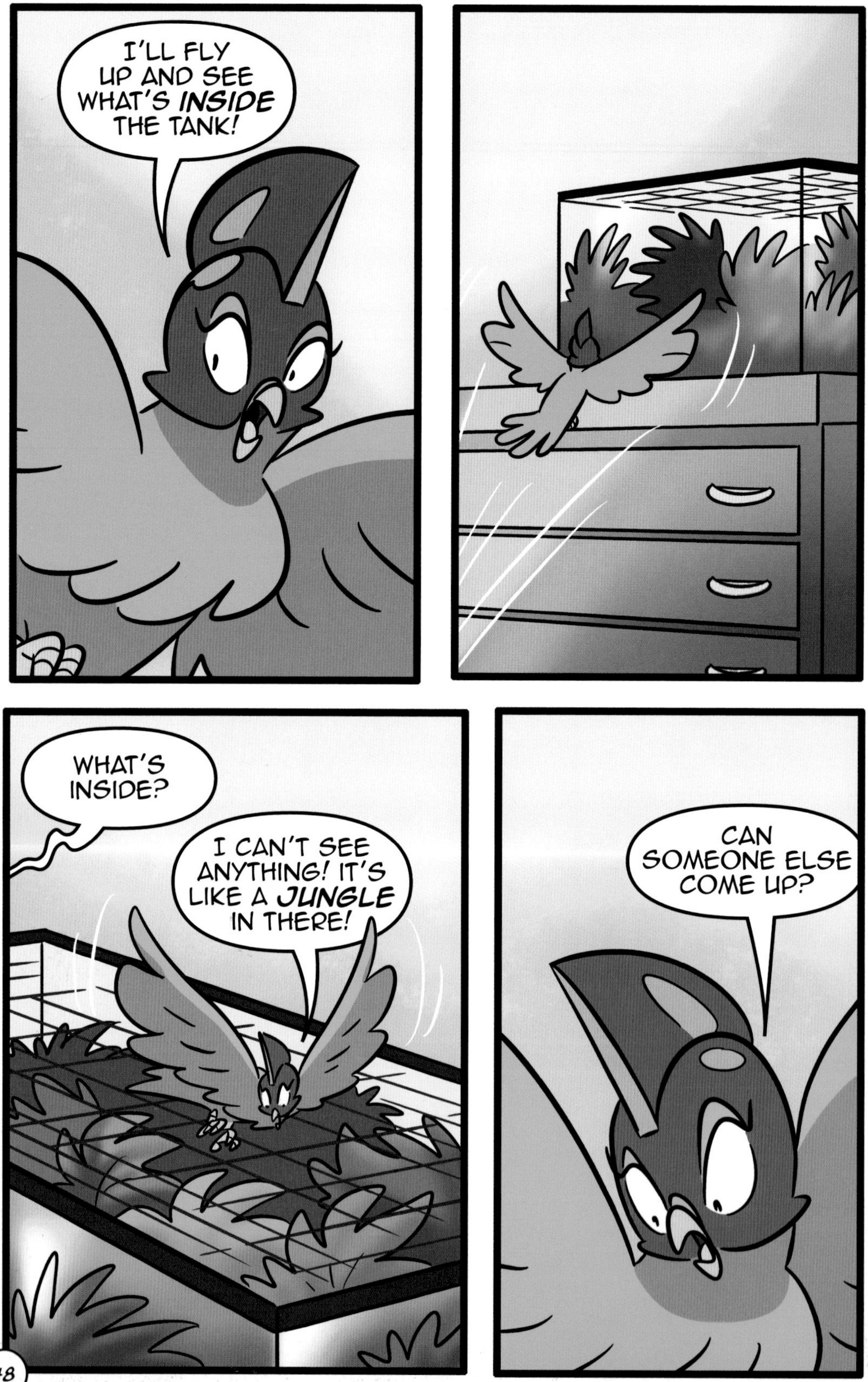
I'LL FLY UP AND SEE WHAT'S *INSIDE* THE TANK!
WHAT'S INSIDE?
I CAN'T SEE ANYTHING! IT'S LIKE A *JUNGLE* IN THERE!
CAN SOMEONE ELSE COME UP?

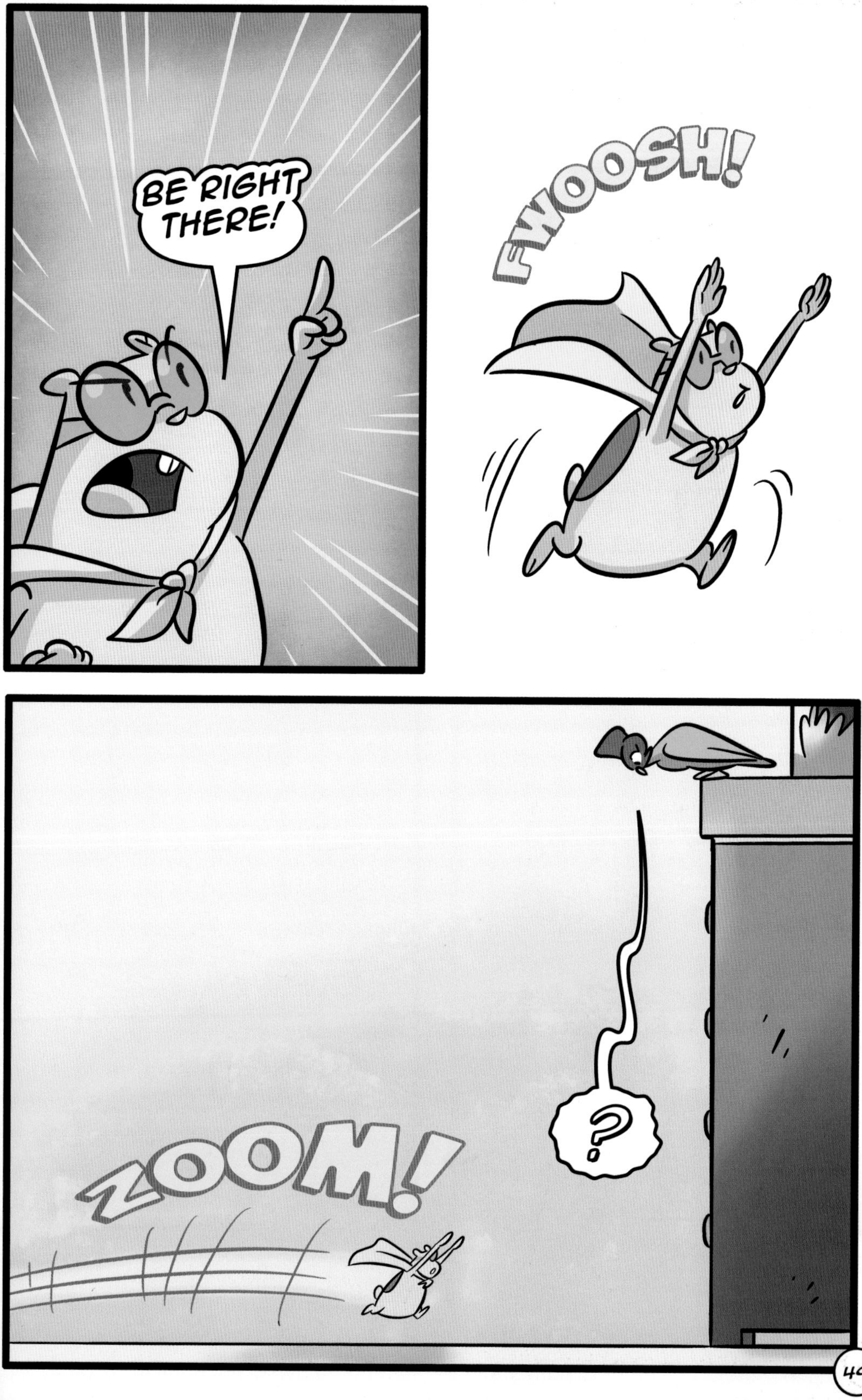
BE RIGHT THERE!
FWOOSH!
?
ZOOM!

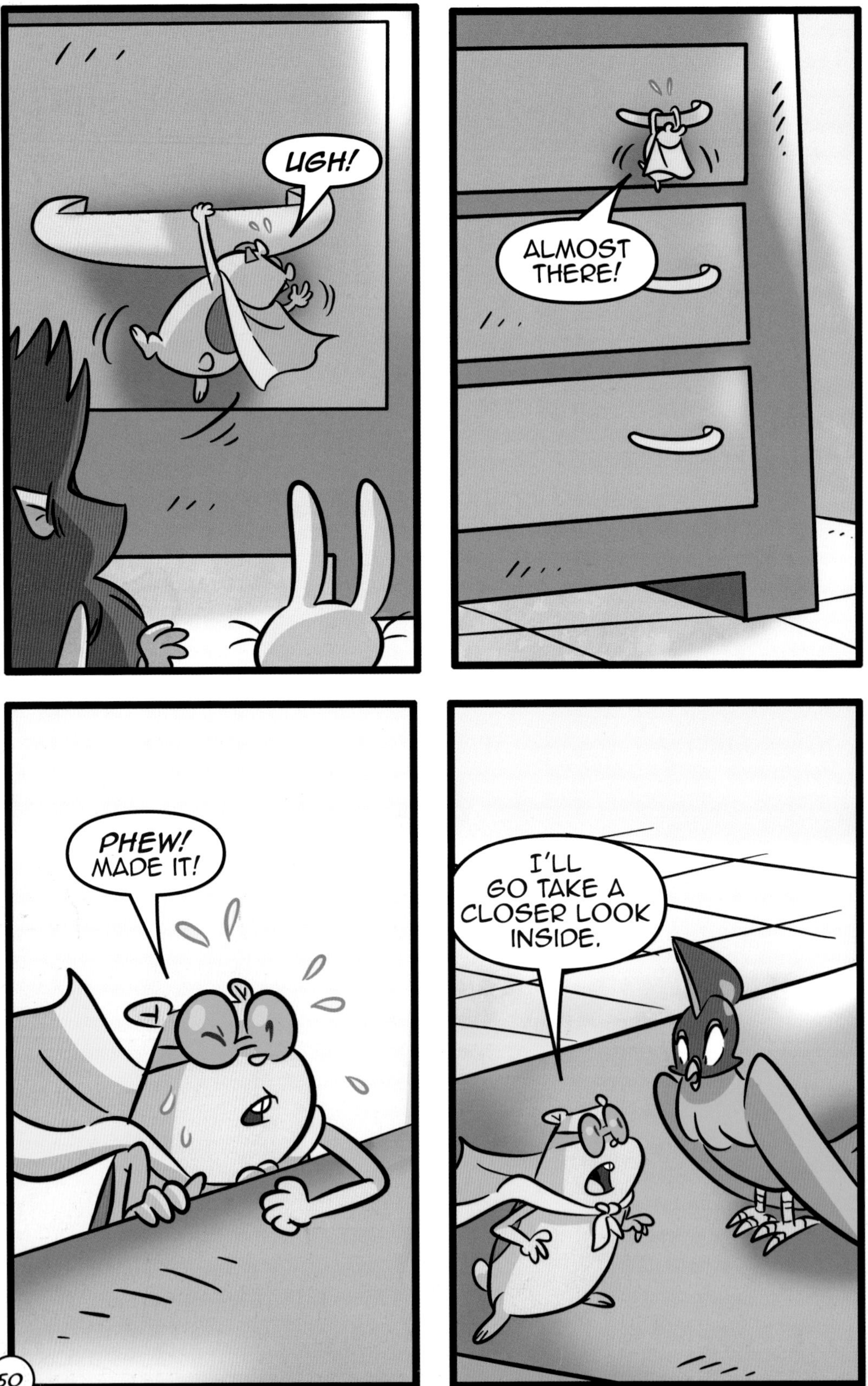
UGH!
ALMOST THERE!
PHEW! MADE IT!
I'LL GO TAKE A CLOSER LOOK INSIDE.

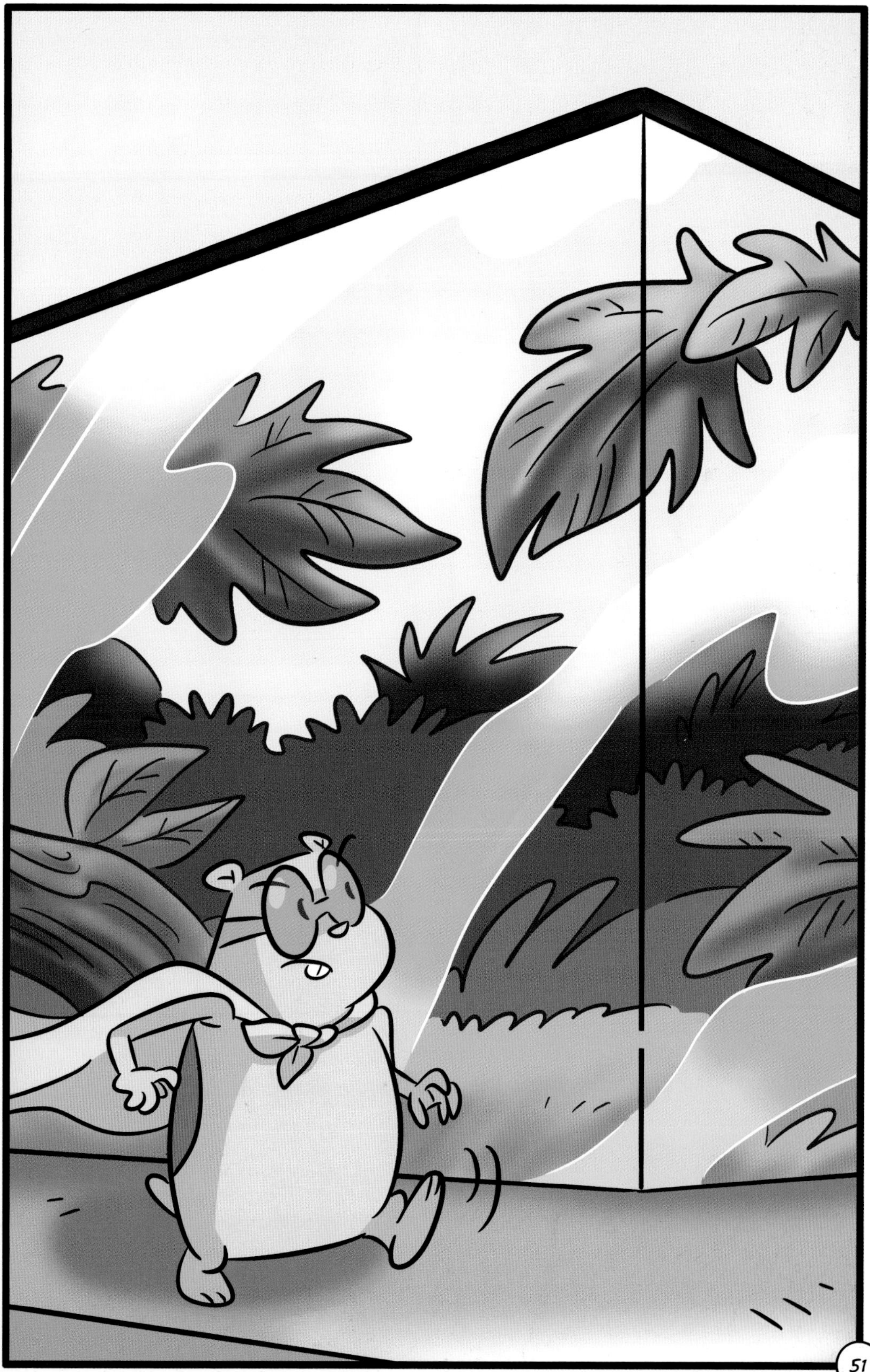

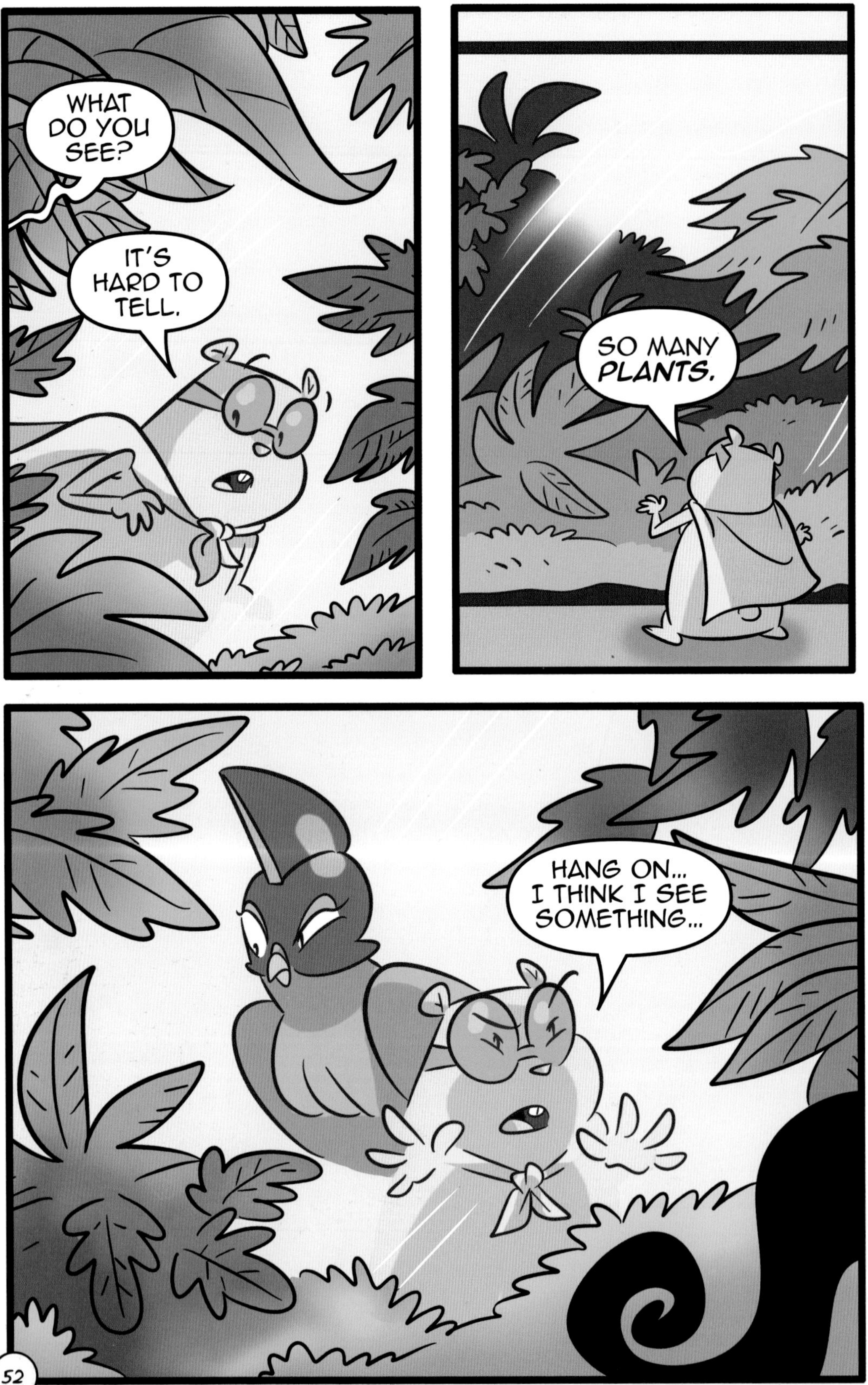
WHAT DO YOU SEE?
IT'S HARD TO TELL.
SO MANY PLANTS.
HANG ON... I THINK I SEE SOMETHING...

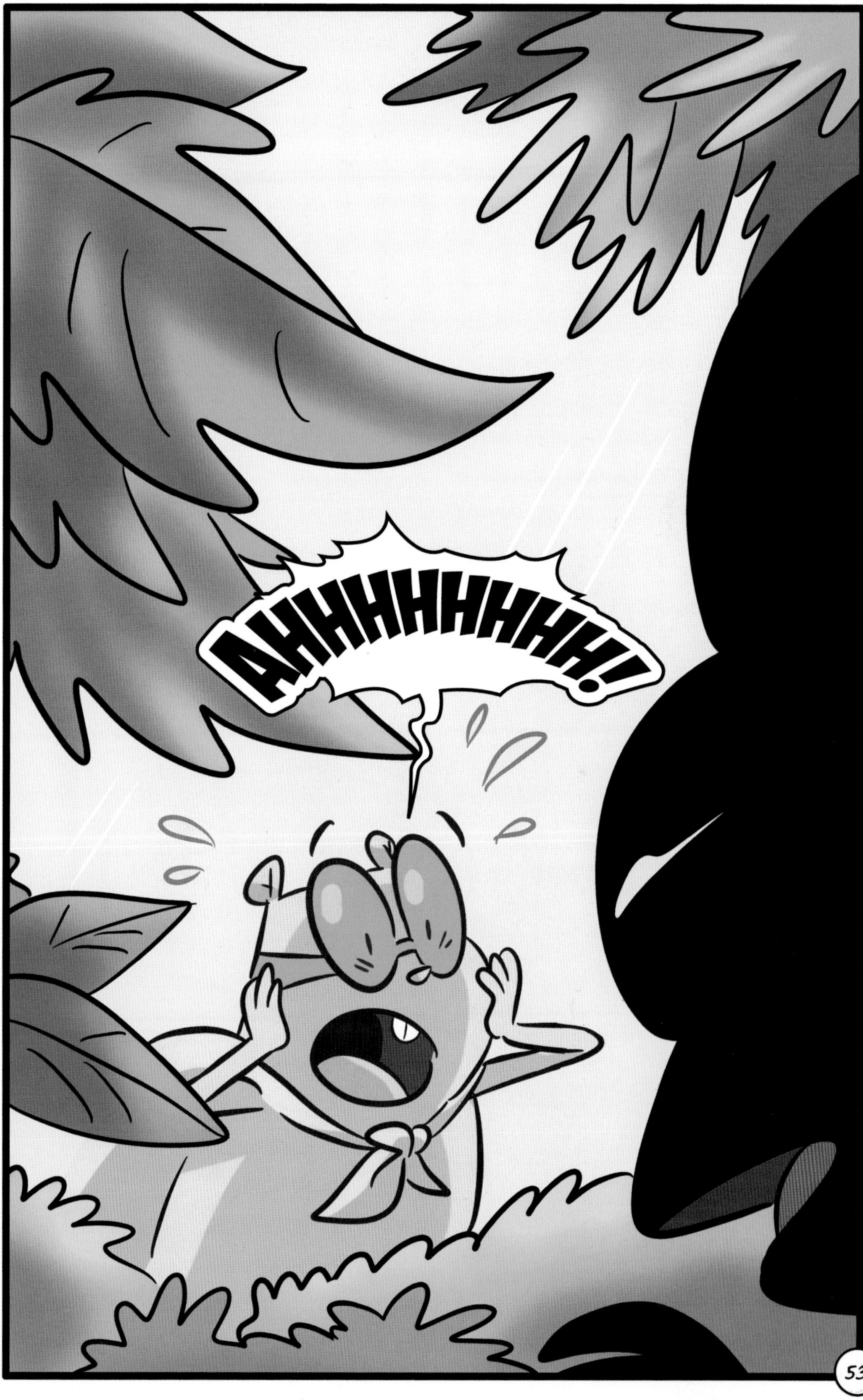
AHHHHHHHHH!

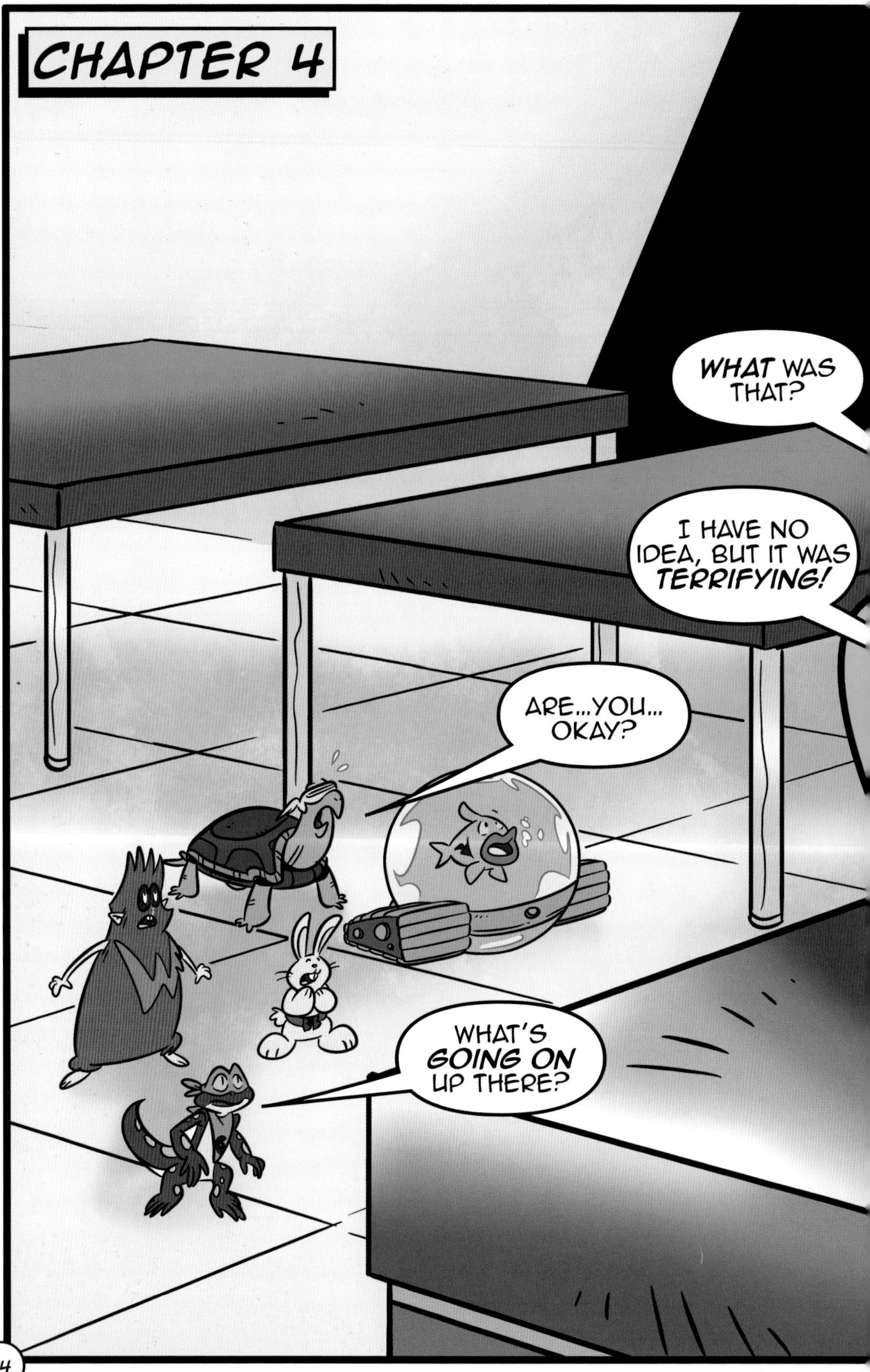
CHAPTER 4
WHAT WAS THAT?
I HAVE NO IDEA, BUT IT WAS TERRIFYING!
ARE...YOU... OKAY?
WHAT'S GOING ON UP THERE?

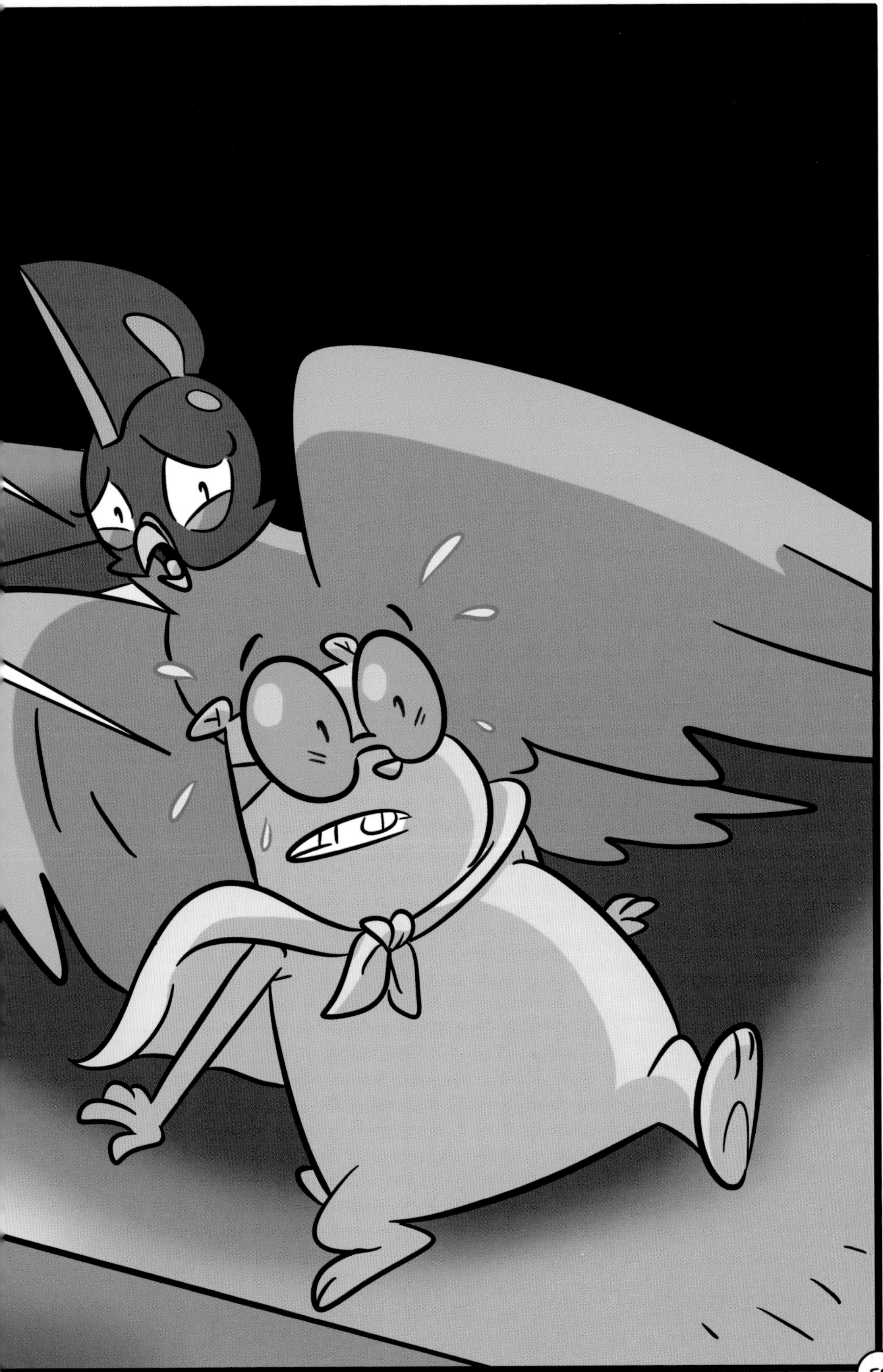

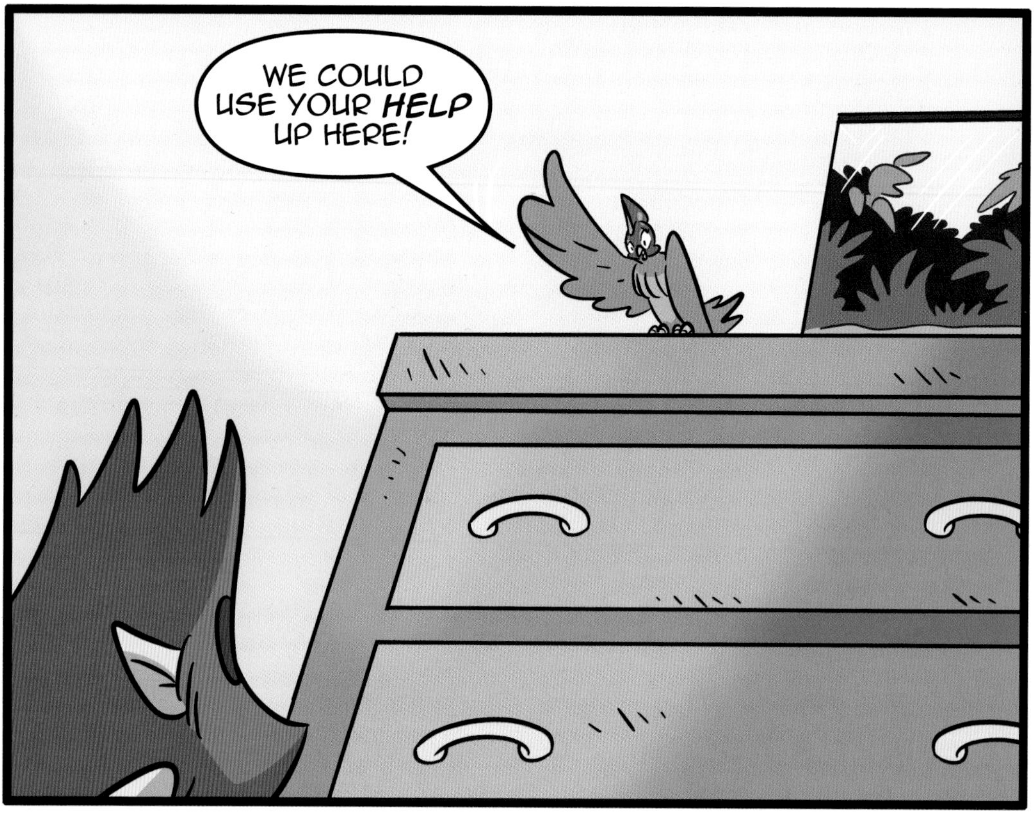
WE COULD USE YOUR **HELP** UP HERE!

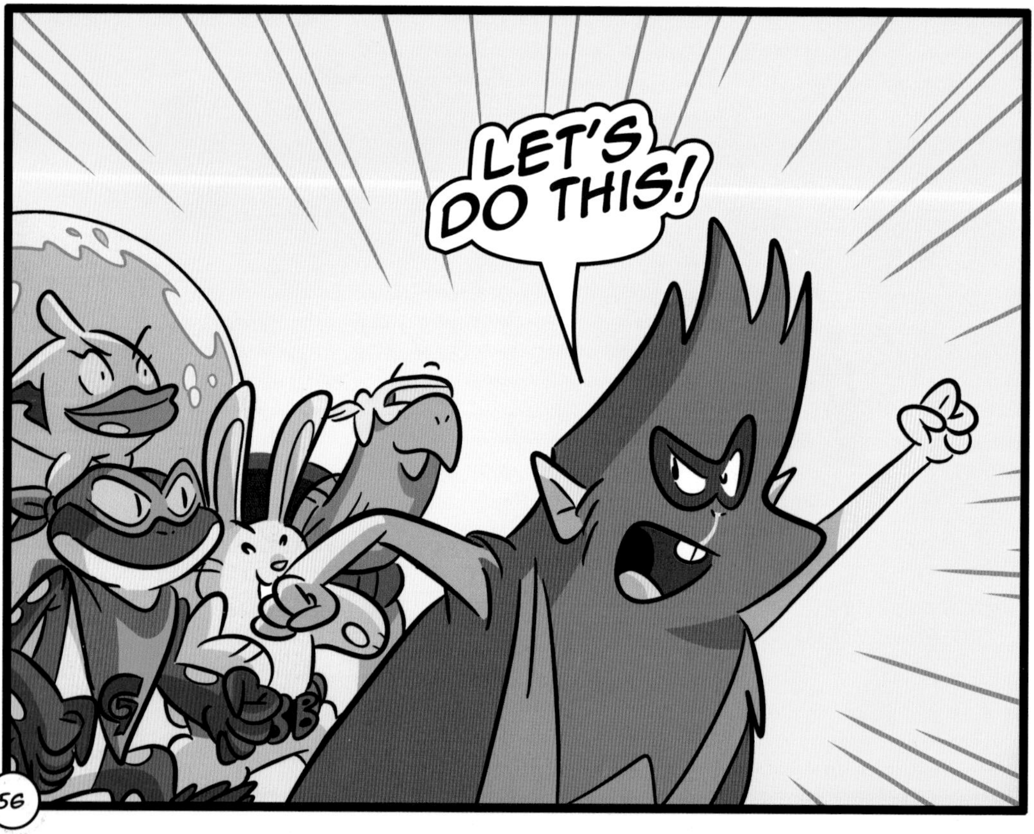
LET'S DO THIS!

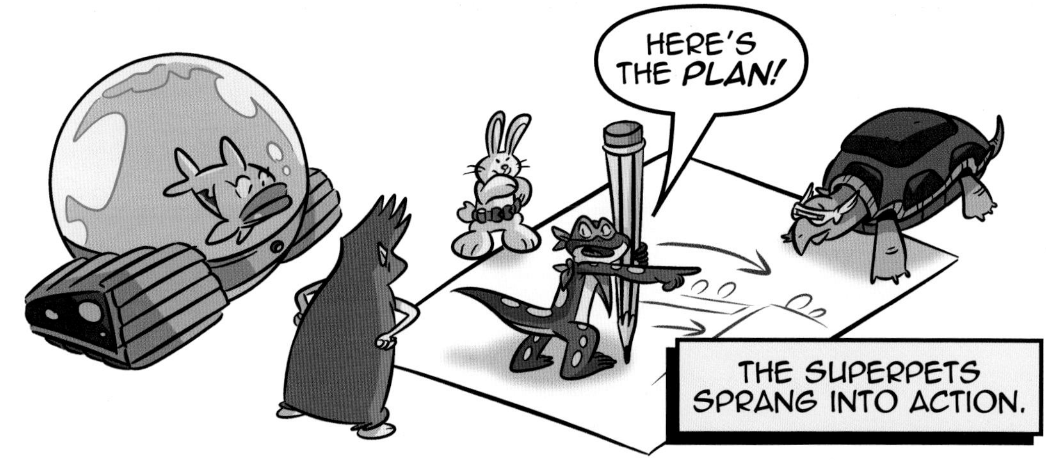
HERE'S THE PLAN!
THE SUPERPETS SPRANG INTO ACTION.

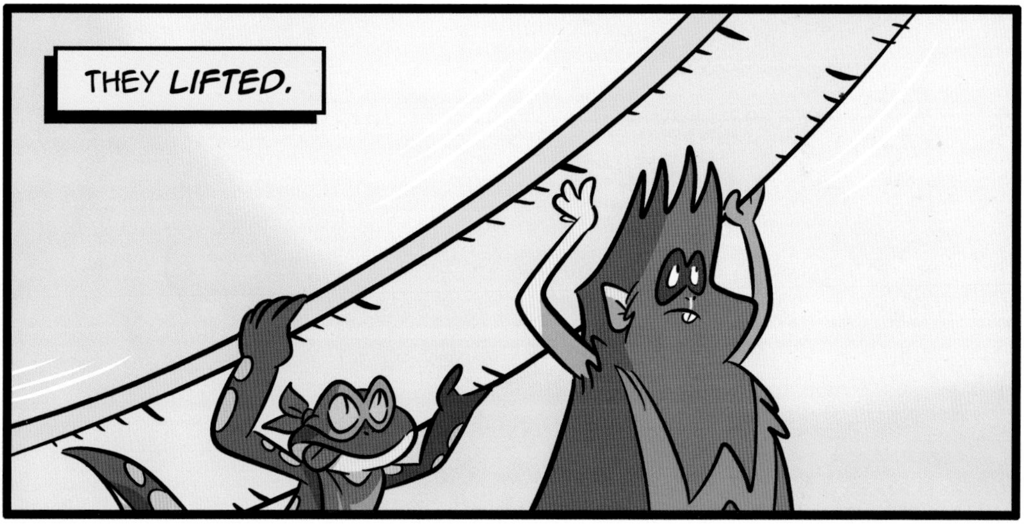
THEY LIFTED.

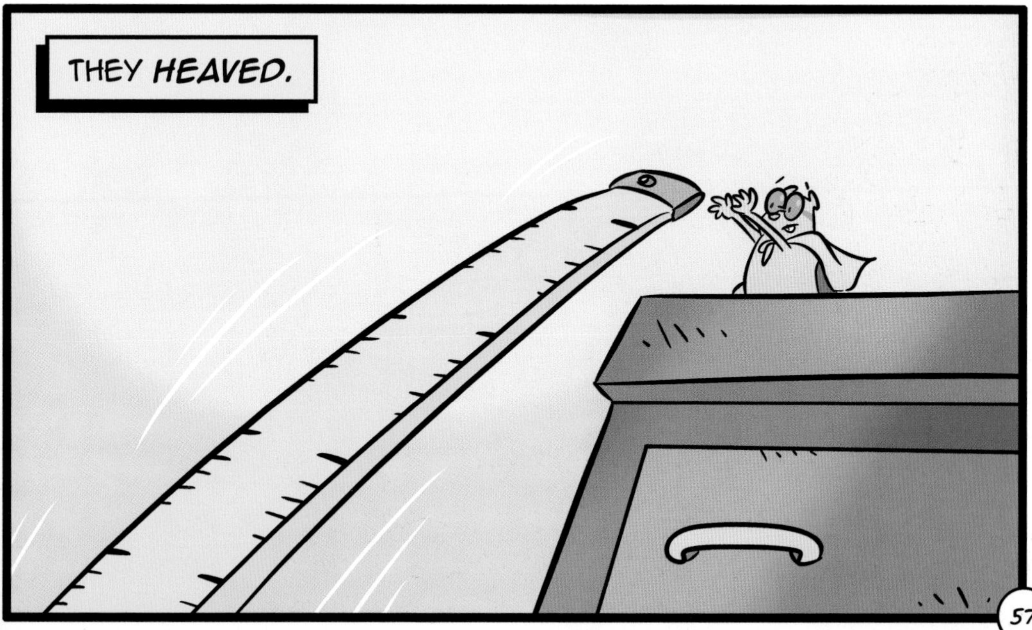
THEY HEAVED.

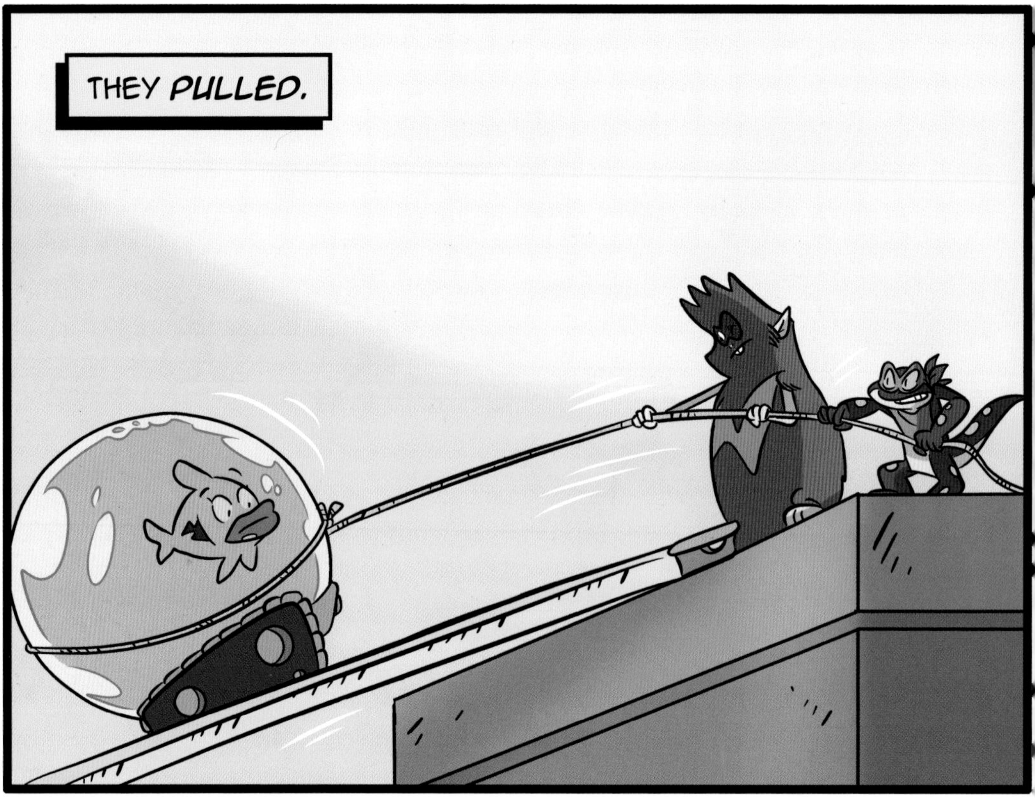
THEY PULLED.

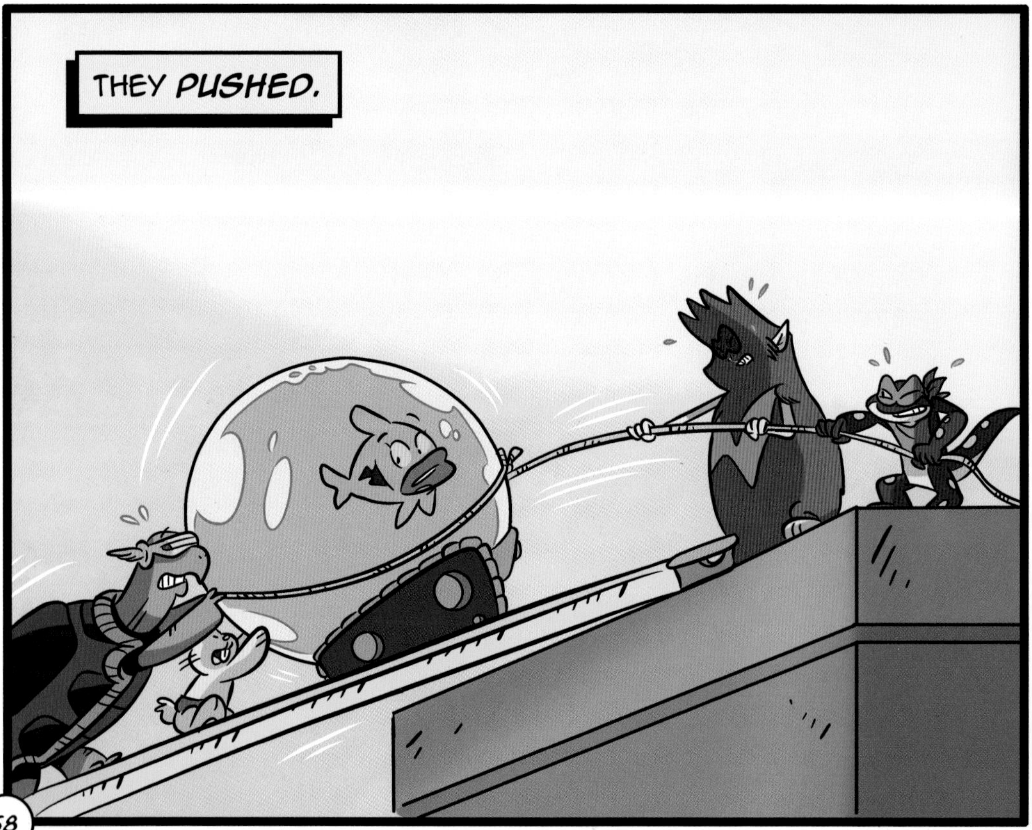
THEY PUSHED.

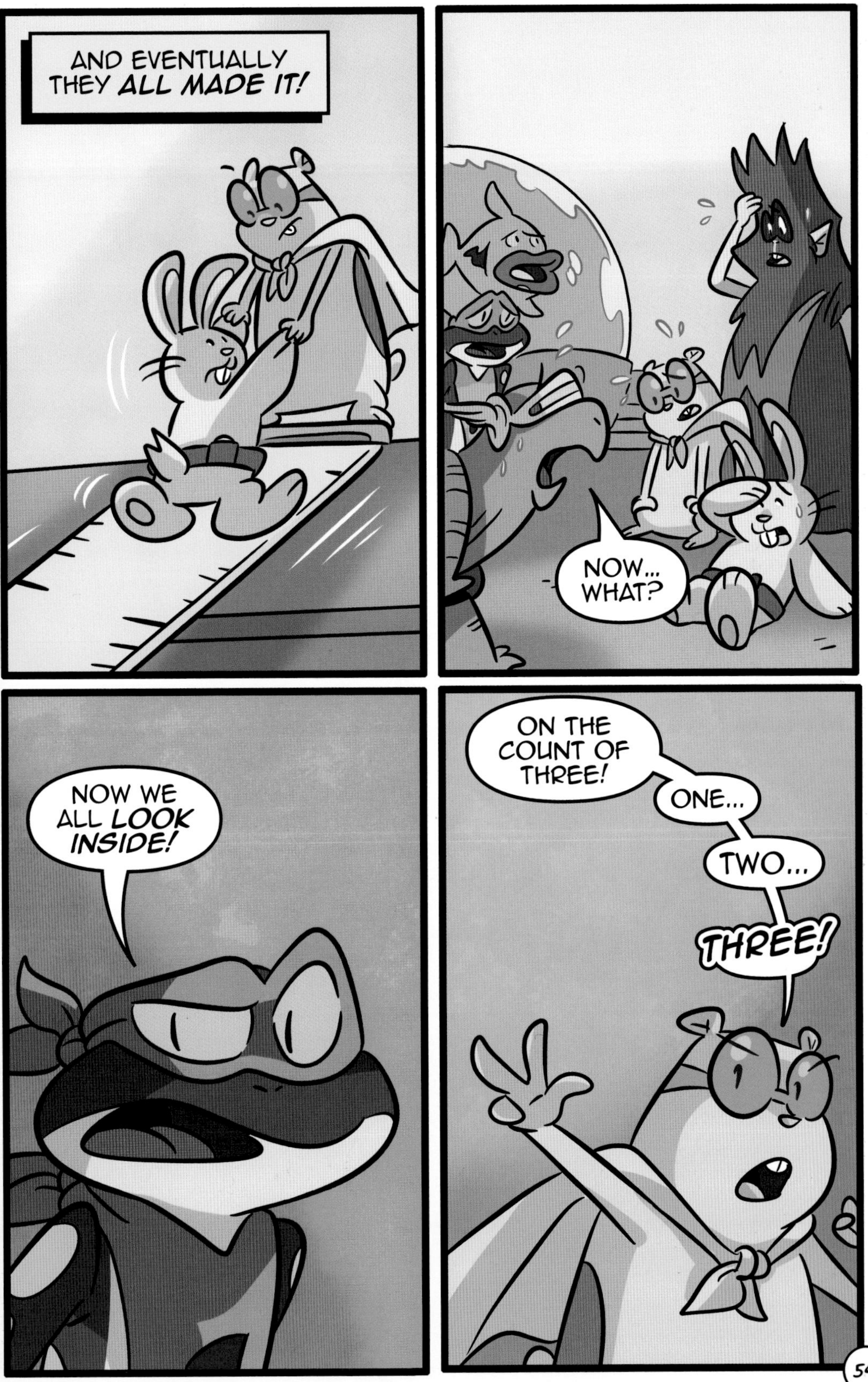
AND EVENTUALLY THEY ALL MADE IT!
NOW... WHAT?
NOW WE ALL LOOK INSIDE!
ON THE COUNT OF THREE!
ONE...
TWO...
THREE!

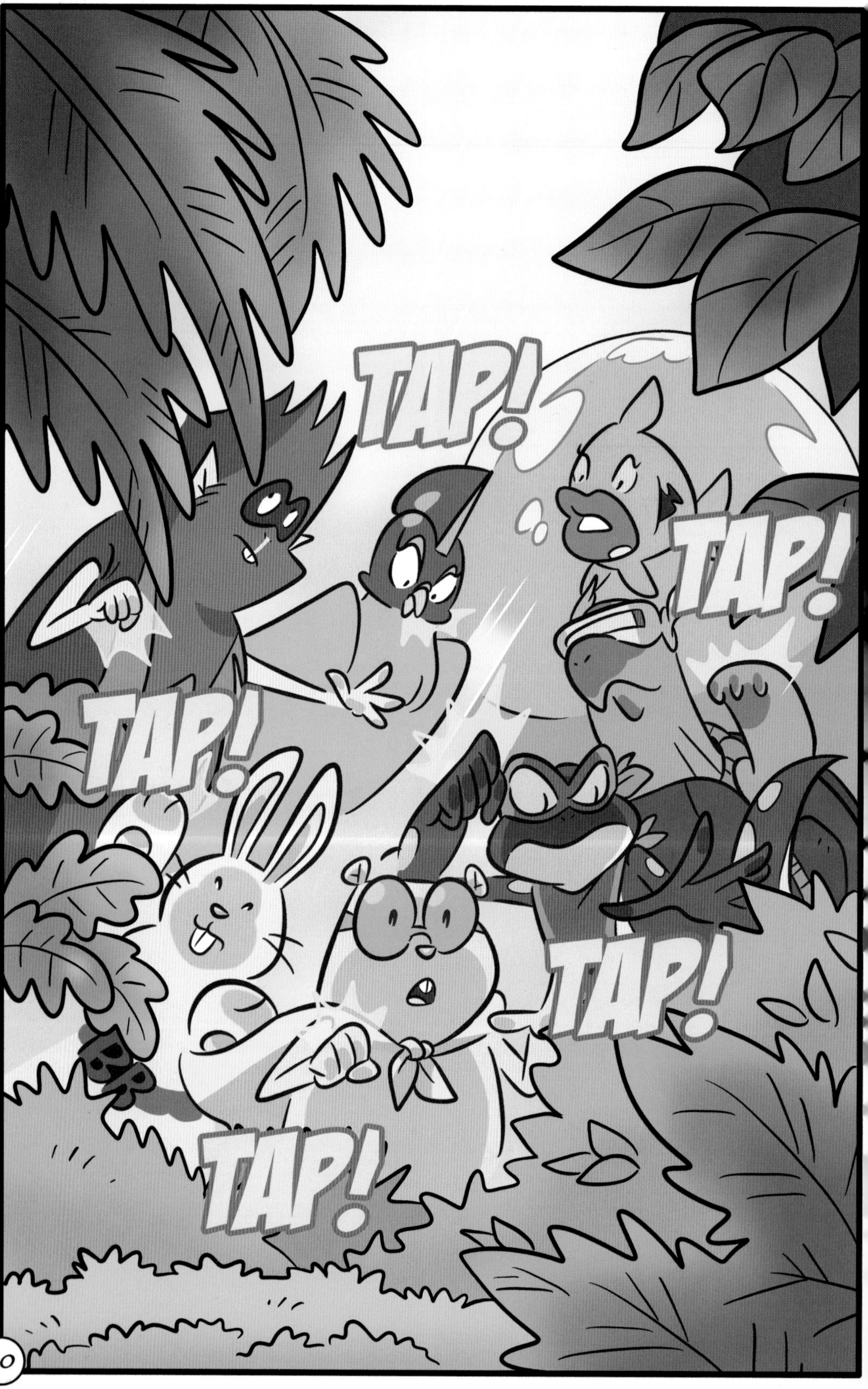
TAP!
TAP!
TAP!
TAP!
TAP!

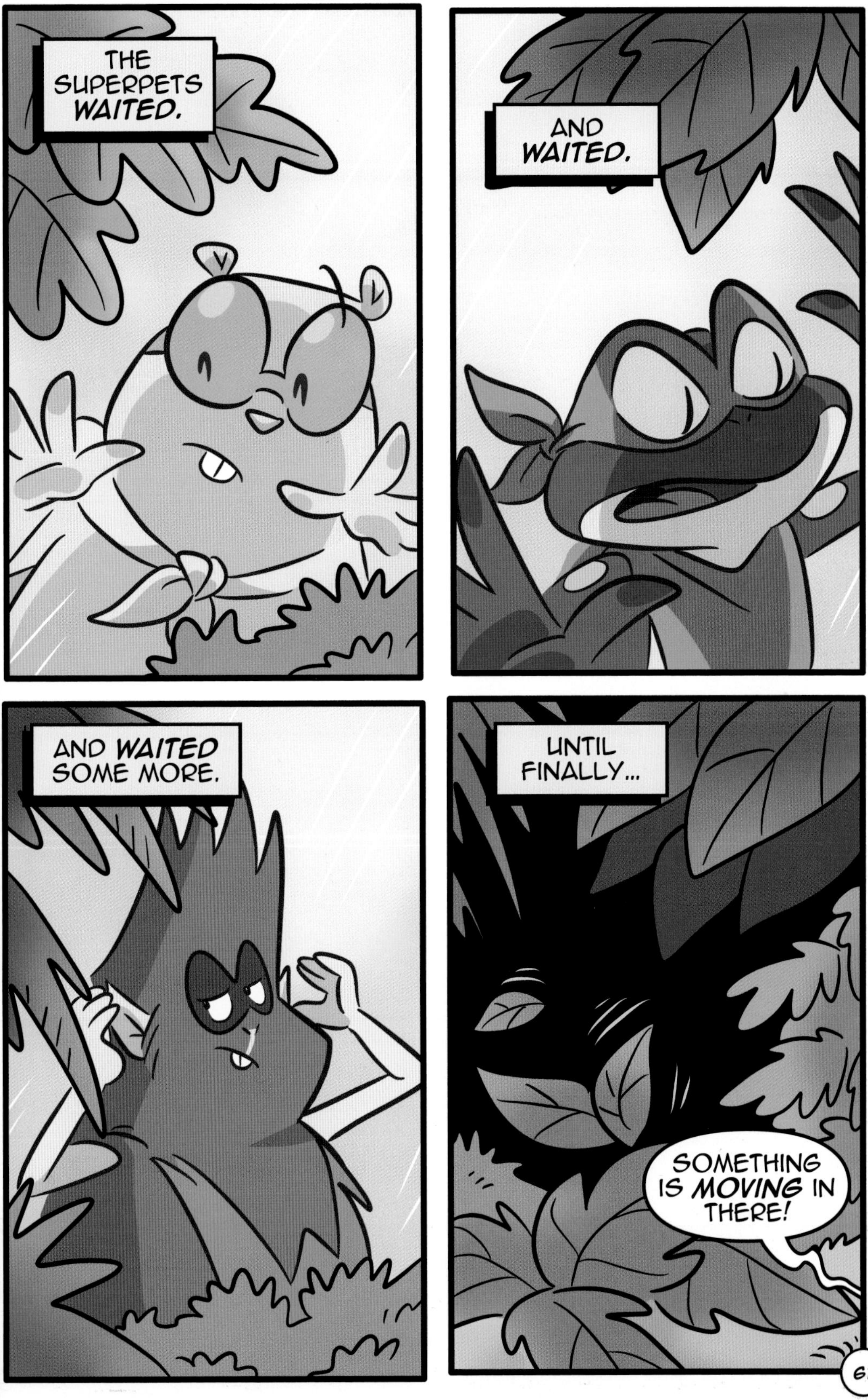
THE SUPERPETS WAITED.
AND WAITED.
AND WAITED SOME MORE.
UNTIL FINALLY...
SOMETHING IS MOVING IN THERE!

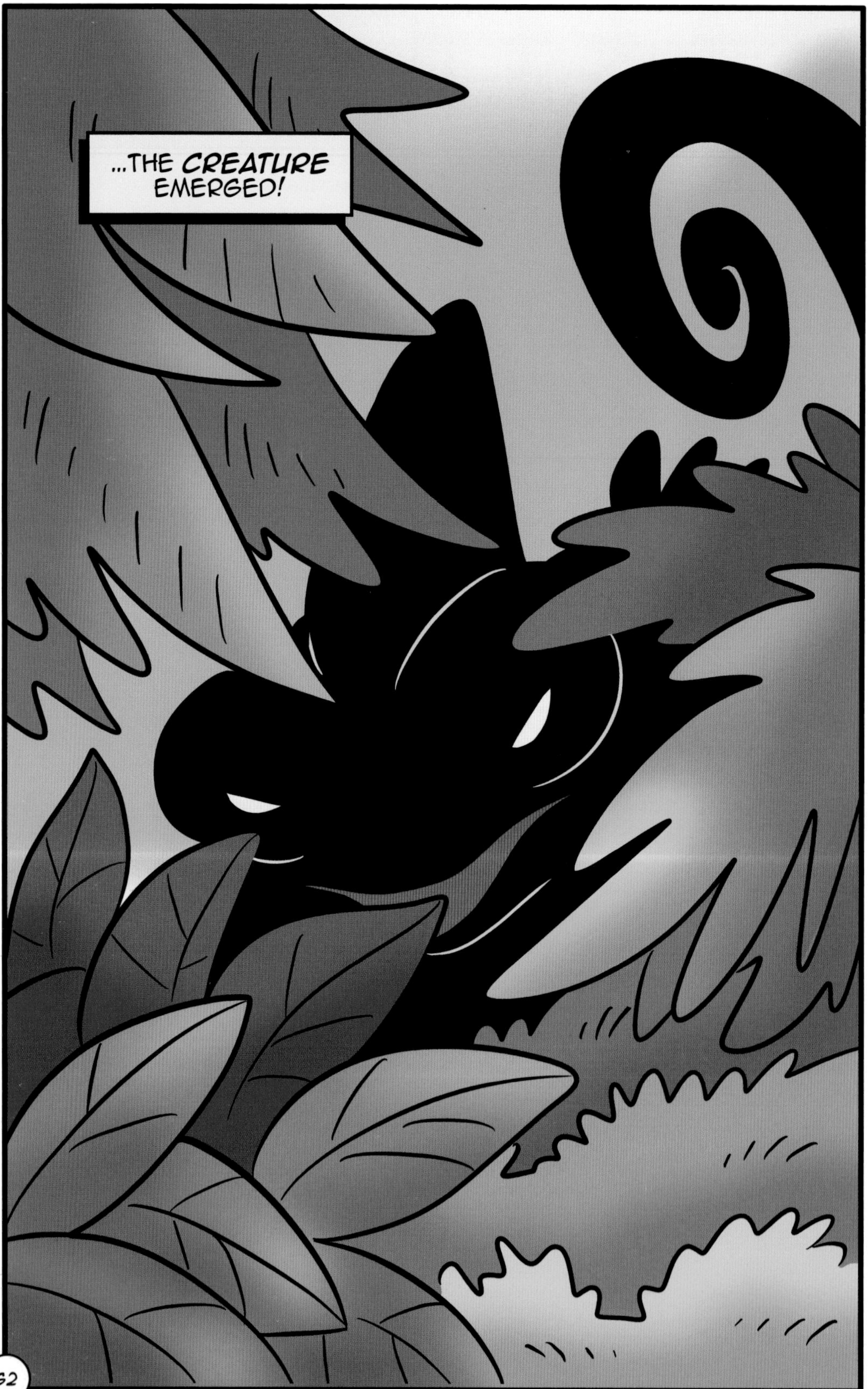
...THE CREATURE EMERGED!

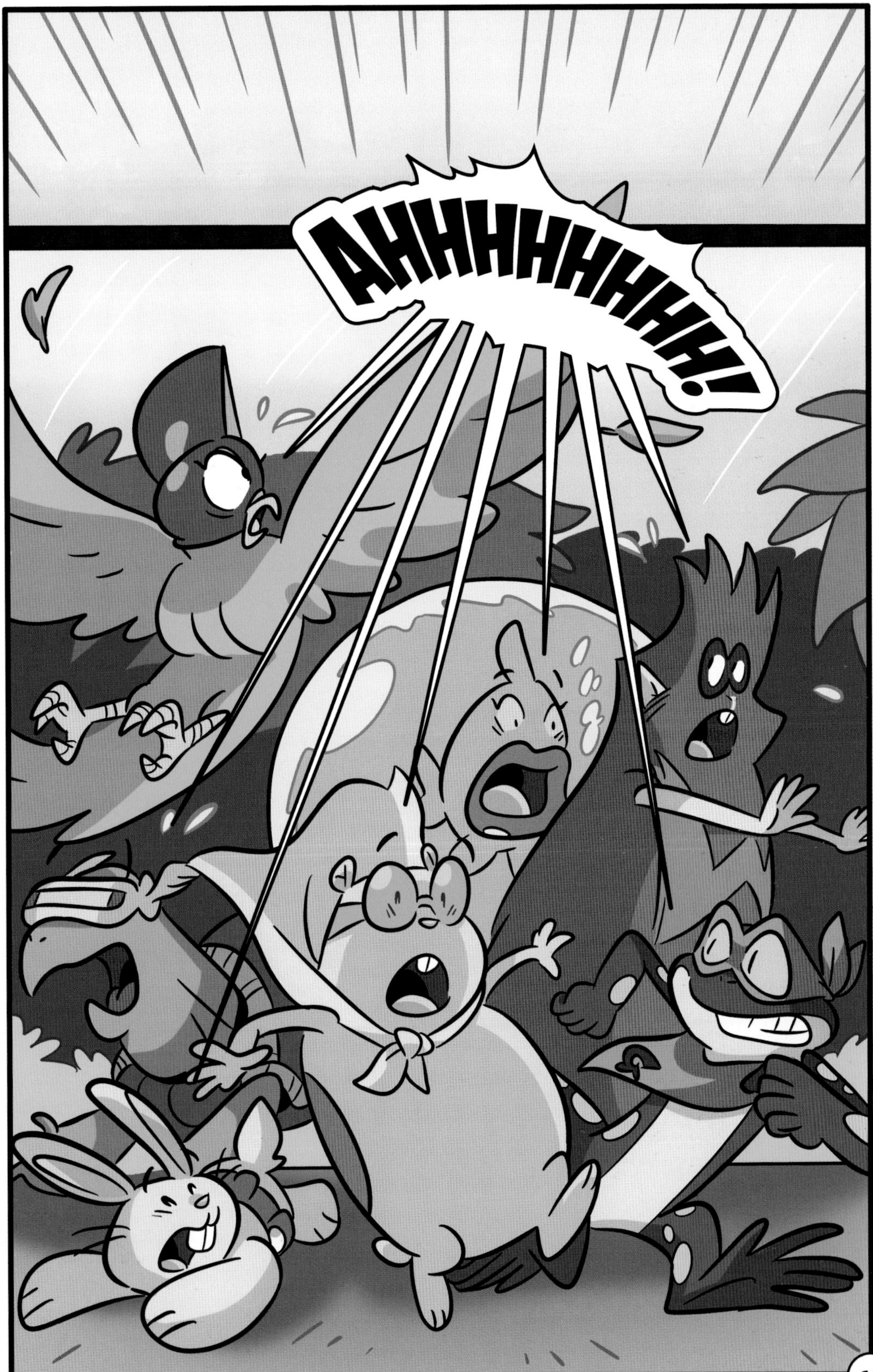
AHHHHHHHH!

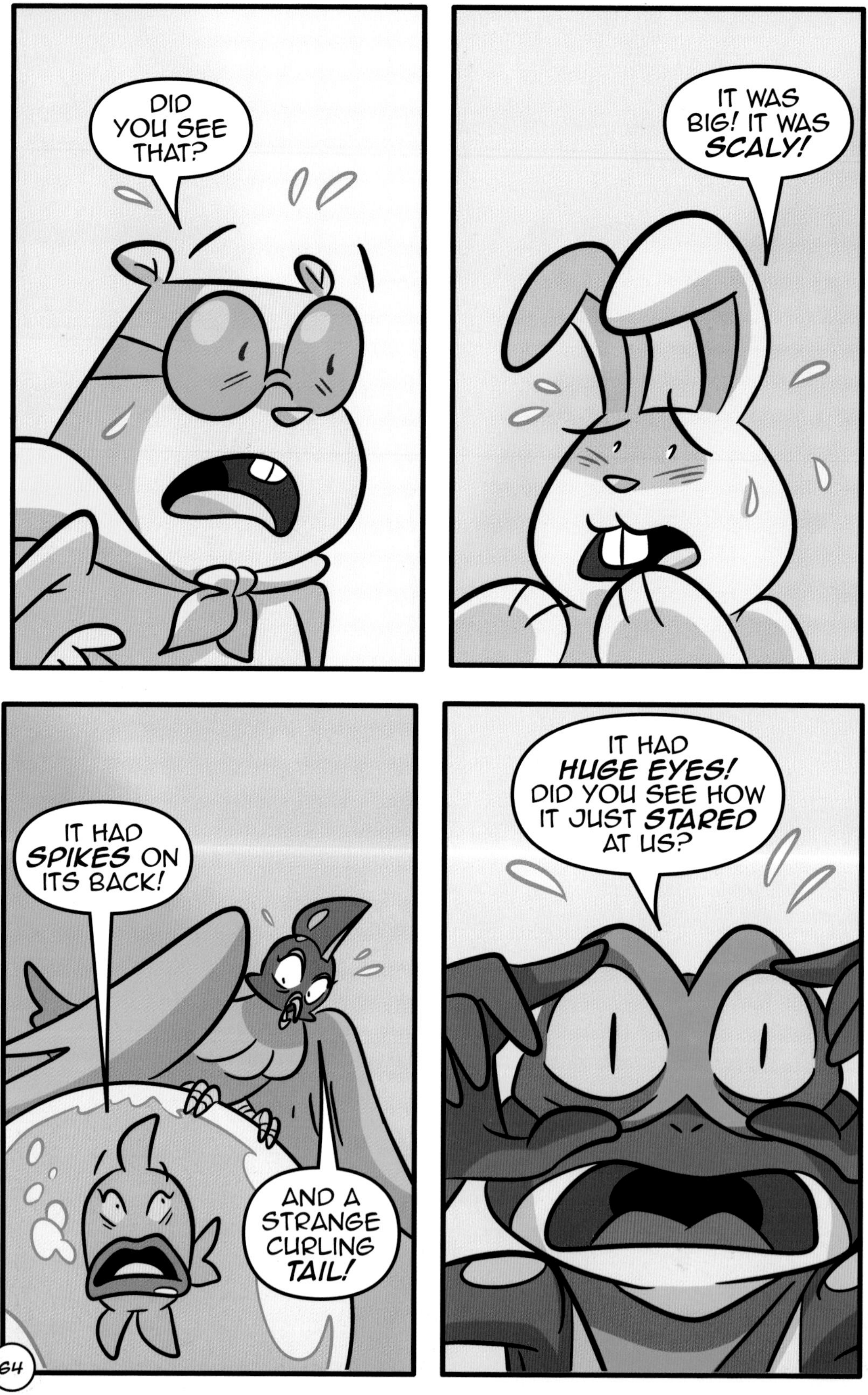
DID YOU SEE THAT?
IT WAS BIG! IT WAS SCALY!
IT HAD SPIKES ON ITS BACK!
AND A STRANGE CURLING TAIL!
IT HAD HUGE EYES! DID YOU SEE HOW IT JUST STARED AT US?

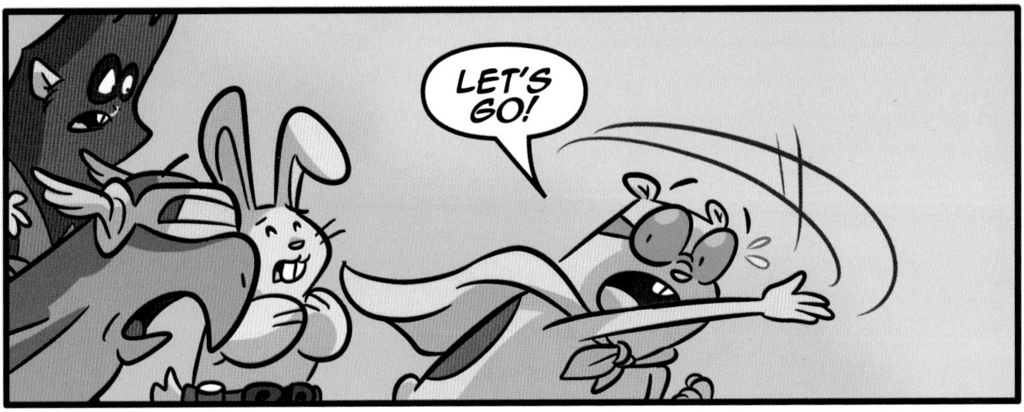
LET'S GO!

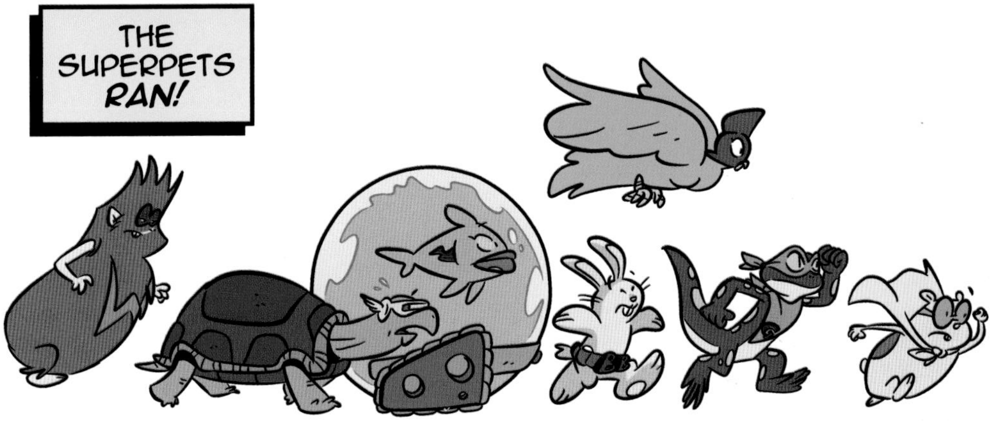
THE SUPERPETS *RAN!*

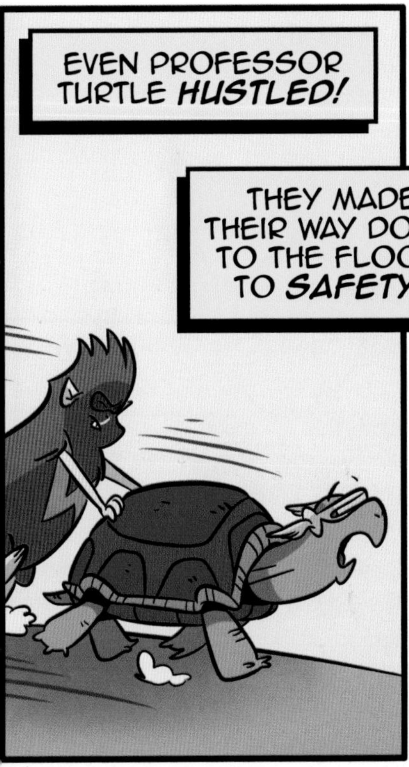
EVEN PROFESSOR TURTLE *HUSTLED!*
THEY MADE THEIR WAY DOWN TO THE FLOOR. TO *SAFETY!*

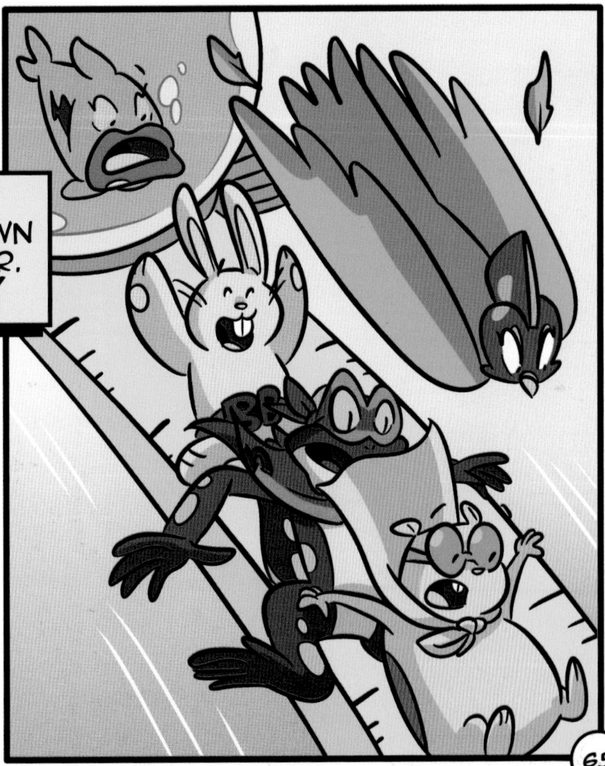

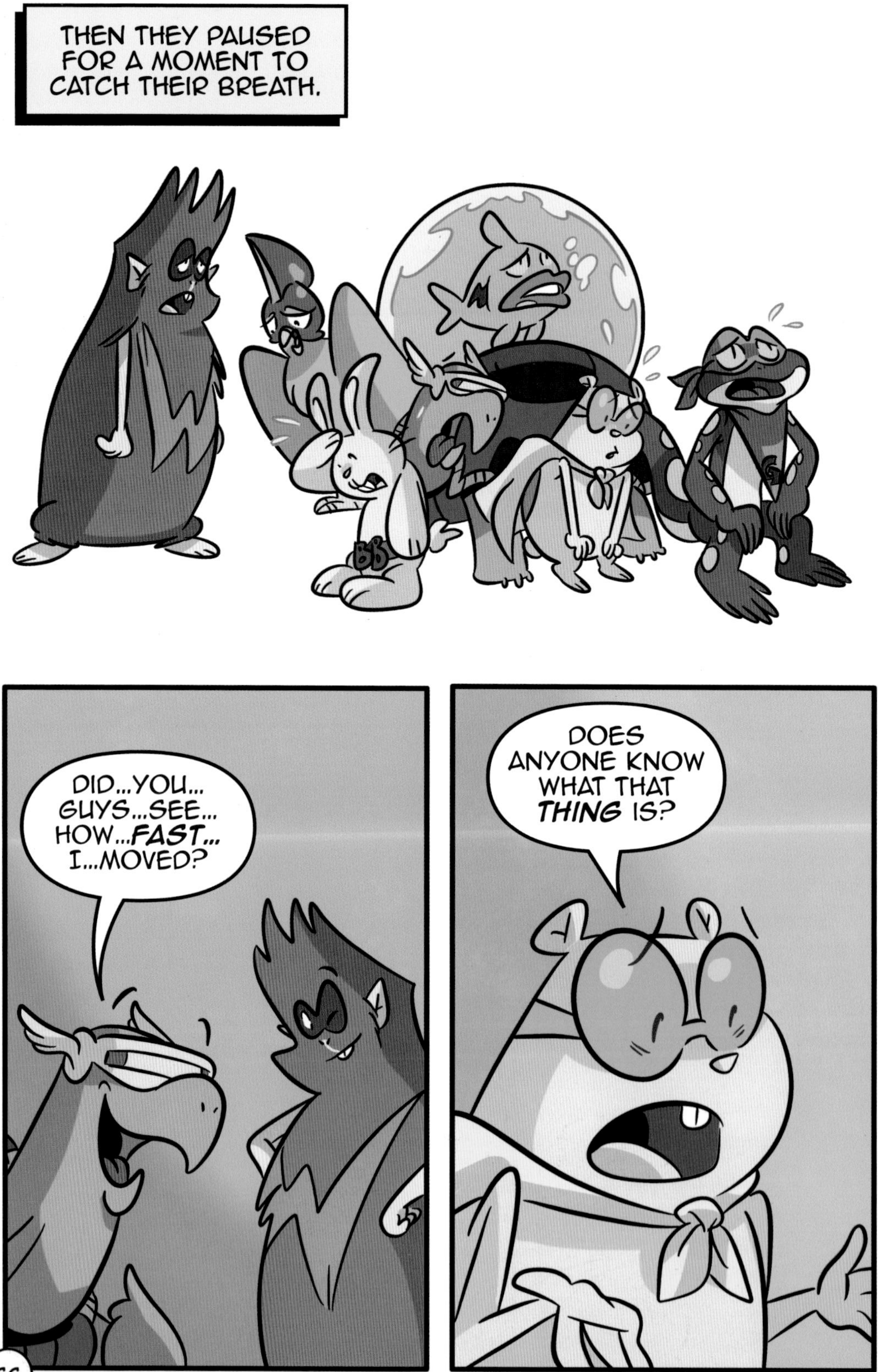
THEN THEY PAUSED FOR A MOMENT TO CATCH THEIR BREATH.
DID...YOU... GUYS...SEE... HOW...*FAST*... I...MOVED?
DOES ANYONE KNOW WHAT THAT *THING* IS?

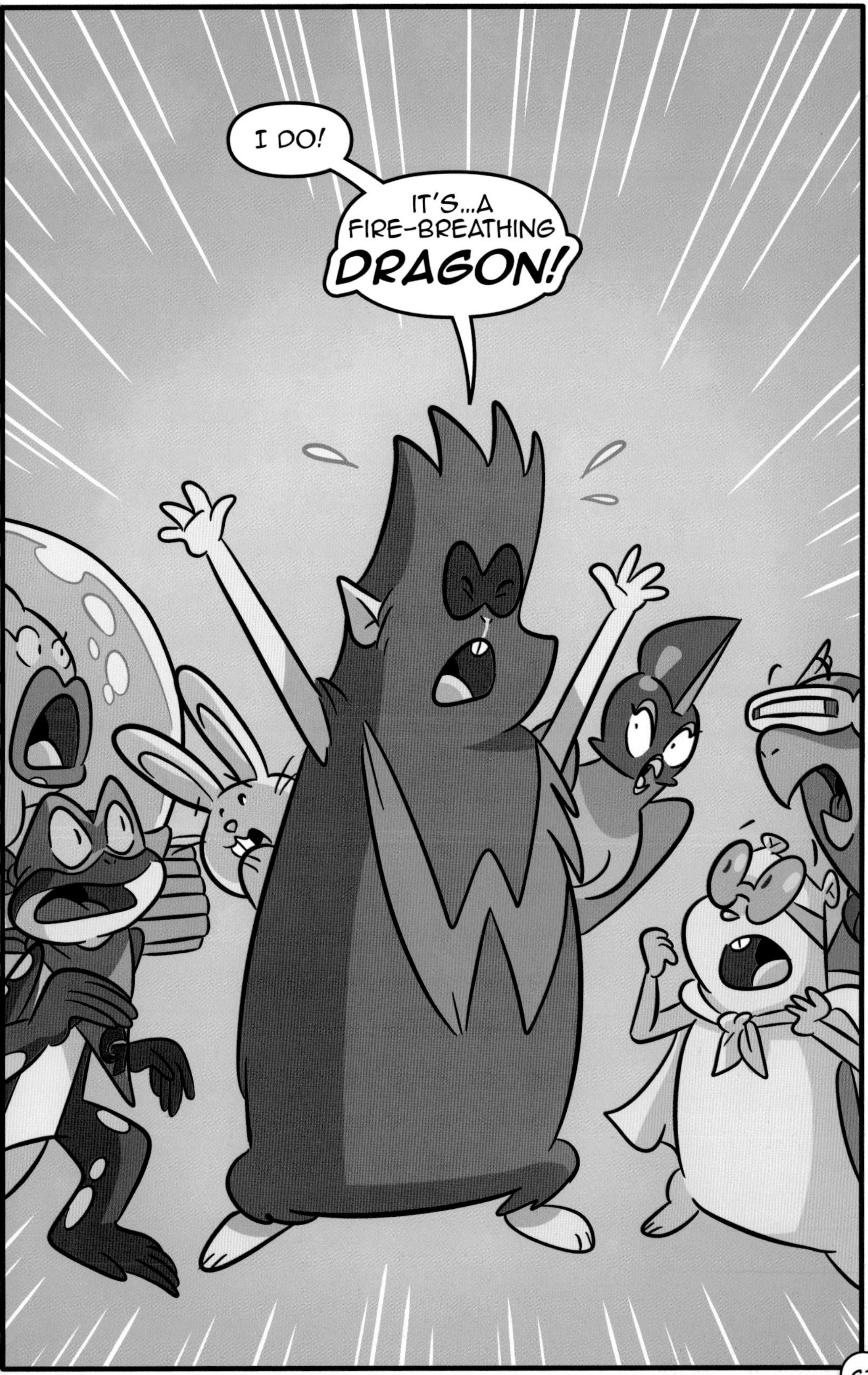
I DO!
IT'S...A FIRE-BREATHING DRAGON!

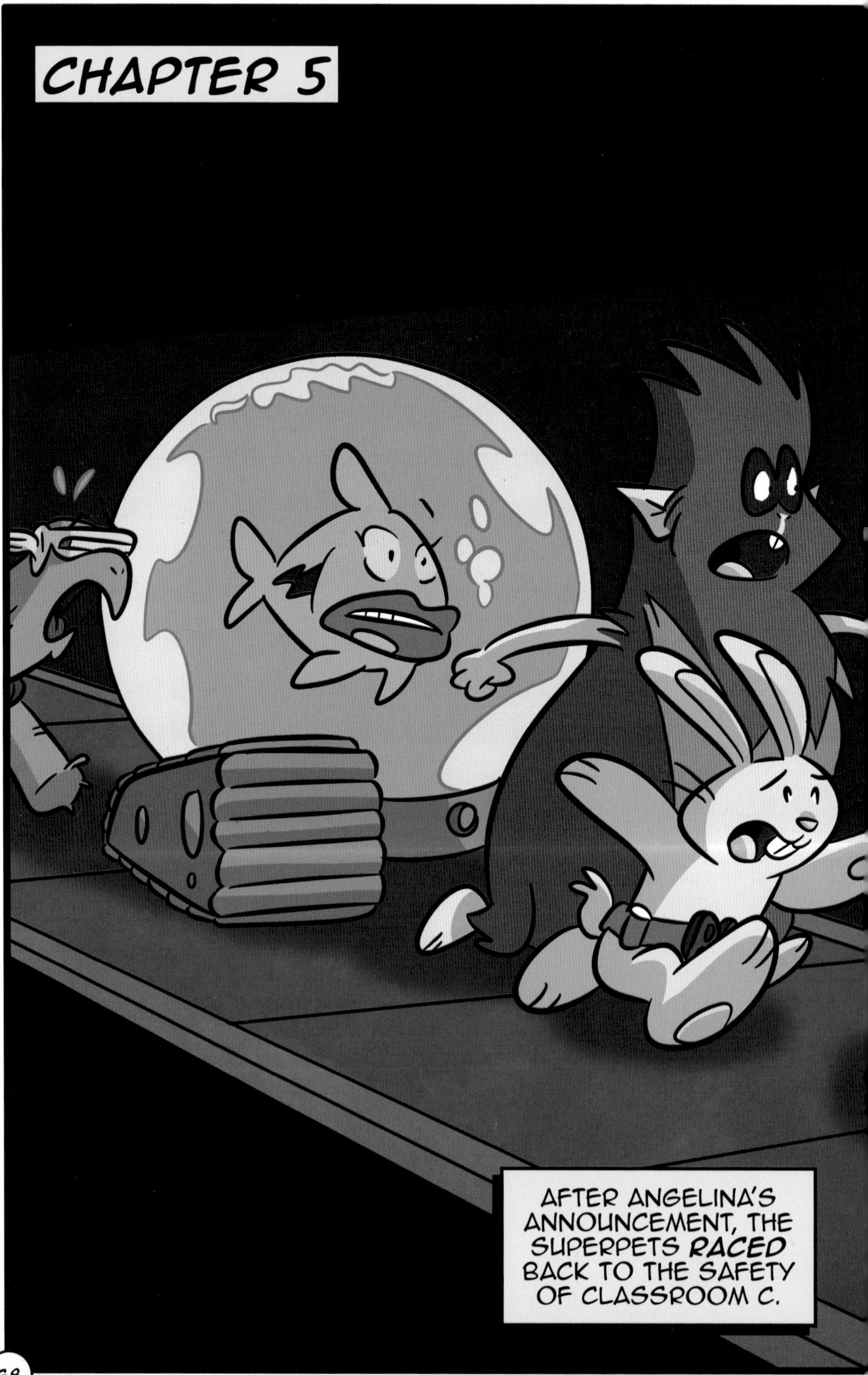
CHAPTER 5
AFTER ANGELINA'S ANNOUNCEMENT, THE SUPERPETS *RACED* BACK TO THE SAFETY OF CLASSROOM C.

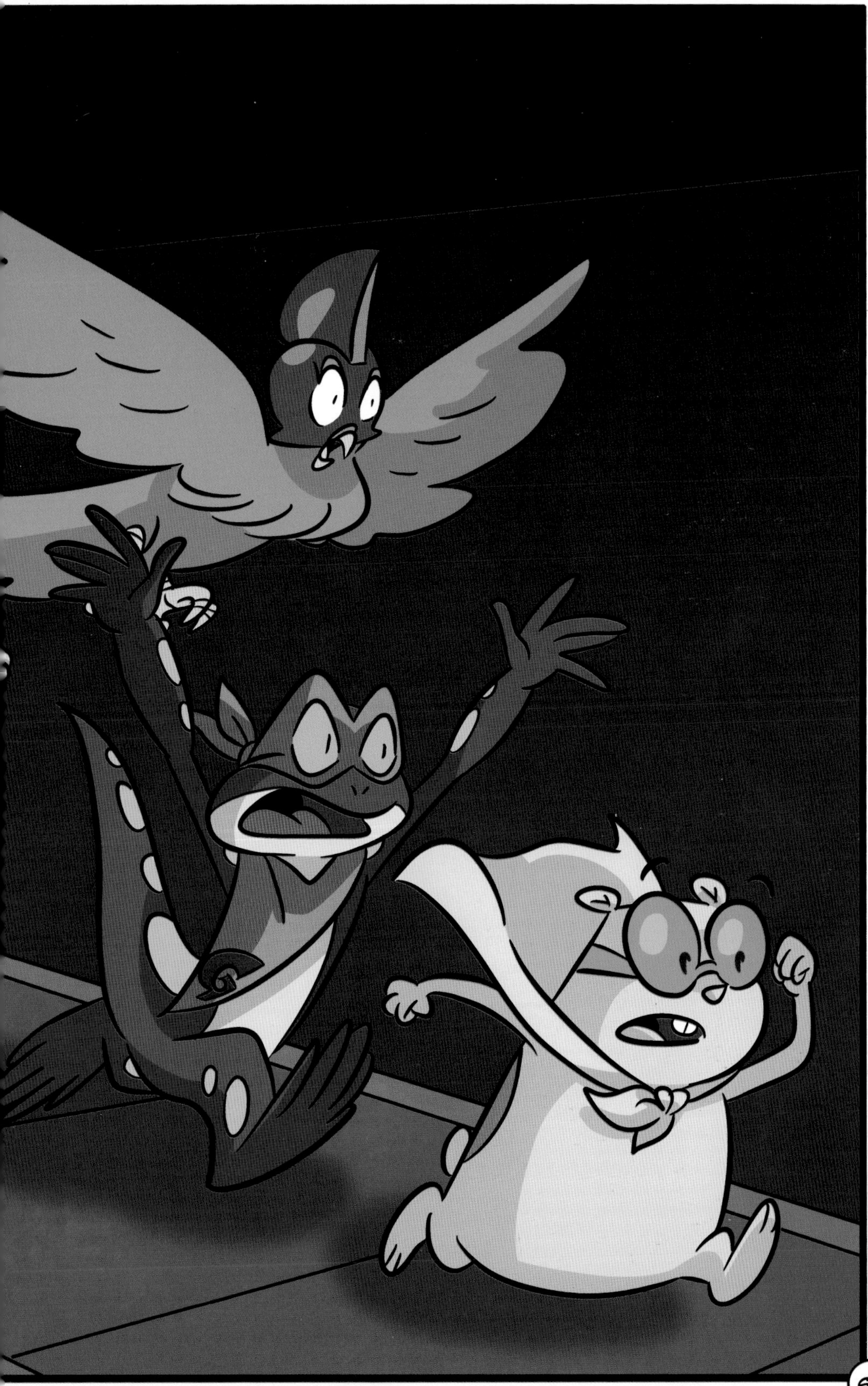

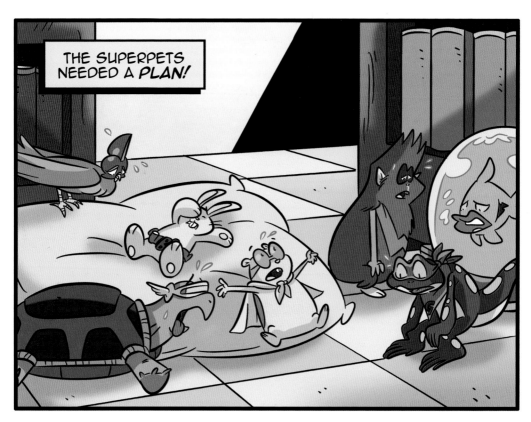

THE SUPERPETS NEEDED A *PLAN!*

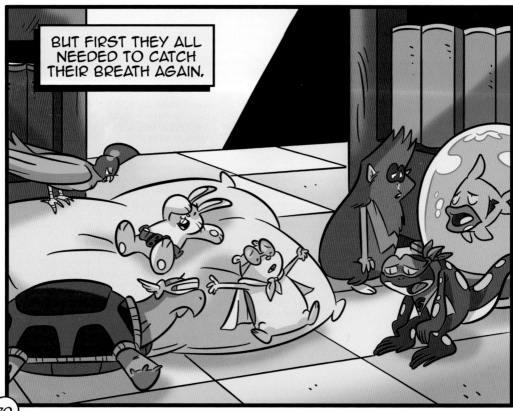

BUT FIRST THEY ALL NEEDED TO CATCH THEIR BREATH AGAIN.

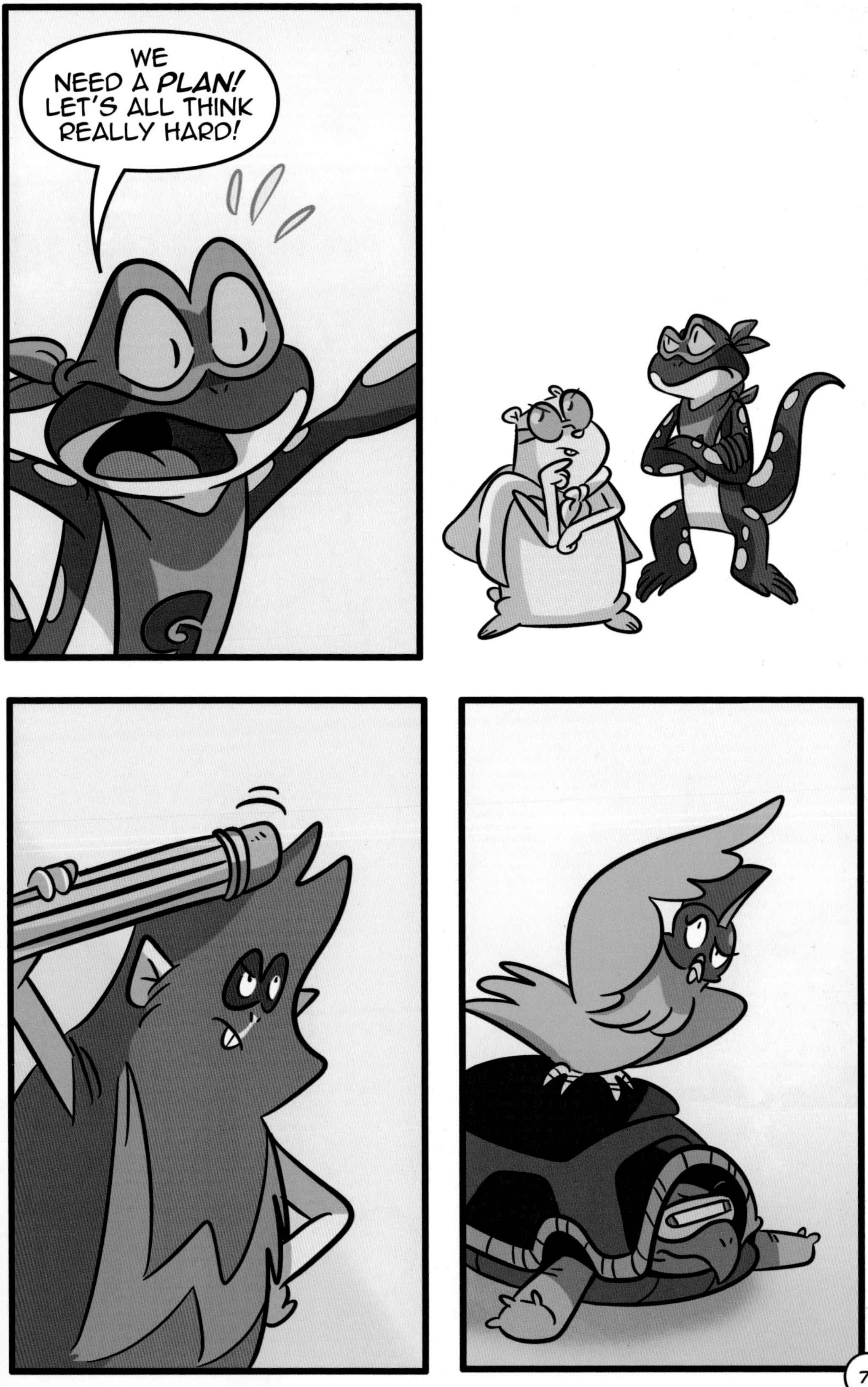
WE NEED A PLAN! LET'S ALL THINK REALLY HARD!

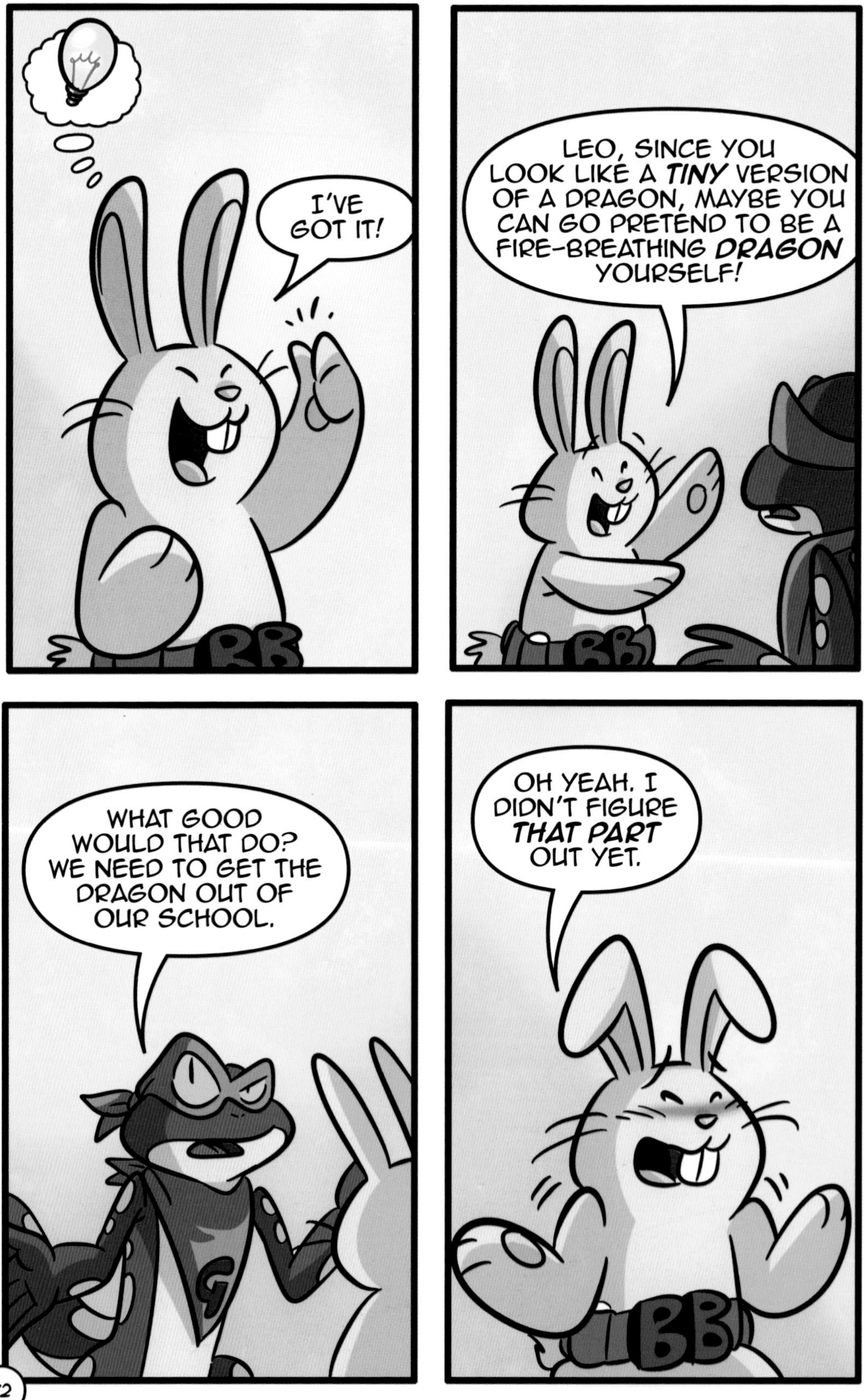
I'VE GOT IT!
LEO, SINCE YOU LOOK LIKE A *TINY* VERSION OF A DRAGON, MAYBE YOU CAN GO PRETEND TO BE A FIRE-BREATHING *DRAGON* YOURSELF!
WHAT GOOD WOULD THAT DO? WE NEED TO GET THE DRAGON OUT OF OUR SCHOOL.
OH YEAH. I DIDN'T FIGURE *THAT PART* OUT YET.

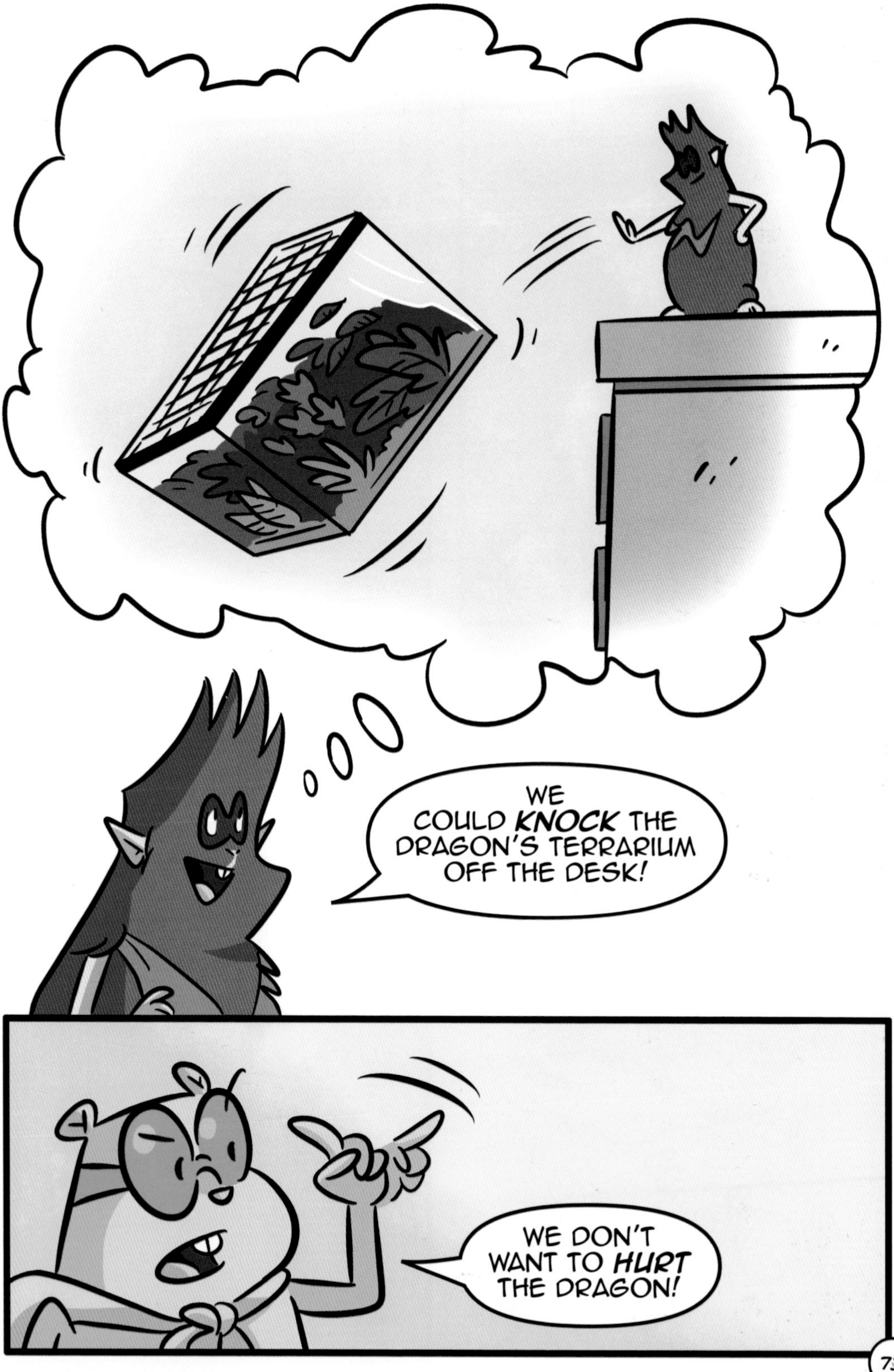
WE COULD **KNOCK** THE DRAGON'S TERRARIUM OFF THE DESK!
WE DON'T WANT TO ***HURT*** THE DRAGON!

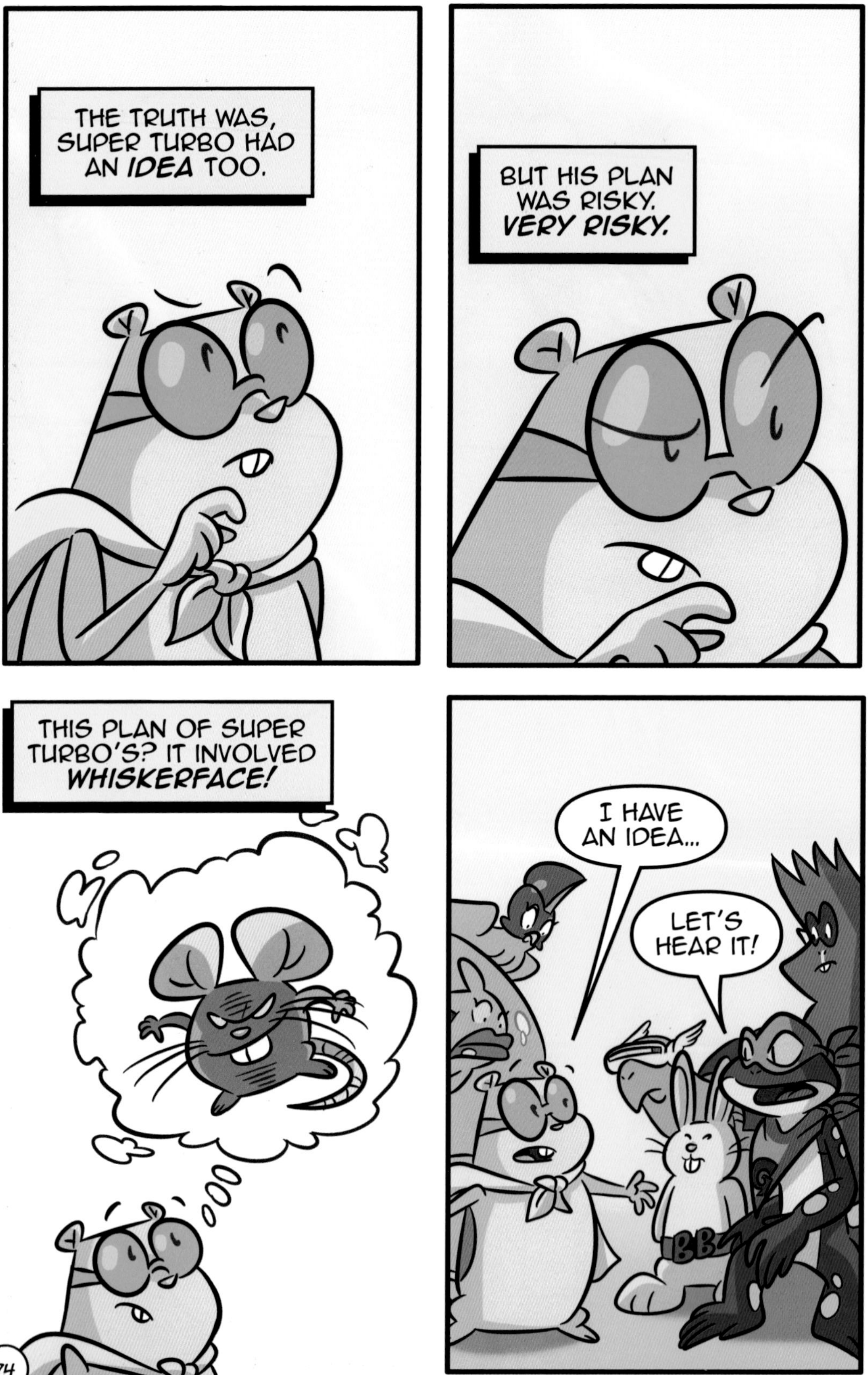
THE TRUTH WAS, SUPER TURBO HAD AN IDEA TOO.
BUT HIS PLAN WAS RISKY. VERY RISKY.
THIS PLAN OF SUPER TURBO'S? IT INVOLVED WHISKERFACE!
I HAVE AN IDEA...
LET'S HEAR IT!
BB

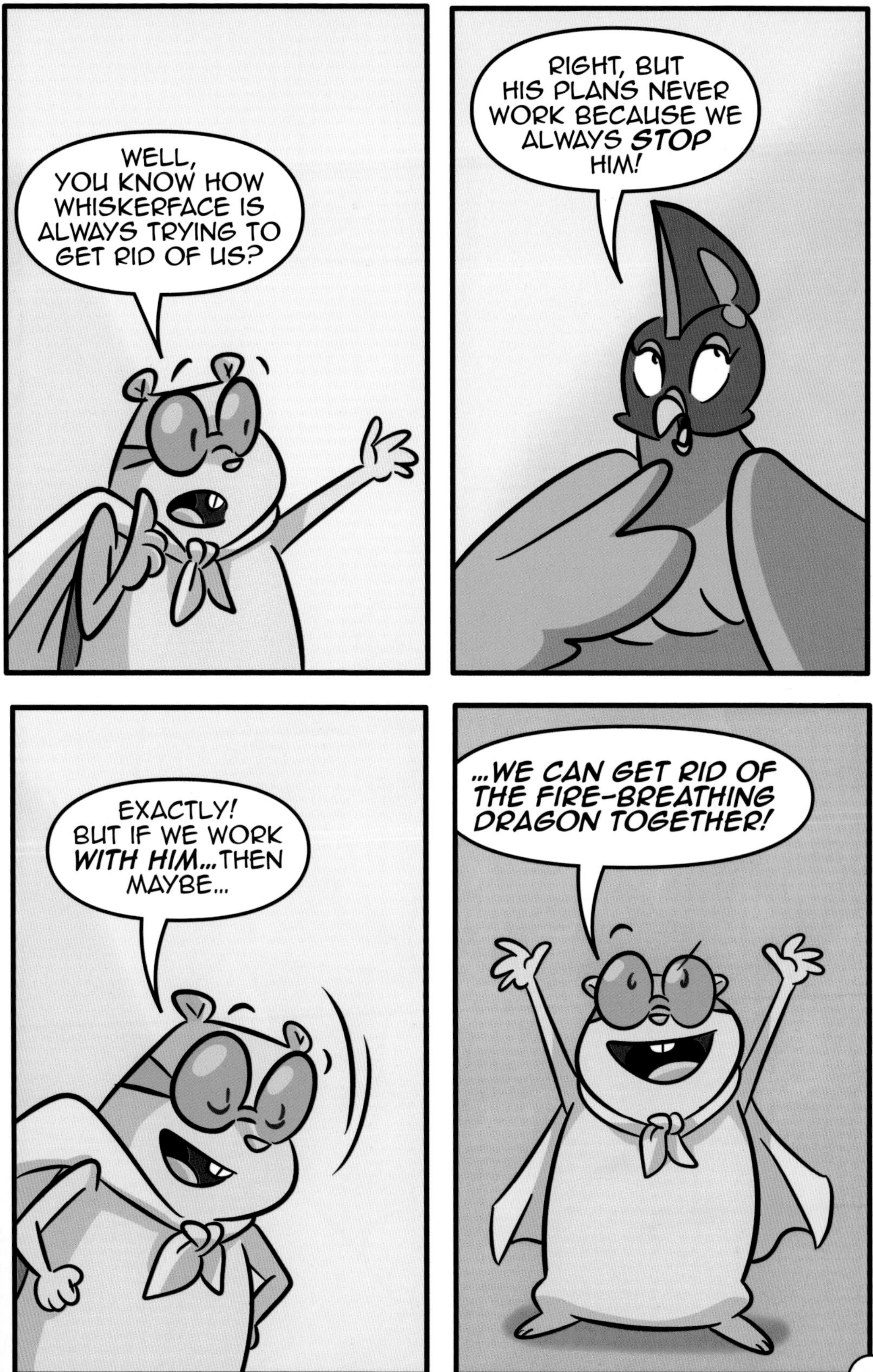
WELL, YOU KNOW HOW WHISKERFACE IS ALWAYS TRYING TO GET RID OF US?
RIGHT, BUT HIS PLANS NEVER WORK BECAUSE WE ALWAYS STOP HIM!
EXACTLY! BUT IF WE WORK WITH HIM...THEN MAYBE...
...WE CAN GET RID OF THE FIRE-BREATHING DRAGON TOGETHER!

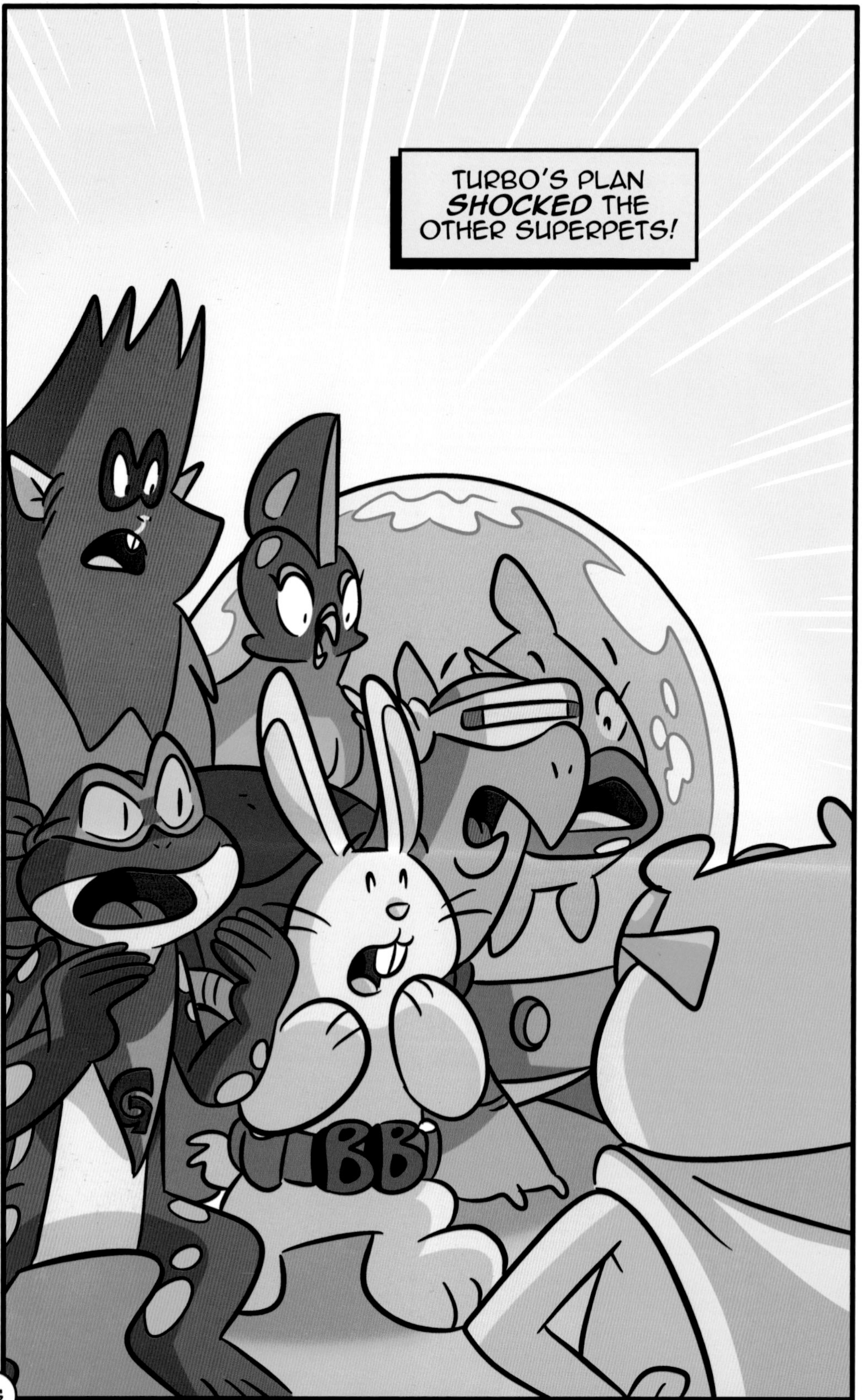
TURBO'S PLAN *SHOCKED* THE OTHER SUPERPETS!
BB

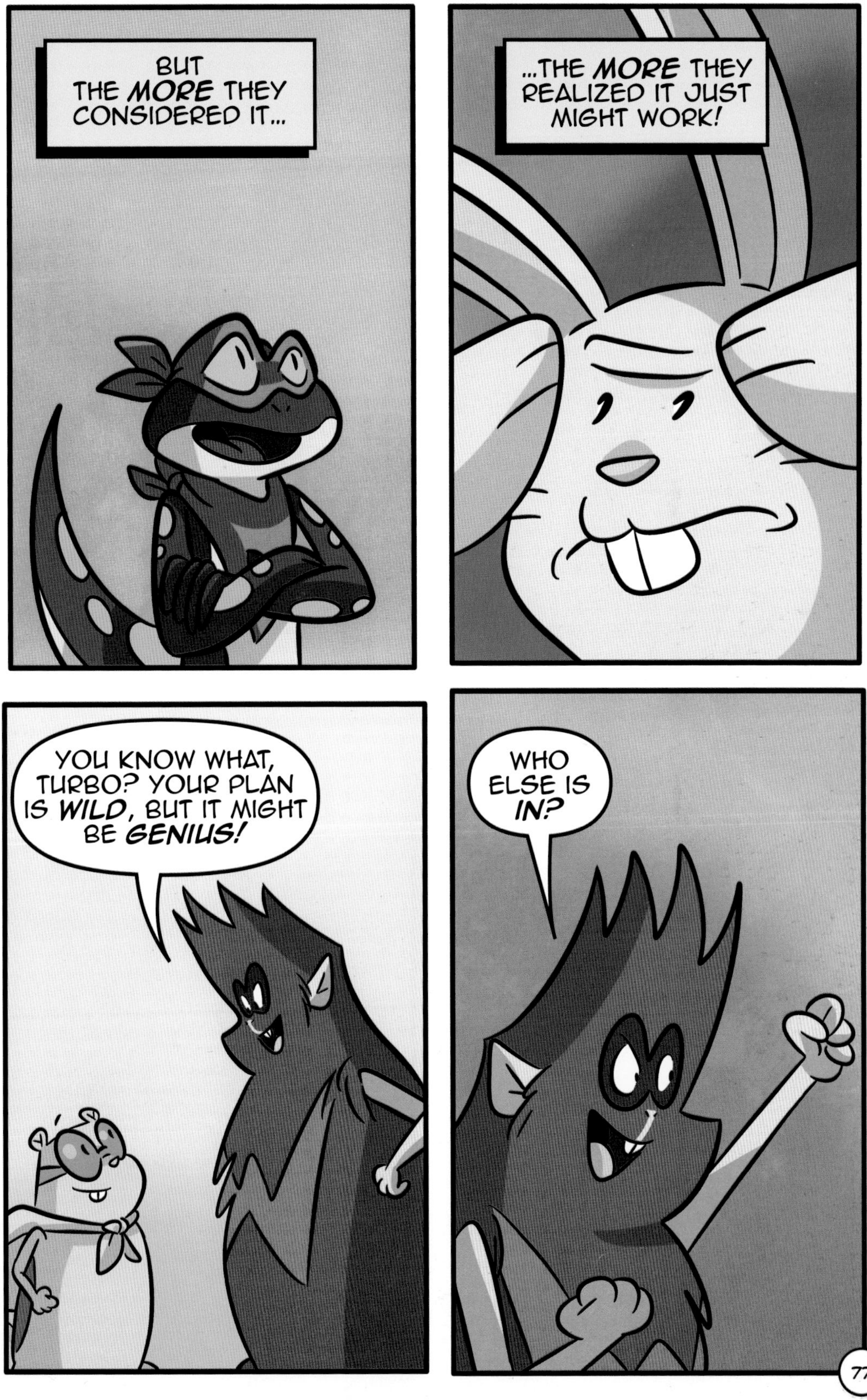
BUT THE *MORE* THEY CONSIDERED IT...
...THE *MORE* THEY REALIZED IT JUST MIGHT WORK!
YOU KNOW WHAT, TURBO? YOUR PLAN IS *WILD*, BUT IT MIGHT BE *GENIUS!*
WHO ELSE IS *IN?*

COUNT *ME* IN!

US TOO!

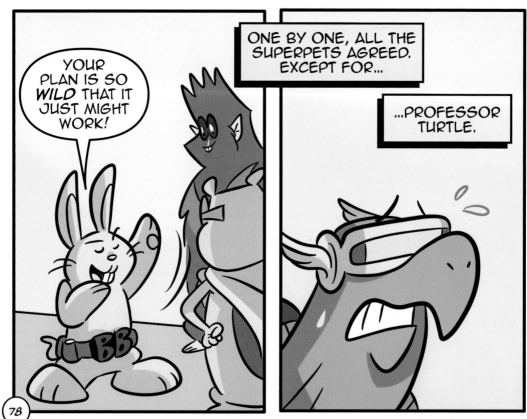

YOUR PLAN IS SO *WILD* THAT IT JUST MIGHT WORK!

ONE BY ONE, ALL THE SUPERPETS AGREED. EXCEPT FOR...

...PROFESSOR TURTLE.

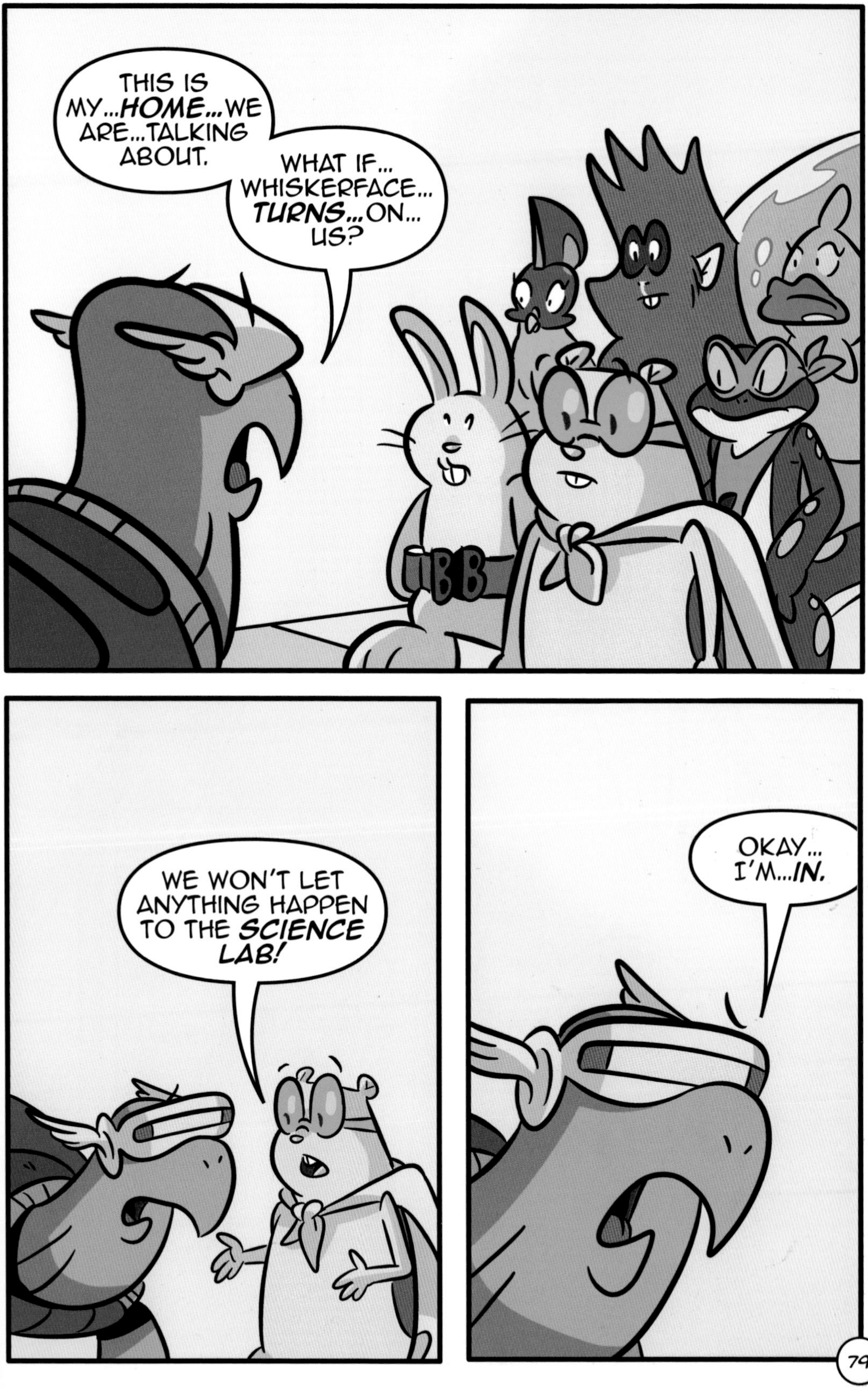
THIS IS MY...HOME...WE ARE...TALKING ABOUT.
WHAT IF... WHISKERFACE... TURNS...ON... US?
WE WON'T LET ANYTHING HAPPEN TO THE SCIENCE LAB!
OKAY... I'M...IN.

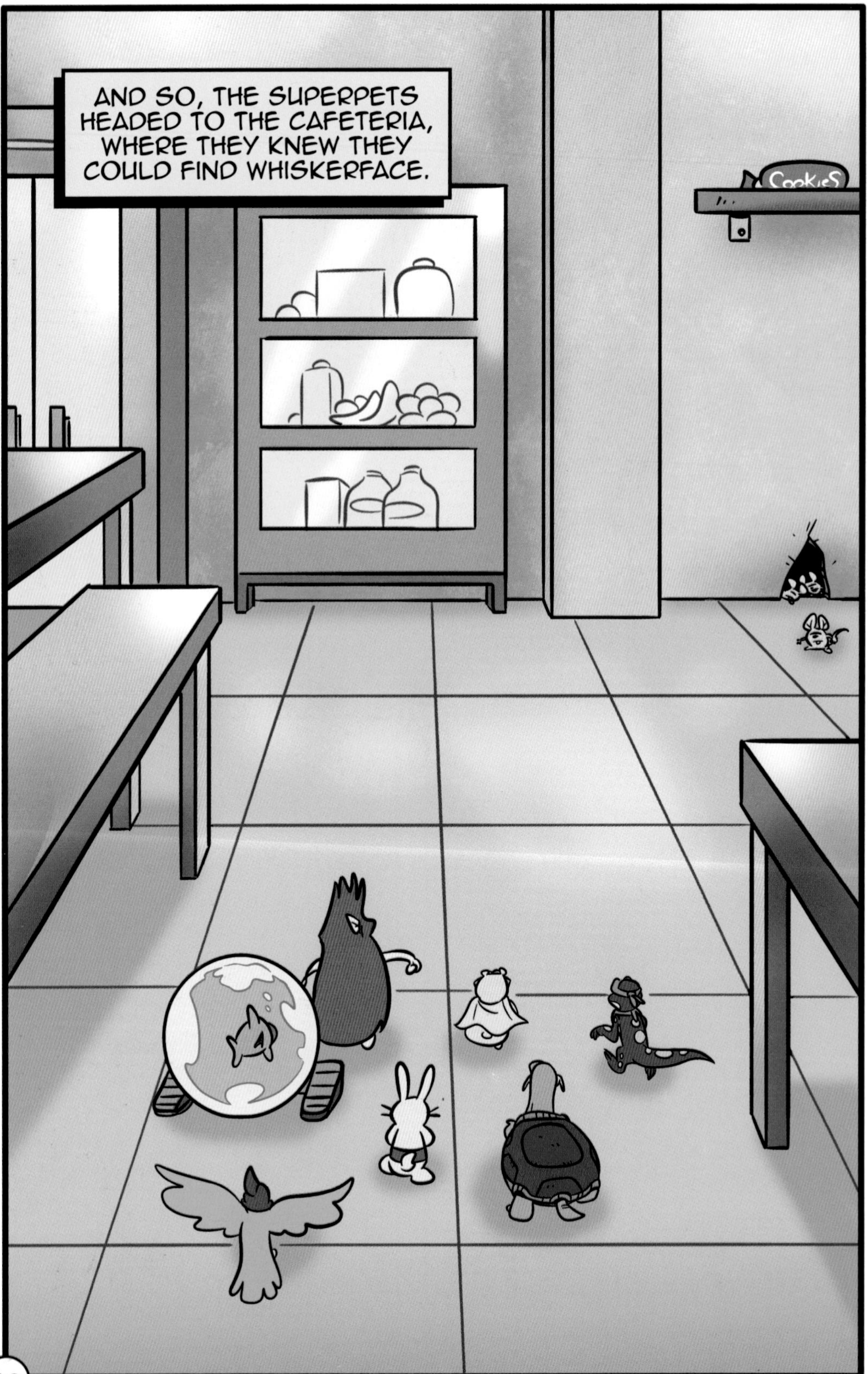
AND SO, THE SUPERPETS HEADED TO THE CAFETERIA, WHERE THEY KNEW THEY COULD FIND WHISKERFACE.
Cookies

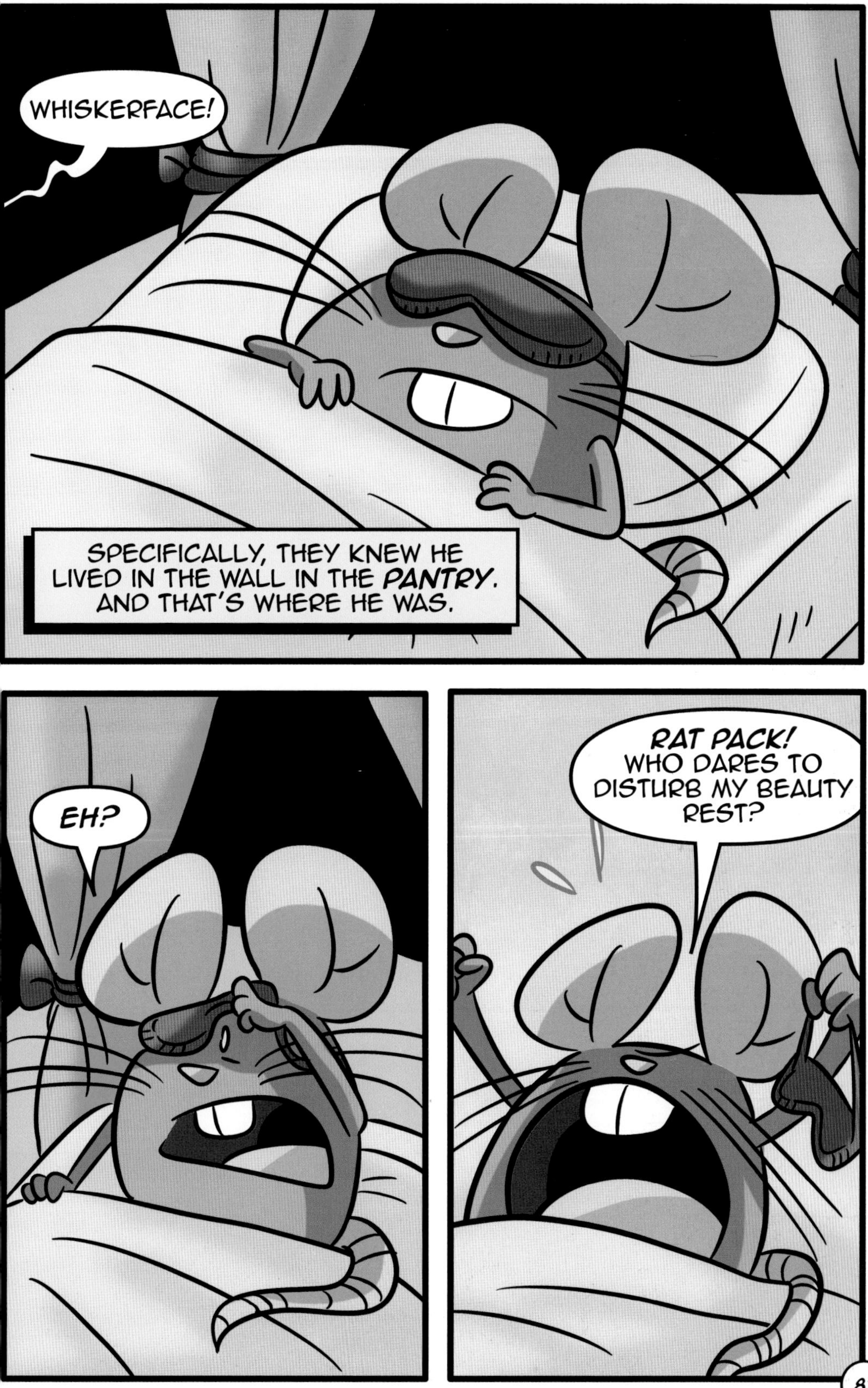
WHISKERFACE!
SPECIFICALLY, THEY KNEW HE LIVED IN THE WALL IN THE *PANTRY*. AND THAT'S WHERE HE WAS.
EH?
RAT PACK! WHO DARES TO DISTURB MY BEAUTY REST?

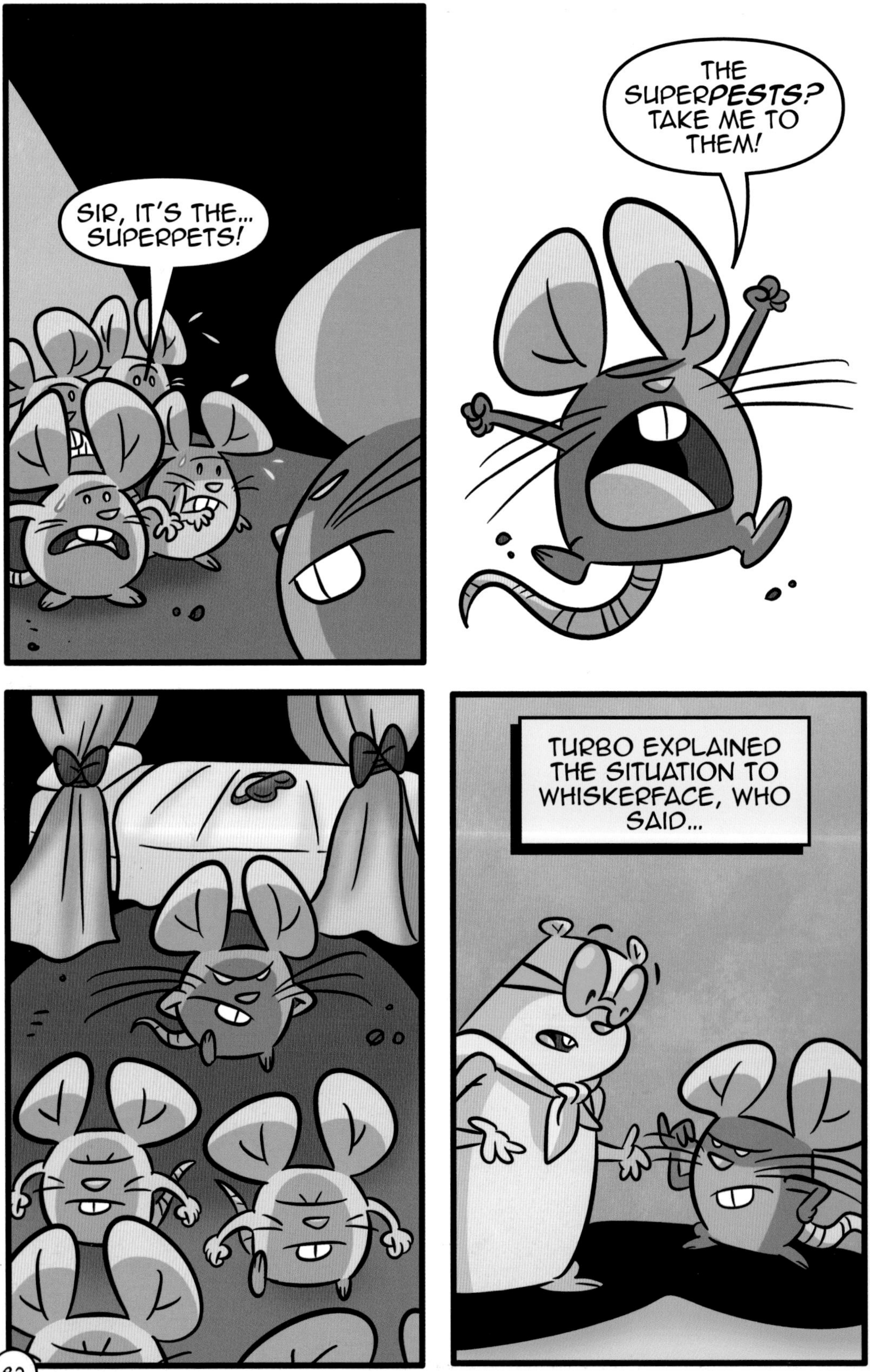
SIR, IT'S THE... SUPERPETS!
THE SUPERPESTS? TAKE ME TO THEM!
TURBO EXPLAINED THE SITUATION TO WHISKERFACE, WHO SAID...

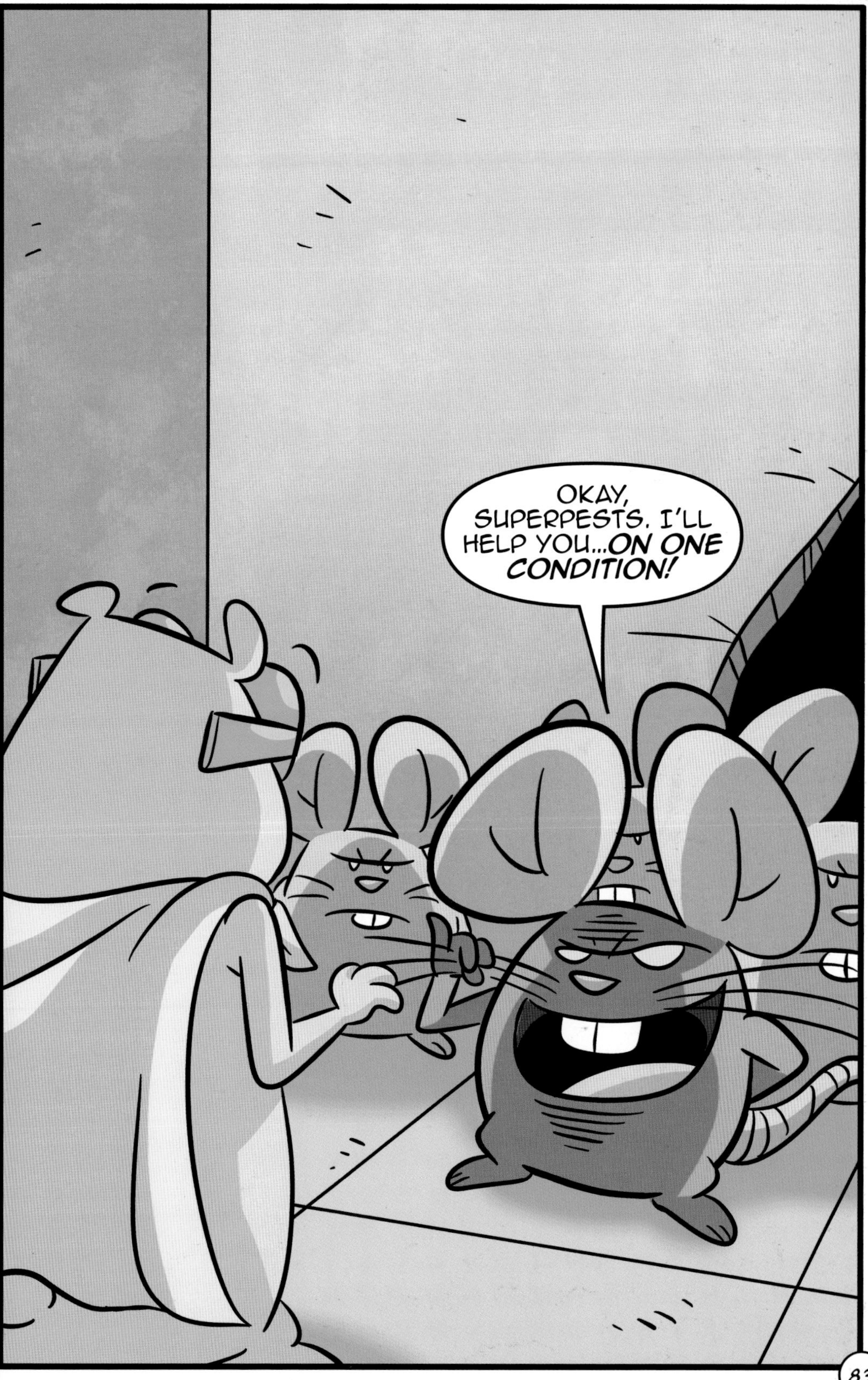
OKAY, SUPERPESTS. I'LL HELP YOU...**ON ONE CONDITION!**

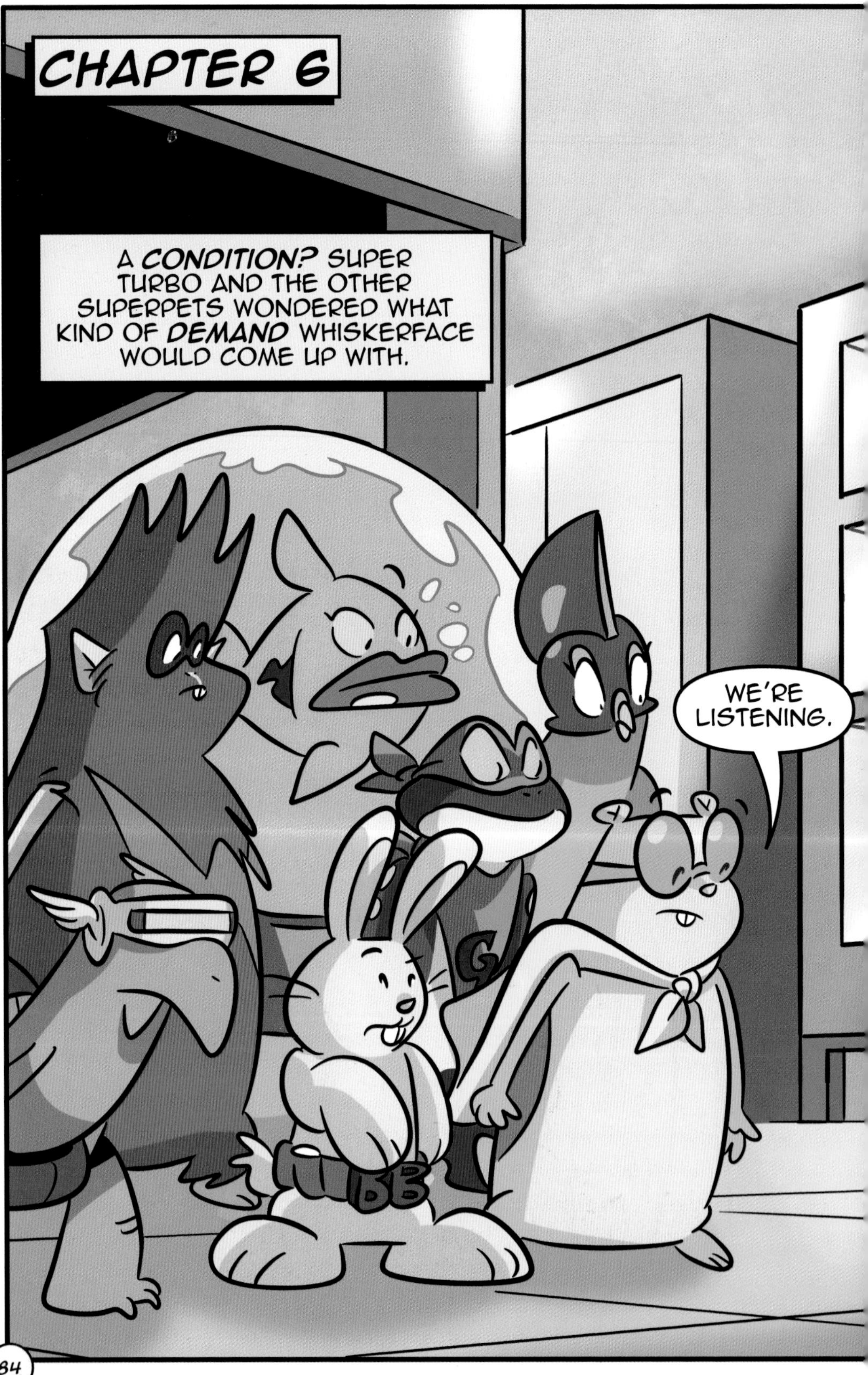
CHAPTER 6
A *CONDITION?* SUPER TURBO AND THE OTHER SUPERPETS WONDERED WHAT KIND OF *DEMAND* WHISKERFACE WOULD COME UP WITH.
WE'RE LISTENING.

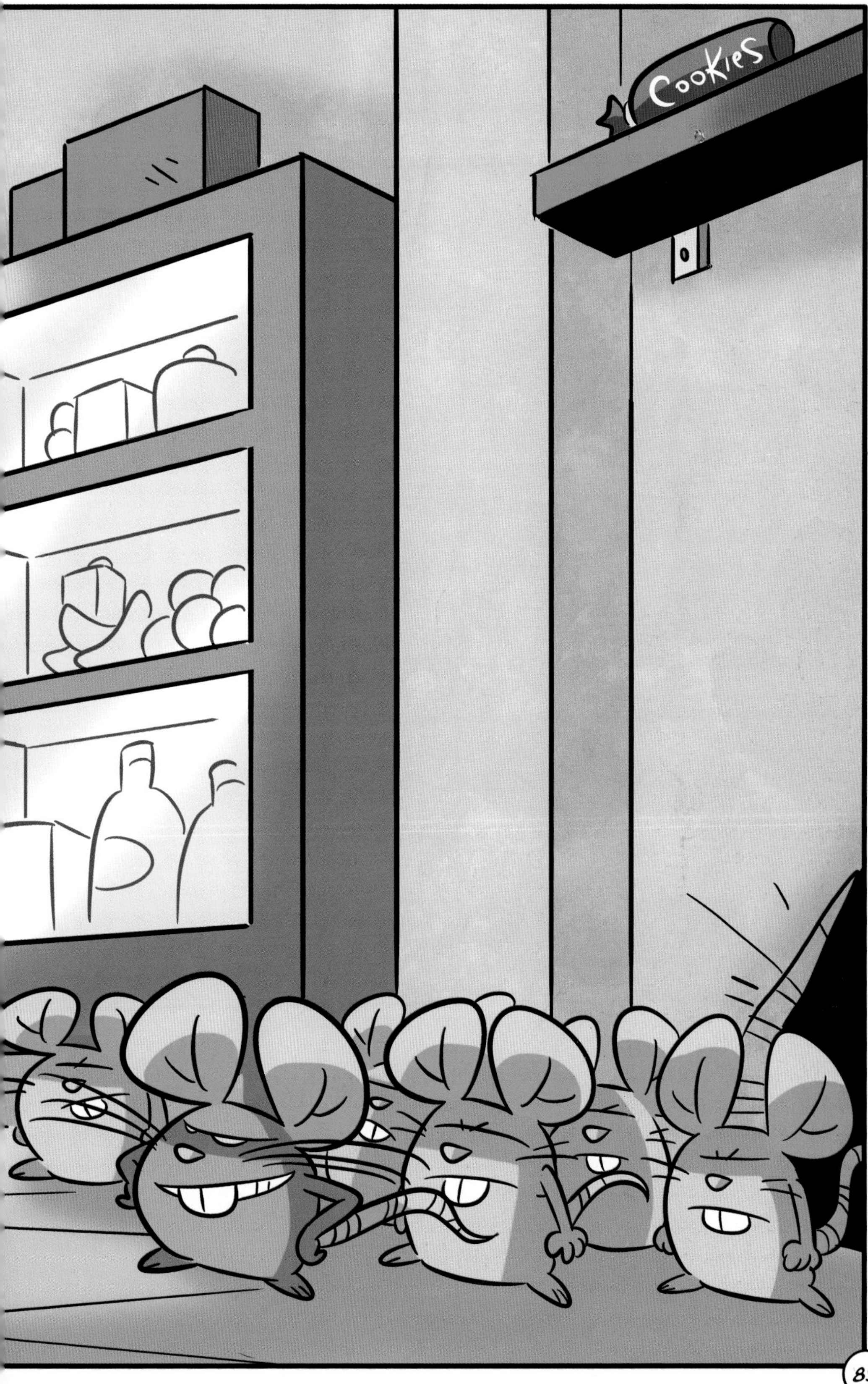
Cookies

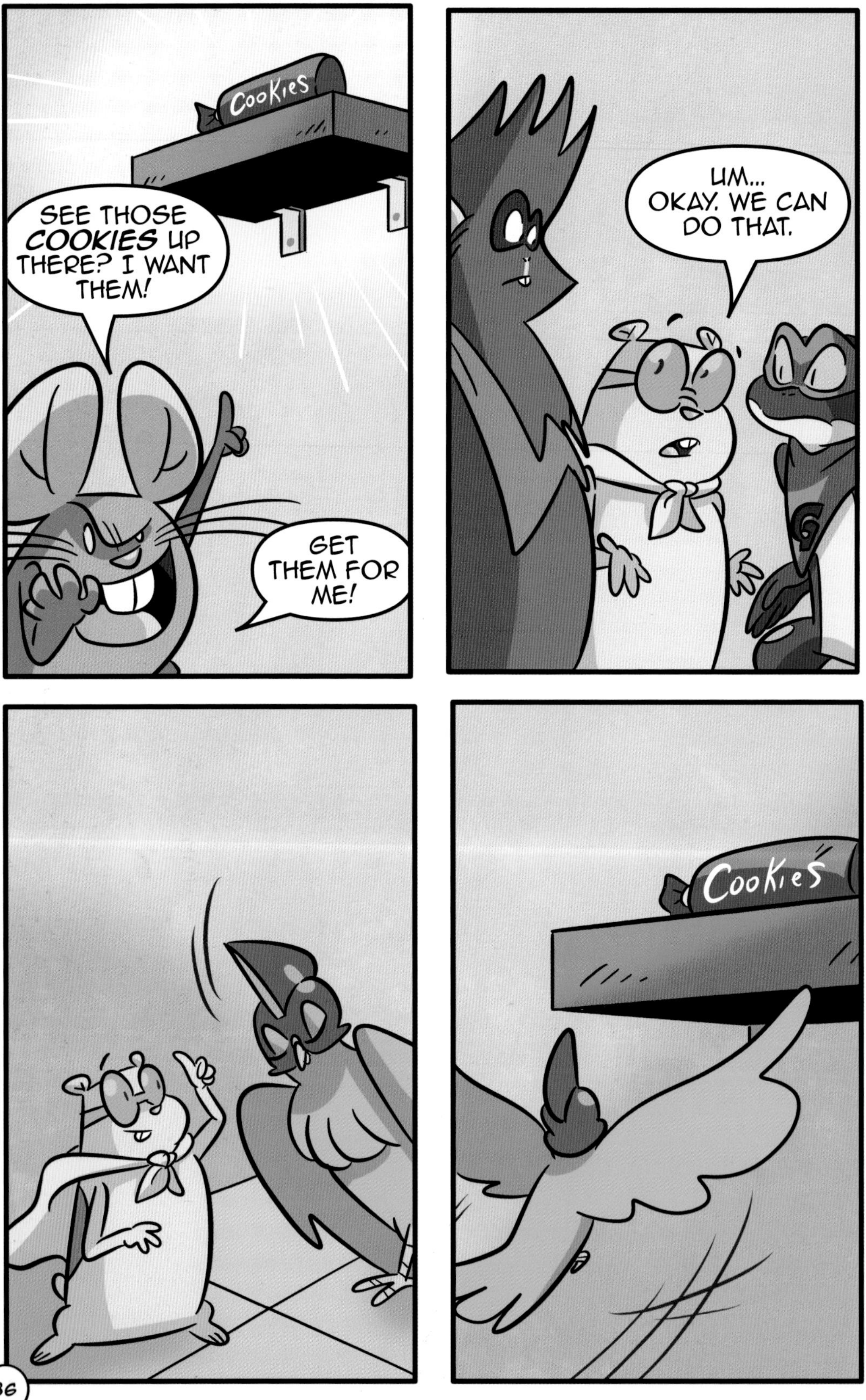
Cookies
SEE THOSE COOKIES UP THERE? I WANT THEM!
GET THEM FOR ME!
UM... OKAY. WE CAN DO THAT.
Cookies

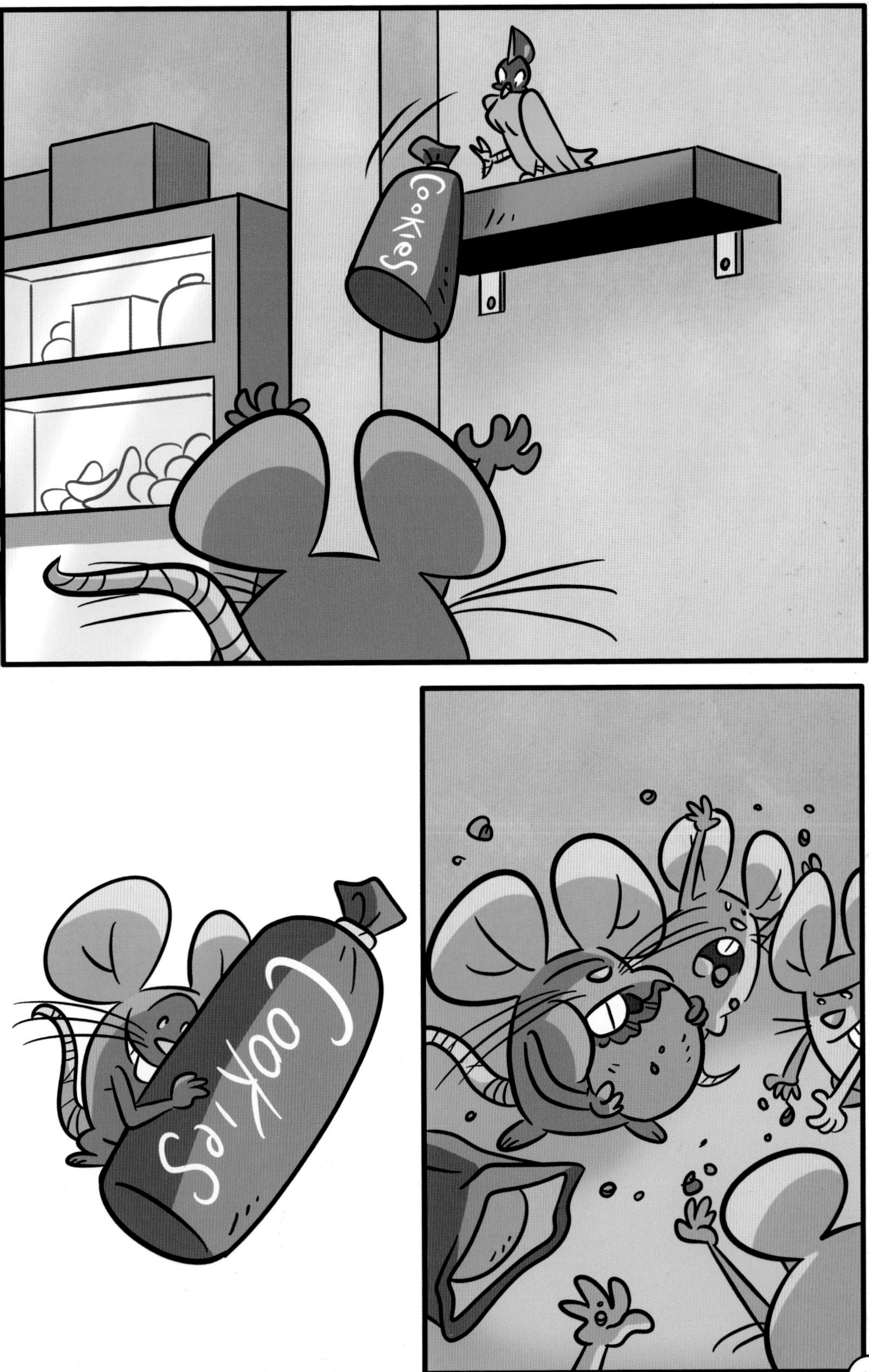
CooKies
CooKies

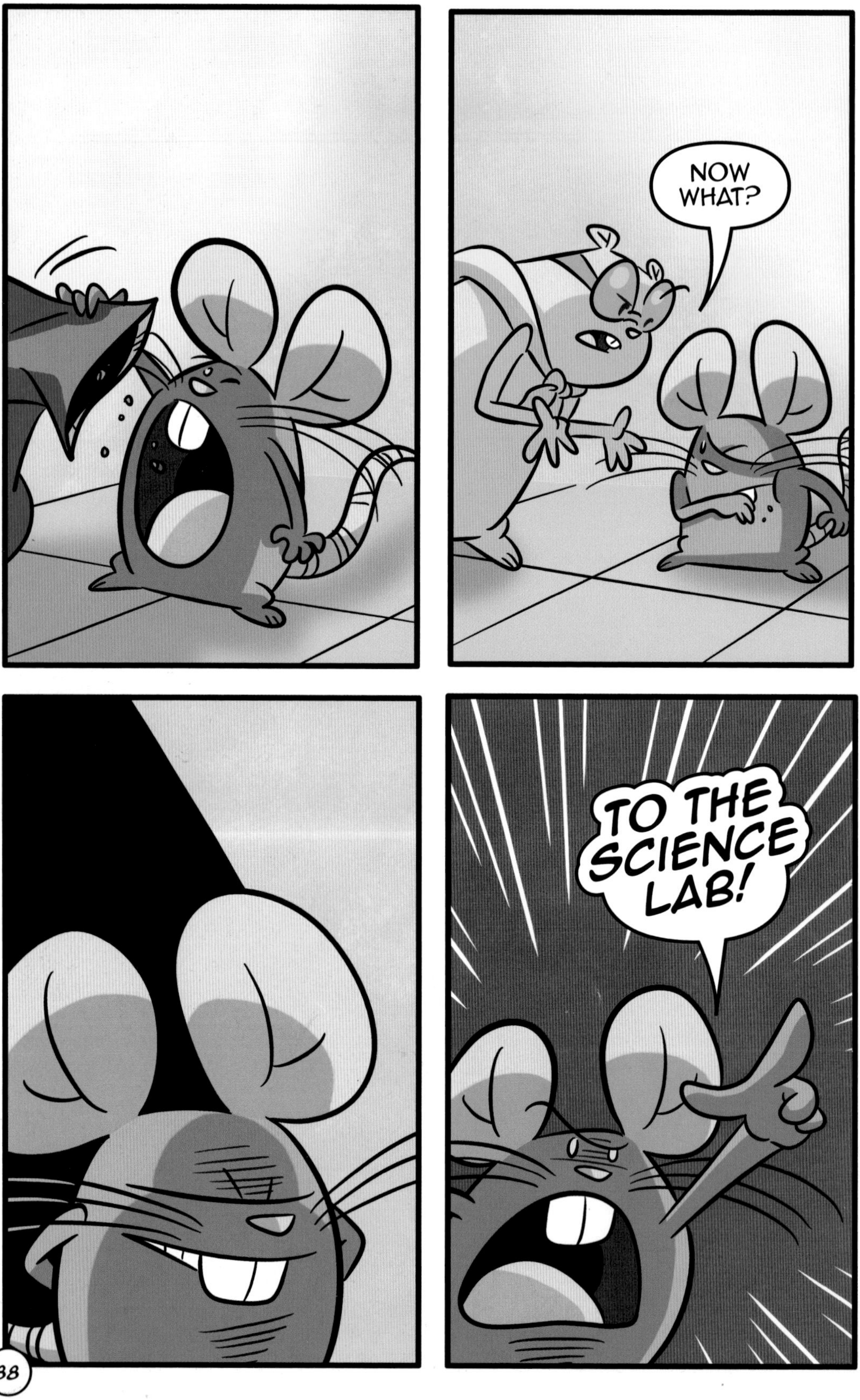
NOW WHAT?
TO THE SCIENCE LAB!

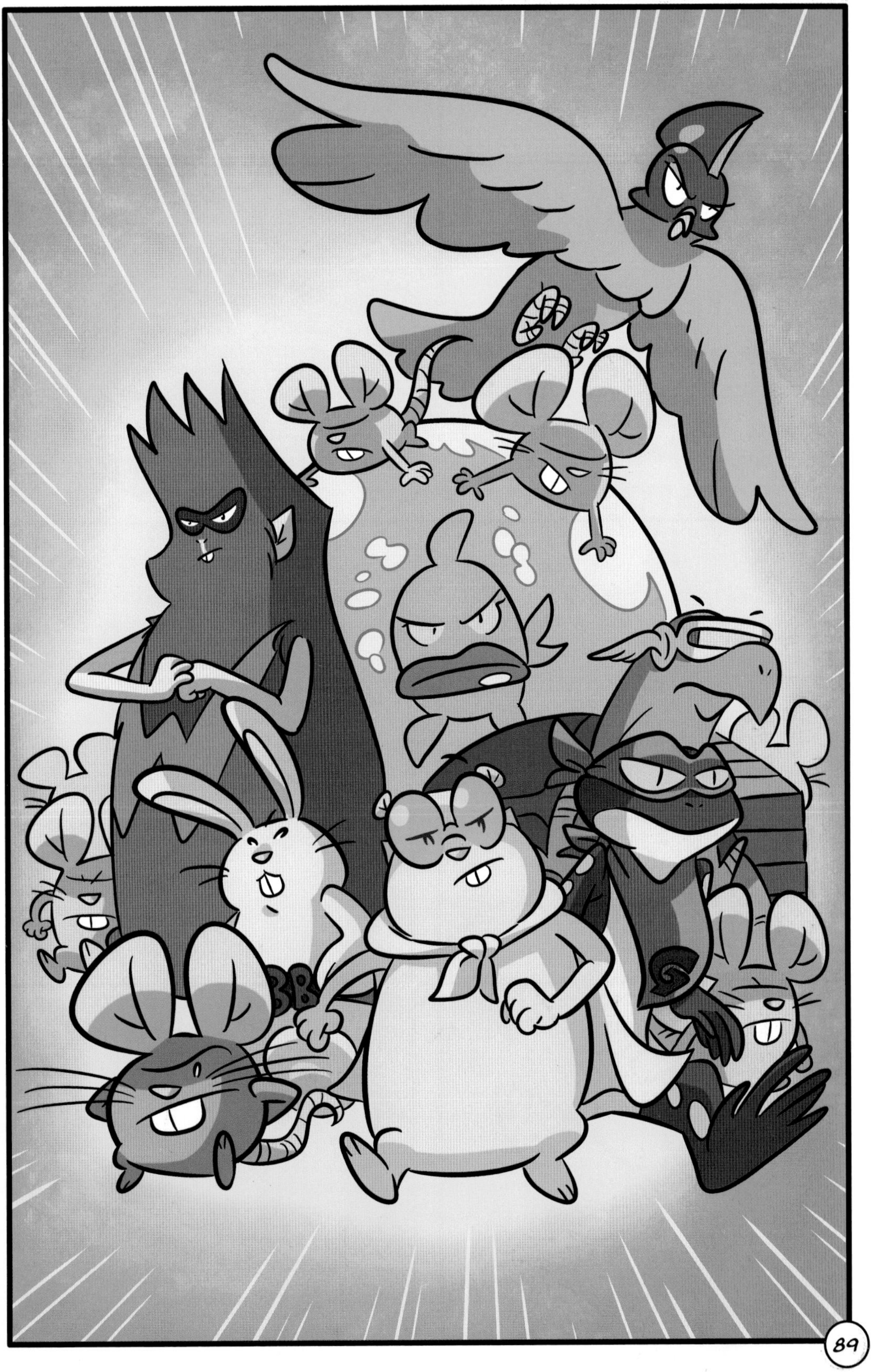

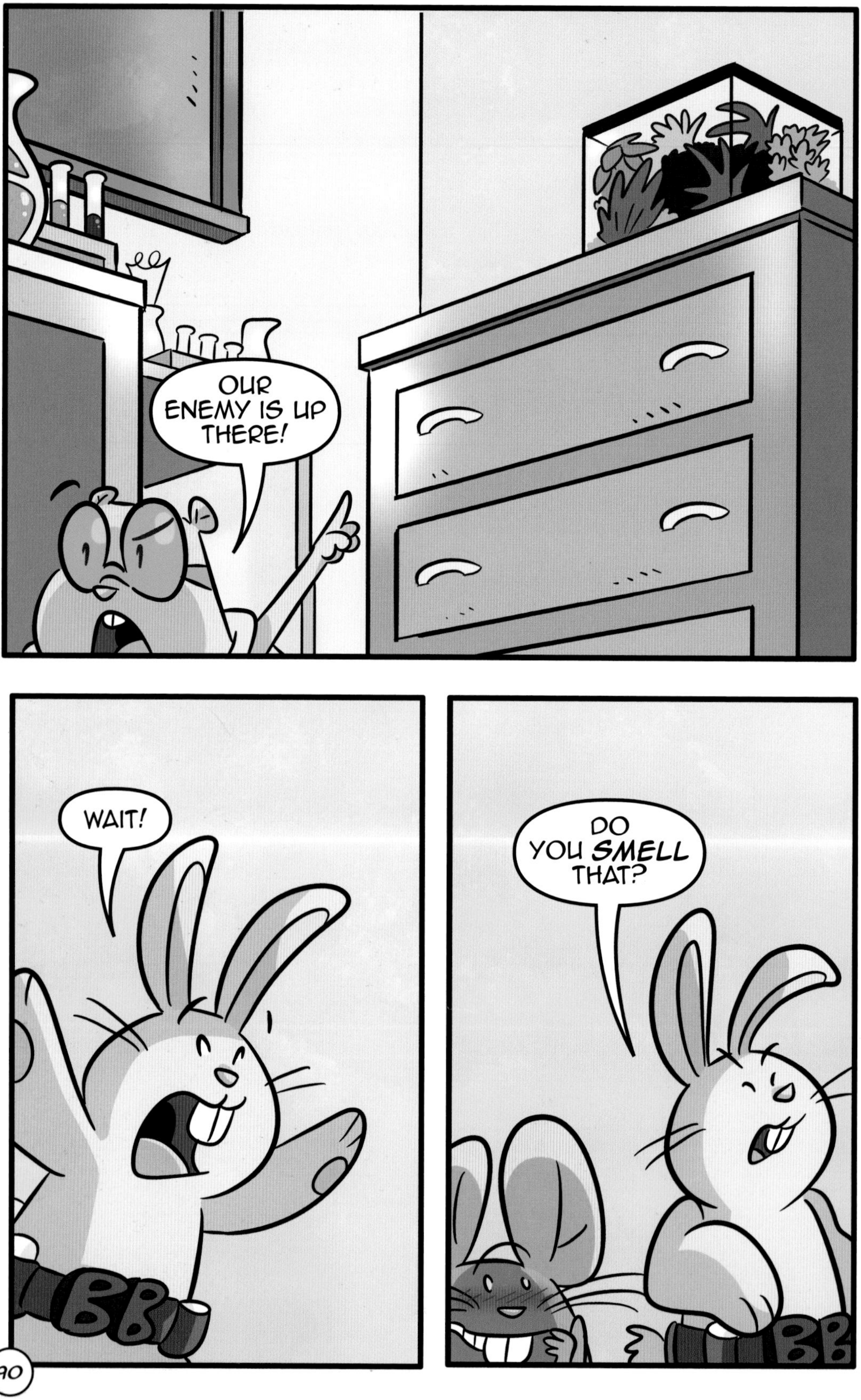
OUR ENEMY IS UP THERE!
WAIT!
DO YOU SMELL THAT?

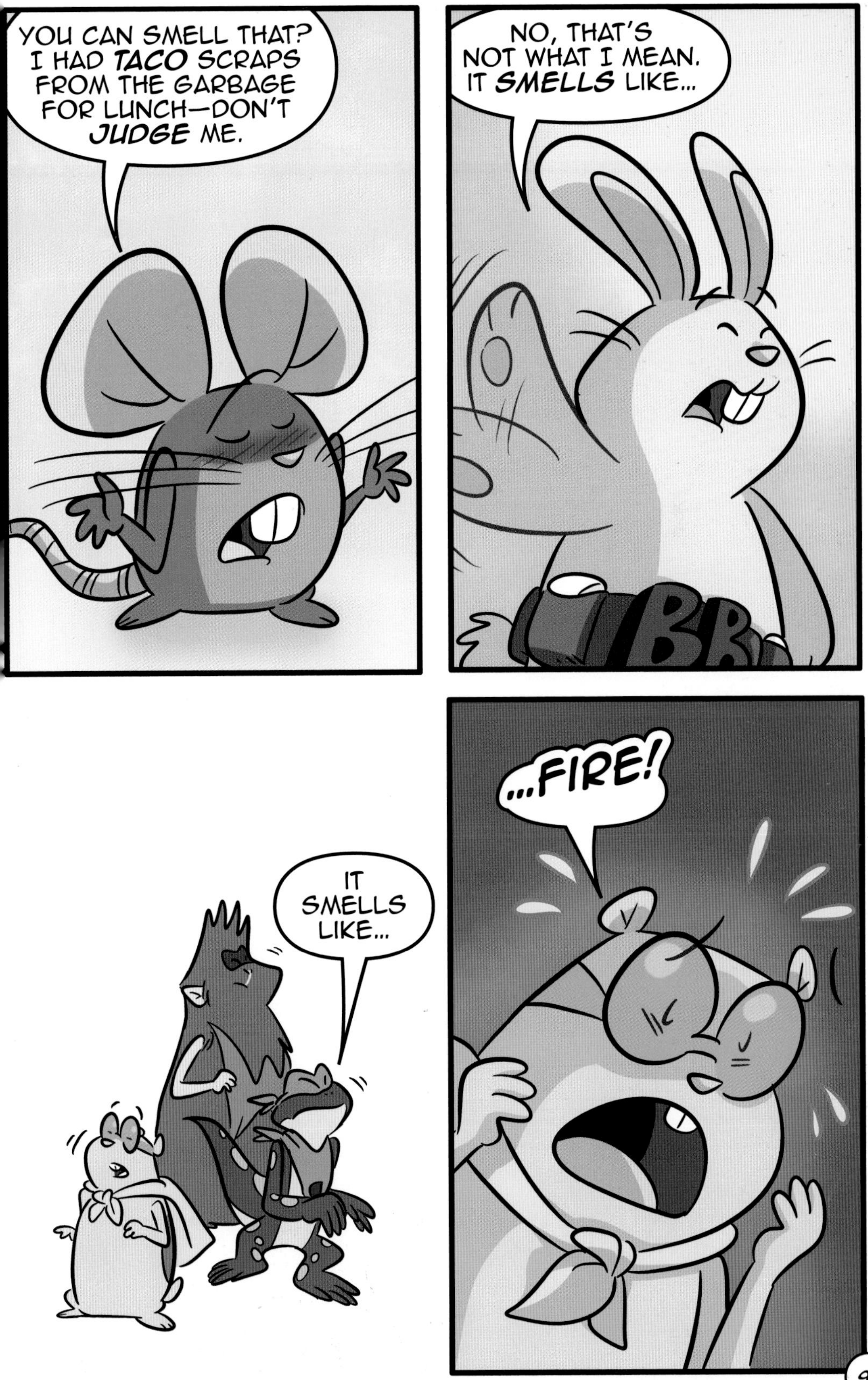
YOU CAN SMELL THAT? I HAD TACO SCRAPS FROM THE GARBAGE FOR LUNCH—DON'T JUDGE ME.
NO, THAT'S NOT WHAT I MEAN. IT SMELLS LIKE...
IT SMELLS LIKE...
...FIRE!

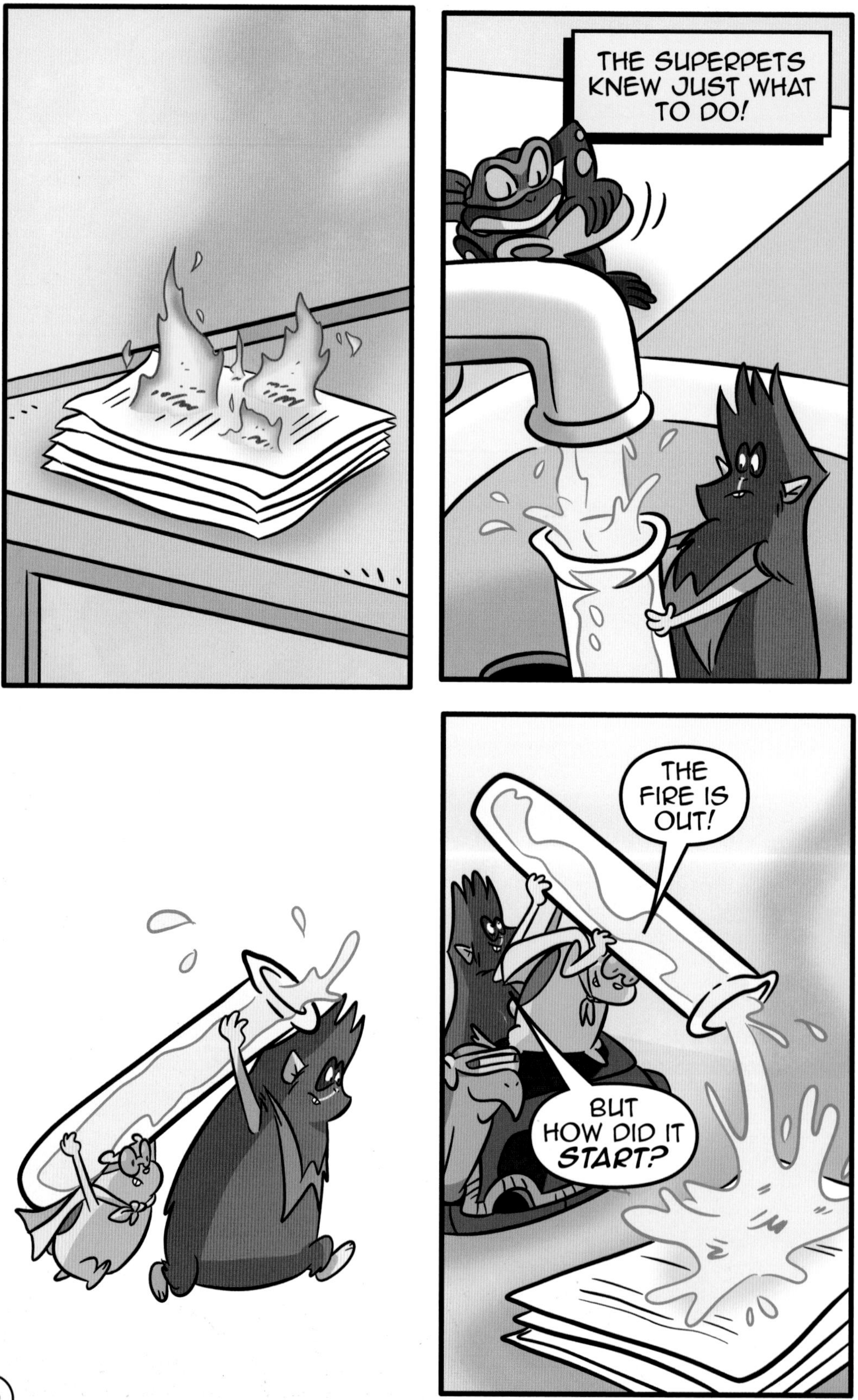
THE SUPERPETS KNEW JUST WHAT TO DO!
THE FIRE IS OUT!
BUT HOW DID IT START?

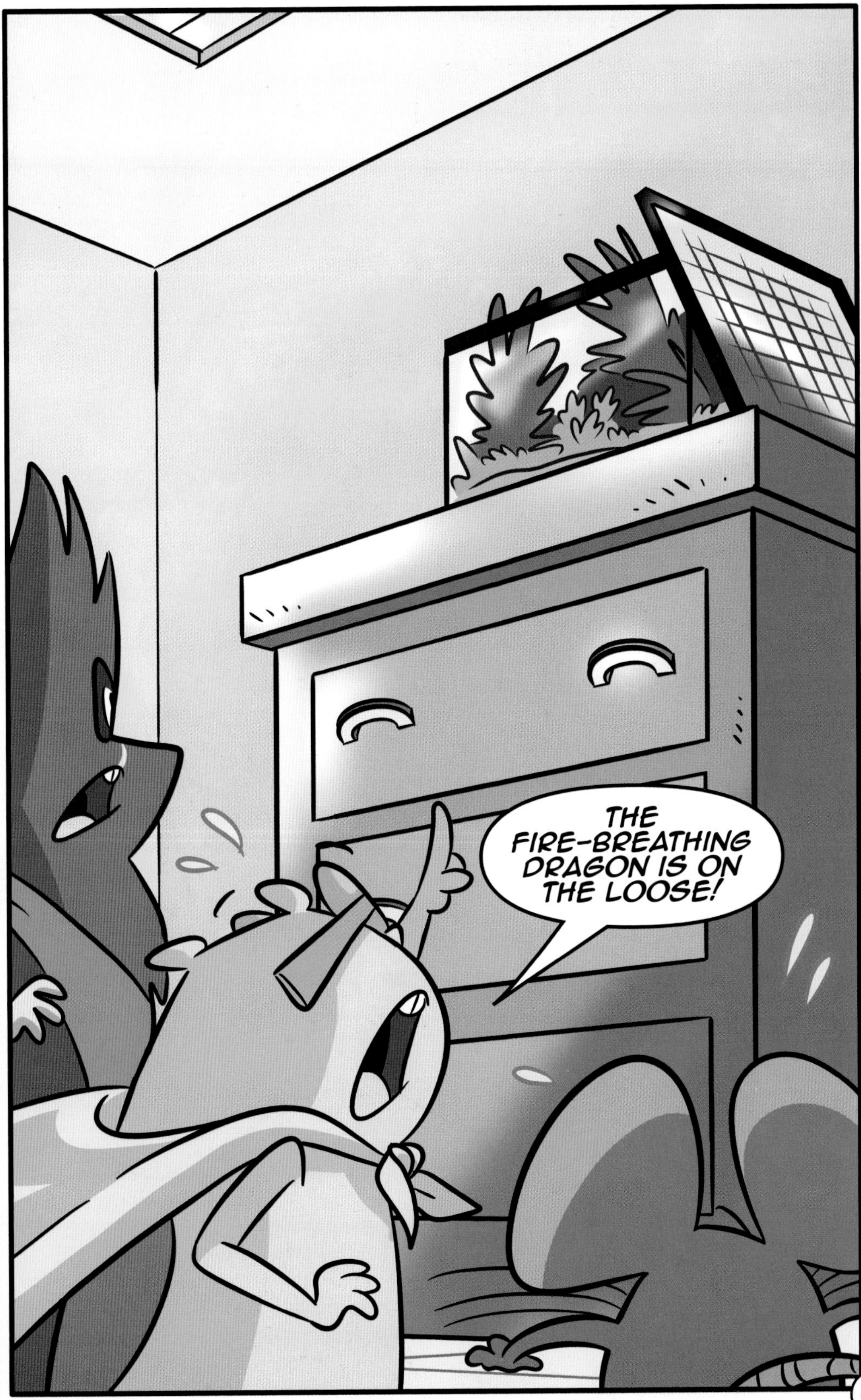
THE FIRE-BREATHING DRAGON IS ON THE LOOSE!

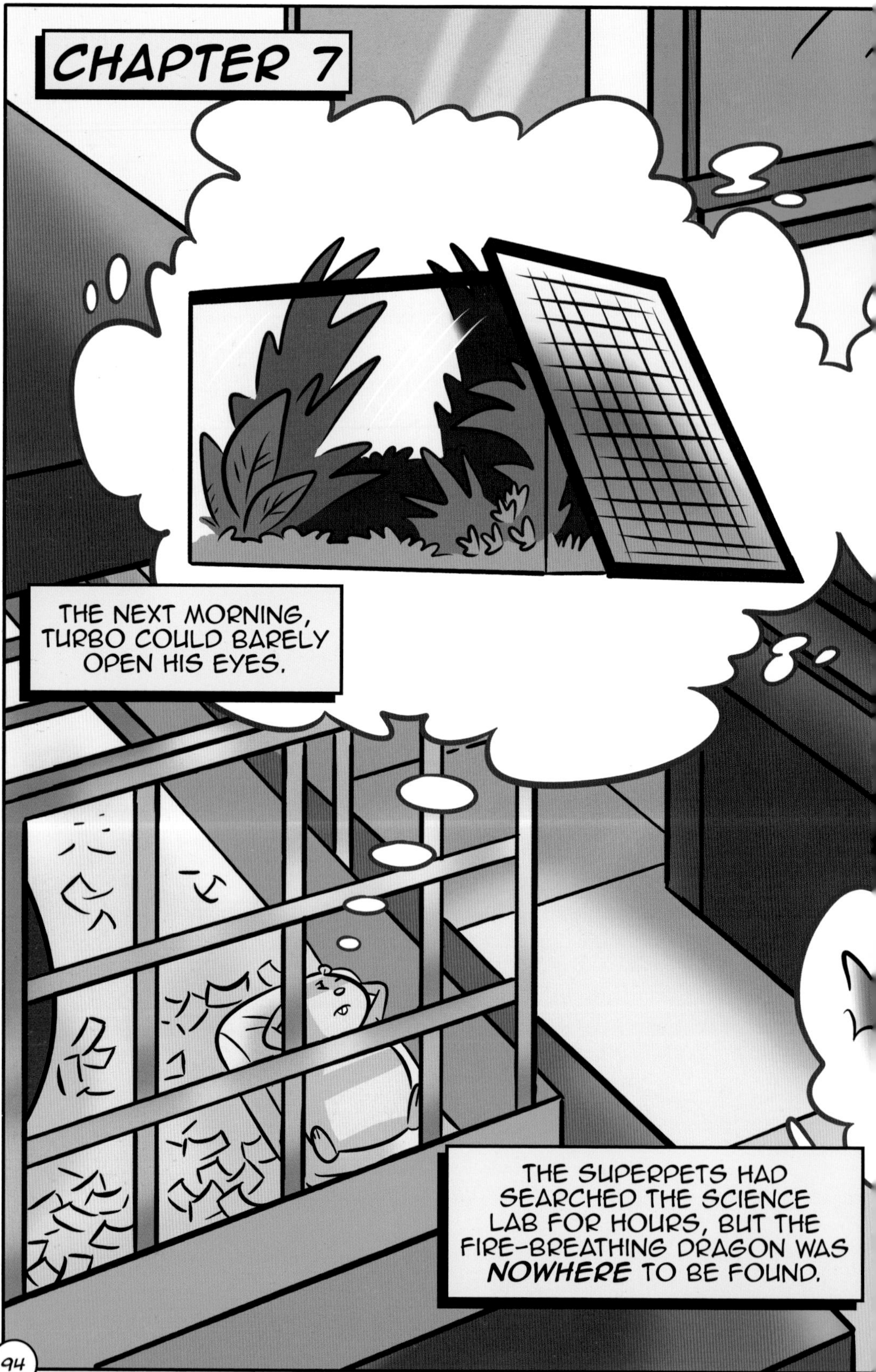
CHAPTER 7
THE NEXT MORNING, TURBO COULD BARELY OPEN HIS EYES.
THE SUPERPETS HAD SEARCHED THE SCIENCE LAB FOR HOURS, BUT THE FIRE-BREATHING DRAGON WAS *NOWHERE* TO BE FOUND.

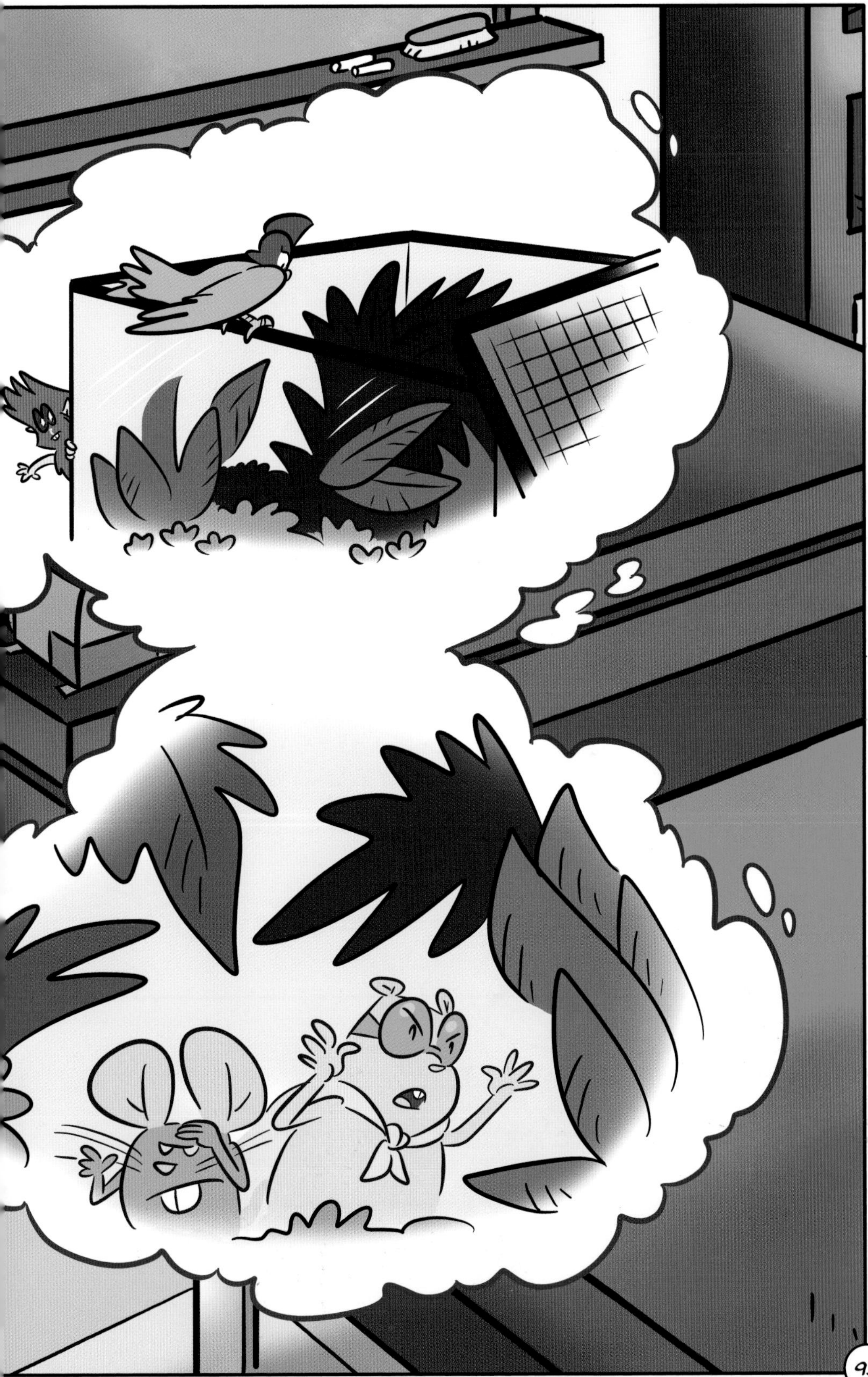

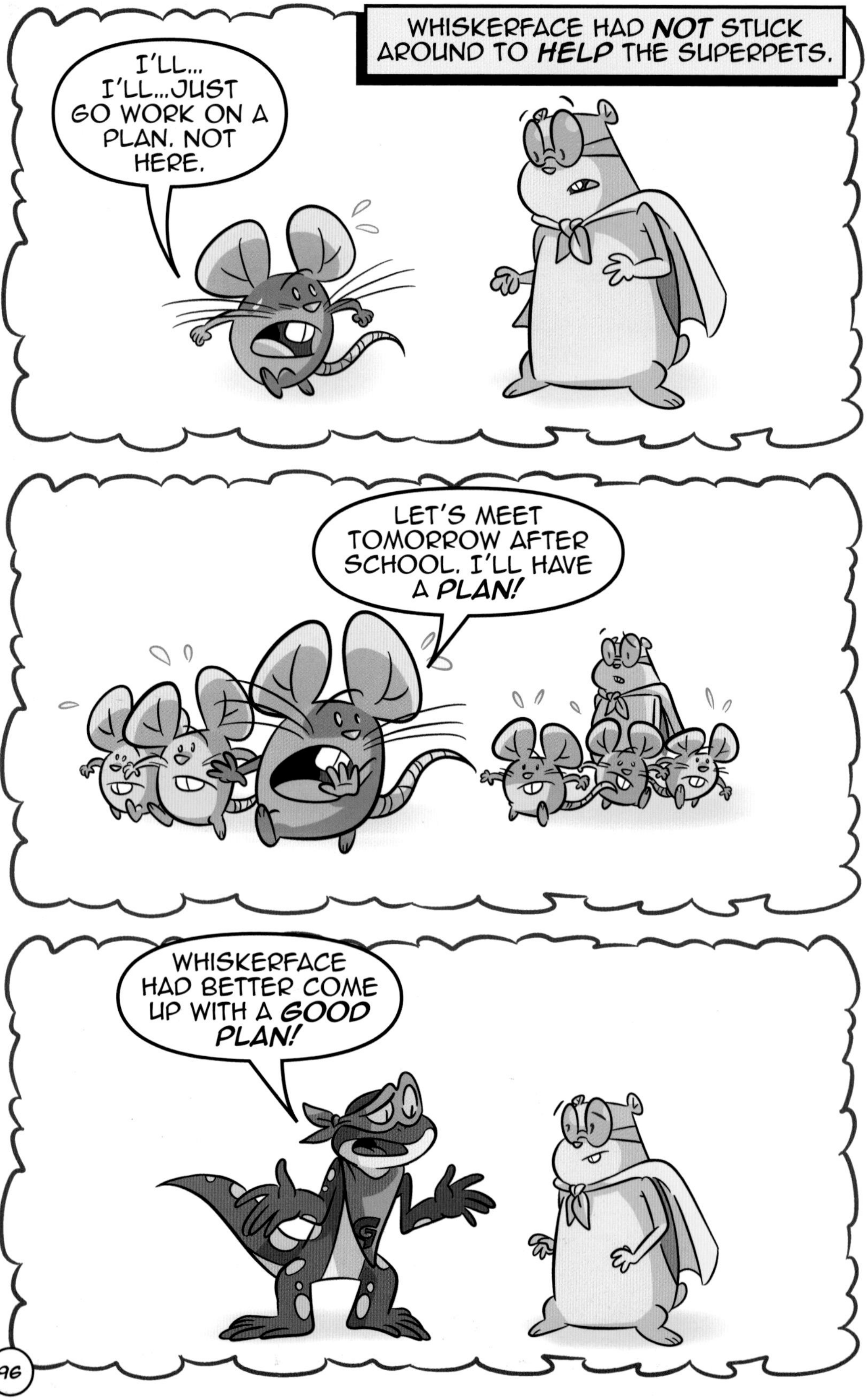
WHISKERFACE HAD **NOT** STUCK AROUND TO **HELP** THE SUPERPETS.
I'LL... I'LL...JUST GO WORK ON A PLAN. NOT HERE.
LET'S MEET TOMORROW AFTER SCHOOL. I'LL HAVE A **PLAN!**
WHISKERFACE HAD BETTER COME UP WITH A **GOOD PLAN!**

IT HAD BEEN A LONG NIGHT. AND TURBO WAS *EXHAUSTED.*

AND SO WERE ALL THE OTHER SUPERPETS. SINCE THEY HAD NOWHERE TO BE UNTIL AFTER SCHOOL, MOST OF THEM SPENT THE DAY *SLEEPING.*

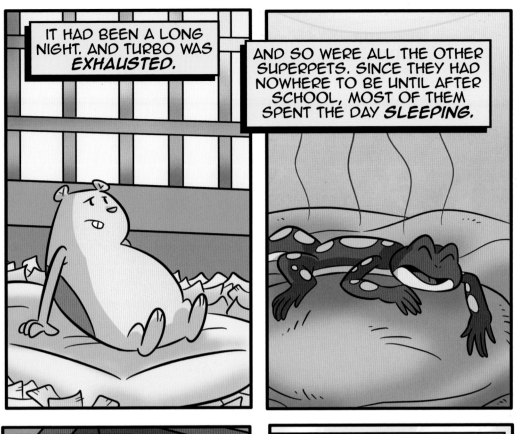

BUT NOT ALL THE SUPERPETS.

NO PAIN, NO GAIN.

WARREN, HOWEVER, WAS CATCHING UP ON HIS *SLEEP.*

WHICH WAS WHY HE MISSED IT WHEN DR. GARFIELD SAID *THIS...*

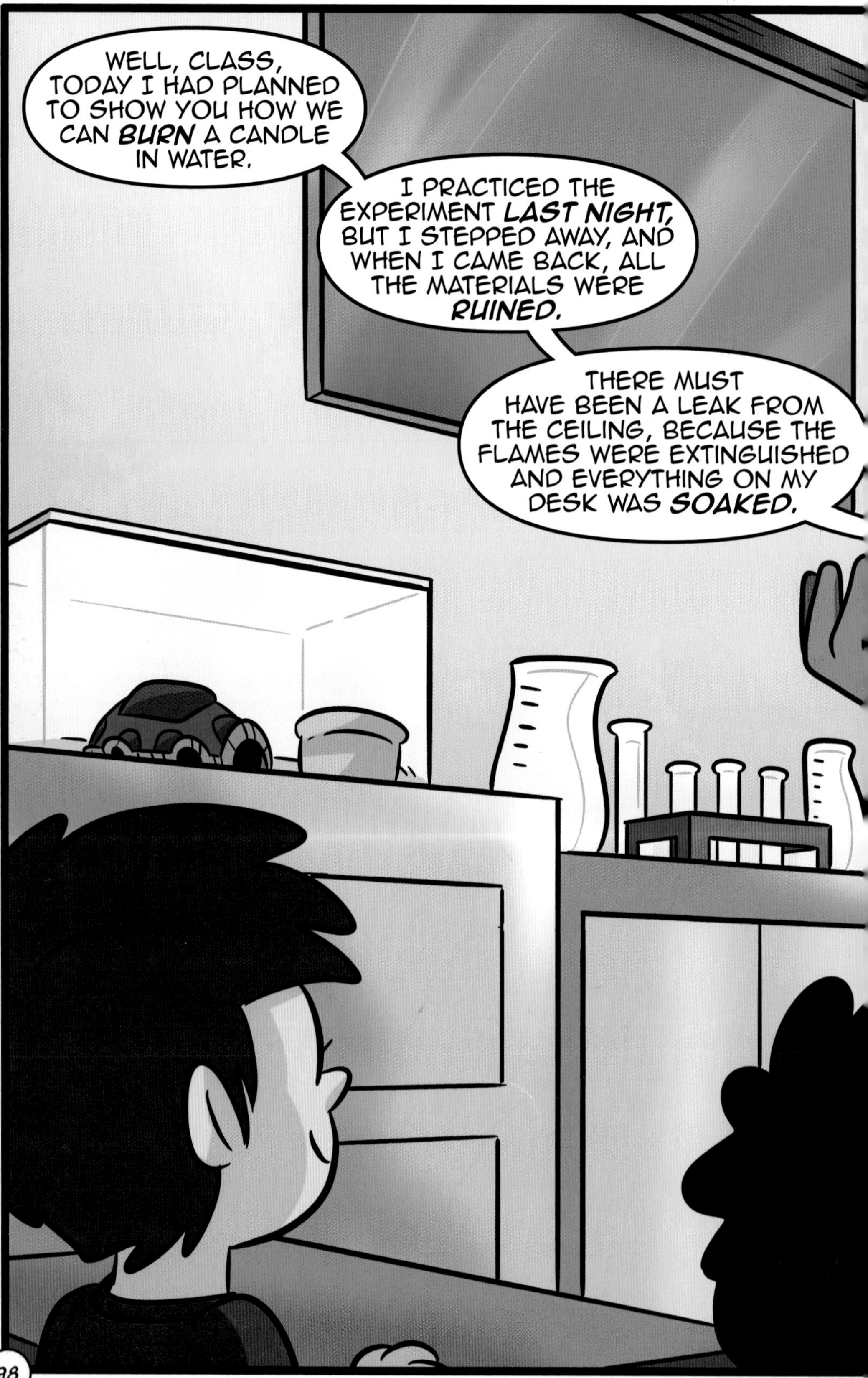
WELL, CLASS, TODAY I HAD PLANNED TO SHOW YOU HOW WE CAN BURN A CANDLE IN WATER.
I PRACTICED THE EXPERIMENT LAST NIGHT, BUT I STEPPED AWAY, AND WHEN I CAME BACK, ALL THE MATERIALS WERE RUINED.
THERE MUST HAVE BEEN A LEAK FROM THE CEILING, BECAUSE THE FLAMES WERE EXTINGUISHED AND EVERYTHING ON MY DESK WAS SOAKED.

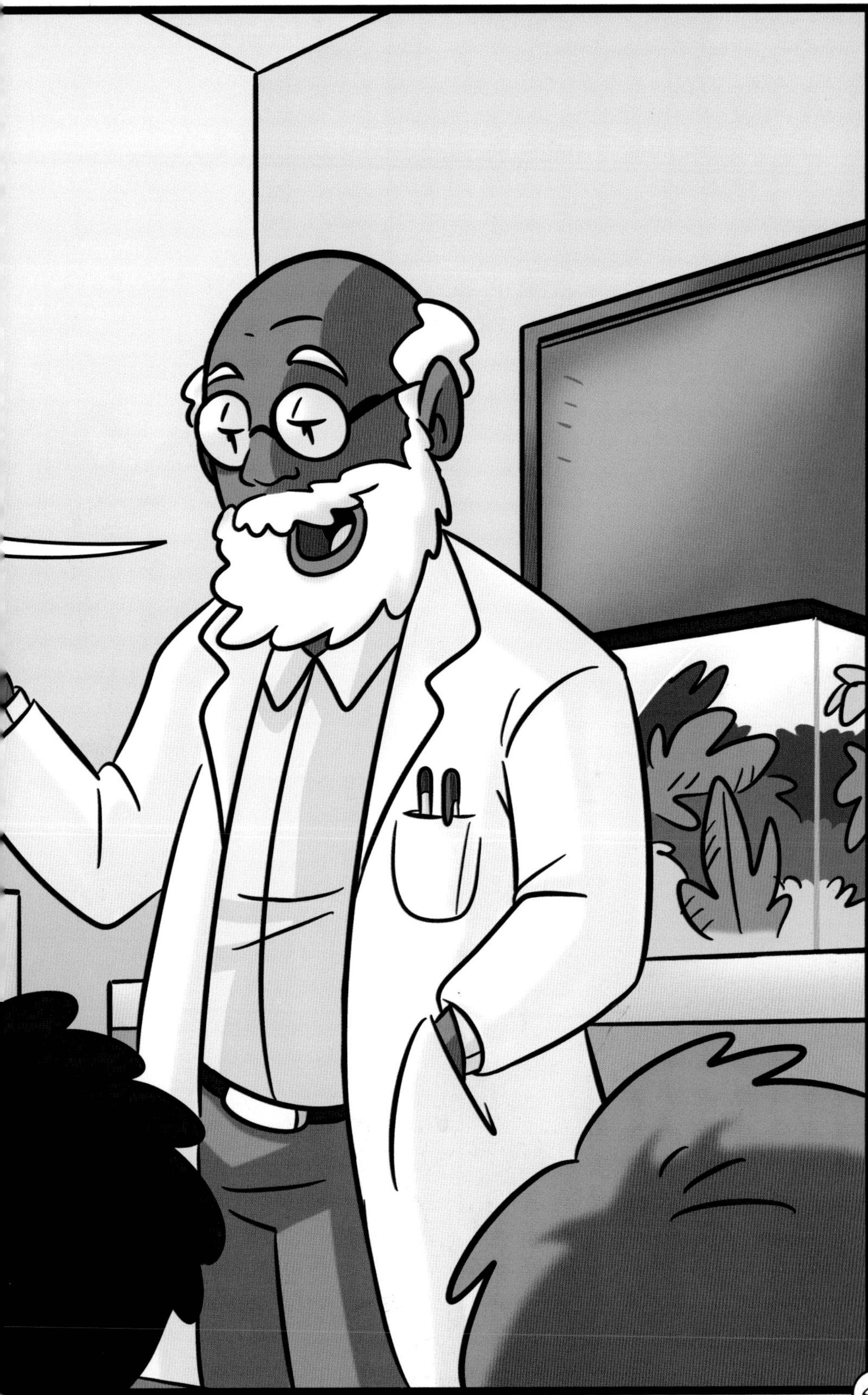

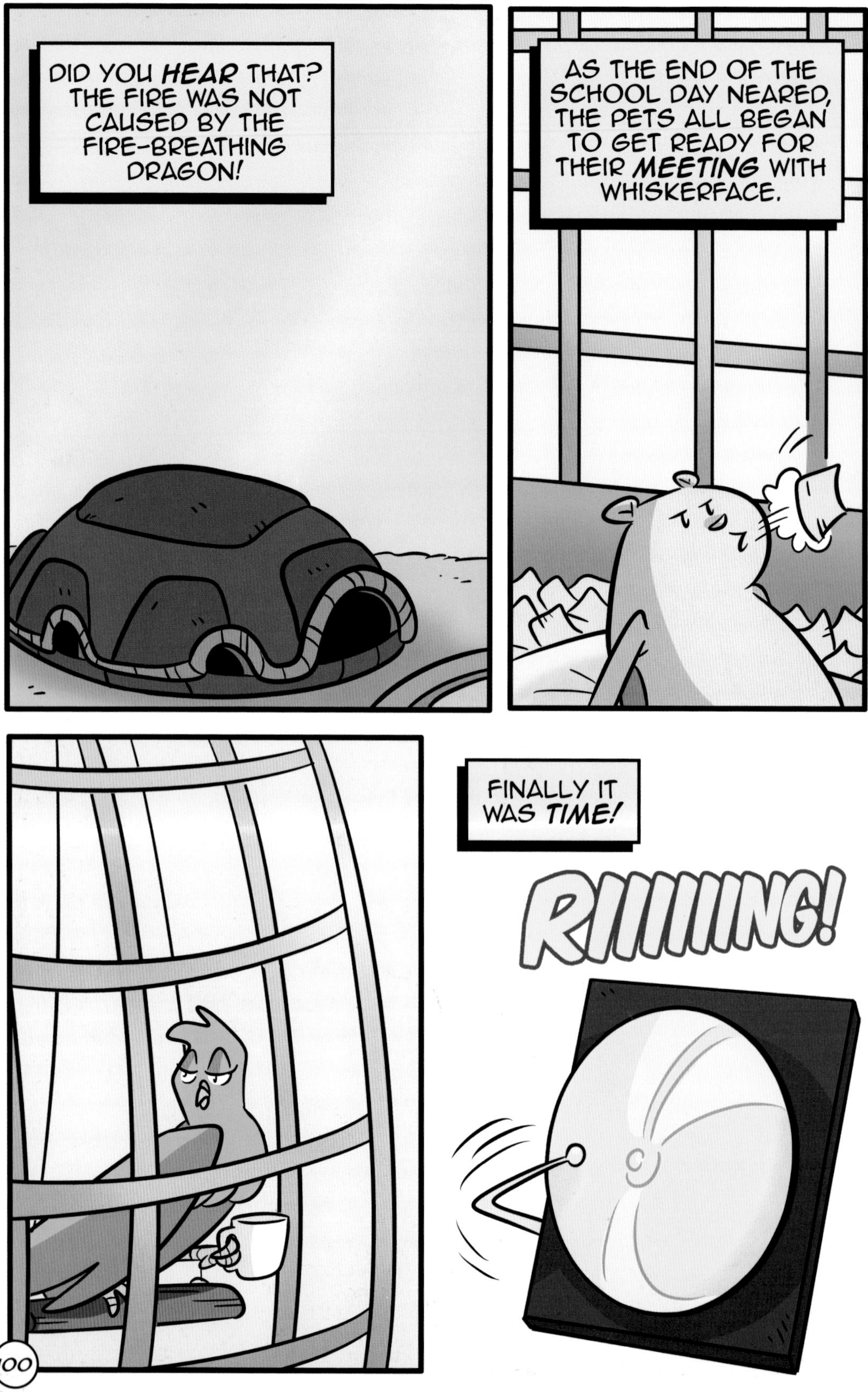
DID YOU *HEAR* THAT? THE FIRE WAS NOT CAUSED BY THE FIRE-BREATHING DRAGON!
AS THE END OF THE SCHOOL DAY NEARED, THE PETS ALL BEGAN TO GET READY FOR THEIR *MEETING* WITH WHISKERFACE.
FINALLY IT WAS *TIME!*
RIIIIIING!

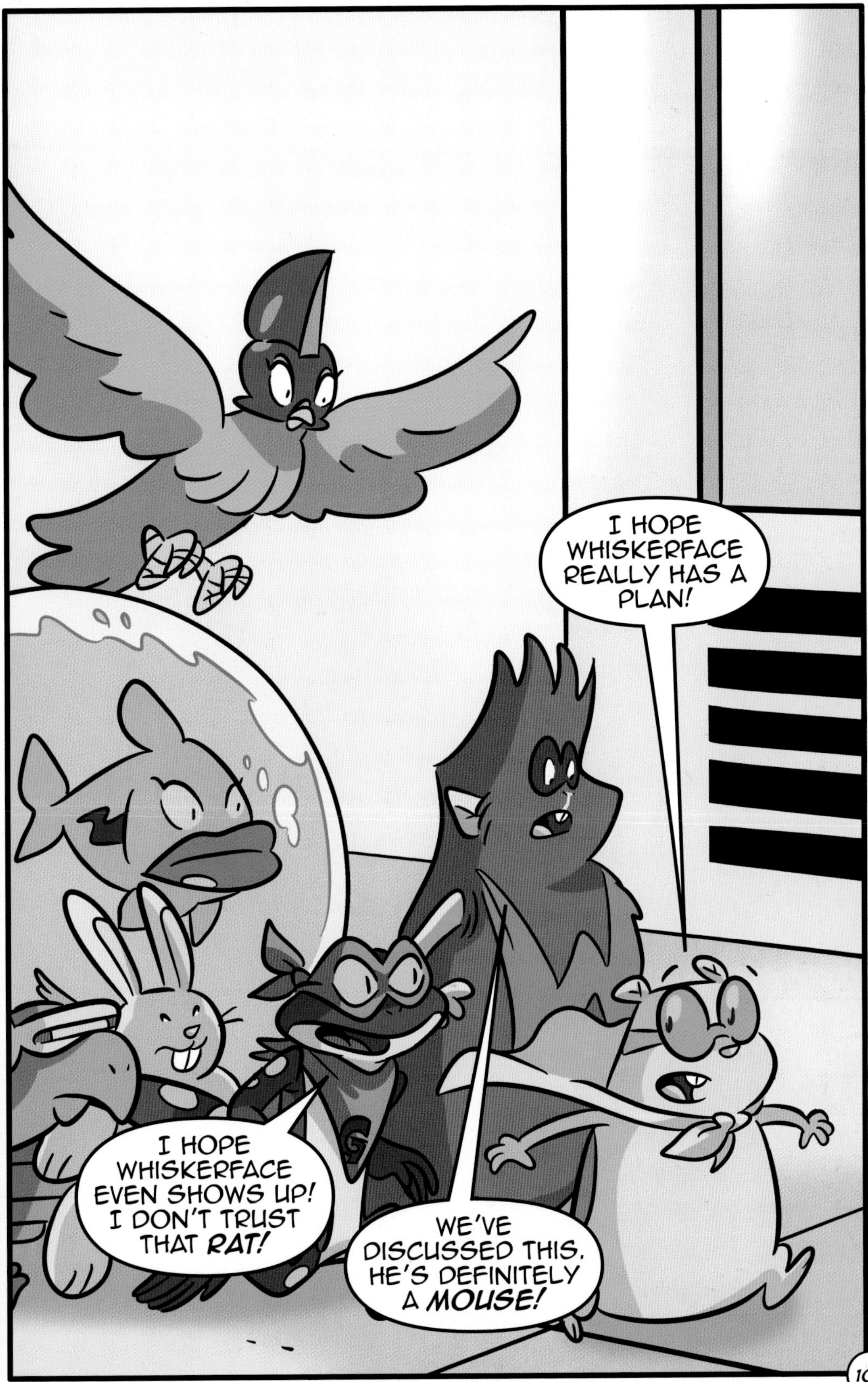
I HOPE WHISKERFACE REALLY HAS A PLAN!
I HOPE WHISKERFACE EVEN SHOWS UP! I DON'T TRUST THAT RAT!
WE'VE DISCUSSED THIS. HE'S DEFINITELY A MOUSE!

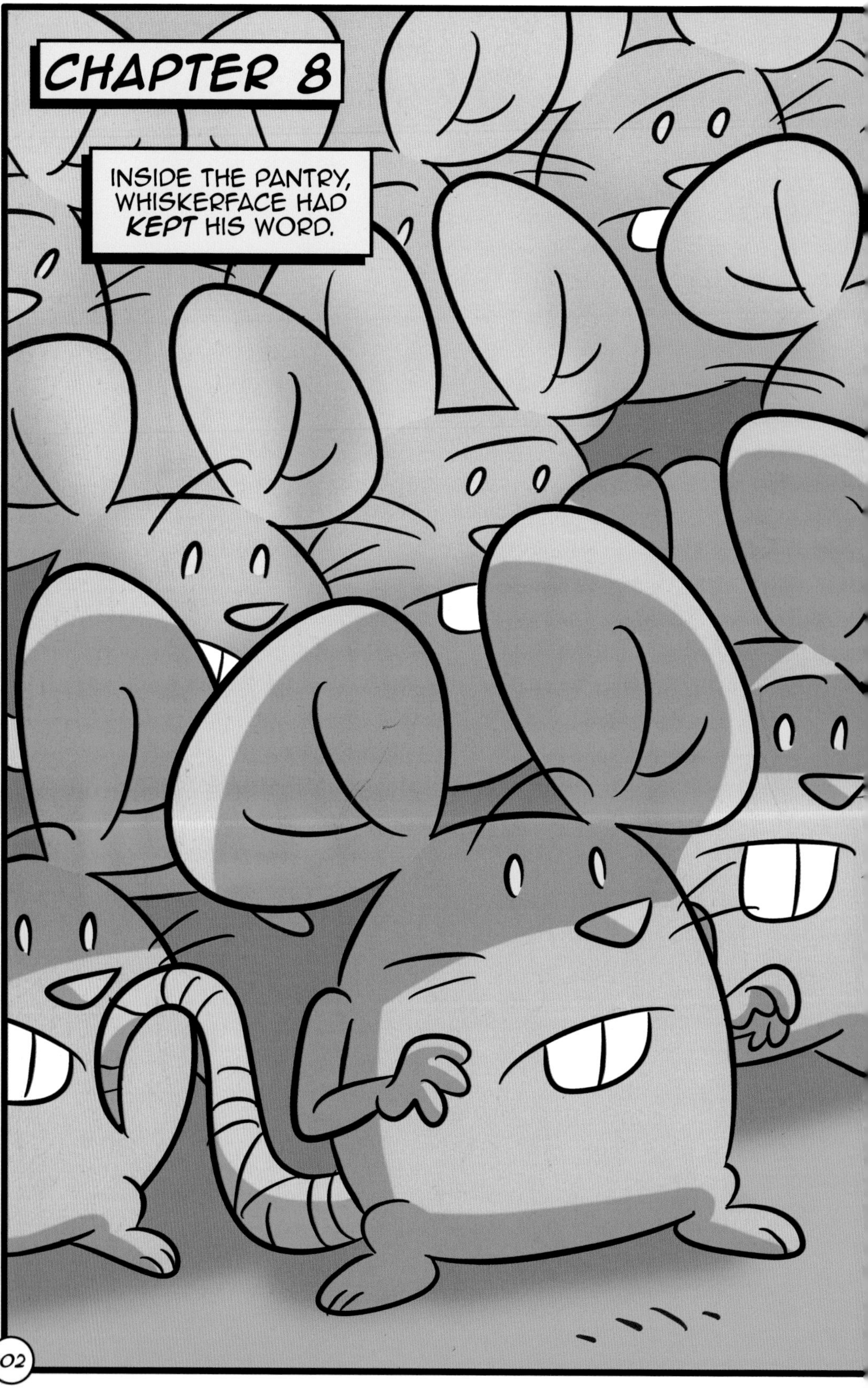
CHAPTER 8
INSIDE THE PANTRY, WHISKERFACE HAD KEPT HIS WORD.

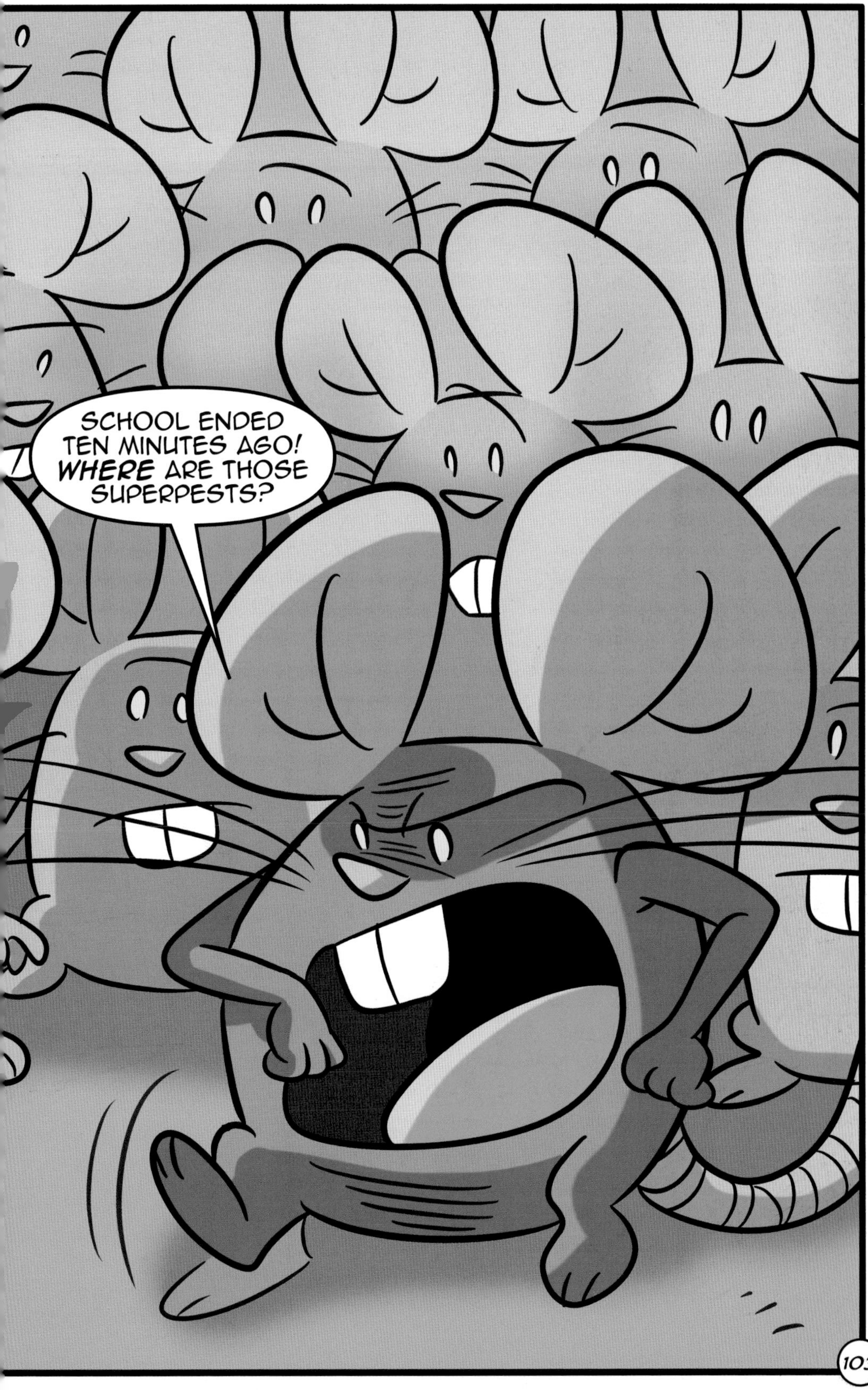
SCHOOL ENDED TEN MINUTES AGO! *WHERE* ARE THOSE SUPERPESTS?

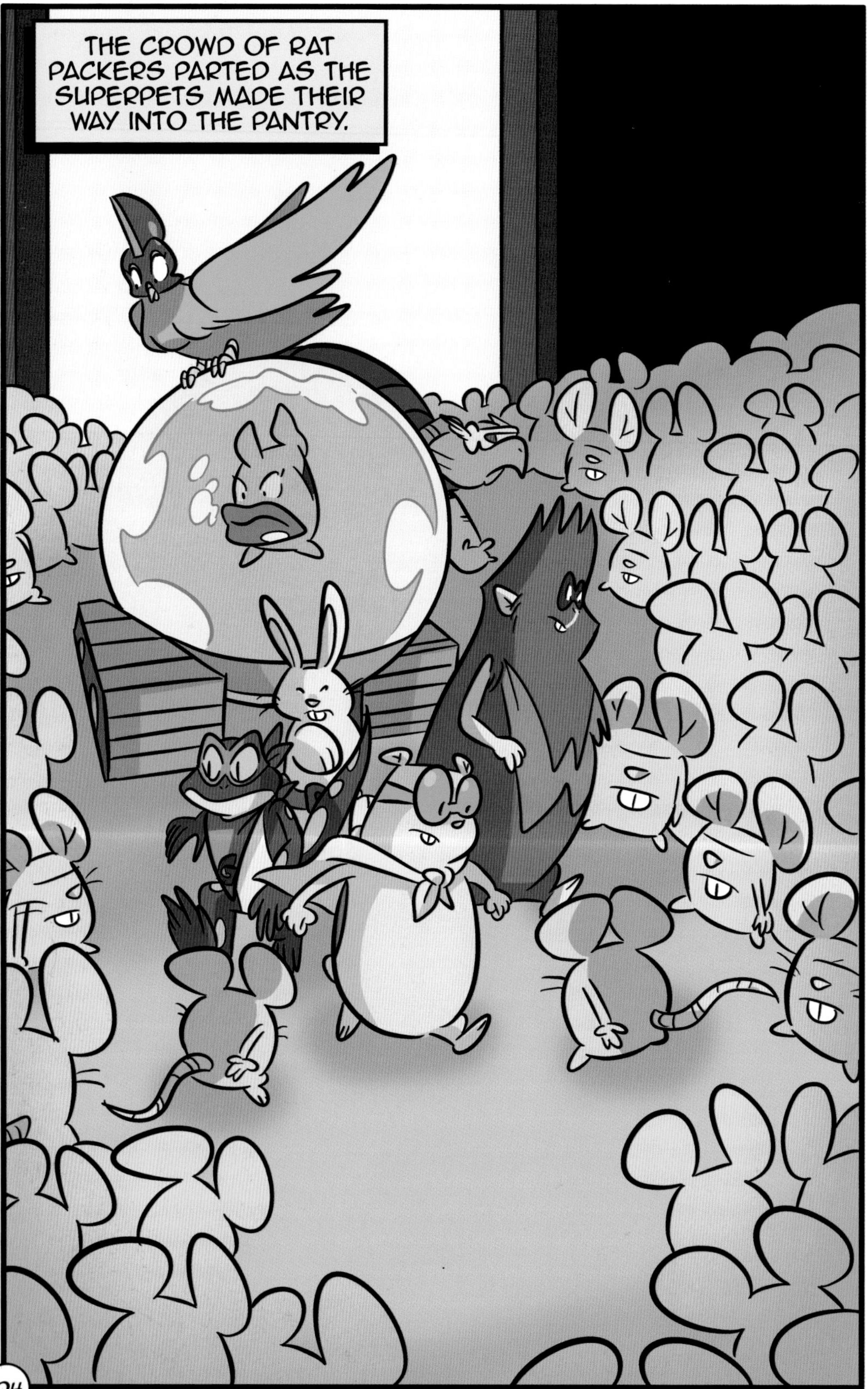
THE CROWD OF RAT PACKERS PARTED AS THE SUPERPETS MADE THEIR WAY INTO THE PANTRY.

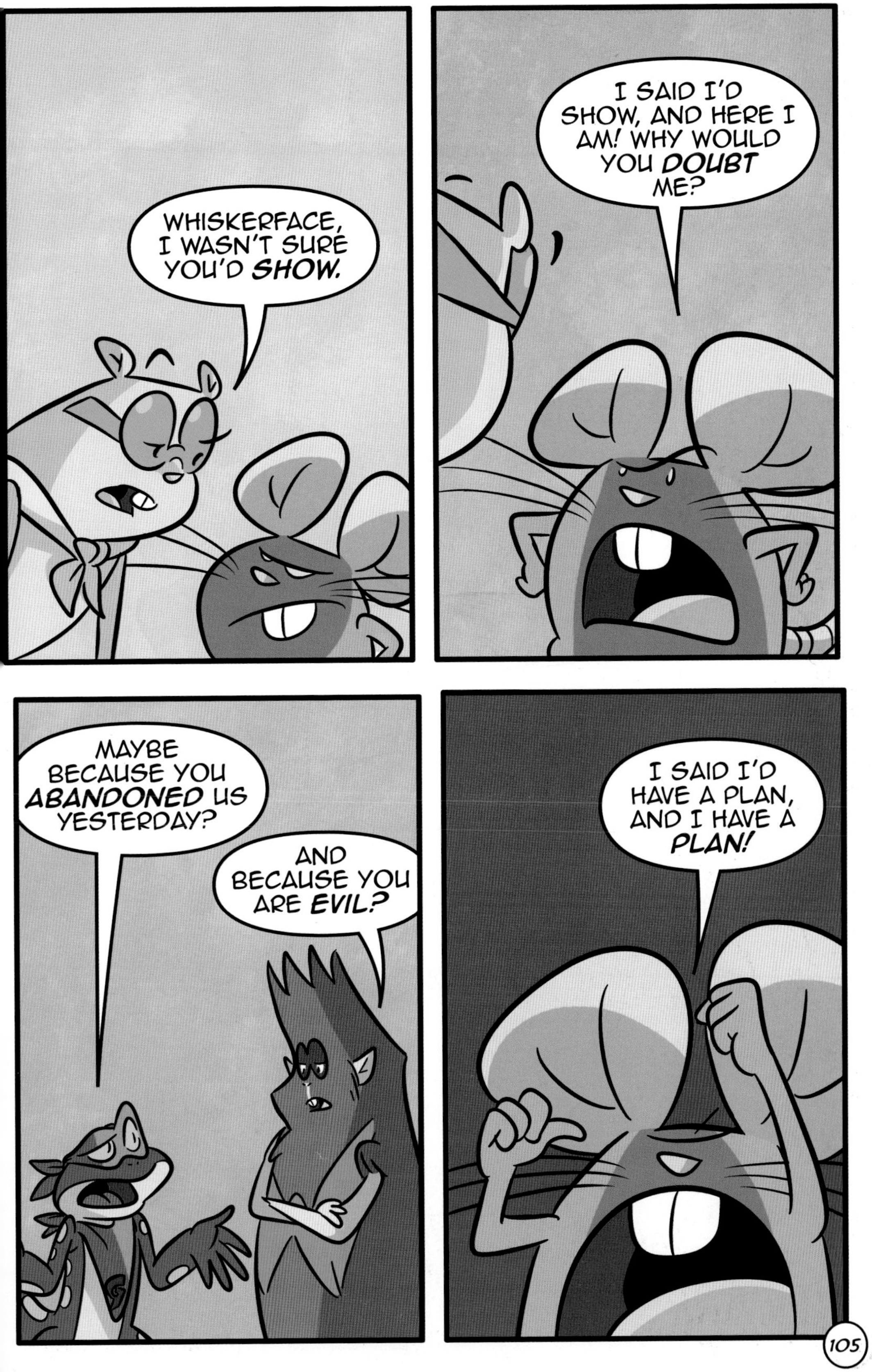
WHISKERFACE, I WASN'T SURE YOU'D **SHOW.**
I SAID I'D SHOW, AND HERE I AM! WHY WOULD YOU **DOUBT** ME?
MAYBE BECAUSE YOU **ABANDONED** US YESTERDAY?
AND BECAUSE YOU ARE **EVIL?**
I SAID I'D HAVE A PLAN, AND I HAVE A **PLAN!**

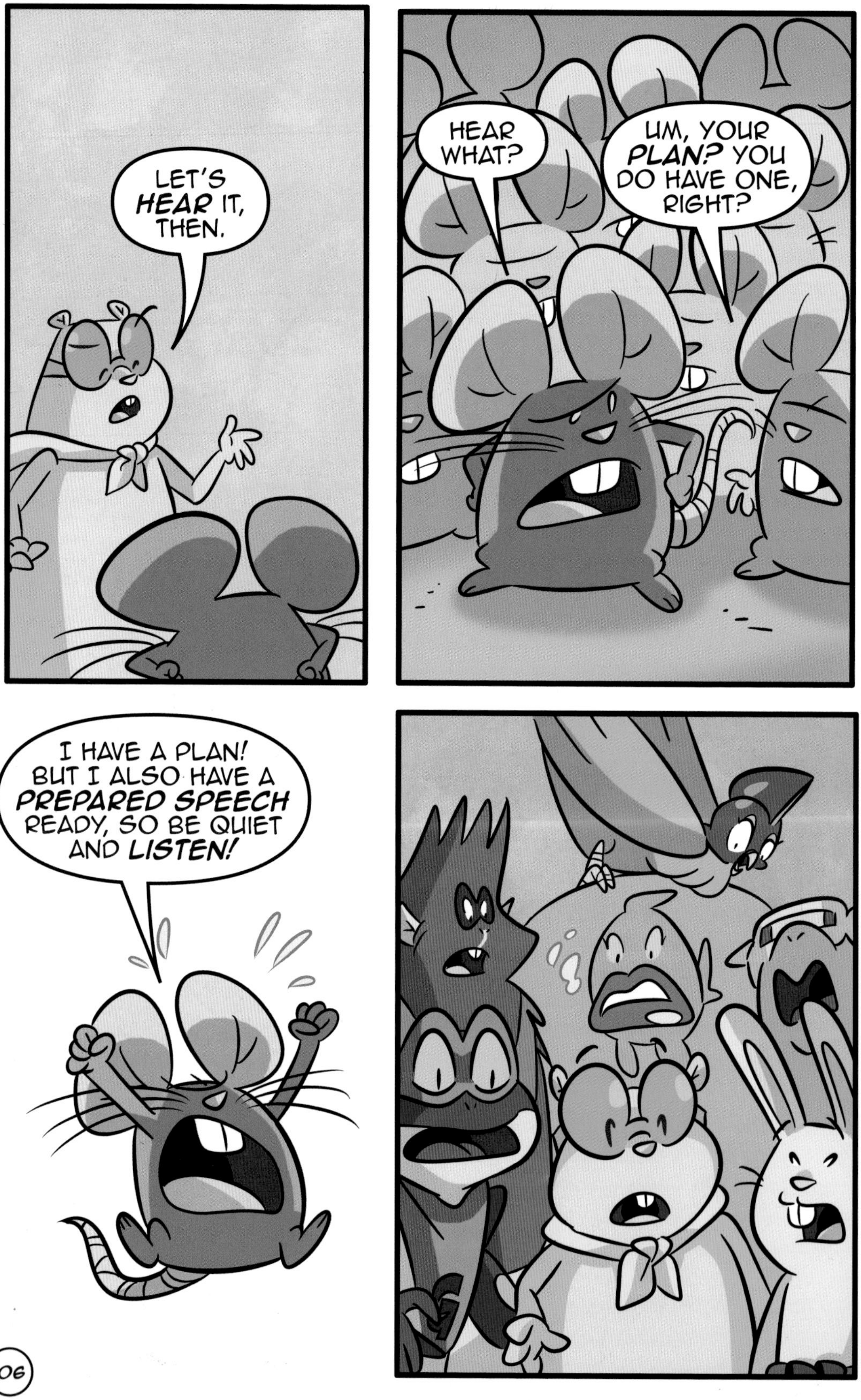
LET'S HEAR IT, THEN.
HEAR WHAT?
UM, YOUR PLAN? YOU DO HAVE ONE, RIGHT?
I HAVE A PLAN! BUT I ALSO HAVE A PREPARED SPEECH READY, SO BE QUIET AND LISTEN!

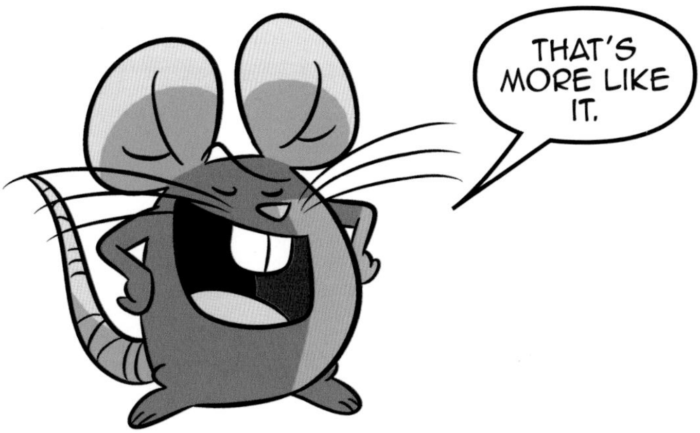
THAT'S MORE LIKE IT.

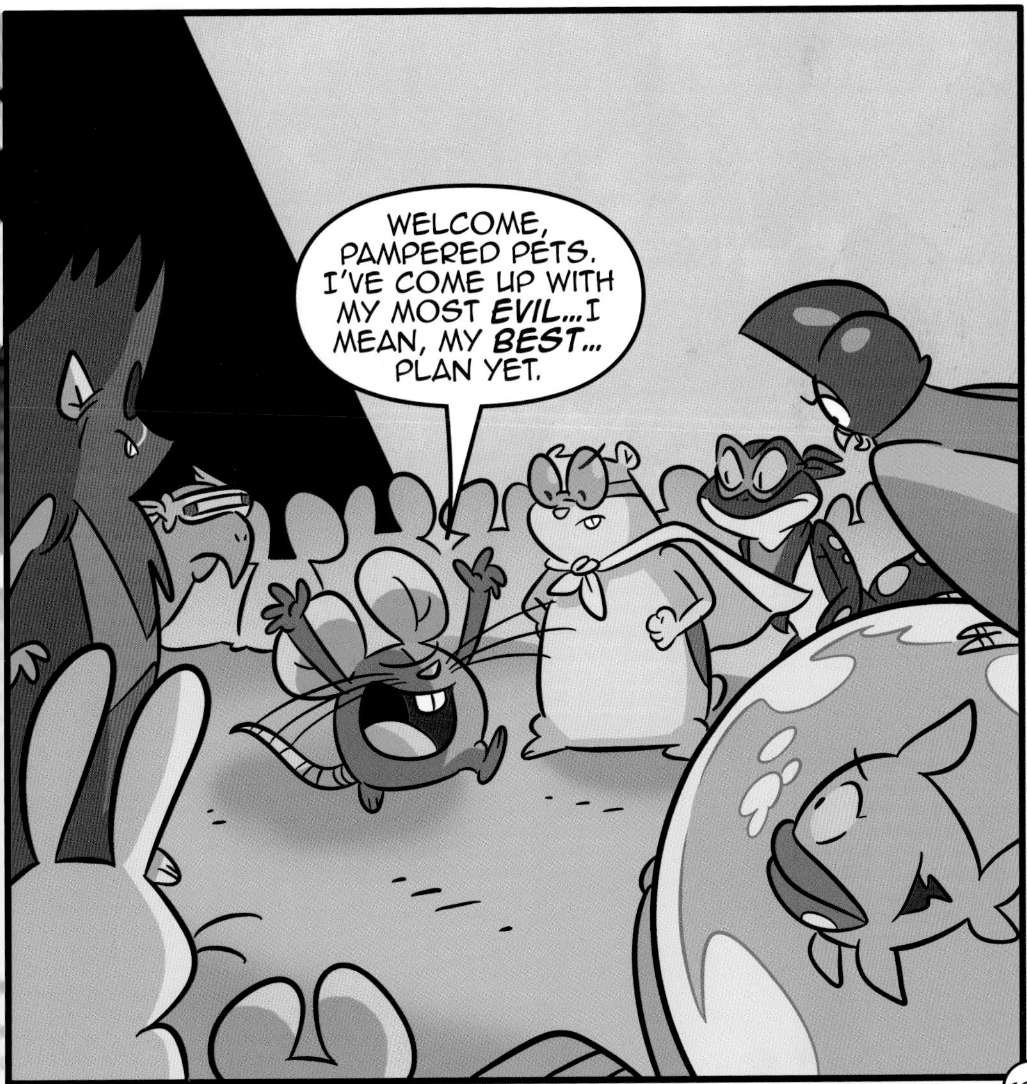
WELCOME, PAMPERED PETS. I'VE COME UP WITH MY MOST EVIL...I MEAN, MY BEST... PLAN YET.

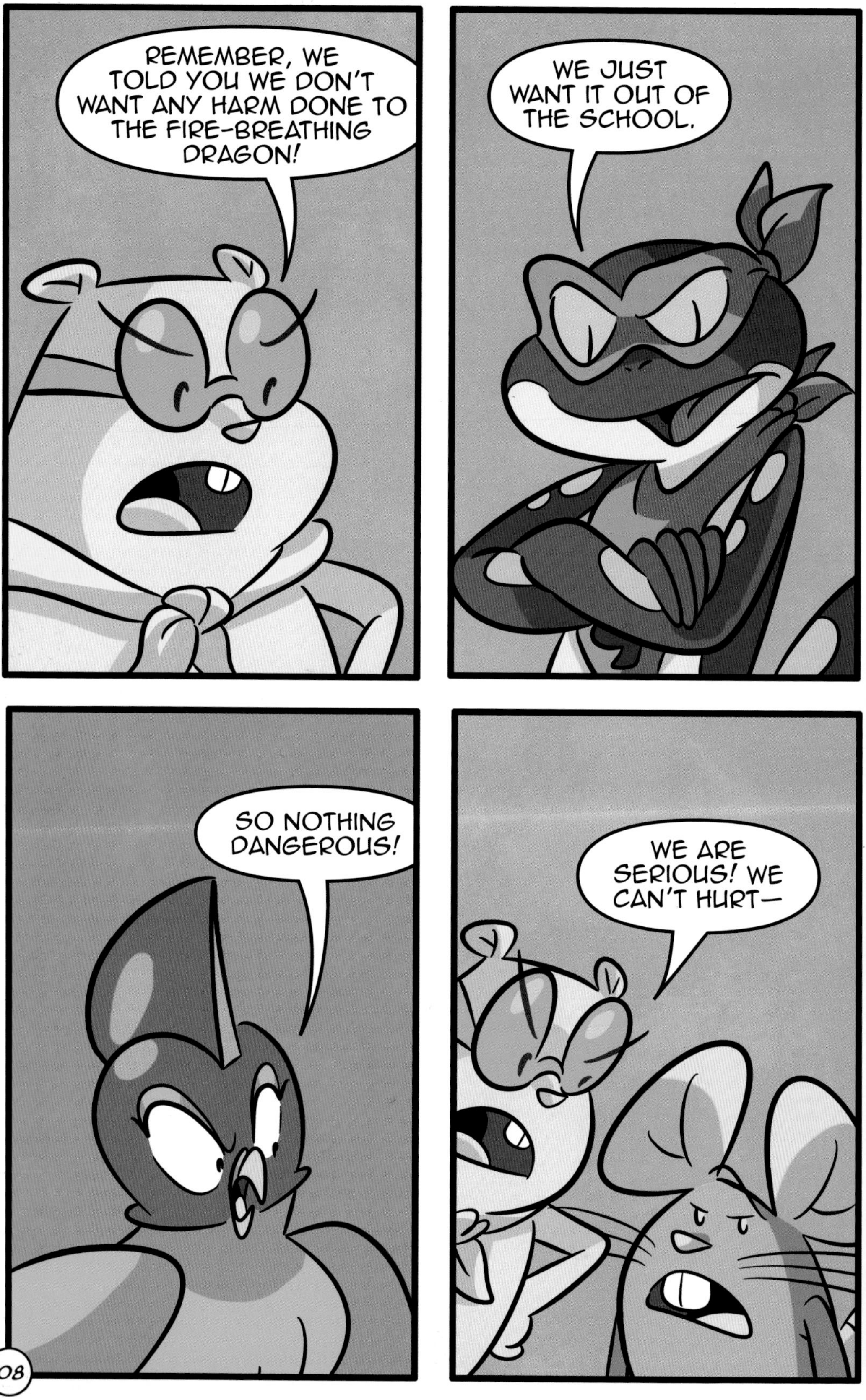
REMEMBER, WE TOLD YOU WE DON'T WANT ANY HARM DONE TO THE FIRE-BREATHING DRAGON!
WE JUST WANT IT OUT OF THE SCHOOL.
SO NOTHING DANGEROUS!
WE ARE SERIOUS! WE CAN'T HURT—

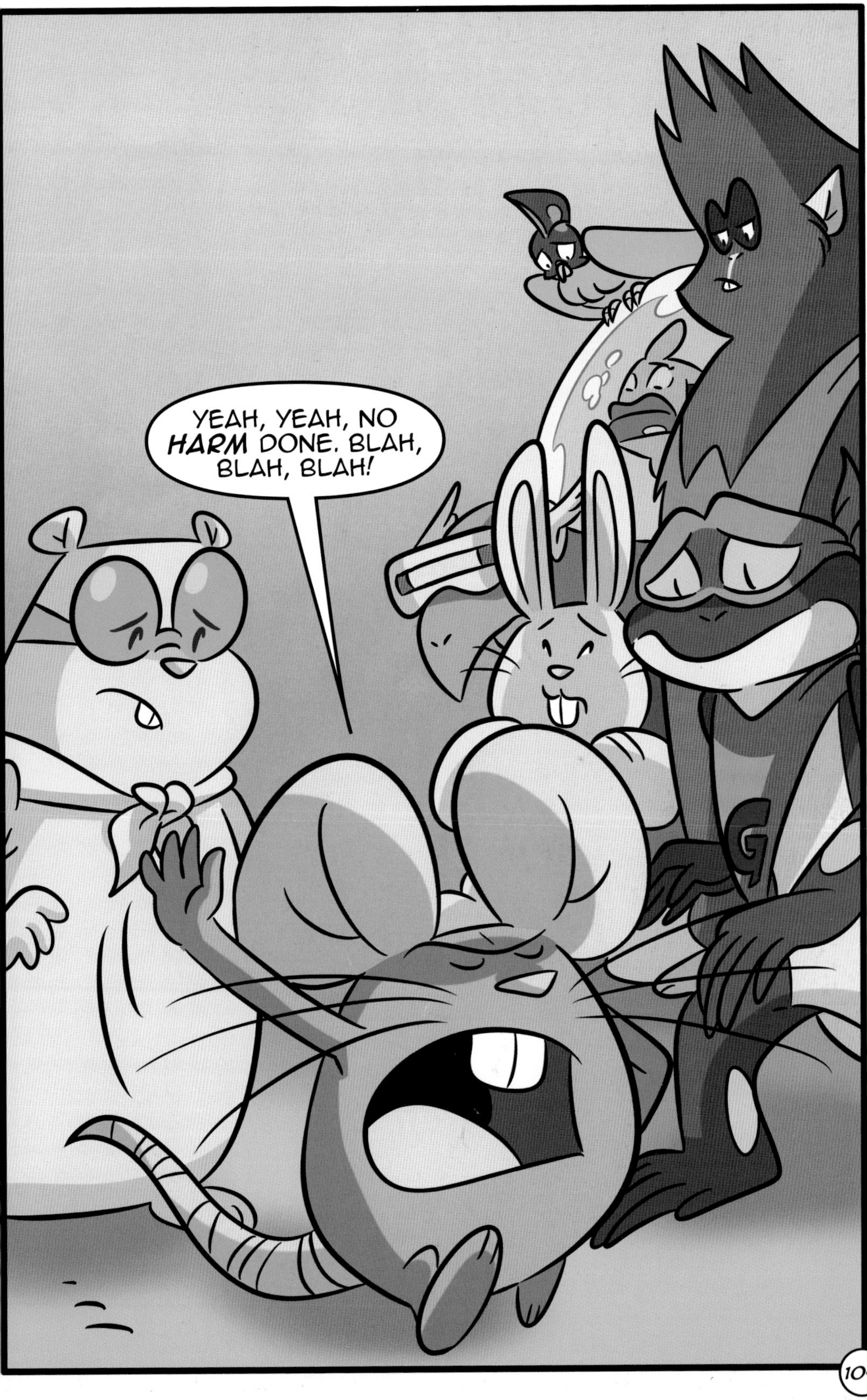
YEAH, YEAH, NO HARM DONE. BLAH, BLAH, BLAH!

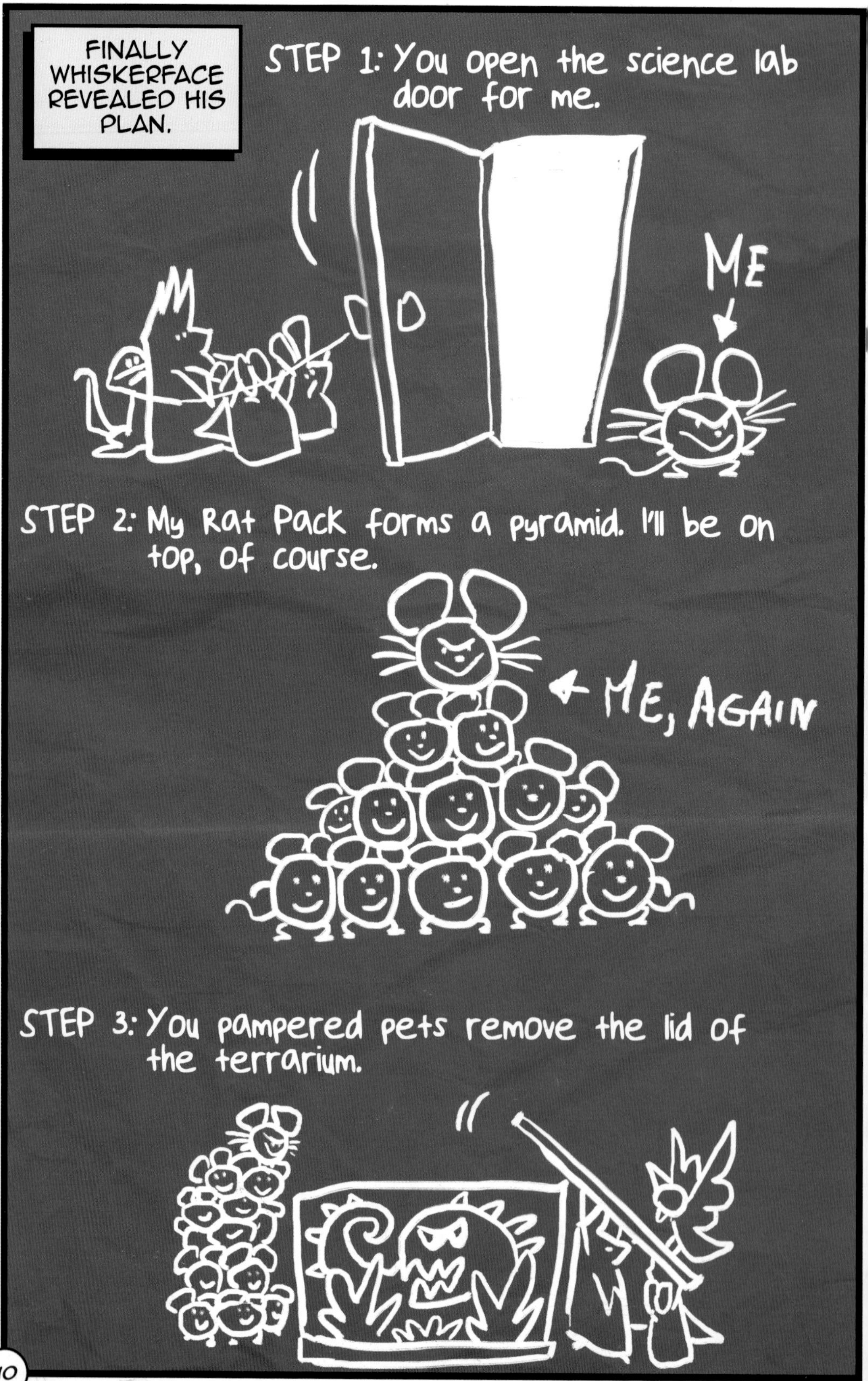
FINALLY WHISKERFACE REVEALED HIS PLAN.
STEP 1: You open the science lab door for me.
ME
STEP 2: My Rat Pack forms a pyramid. I'll be on top, of course.
ME, AGAIN
STEP 3: You pampered pets remove the lid of the terrarium.

STEP 4: I use a feather to tickle the
fire-breathing dragon.

STEP 5: While it's laughing, we tie it up.

STEP 6: We lift the dragon out of the terrarium
and toss it out the window.

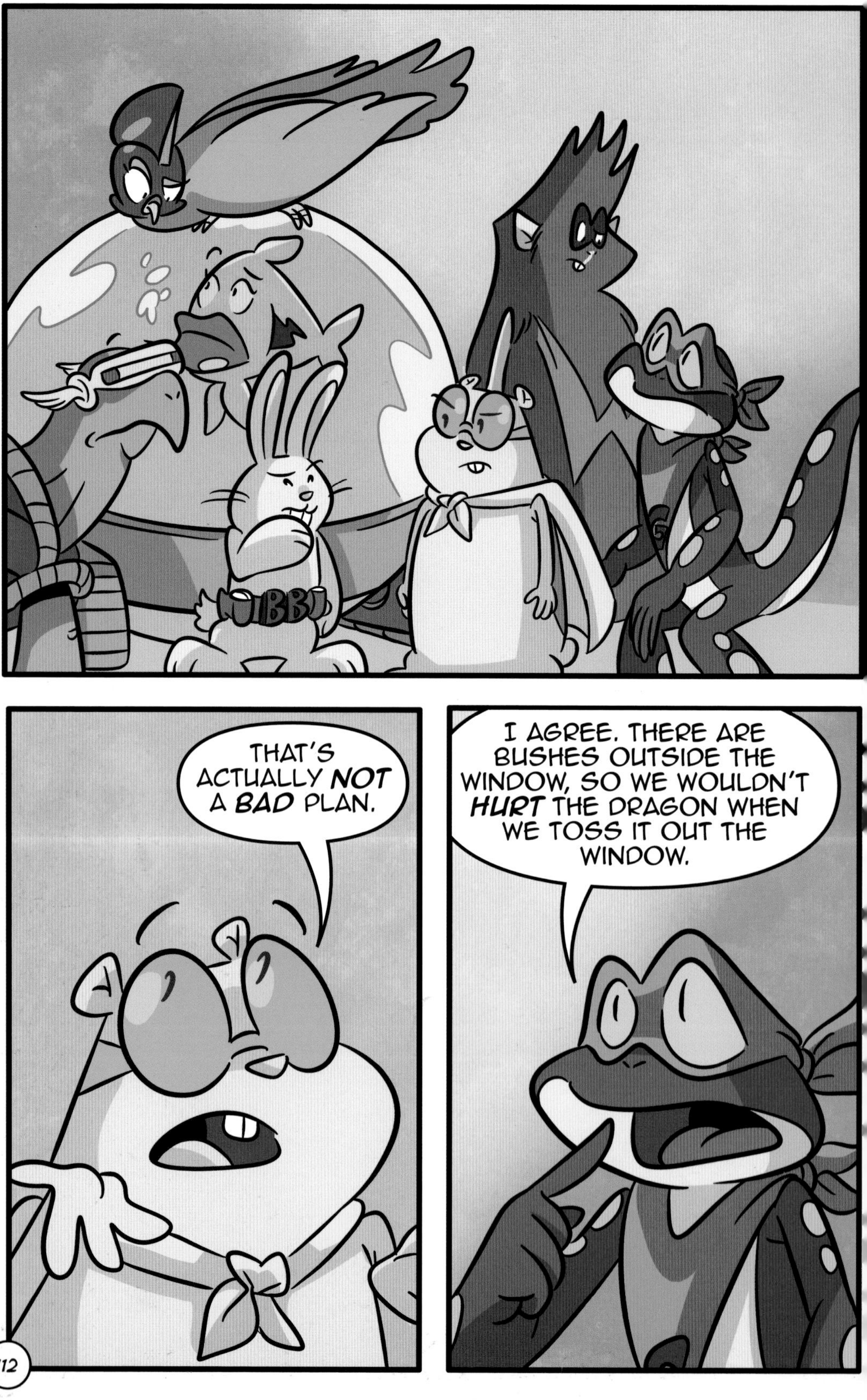
THAT'S ACTUALLY **NOT** A **BAD** PLAN.
I AGREE. THERE ARE BUSHES OUTSIDE THE WINDOW, SO WE WOULDN'T **HURT** THE DRAGON WHEN WE TOSS IT OUT THE WINDOW.

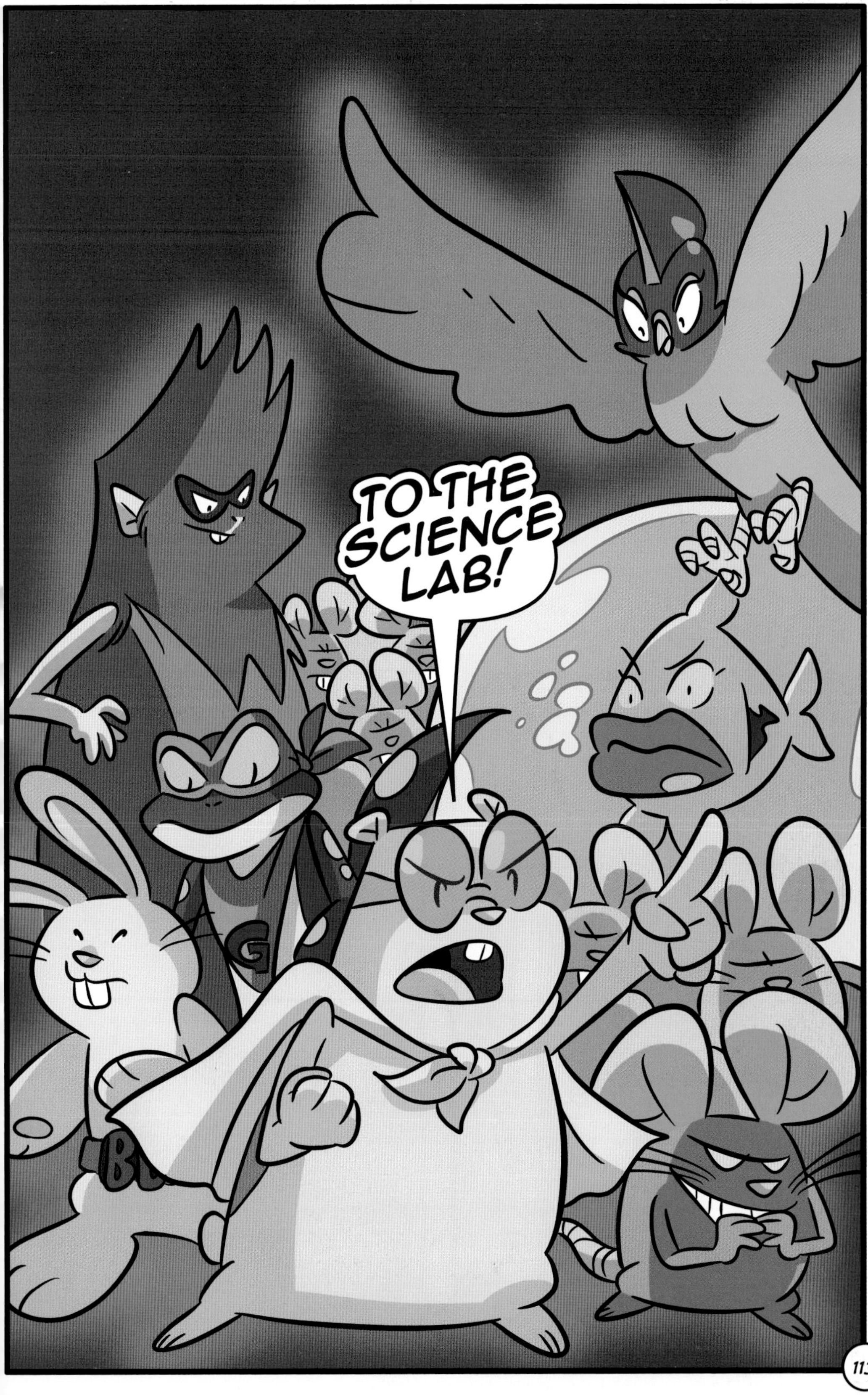
TO THE SCIENCE LAB!

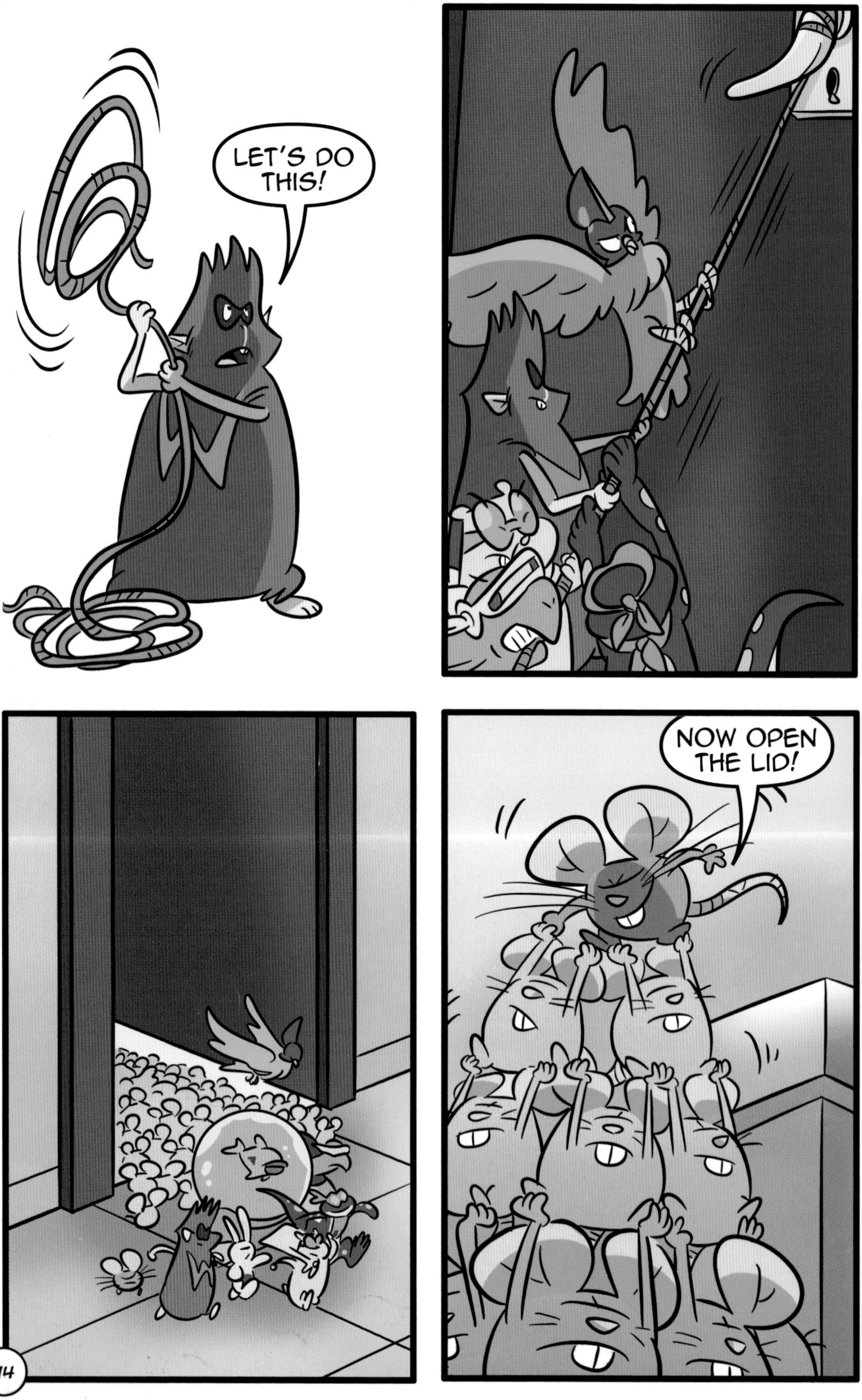
LET'S DO THIS!
NOW OPEN THE LID!

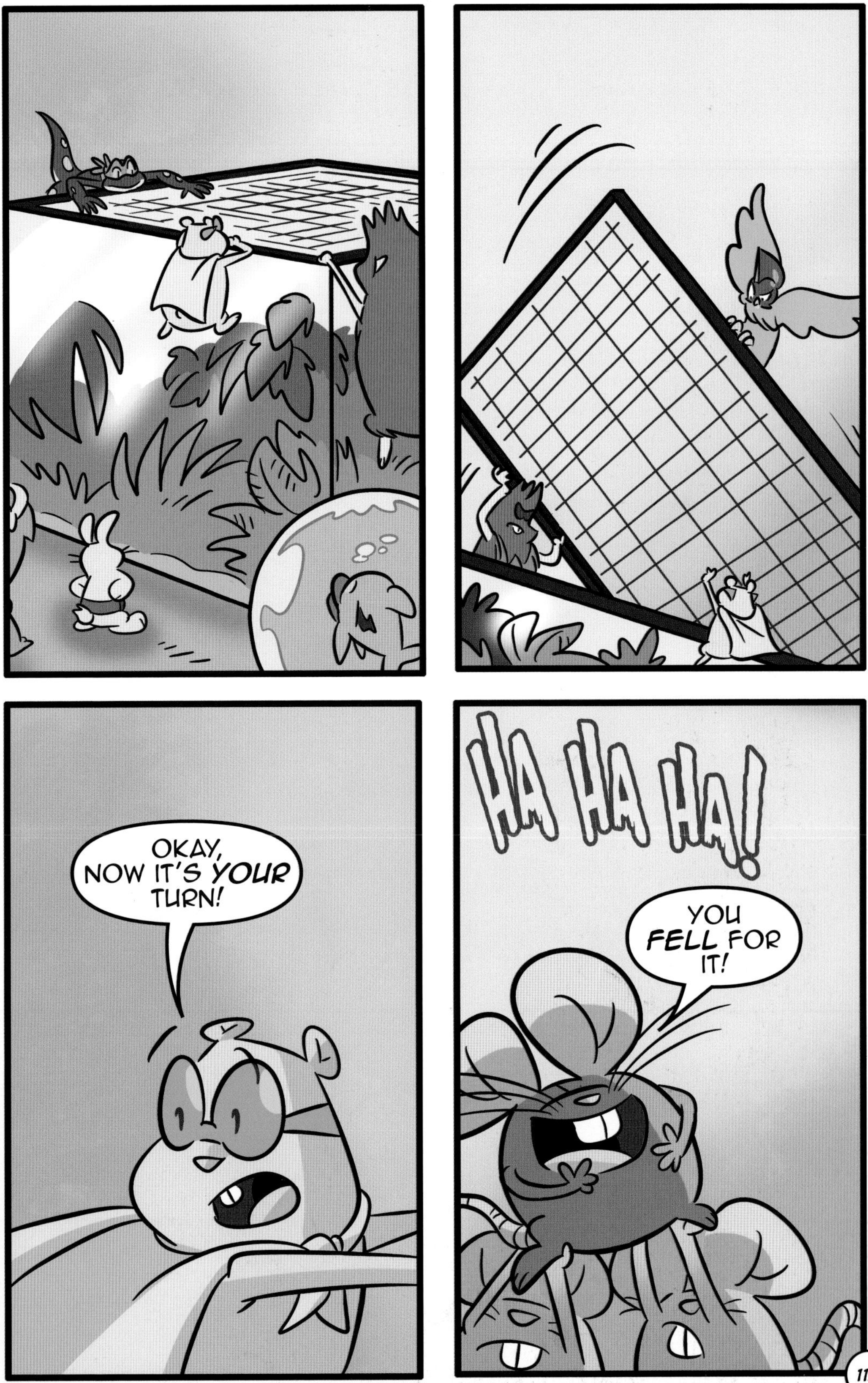
OKAY, NOW IT'S YOUR TURN!
HA HA HA!
YOU FELL FOR IT!

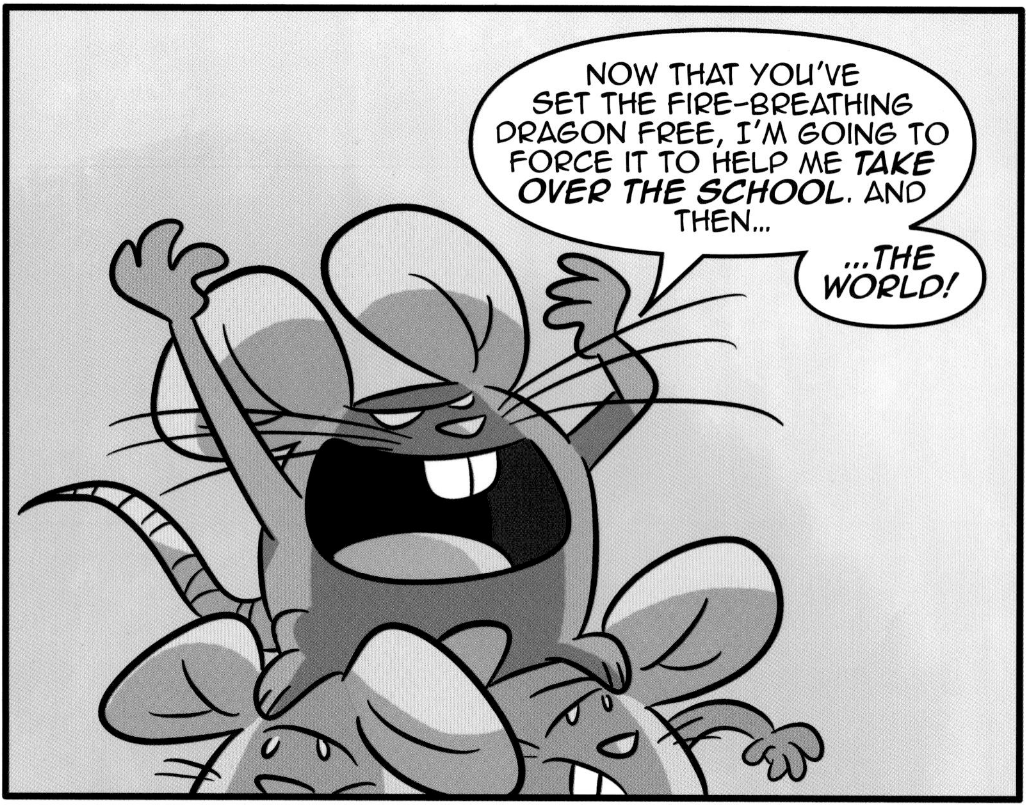
NOW THAT YOU'VE SET THE FIRE-BREATHING DRAGON FREE, I'M GOING TO FORCE IT TO HELP ME TAKE OVER THE SCHOOL. AND THEN...
...THE WORLD!

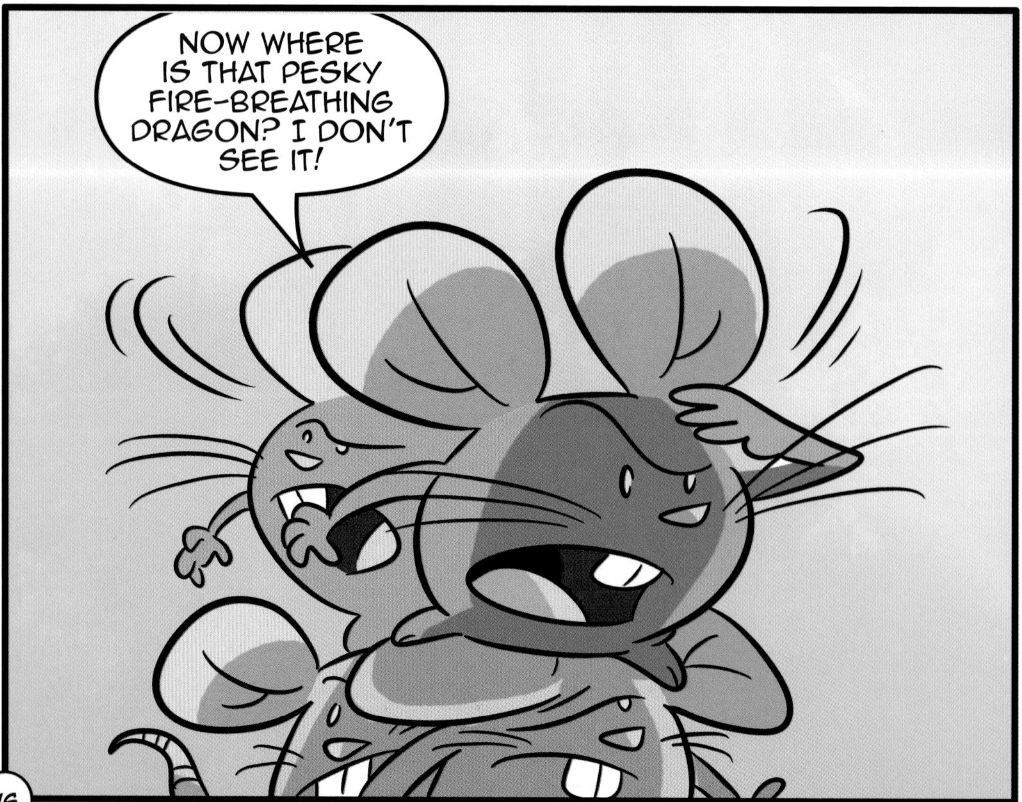
NOW WHERE IS THAT PESKY FIRE-BREATHING DRAGON? I DON'T SEE IT!

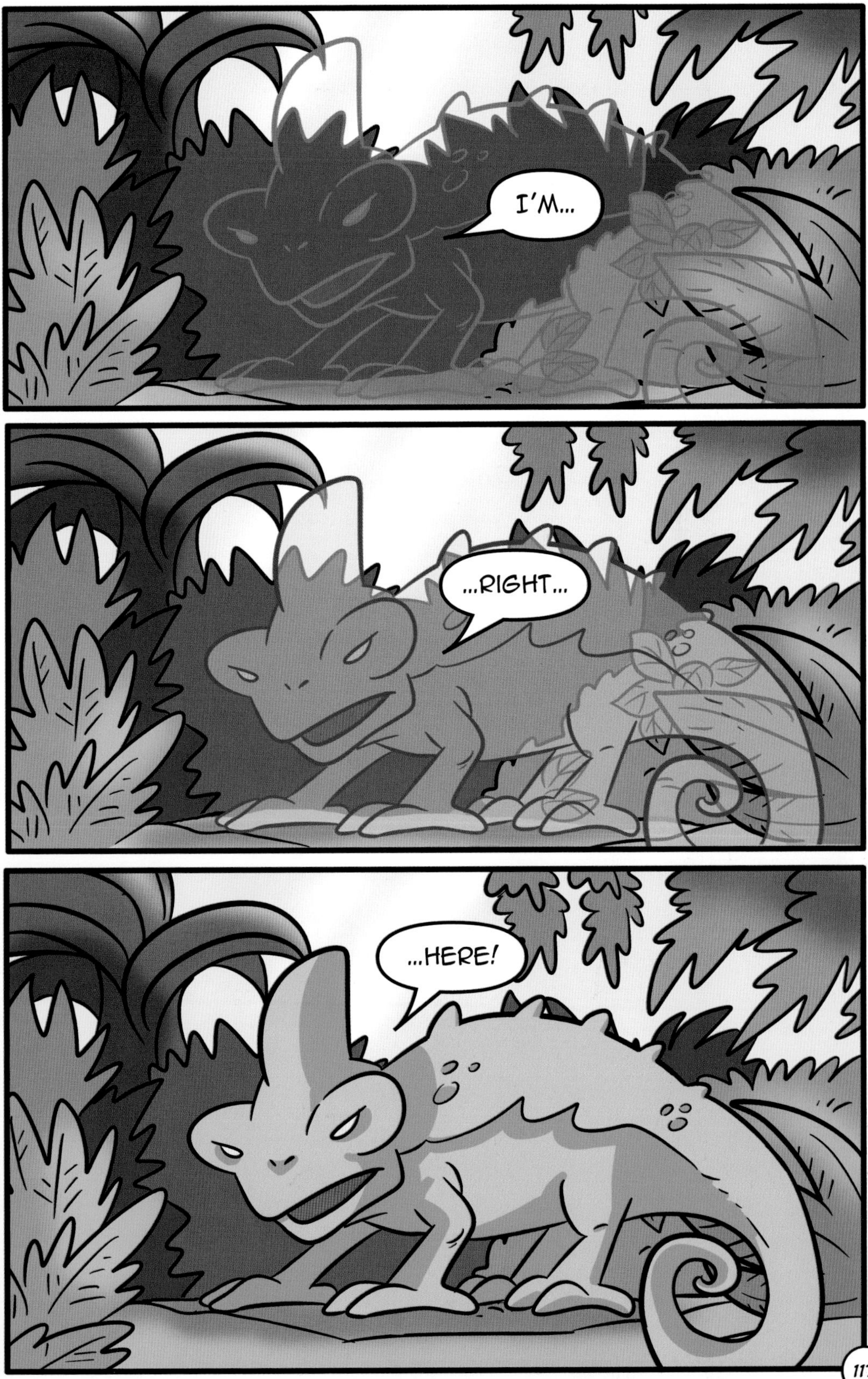
I'M...
...RIGHT...
...HERE!

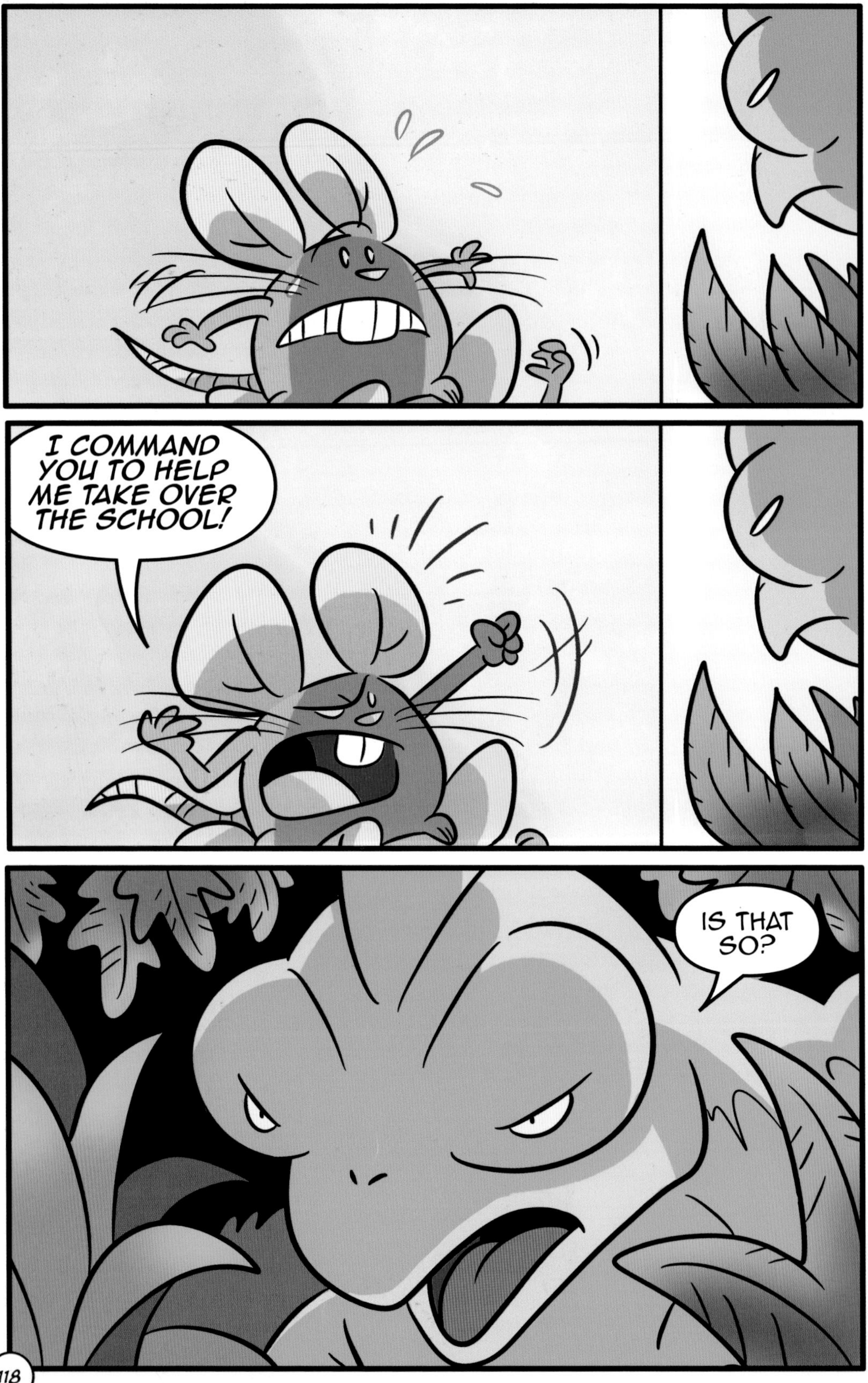
I COMMAND YOU TO HELP ME TAKE OVER THE SCHOOL!
IS THAT SO?

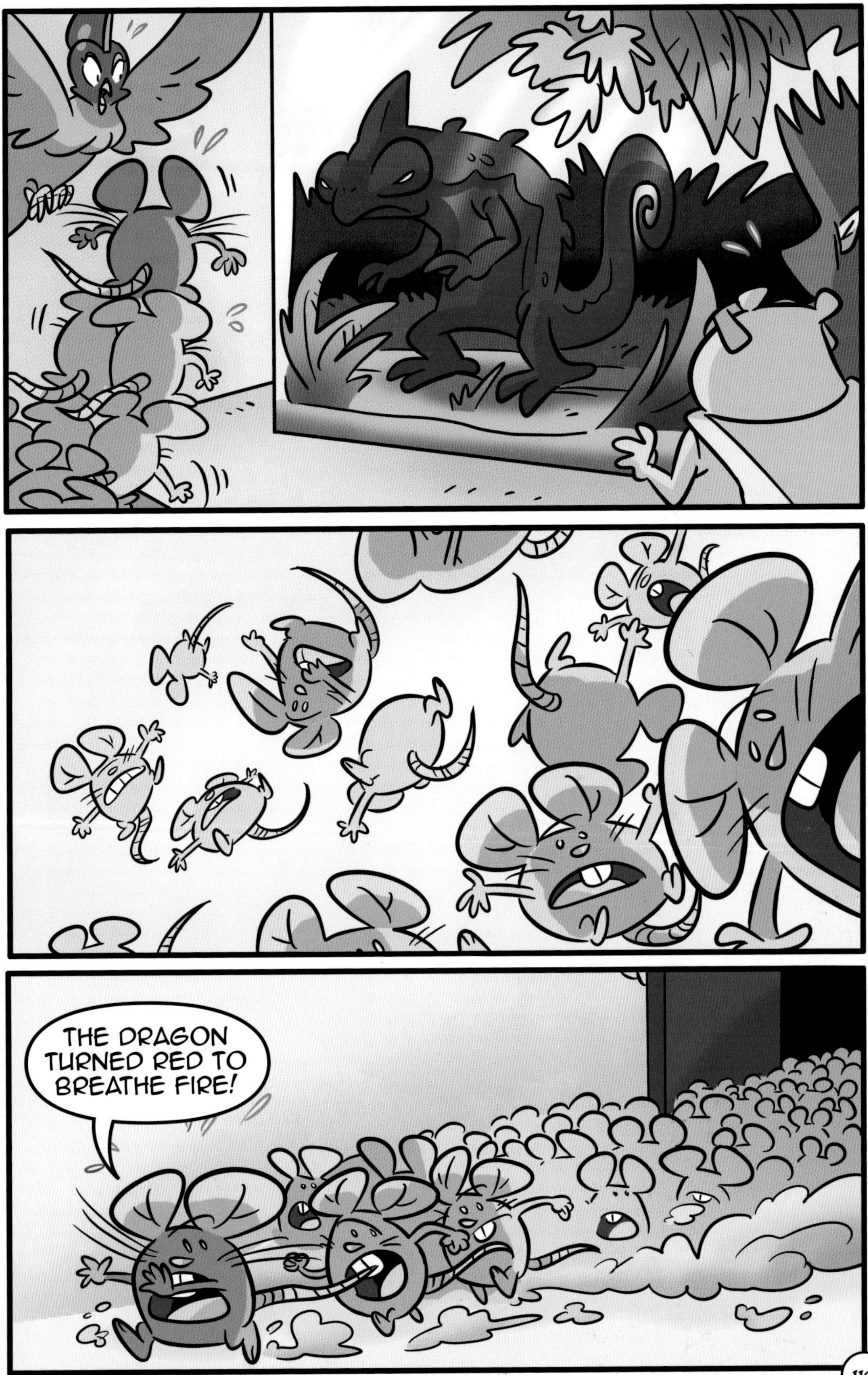
THE DRAGON TURNED RED TO BREATHE FIRE!

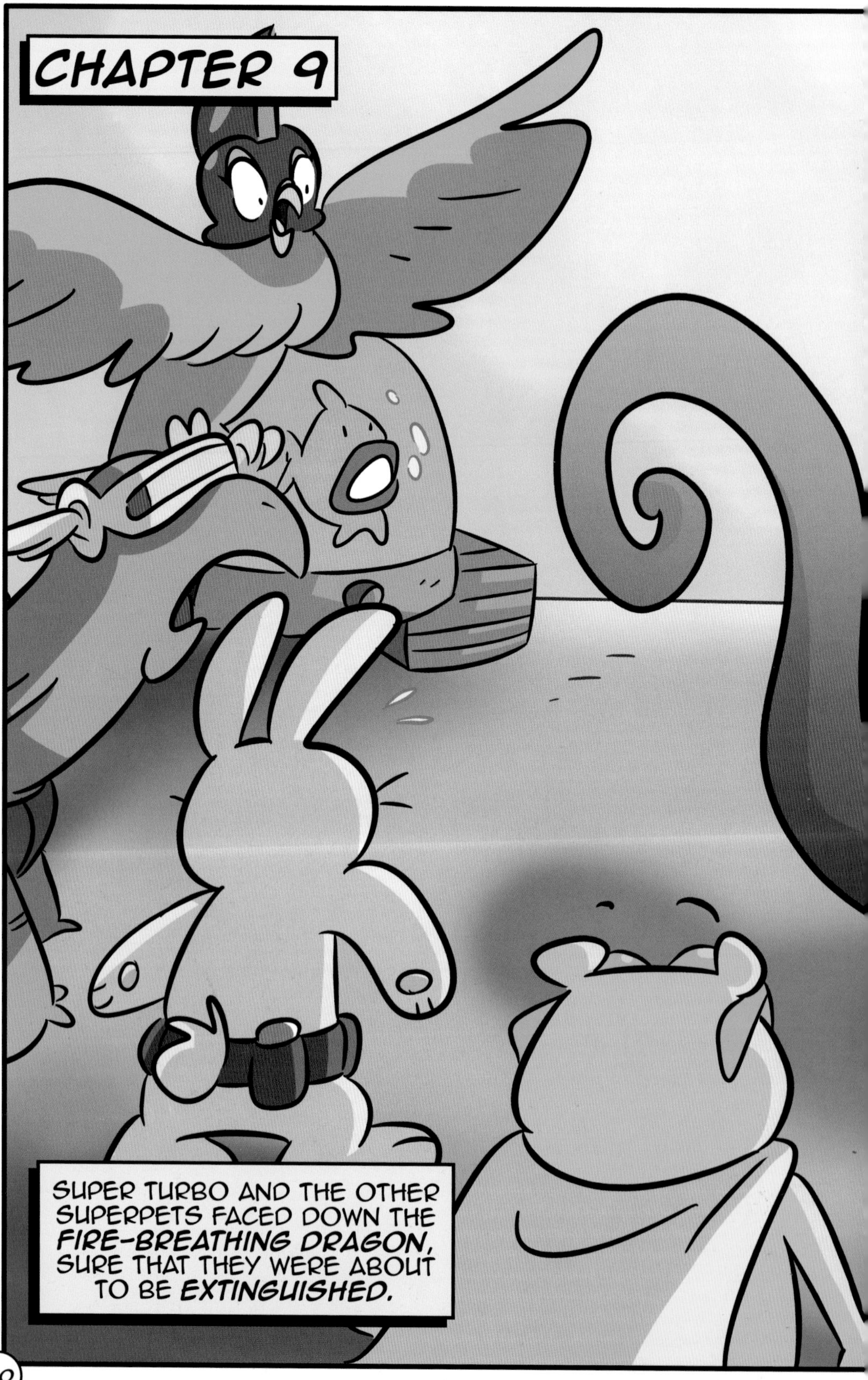
CHAPTER 9
SUPER TURBO AND THE OTHER SUPERPETS FACED DOWN THE *FIRE-BREATHING DRAGON*, SURE THAT THEY WERE ABOUT TO BE *EXTINGUISHED.*

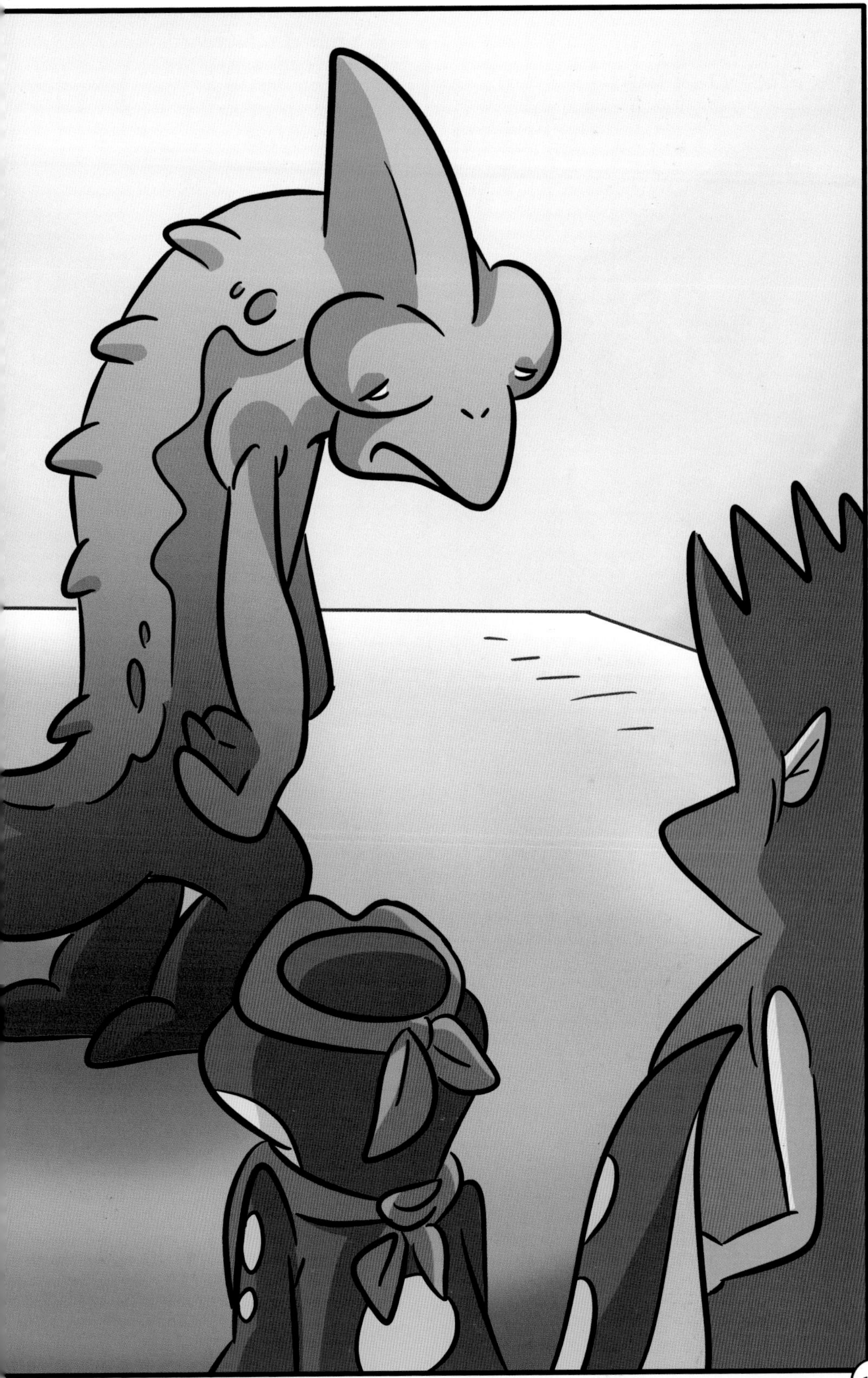

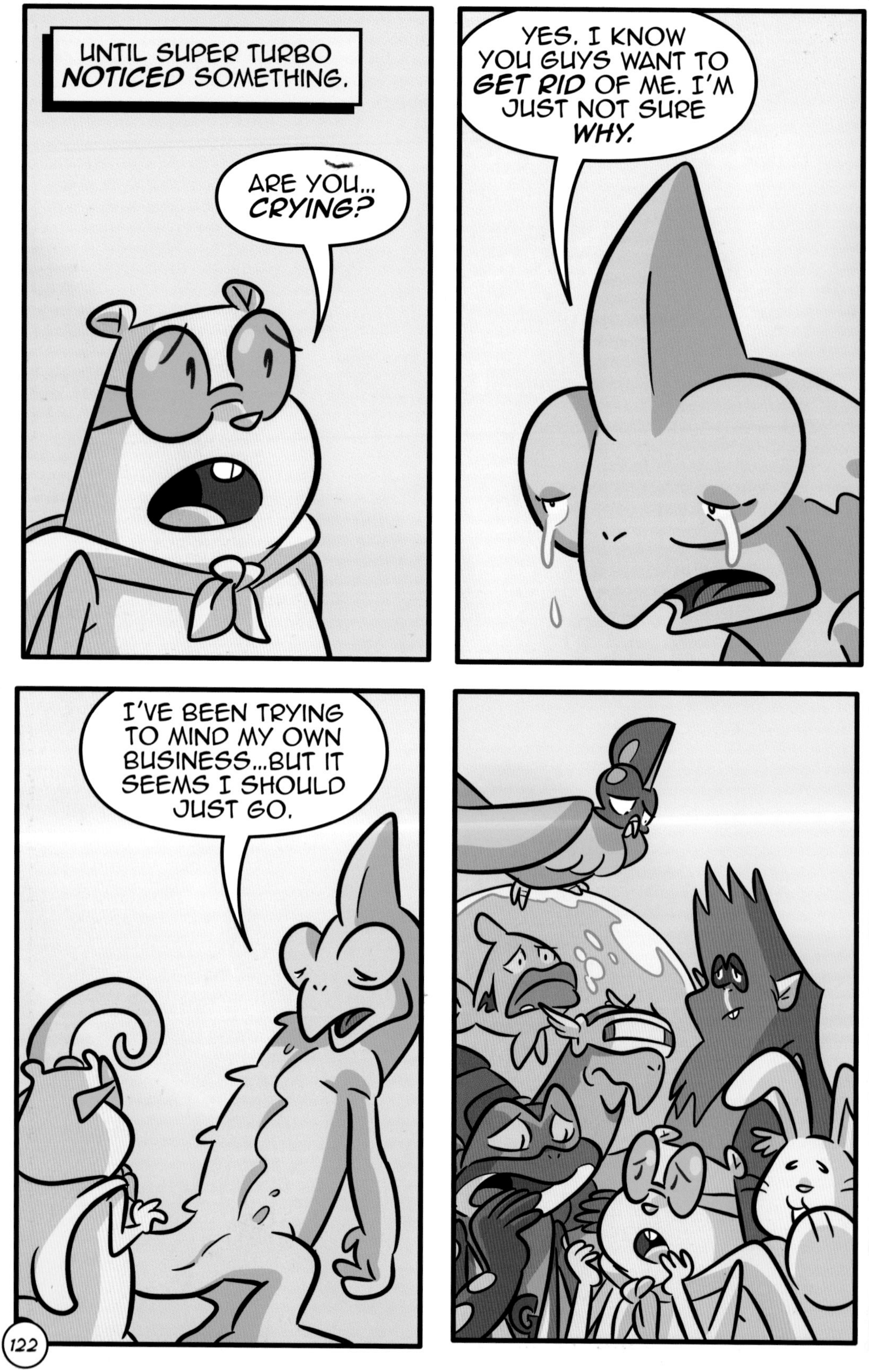
UNTIL SUPER TURBO *NOTICED* SOMETHING.
ARE YOU... *CRYING?*
YES. I KNOW YOU GUYS WANT TO *GET RID* OF ME. I'M JUST NOT SURE *WHY.*
I'VE BEEN TRYING TO MIND MY OWN BUSINESS...BUT IT SEEMS I SHOULD JUST GO.

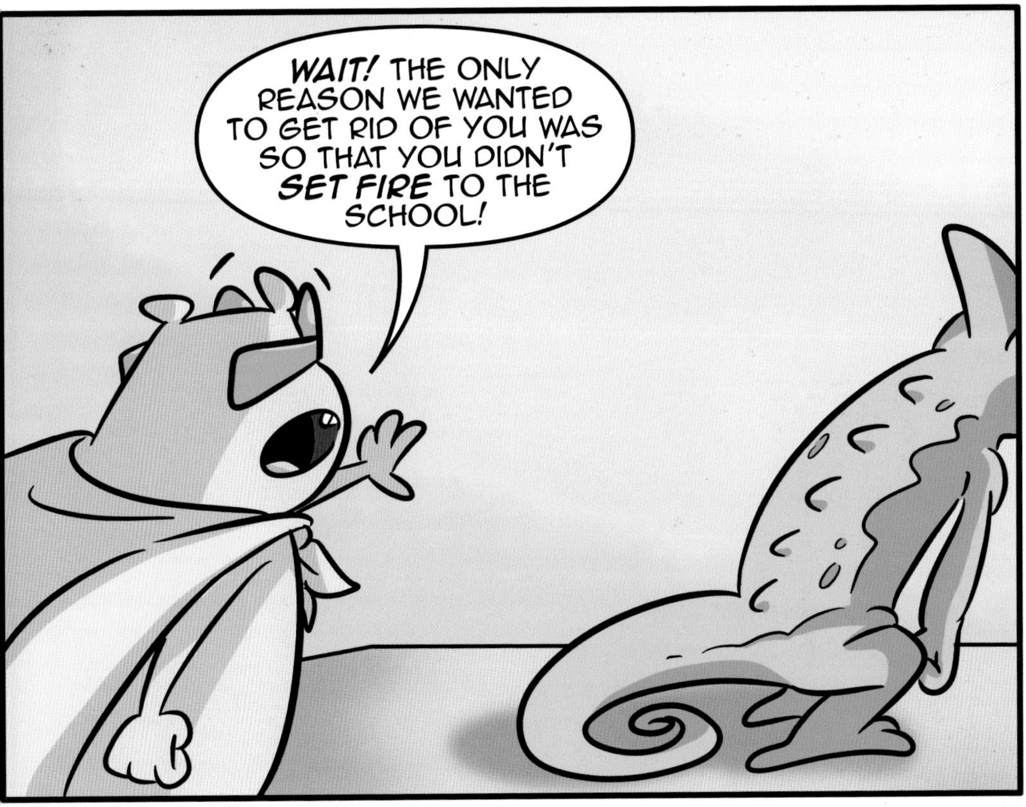
WAIT! THE ONLY REASON WE WANTED TO GET RID OF YOU WAS SO THAT YOU DIDN'T SET FIRE TO THE SCHOOL!

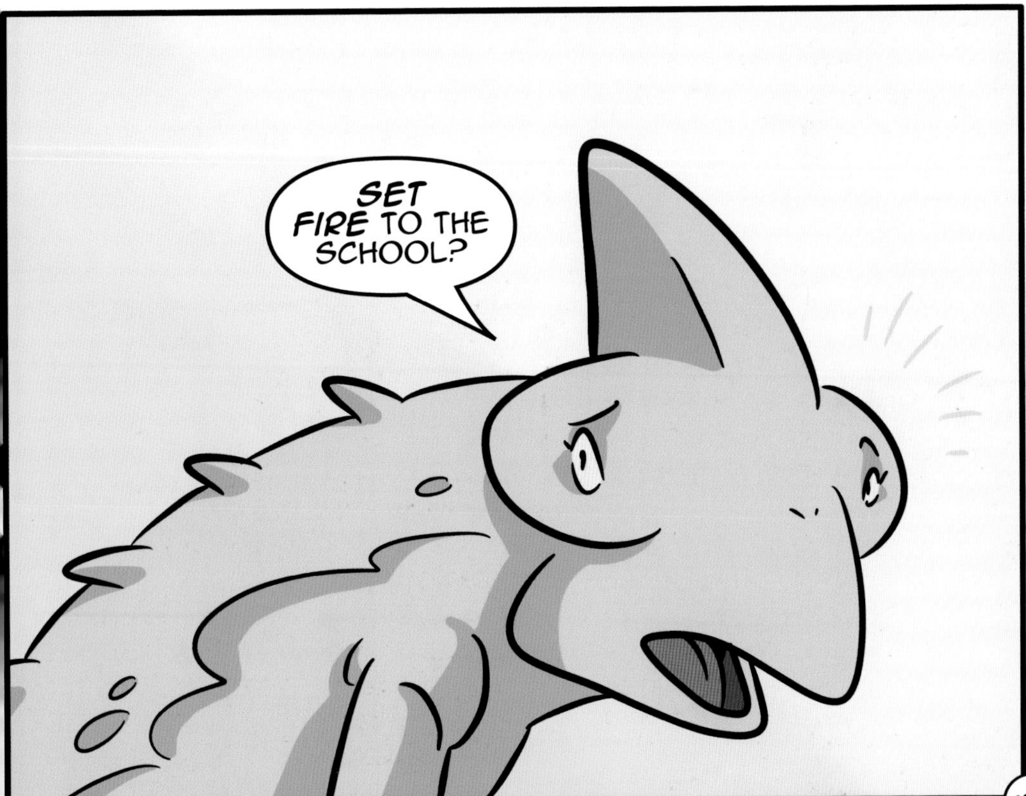
SET FIRE TO THE SCHOOL?

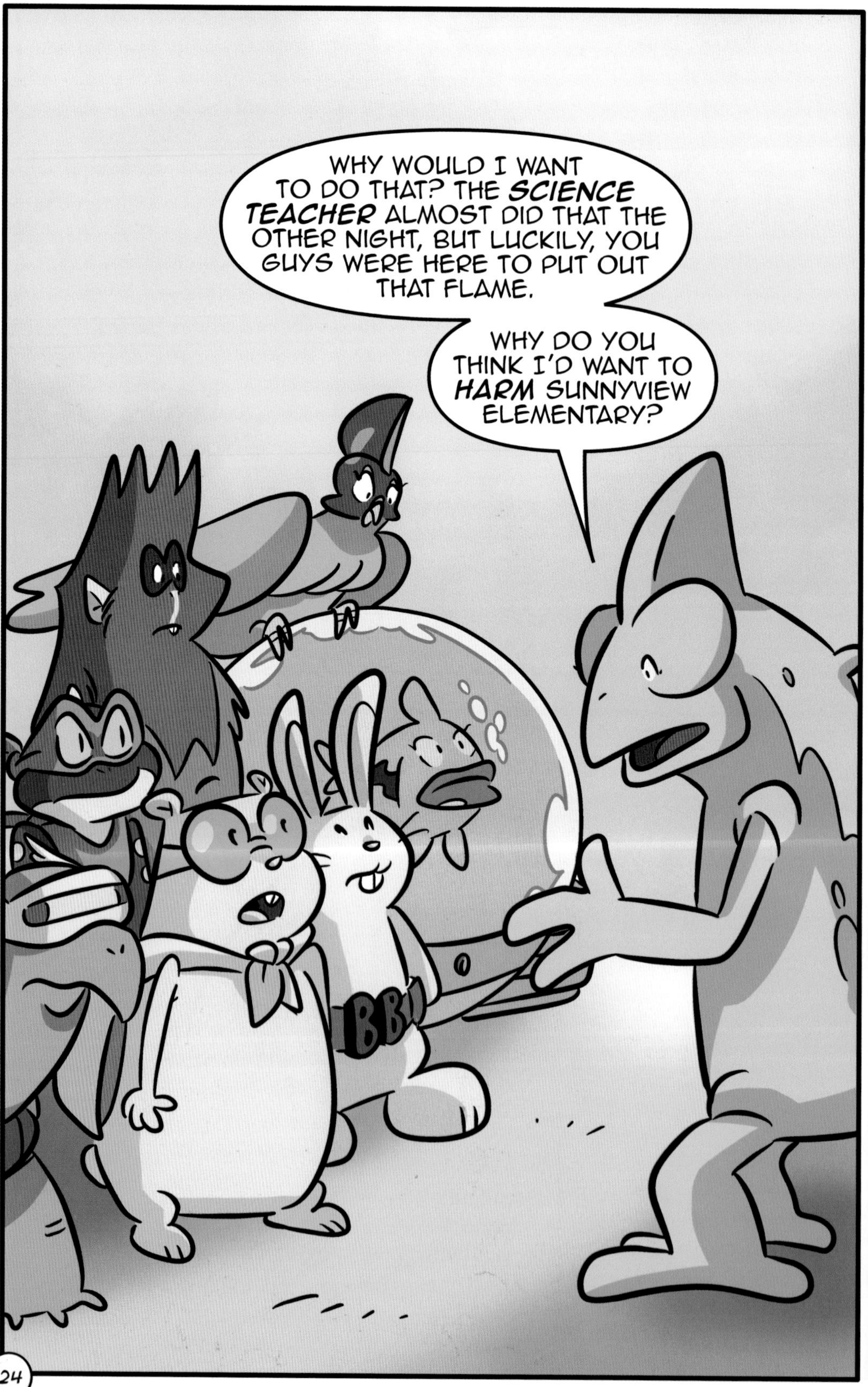
WHY WOULD I WANT TO DO THAT? THE SCIENCE TEACHER ALMOST DID THAT THE OTHER NIGHT, BUT LUCKILY, YOU GUYS WERE HERE TO PUT OUT THAT FLAME.
WHY DO YOU THINK I'D WANT TO HARM SUNNYVIEW ELEMENTARY?
BB

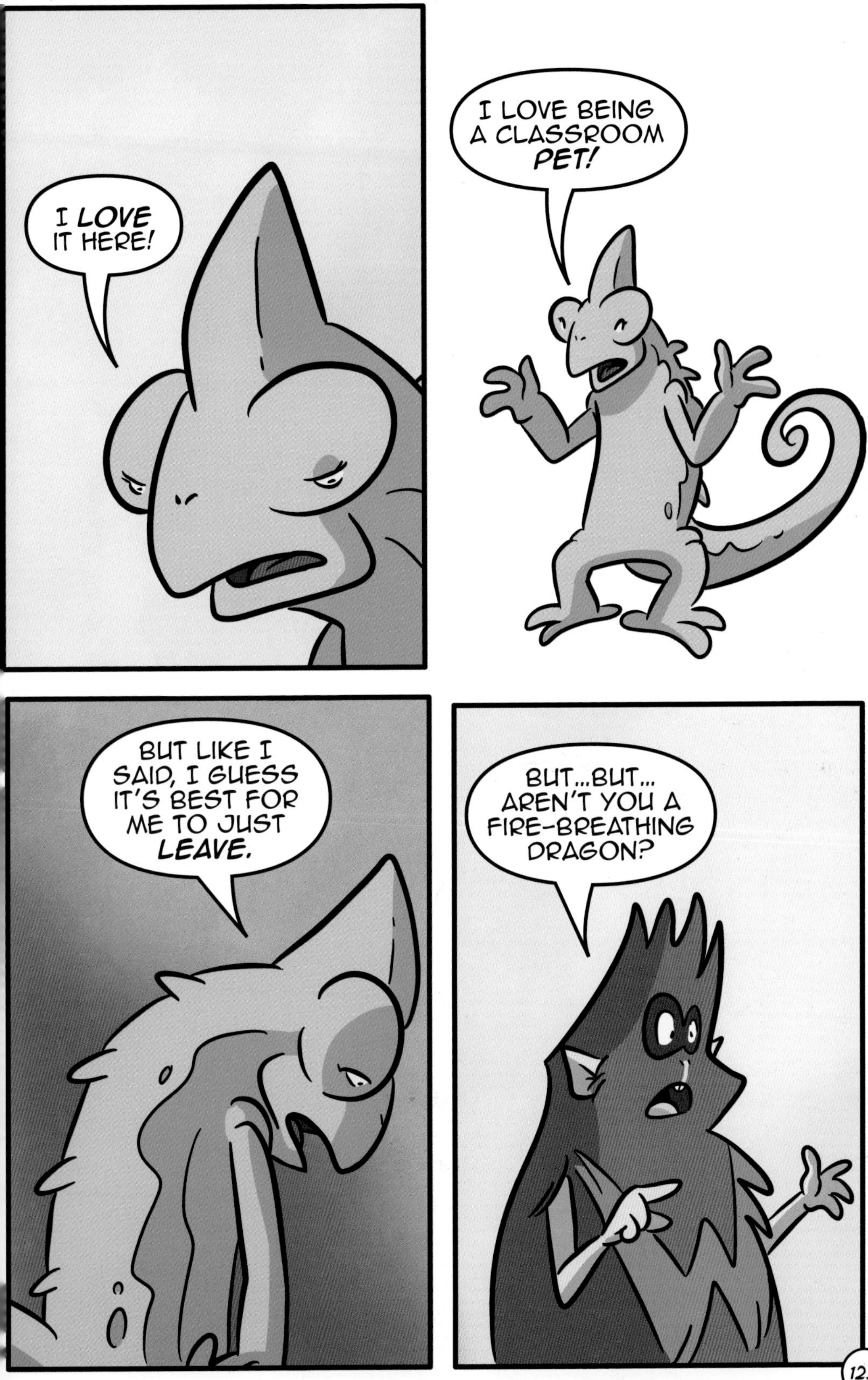
I LOVE IT HERE!
I LOVE BEING A CLASSROOM PET!
BUT LIKE I SAID, I GUESS IT'S BEST FOR ME TO JUST LEAVE.
BUT...BUT... AREN'T YOU A FIRE-BREATHING DRAGON?

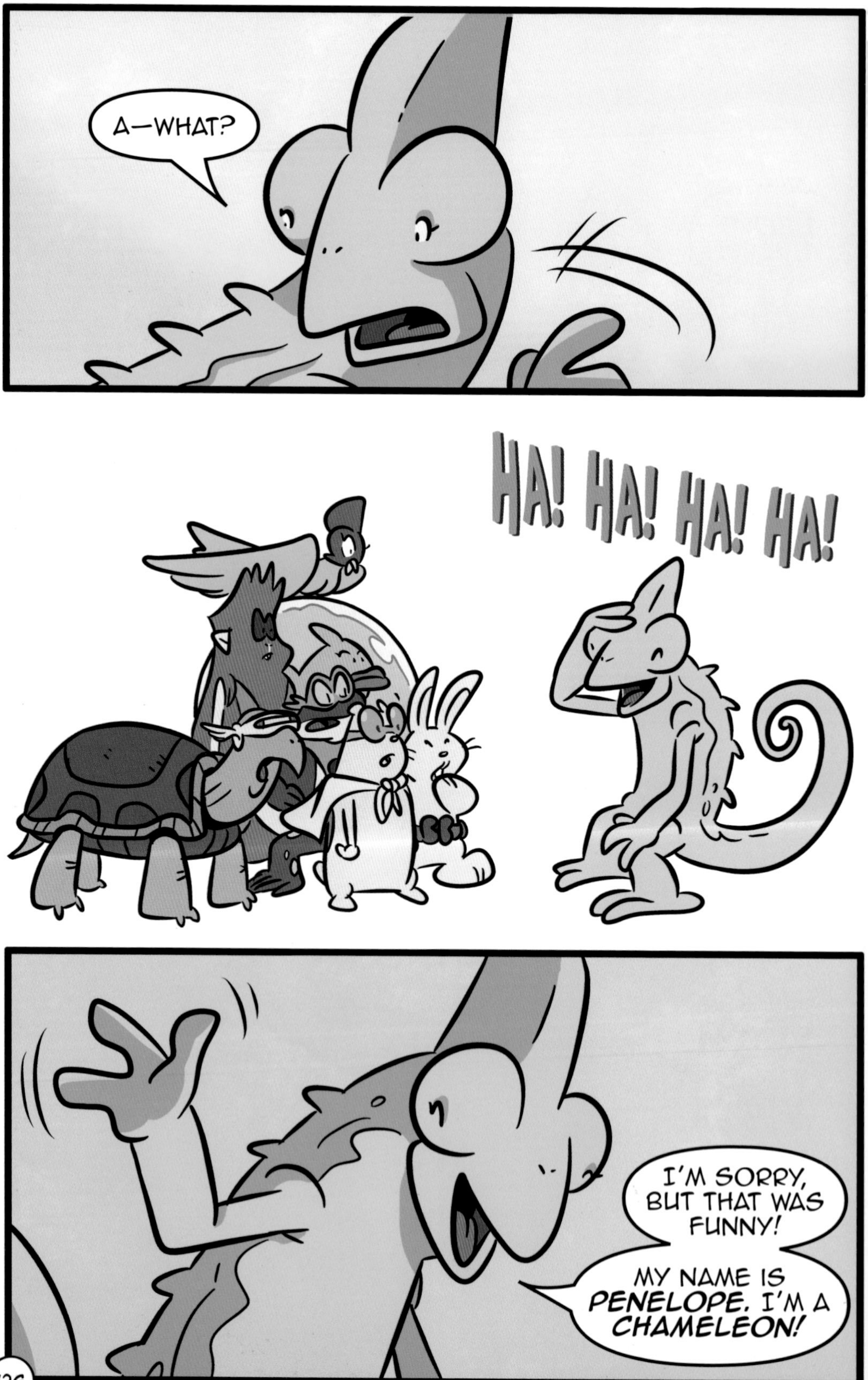
A—WHAT?
HA! HA! HA! HA!
I'M SORRY, BUT THAT WAS FUNNY!
MY NAME IS PENELOPE. I'M A CHAMELEON!

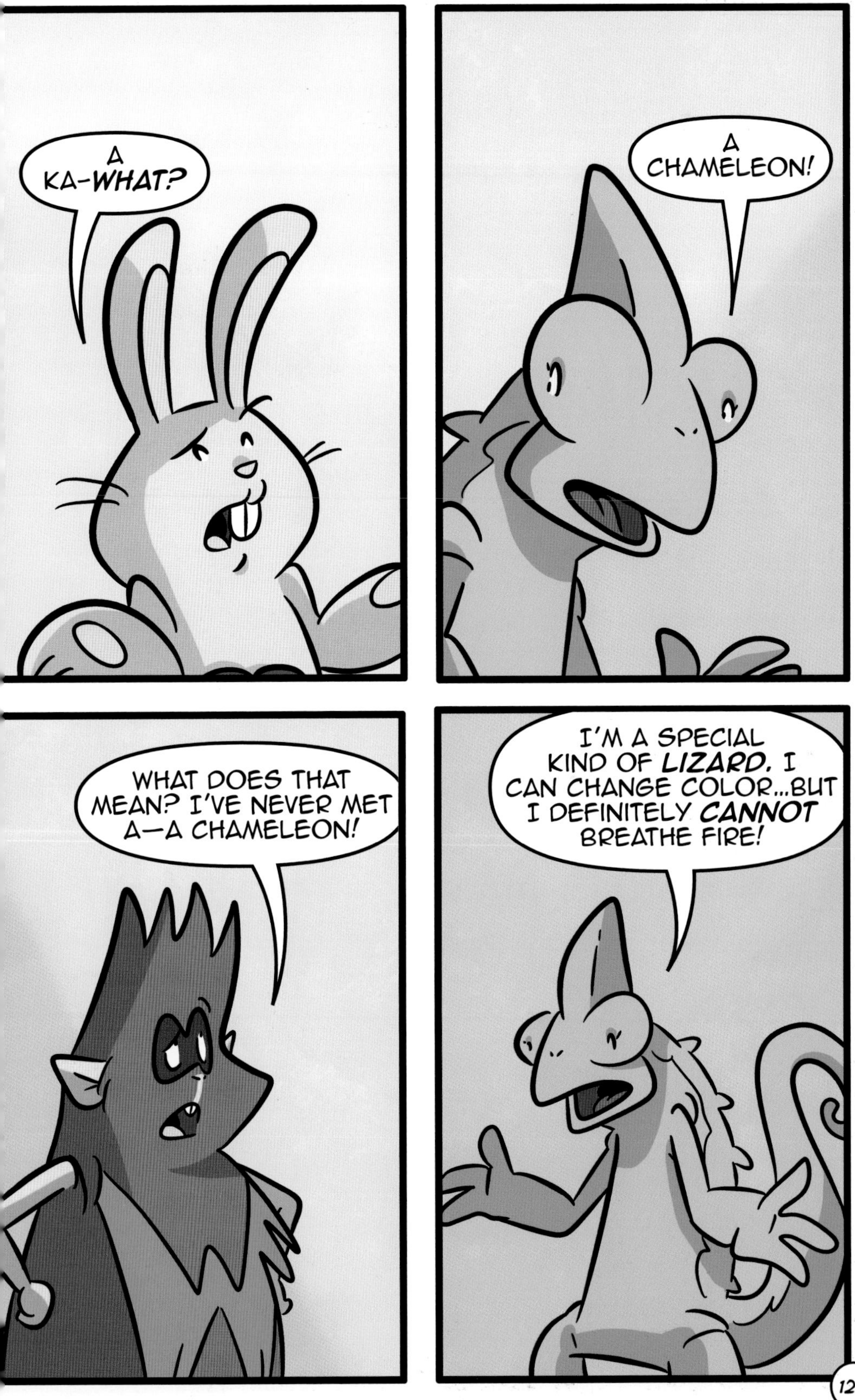
A KA-WHAT?
A CHAMELEON!
WHAT DOES THAT MEAN? I'VE NEVER MET A—A CHAMELEON!
I'M A SPECIAL KIND OF LIZARD. I CAN CHANGE COLOR...BUT I DEFINITELY CANNOT BREATHE FIRE!

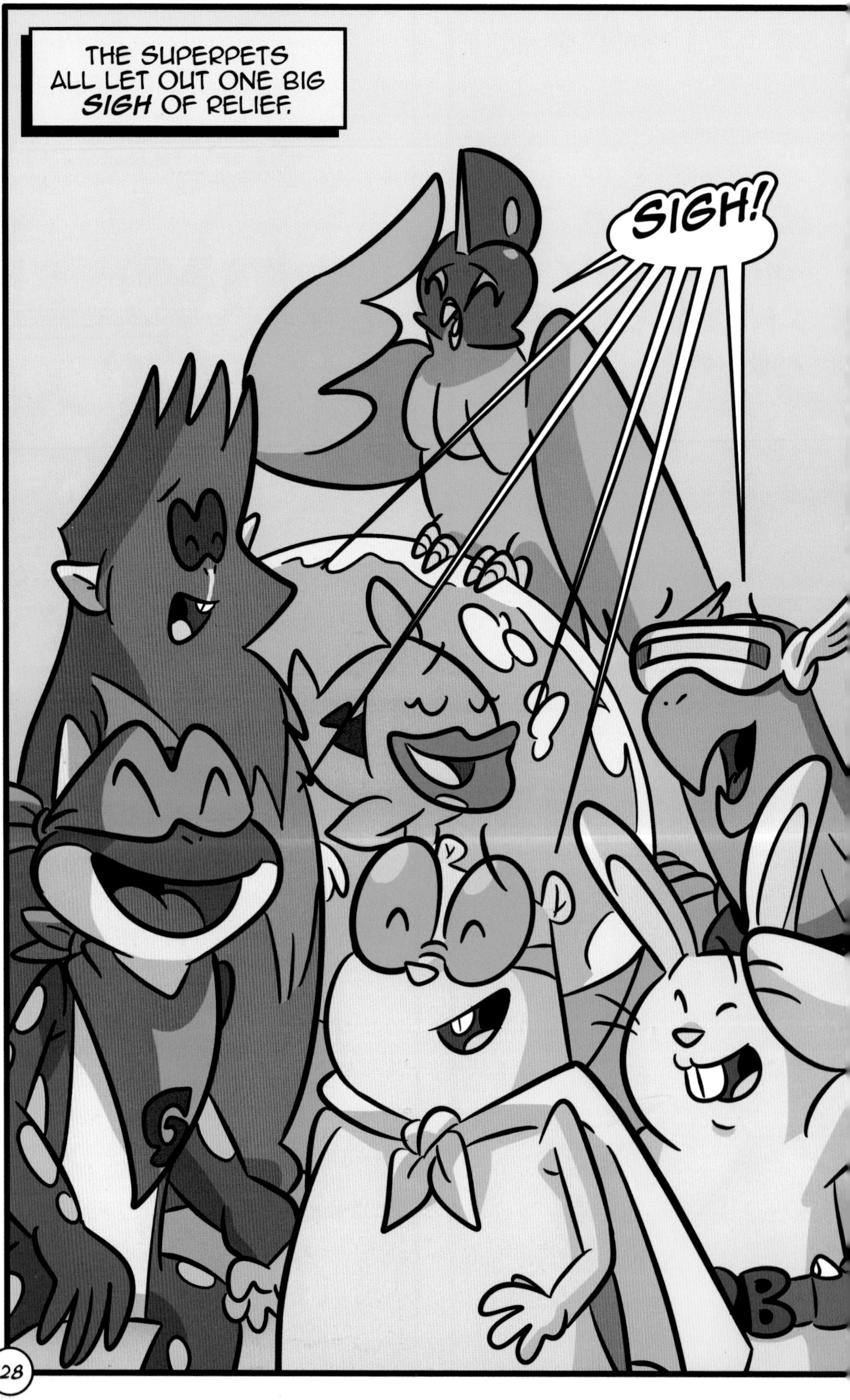
THE SUPERPETS ALL LET OUT ONE BIG SIGH OF RELIEF.
SIGH!

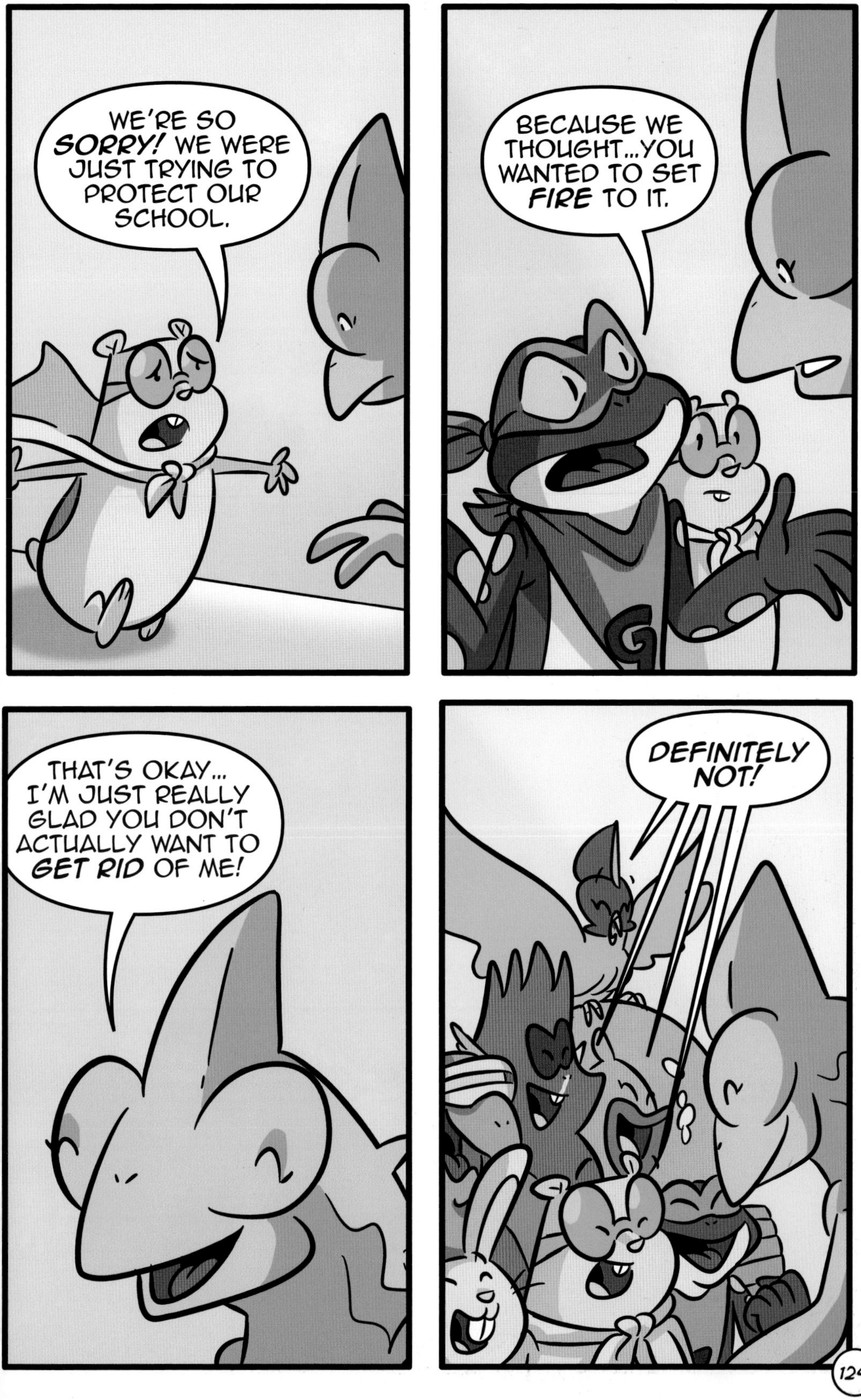
WE'RE SO SORRY! WE WERE JUST TRYING TO PROTECT OUR SCHOOL.
BECAUSE WE THOUGHT...YOU WANTED TO SET FIRE TO IT.
THAT'S OKAY... I'M JUST REALLY GLAD YOU DON'T ACTUALLY WANT TO GET RID OF ME!
DEFINITELY NOT!

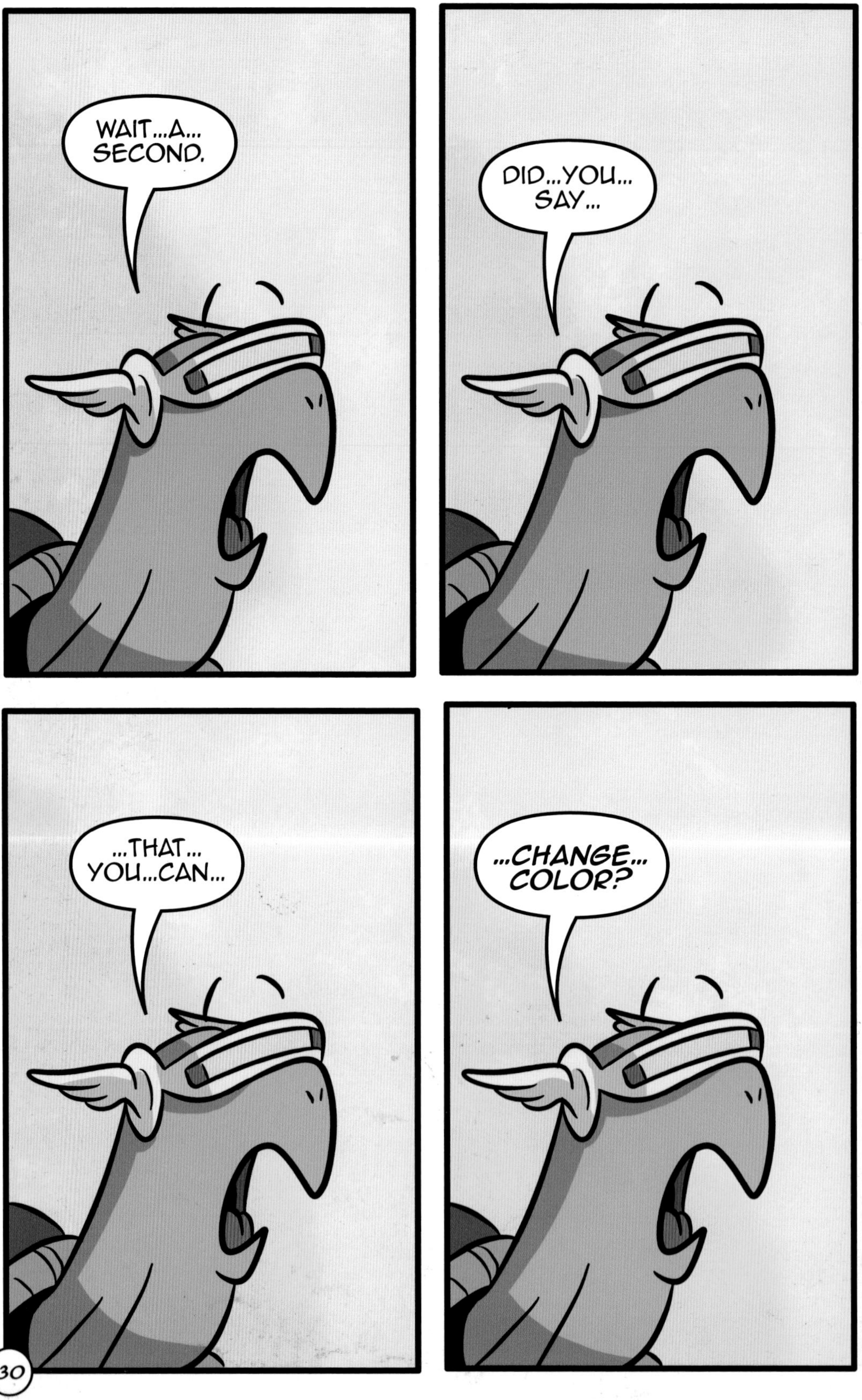
WAIT...A... SECOND.
DID...YOU... SAY...
...THAT... YOU...CAN...
...CHANGE... COLOR?

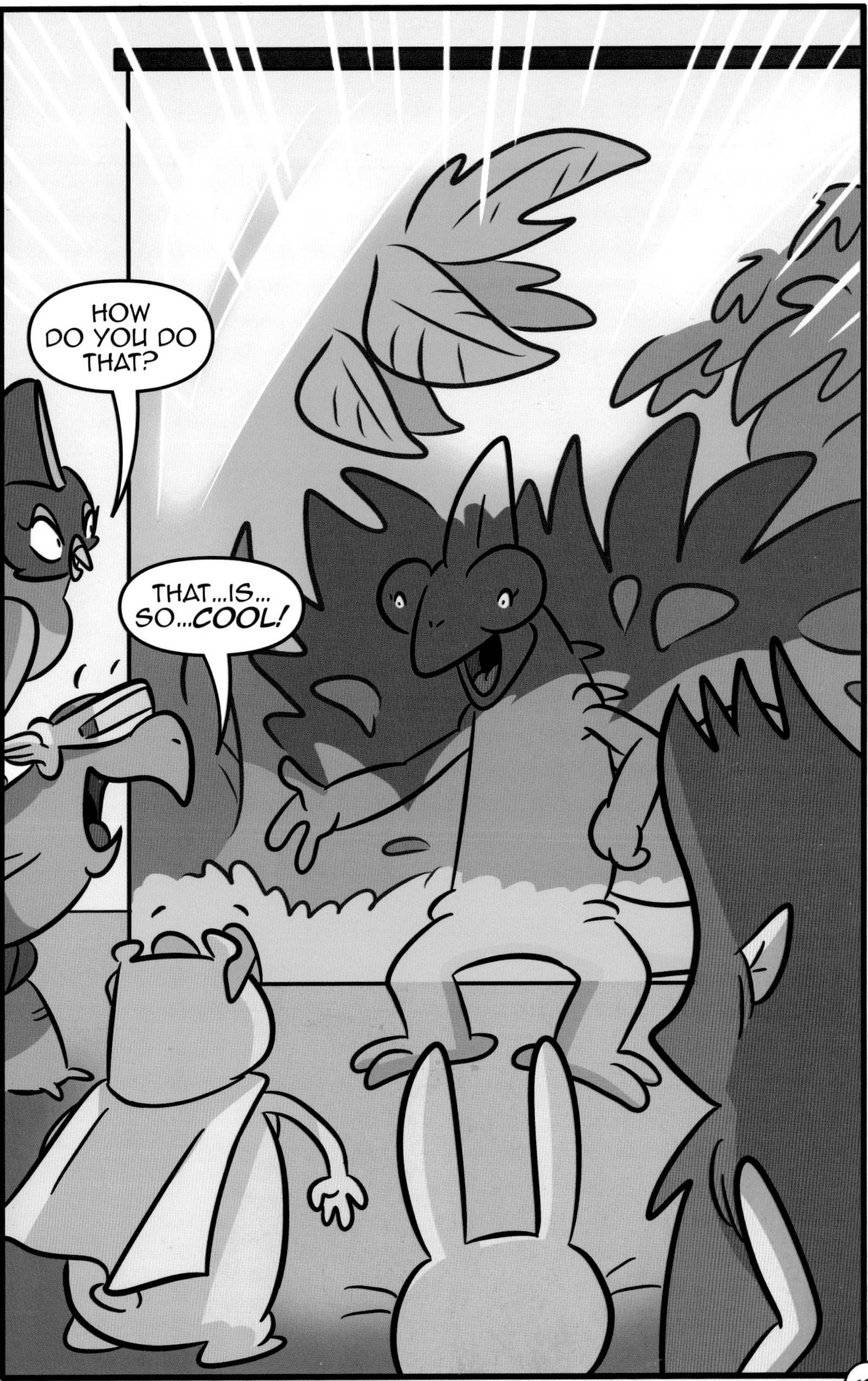
HOW DO YOU DO THAT?
THAT...IS... SO...COOL!

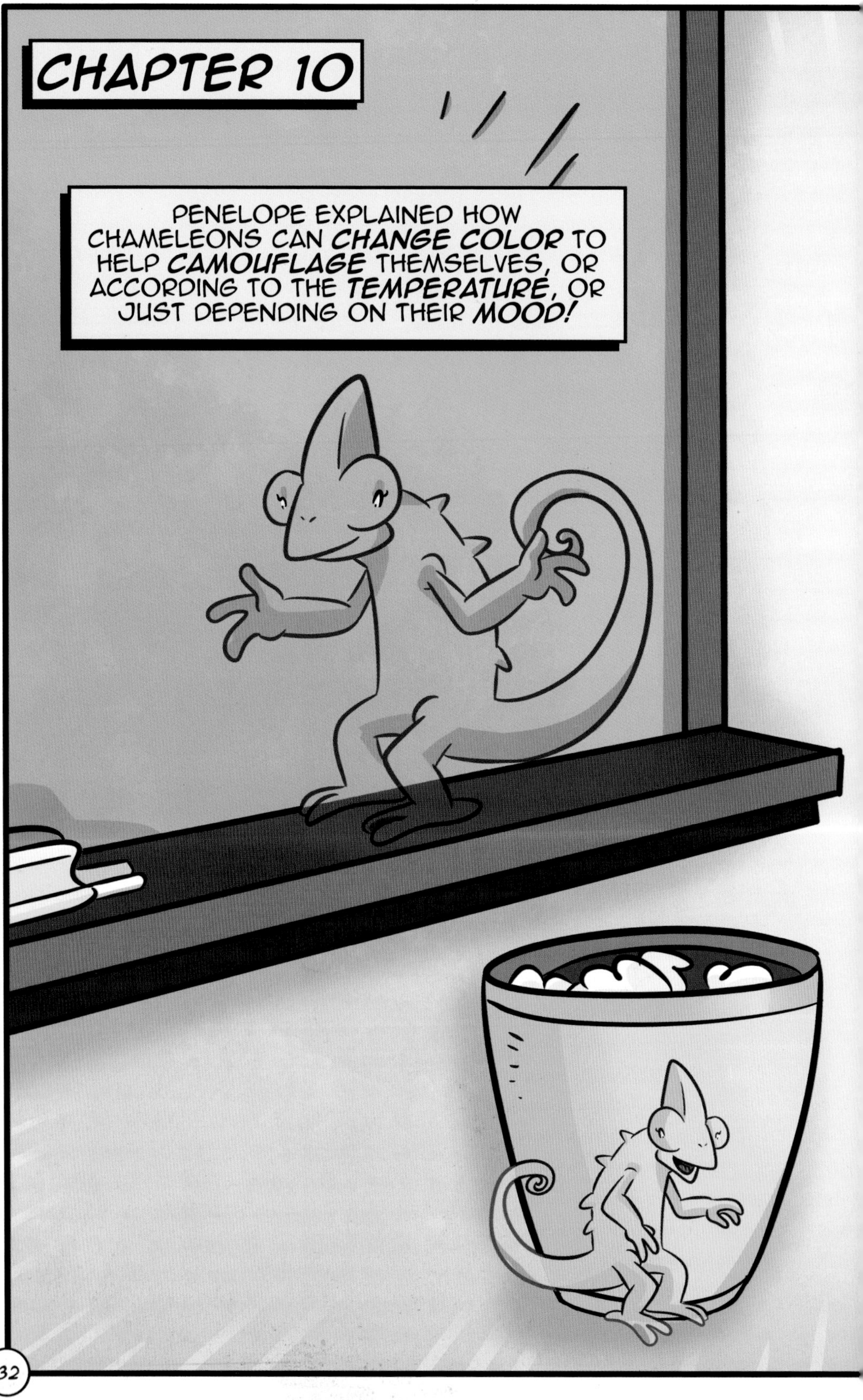
CHAPTER 10
PENELOPE EXPLAINED HOW CHAMELEONS CAN CHANGE COLOR TO HELP CAMOUFLAGE THEMSELVES, OR ACCORDING TO THE TEMPERATURE, OR JUST DEPENDING ON THEIR MOOD!

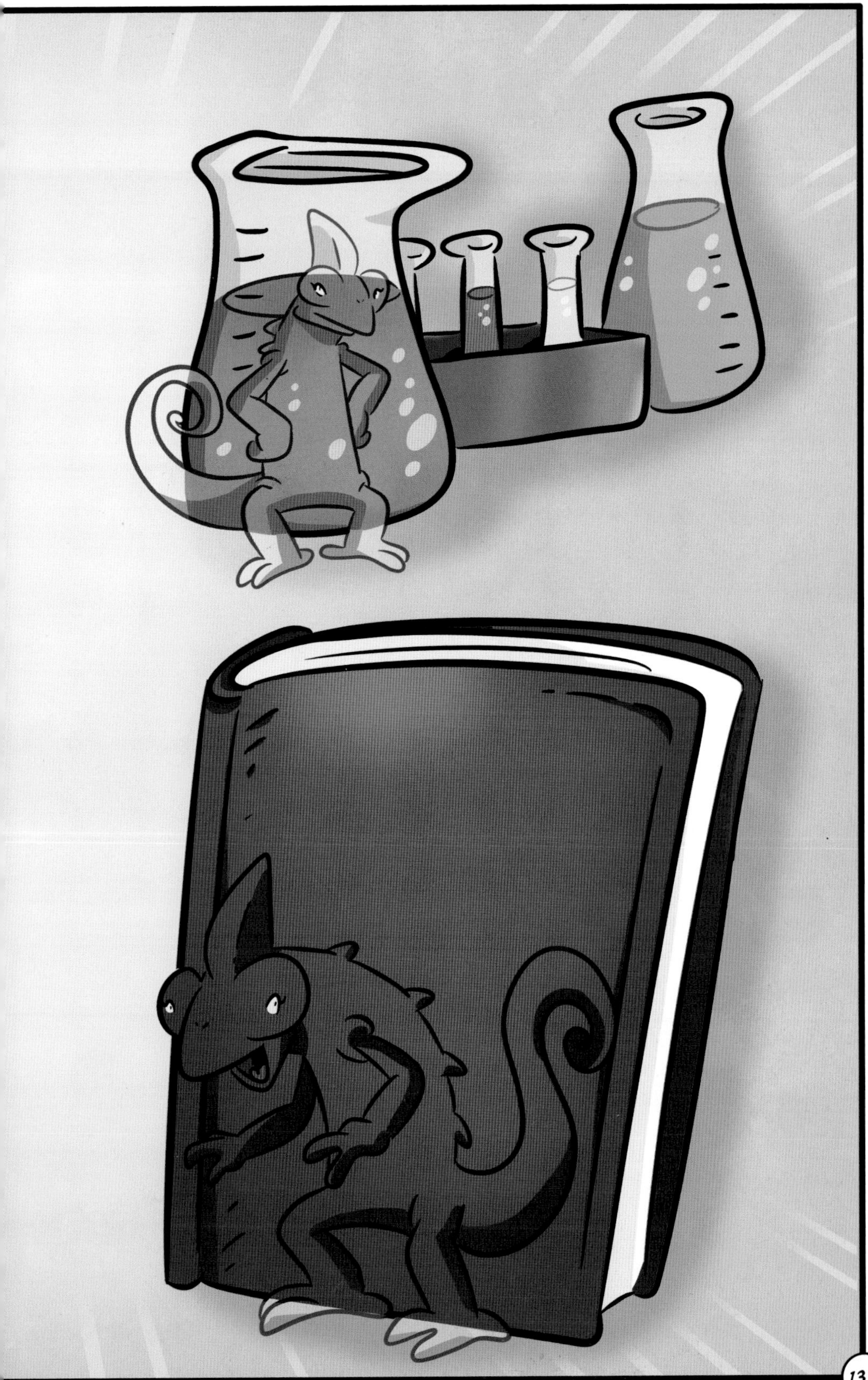

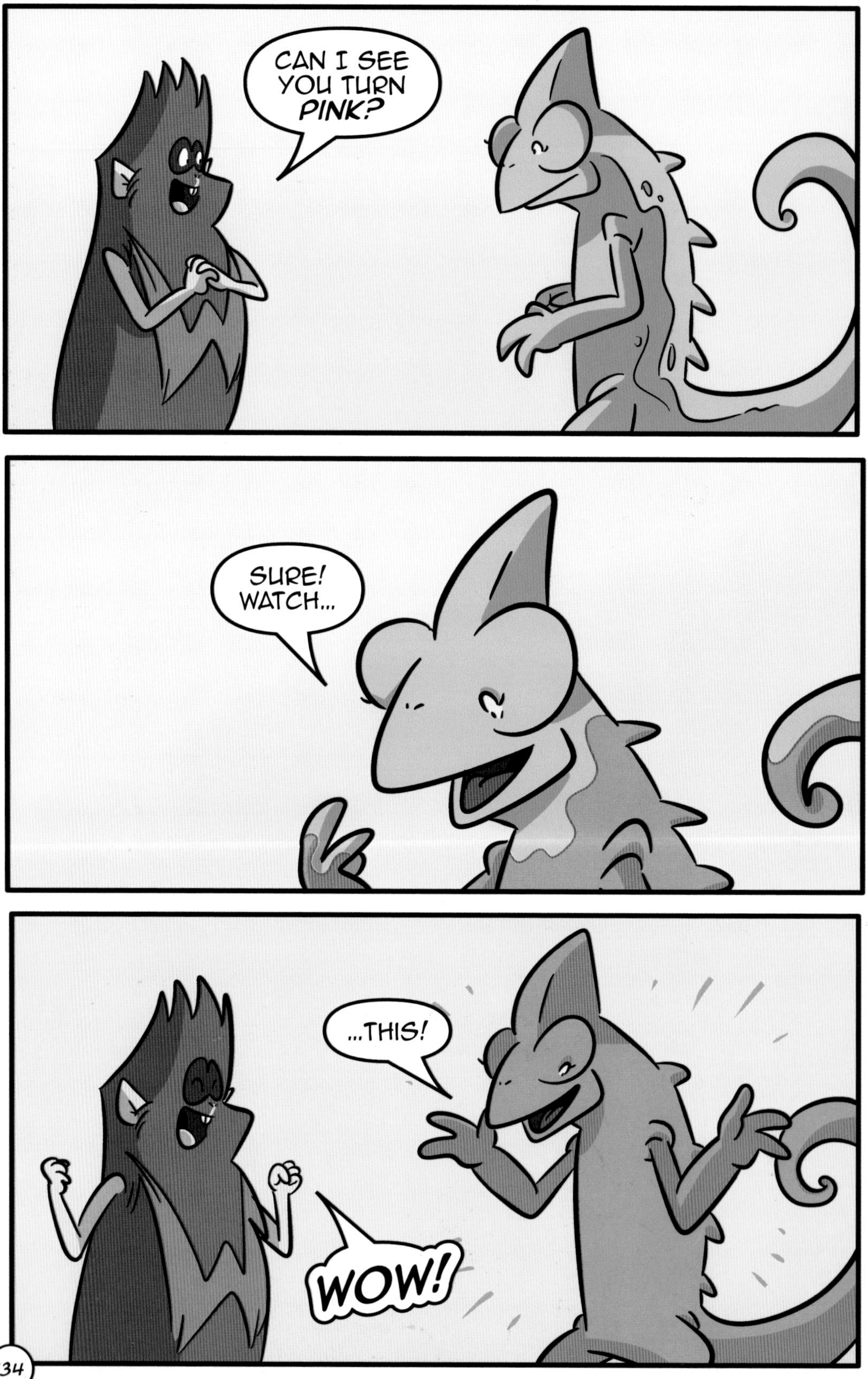
CAN I SEE YOU TURN PINK?
SURE! WATCH...
...THIS!
WOW!

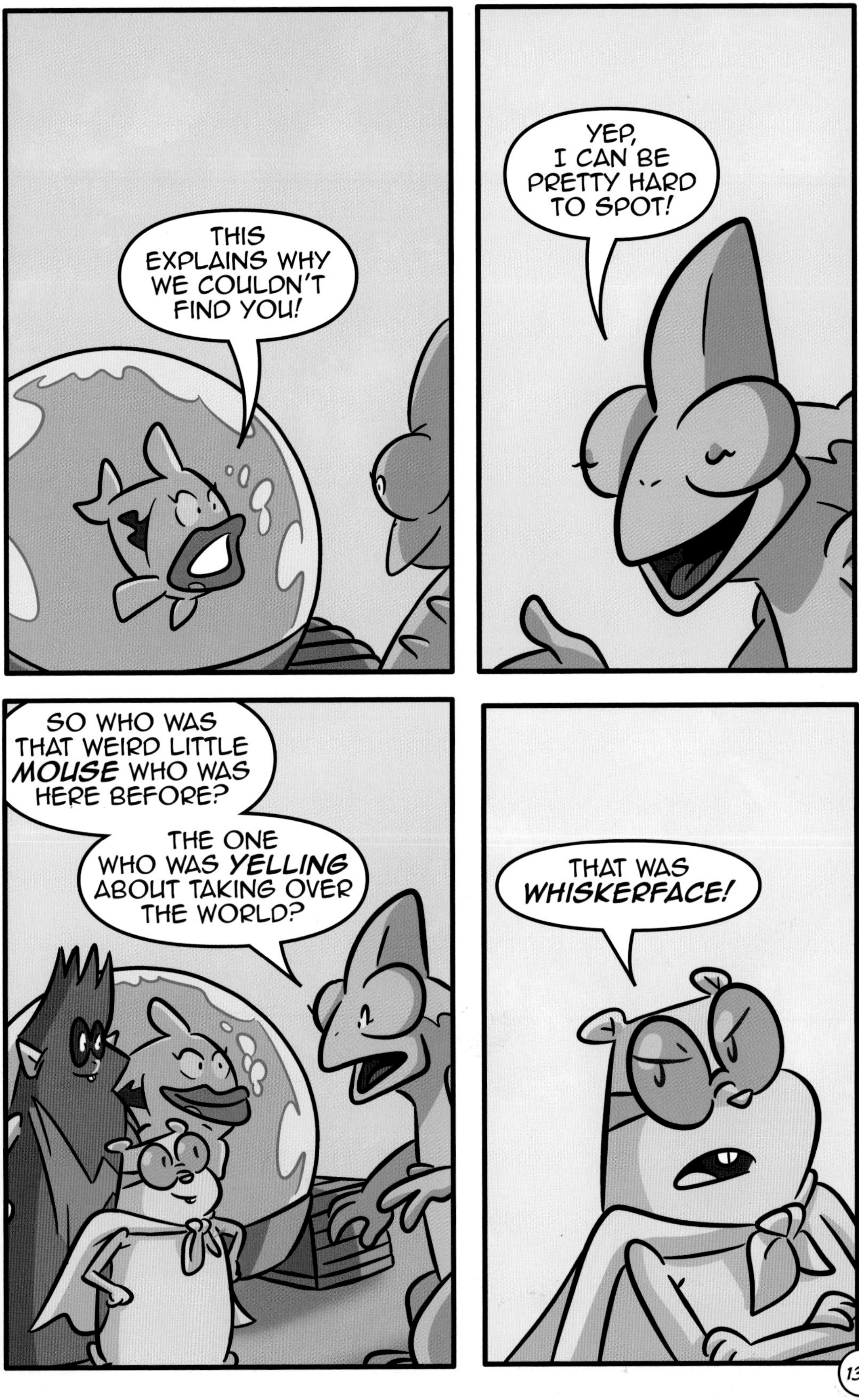
THIS EXPLAINS WHY WE COULDN'T FIND YOU!
YEP, I CAN BE PRETTY HARD TO SPOT!
SO WHO WAS THAT WEIRD LITTLE *MOUSE* WHO WAS HERE BEFORE?
THE ONE WHO WAS *YELLING* ABOUT TAKING OVER THE WORLD?
THAT WAS *WHISKERFACE!*

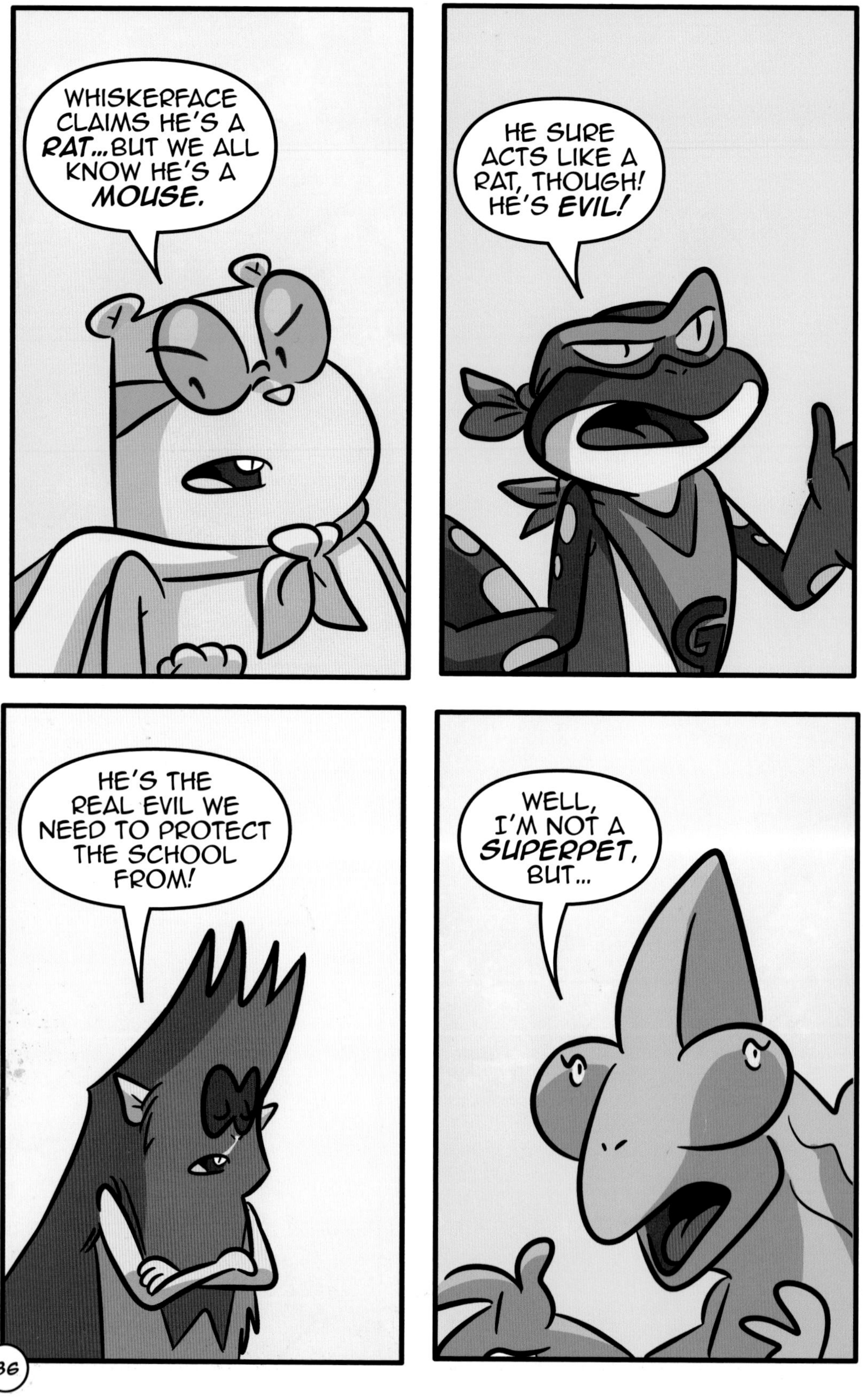
WHISKERFACE CLAIMS HE'S A *RAT*...BUT WE ALL KNOW HE'S A *MOUSE*.
HE SURE ACTS LIKE A RAT, THOUGH! HE'S *EVIL!*
HE'S THE REAL EVIL WE NEED TO PROTECT THE SCHOOL FROM!
WELL, I'M NOT A *SUPERPET*, BUT...

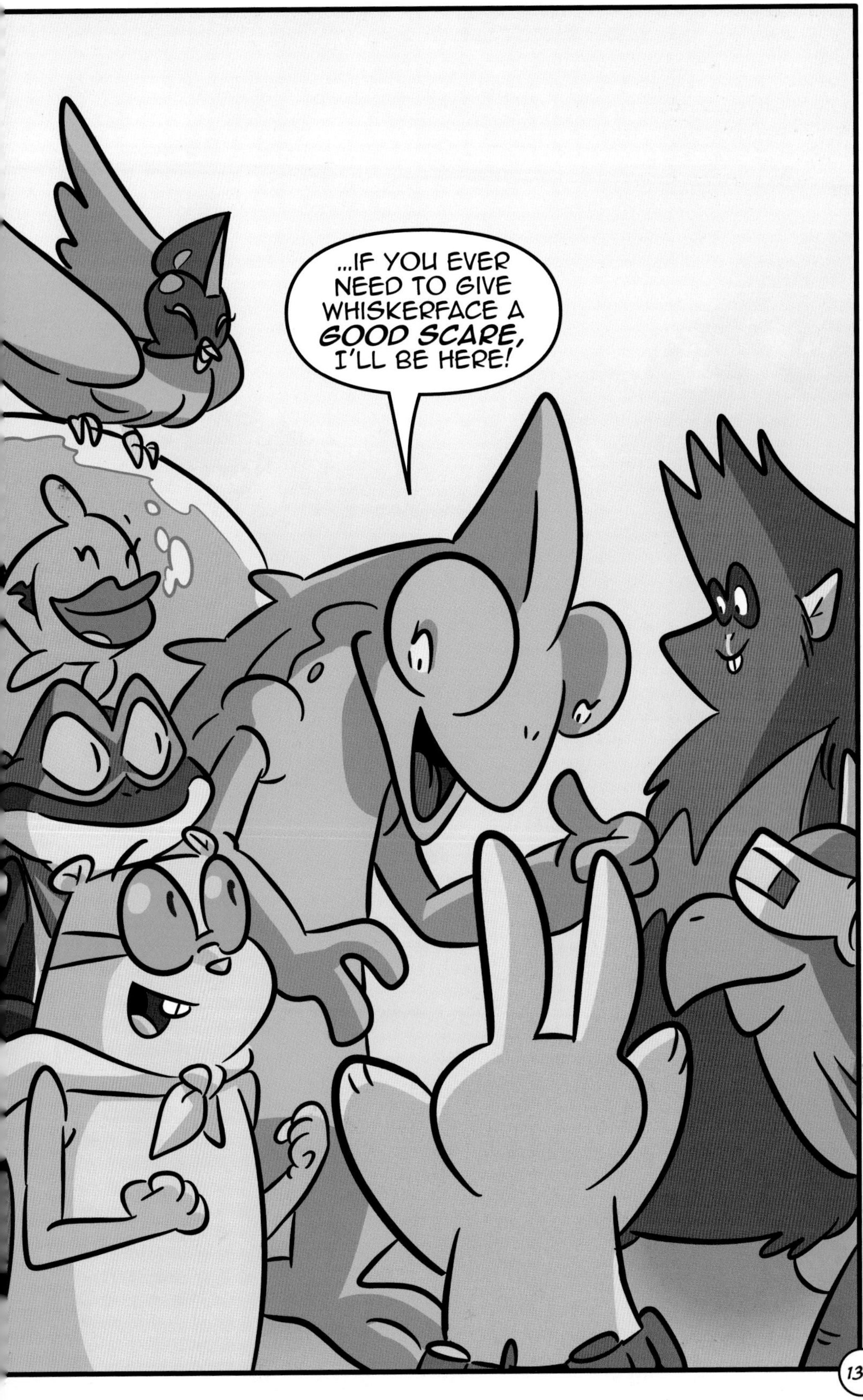
...IF YOU EVER NEED TO GIVE WHISKERFACE A GOOD SCARE, I'LL BE HERE!

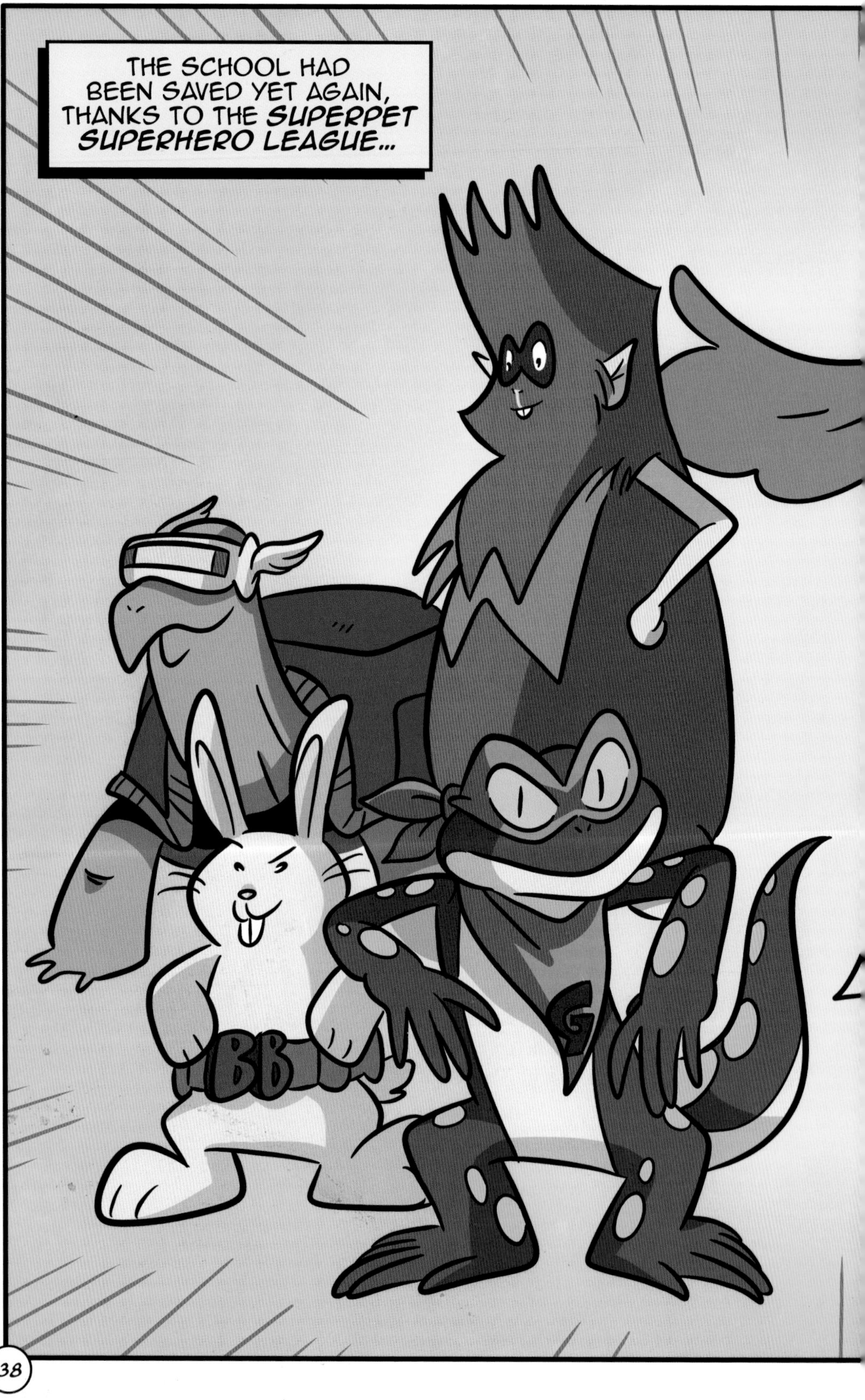
THE SCHOOL HAD BEEN SAVED YET AGAIN, THANKS TO THE *SUPERPET SUPERHERO LEAGUE...*
BB
G

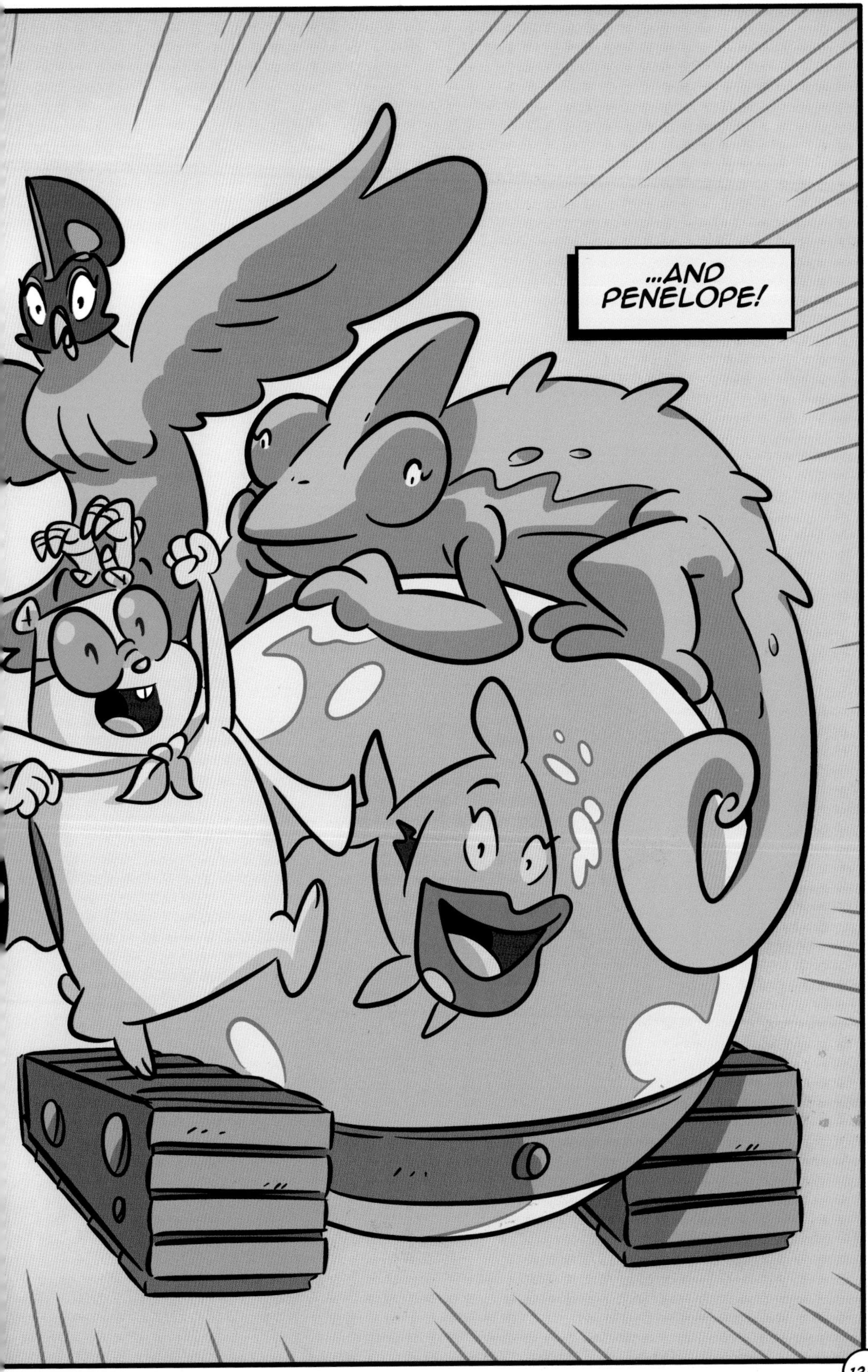
...AND PENELOPE!

CAN'T GET ENOUGH OF THE
SUPERPET SUPERHERO LEAGUE?
CHECK OUT THEIR NEXT
ADVENTURE...

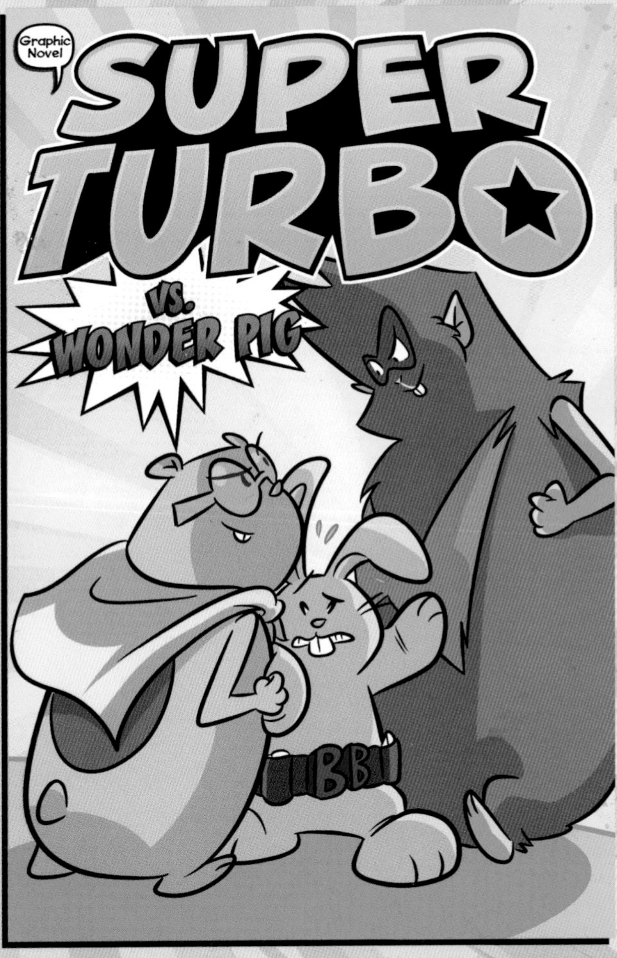
Graphic Novel
SUPER TURBO
VS. WONDER PIG
BB

TURN THE PAGE FOR A SNEAK PEEK...

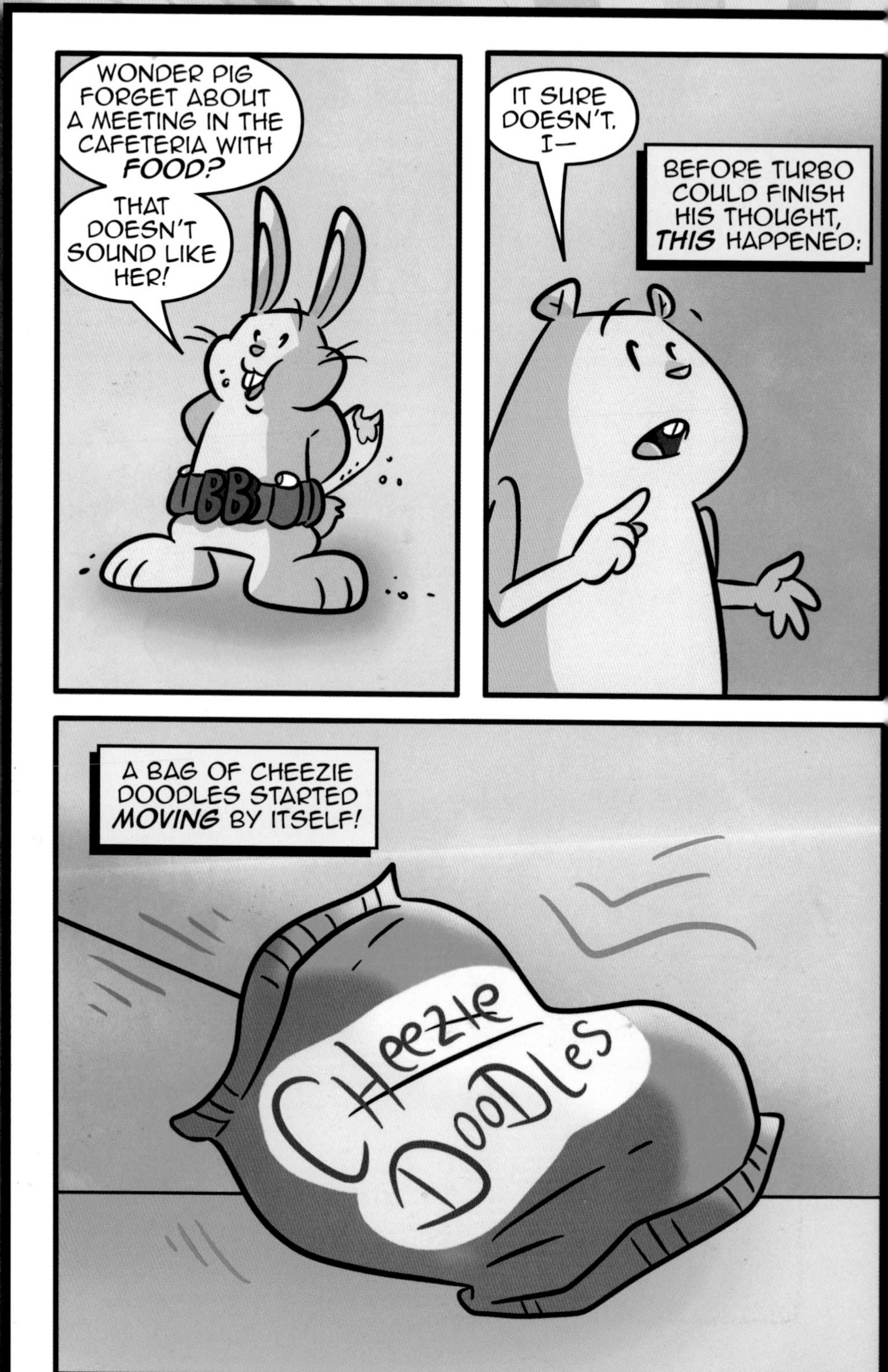
WONDER PIG FORGET ABOUT A MEETING IN THE CAFETERIA WITH *FOOD?*
THAT DOESN'T SOUND LIKE HER!
IT SURE DOESN'T. I—
BEFORE TURBO COULD FINISH HIS THOUGHT, *THIS* HAPPENED:
A BAG OF CHEEZIE DOODLES STARTED *MOVING* BY ITSELF!
Cheezie Doodles

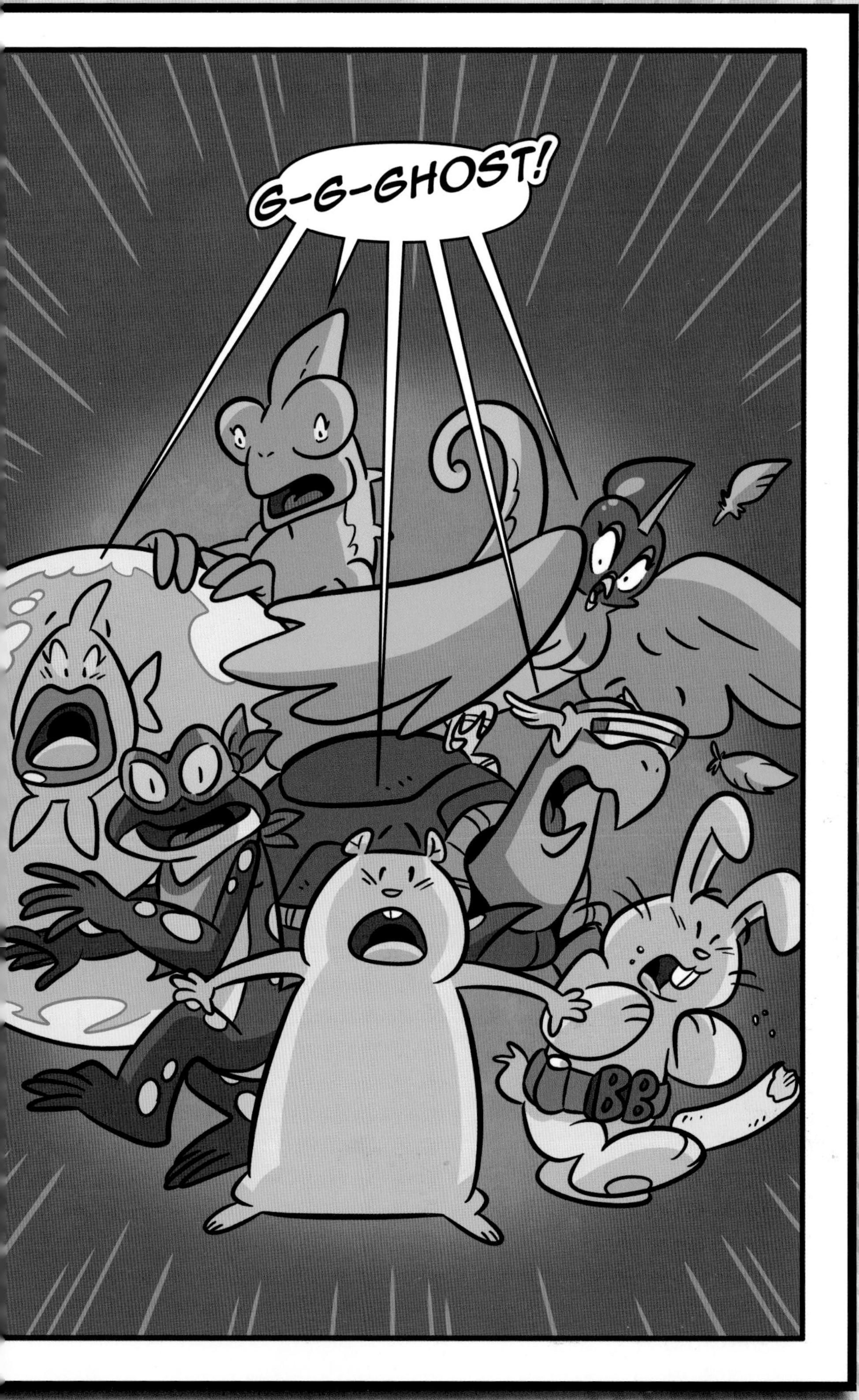
G-G-GHOST!